THE WORTHINGTON WIFE

Center Point
Large Print

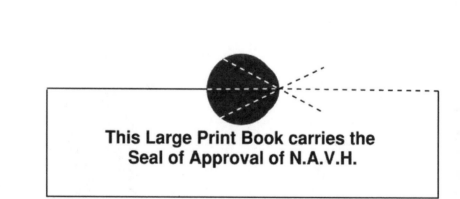

**This Large Print Book carries the
Seal of Approval of N.A.V.H.**

THE WORTHINGTON WIFE

Sharon Page

CENTER POINT LARGE PRINT
THORNDIKE, MAINE

This Center Point Large Print edition
is published in the year 2017 by arrangement with
Harlequin Books S.A.

The text of this Large Print edition is unabridged.
In other aspects, this book may vary
from the original edition.
Printed in the United States of America
on permanent paper.
Set in 16-point Times New Roman type.

ISBN: 978-1-68324-379-3

Library of Congress Cataloging-in-Publication Data

Names: Page, Sharon, author.
Title: The Worthington wife / Sharon Page.
Description: Center Point Large Print edition. | Thorndike, Maine : Center Point Large Print, 2017.
Identifiers: LCCN 2017004024 | ISBN 9781683243793
    (hardcover : alk. paper)
Subjects: LCSH: Large type books. | GSAFD: Love stories.
Classification: LCC PS3616.A337625 W67 2017 | DDC 813/.6—dc23
LC record available at https://lccn.loc.gov/2017004024

THE
WORTHINGTON
WIFE

1

The American Heir

The Estate of Brideswell Abbey
June, 1925

"I don't *care* about scandal, Nigel." Lady Julia Hazelton marched up to the desk in the study of her brother, the Duke of Langford, and set her palms on the smooth oak edge. "These women lost their husbands to war and now there is *nothing* for them. If they have farms or stores or homes, they are being turned out of them, despite having children to feed and clothe. I can help them. What do you think I will do? Do you really think I'll be inspired, after spending time with a fallen woman, to stand outside the village public house, plying the trade?"

"Good God, Julia!" Her brother, startlingly handsome with raven-black hair and brilliant blue eyes, jolted in his chair. Fortunately he had a secure grip on the very precious bundle he held. Nigel wore his tweeds, but a lacy blanket hung over his shoulder. Napping on his shoulder was his eleven-month-old son, holding his father's strong hands.

Nigel blushed scarlet. "The fact you know so much about such things speaks for itself."

"I thought Zoe finally cured you of your stuffiness, Nigel," Julia said.

Zoe was her brother's American bride, the "American Duchess" famous in the British newspapers—once famous for her wild style of living, now famous for her brilliance in investing and in turning Brideswell into the most modern yet beautiful house in England.

Cradling his son, Nigel said, "Julia, I agree that the plight of the war widows is terrible. But the responsibility for it doesn't rest on your shoulders. You have been loaning money to them out of your pin money—"

"What I am supposed to do? Simply pretend I don't see the women who look as if they've lost their souls, because they are hoping some man gives them a few pennies to—to poke at them?"

"Julia! Where, for the love of God, did you learn expressions like that?"

"Nigel, there was a war on. I'm afraid that one of the casualties of war is innocence. You were there. You know how brave those men were, and how wrong it is that they are dead."

"I know that. As a result, Zoe and I have given to many charities—"

"But once these women sell themselves, they don't go to charities for help. Some of these women were left alone, with babies even younger than Nicholas. I would go to terrible lengths if my child was starving."

8

"Yes, but—"

"These women do not have a choice. With money, they would!"

"Yes, but—"

"Many of them have skills—they have run households and farms."

"Yes, but—"

"They could start businesses. They could better themselves. They could give futures to their children."

This time her brother didn't bother with a *yes, but*.

"Julia, this work is not helping your marriage prospects."

"Oh, *that's* what you all are worried about."

Now that Zoe and Nigel were married and Julia's dowry was restored—from the investments made from Zoe's fortune—her brother, her mother and her grandmother wanted to see her wed.

"I've lost two men that I loved, Nigel. I lost Anthony to the Battle of the Somme. And Dougal to the idiocy of our class system. Frankly, I've given up on getting married."

Nigel shifted his son in his arms. "Don't, Julia."

"Well, I have." Julia crossed her arms over her chest defiantly. "But I can still do something *worthwhile*. I have the power to help these women. No bank would loan them money. But—"

She knew people thought her to be a cool, controlled, reserved English lady, but there were times when her heart hammered passionately and she was willing to fight to the ends of the earth if she had to. Two years ago, accompanied by her American sister-in-law, Zoe, Julia had begun to be daring. She had put mourning behind her and taken risks, only to have her heart broken again, this time by the brilliant Dr. Dougal Campbell, who believed they could never bridge the divide between their positions. She'd retreated back into the world she knew. She'd hidden all her emotion behind ladylike behavior.

Until now. Last week, she had seen a woman named Ellen Lambert struck by a brute of a man on the village street. The man had run when Julia approached, waving her umbrella and shouting for help. She'd learned Ellen's story and Julia had seen, with horror, how insulated her life had been.

"But?" Nigel prompted.

"But *I* would. I want a loan against my dowry, Nigel. I can use that to provide money to widows like Ellen Lambert of the village. They can pay it back over a reasonable time and with a reasonable interest."

"Julia, your dowry is there—"

"To bribe men to marry me."

"That is not true. For a start, no man would need a bribe to propose to you."

"Really? No gentleman looked at me twice when the estate was close to bankruptcy and I didn't have the dowry."

Nicholas stirred. Nigel ran his large hand over the baby's small back, gently soothing. "That had nothing to do with it. Everyone knew you were still grieving Anthony and you weren't ready to move on."

Oh, how Julia's heart gave a pang as her brother stroked his son. Without marriage, she would never have such a moment with a child of her own.

Was it worth marrying a man she didn't love to have a child she could love?

Once she would have emphatically said no. Now, with adorable baby Nicholas in the house, a strange madness would sometimes overtake her. She had to *fight* the dangerous idea that marriage without love could somehow work. She knew it didn't. She knew that from living with unhappily married parents.

And she didn't believe she could ever fall in love again. She had been in love twice—she'd lost Anthony to war, and Dr. Campbell when he'd left her to go to the London Hospital. Her heart had been broken twice. She didn't think she could survive a third time.

Nigel looked up from his infant son. "Julia, promise you will not give up on the idea of marriage."

"Nigel, I—" She broke off. Suspicion grew at the hopeful look in her brother's blue eyes. "Oh no. Say you didn't—"

"Did not what?" he asked innocently.

"You didn't invite a prospective husband to the house . . . again?"

"No, no. We are dining at Worthington Park tonight. But a friend of mine is going to be there. A friend from Oxford. An admirable chap. He's now the Earl of Summerhay."

"Nigel, I am not exactly out of love with Dougal yet." She had just received a rather devastating letter from Dougal, but this would give her an excuse. "I am definitely not ready to fall in love with anyone else." That was certainly true. She didn't even think it could ever be possible.

Her brother lifted an autocratic brow. "Dr. Campbell did a sensible thing. You couldn't be a doctor's wife. You should be running a house like Brideswell."

"I think I would have been very happy as a doctor's wife." True, but it was pointless now, wasn't it? "But Dougal believed we could not circumvent the difference in our social positions." In fact, like her brother, Dougal thought she needed a grand estate and a title. "Grandmama and Mother worked at Dougal until he went away to London. Honestly, I wouldn't be surprised if Grandmama paid a gamekeeper to escort Dougal to the train station with a rifle at his back."

"She wants you to be happy."

"No, she does not if her only objection was that she didn't want her oldest granddaughter married to a mere doctor. But Dougal has saved lives. I

12

don't want an earl or a duke. I've realized that I want a hero. When I saw what Dougal could do, I was struck with awe."

Nigel frowned. "But I do not think Dr. Campbell is worthy of you. He should have stayed and fought for you. You are worthy of a dragon slayer. Your doctor may have saved lives, but I don't know if he has enough courage for you, Julia."

"Is your earl a dragon slayer?"

She was surprised by how serious Nigel suddenly looked. "I know what he did in the War, Julia. I think he is."

"So you won't give me my loan?"

"I cannot distract you, can I?"

"No."

He sighed. "I want to see you happily settled, Julia. So my answer has to be no."

She could argue. And fight. Or she could be smart about this. "I will ask Zoe for a loan."

"In this, Zoe will not disagree with me."

"Maybe not. But I can at least try." She turned and walked away.

"Julia."

She paused at the door.

"Summerhay will not be the only eligible man there. Lady Worthington has invited the Duke of Bradstock, my friend from Eton days. Along with Viscount Yorkville. Three intelligent, interesting men."

James, the duke, she knew quite well. One of his

13

many houses was only an hour away by motorcar, and he would visit on school holidays. He had been born to be a duke—he could be rather arrogant. Yorkville, she'd never met.

"Nigel, you can't push me at eligible men at Worthington Park." She sighed. "It's bad form when Lady Carstairs will want to do that with *her* three unmarried daughters."

"Julia, all I am asking you to do is be polite," her brother protested.

"That is all anyone wants me to do. Be polite and ladylike and boring. But I am not giving up."

Then she swept out of his study. But it was not such a dramatic exit—she was leaving to do what was expected of her. To dress for dinner.

But she longed to burst out of her shell. To do something that was more than just wild and frivolous, like dancing and drinking cocktails.

Her sister-in-law, Zoe, could fly airplanes. There were women doctors, singers, artists, clothing designers. A modern woman could now grasp almost any opportunity, take hold of life and become something.

Modern women could change the world. That was what she wanted to do.

That night, the Daimler took Julia, her mother, sister Isobel and grandmother to Worthington Park. Zoe and Nigel followed in Zoe's sporty motor.

The car door was opened by one of Worthington's

footmen. A warm early-summer breeze flirted with the gauzy, bead-strewn hem of her skirt as Julia stepped out on the drive and gazed up at the house that might have been her home.

Brideswell Abbey, the house she'd grown up in, was more square and severe. Worthington was sprawling and inviting. It had a long facade, with two wings that came forward like embracing arms. A massive fountain stood in the middle of the circular drive. In the June sun, the house glowed with warm golden stone and hundreds of windows glinted.

With Mother and Grandmama, Julia walked into the foyer. Her heels clicked on the black marble tiles, the sound soaring to the high domed ceiling and its exquisite art, gilded with gold leaf. The newel post and railing of the stairs gleamed with gilt and the walls were covered partway in white and rose-pink marble. Orchids from the greenhouses and roses spilled out of enormous vases.

Julia handed off her wrap to a footman.

It was in here, in the very open foyer, that Anthony had stolen his first kiss. She had been unwinding her scarf while the butler fetched Anthony's sister Diana, who was Julia's age and a good friend. From behind, Anthony had swept her into his arms. At the soft, wonderful caress of his lips on hers, her heart had raced and she'd almost melted. Then he'd heard the butler returning, so he'd let her go and run off. But he'd thrown her one last look—a look of pure, hungry, masculine longing that had seared her to her toes.

Two days later, he'd proposed to her.

They had walked to the folly—a temple with white marble columns that stood on a hill and overlooked the house. It had been a rainy, wind-swept day, but they'd had so few days before Anthony would be leaving for France and war.

She had been not quite eighteen. For a year, since she had come out, everyone expected she would marry Anthony. But she had still been young and there had been time. Then war had come, and suddenly everyone was afraid there would not be time anymore—not enough time to live.

Anthony had said, "Someday I will be the Earl of Worthington but none of that matters if you aren't with me. Don't say we're too young. I'm old enough to go and fight and I want to know things are settled between us before I go. I love you, Julia. I wish I could marry you before I leave, but I should be back soon, and we'll be married then."

"We will," she had said. "I love you." Then he'd swept her into his arms and kissed her again . . .

Anthony had died at the Somme in 1916.

Julia let out a long soft breath as she, her mother and grandmother walked toward the drawing room. Worthington Park was special to her. For her, it was filled with the happiness and the excitement of her very first love. It was wrapped up in loss, too.

Even running her hand along a banister or taking

16

a seat in a chair gave her a powerful, electrifying jolt of memory and emotion.

"Julia!"

Her friend Diana came forward, her golden hair bouncing around her lovely face. Her huge blue eyes gave her a helpless look, but her painted Cupid's bow lips and pencil-straight sheath of gold beads and lace were thoroughly modern.

Julia knew Diana fought a constant battle with her mother, Lady Worthington, over her shocking use of makeup, but because she bought her cosmetics from the counter at Selfridges, not because makeup was scandalous anymore.

Diana clasped her hands. "Come with me and we'll have a smart cocktail instead of the horrid sweet sherry my mother insists on. I must talk to you!"

Julia followed Diana to one of the bay windows that looked out upon the side lawns. Worthington Park had one of the most ordered gardens in the country. Behind the house, paths followed a delicate design leading through beds to a central fountain.

A footman brought a silver tray with two enormous glasses, truly the size of finger bowls. Bubbles floated up through the liquid, which was tinted pink.

"Champagne cocktails," Diana said. She took several long swallows.

"Diana—" Julia frowned. "You should slow

down." Diana had been drinking much too much of late. They had been in London together last week and she'd rescued a drunken Diana from a party and taken her to the Savoy to keep Diana from getting behind the wheel and driving when she could barely stand.

"It's for courage," Diana protested. "They found the heir and he's coming here to see exactly what he's inherited—what he gets to take away from us."

Diana's ominous words made Julia shiver. The heir to Worthington had been found. After the old earl had died at the end of the War, Anthony's younger brother, John, had inherited the title. Tragically, John Carstairs had died a year ago in a car crash and the hunt had begun for the next in line to the title.

"What do you mean, what he gets to take away from you?"

"Mummy believes this man—who's American—will turn us out to starve. He hates us all."

"For heaven's sake, why?"

Diana drained her cocktail. "It's all very thrilling. His mother was Irish, a maid working in a house in New York City. My grandmother disowned her younger son—my uncle—over the marriage and the family cut off all ties. It left them in poverty. So Mummy fears he will throw us out into poverty now."

"Surely your mother is wrong. That was years ago, and it was not your fault. This man can't still be bitter and mean to be so harsh." Now Julia saw how pale her friend was beneath her rouge. She was truly afraid. "Diana, it would be ridiculous. After a World War, this man must see that family feuds are utterly meaningless. He must have a decent nature that can be appealed to."

"Mummy doesn't think so. And to protect us, Mummy wants me to marry him. He is my cousin, but royal cousins marry all the time, including first cousins. It would all be quite legal."

"This is 1925. No one will force you to marry, Diana, against your will."

Diana laughed a cold, jaded laugh that sent another chill down Julia's spine. "The thing is—I am willing to marry him. By all reports, he's quite handsome. He's going to be an earl. Master of my home. If one of my brothers had become the earl, I would have had to marry to survive. It's what women like us have to do. And this way I can have everything—a rather sexy husband, the title of countess and the home I grew up in."

How strong were these cocktails? "But you haven't even met this man. Don't let your mother push you into something ill-advised."

"I've decided that I really must have a husband. And there are so few men left for us. The War took them from us." Suddenly Diana grasped her forearm. "I need you to help me, Julia. He's arriving in time for dinner, then he's going to stay. I must convince him to propose."

Julia looked at Diana's worried face and huge blue eyes. "I suspect he will fall in love with you the first moment he sees you."

"He won't. He really does hate us because the family cut his father off. Apparently, this Cal holds rather a grudge. He doesn't even use his real name. That's why it took so long to find him. He goes by his mother's maiden name of Brody."

The footman came past and Diana snatched another cocktail. "I think convincing him to marry me might prove a challenge. Because, you see, I have to convince him to like me."

"Why shouldn't he like you?"

"Because . . . well, isn't it obvious? He will see me as the privileged daughter who had everything while his family lived in squalor. I need to be more like you, Julia. Doing good works and such. Mummy is going to try every trick in the book to force a marriage, but her ideas will be crude and obvious. They will be the kind of plots intended to work on Englishmen with a sense of honor and obligation. I don't think that's going to work on an angry American."

"I don't understand what you mean."

Diana waved her hand and champagne sloshed over the glass. "Oh, Mummy would think that if the American was found in my bedroom, he would feel he had to marry me. She's dreadfully Victorian when it comes to scheming. My plan is to be the sort of woman he can admire. Of course I have no idea what sort of woman that is. Maybe it isn't the noble saint. Maybe he would like a bad girl. You observe people and understand them. Figure out the kind of woman he wants and help me to convince him I'm that woman."

"Diana, this is mad. How can you possibly want to marry a man you do not know—" *and apparently fear* "—based on trying to be someone you are not?"

The Countess of Worthington was approaching and Diana put her lips right beside Julia's ear. "Darling, I'm pregnant," she whispered. "I have to marry. I *have* to."

Pregnant? Julia floundered to think of something to say, but Diana looked to the door and said, in husky tones, "Oh Lord, it's the American. He's arrived."

The butler, Wiggins, looked as if he'd sucked on a lemon, but he cleared his throat, gave a glance of complete disdain at the astonishing-looking man beside him—he had to look up to do it—and announced, "His lordship, the Earl of Worthington."

"It's Cal," the man said. A slow, wicked grin curved his mouth as if he was enjoying himself immensely.

"Oh, good heavens," the countess moaned quietly. "He looks like he was found in a ditch. *How* can this man be the earl instead of my sons?" Unsteady suddenly, she almost fell over. Julia hastened to the countess's side and supported her.

The man who called himself Cal stood well over six feet tall. A threadbare blue sweater stretched across his chest, topped by a worn and faded leather coat. He wore a laborer's rough trousers. His black boots had never seen a lick of polish.

His tanned face set off his golden hair, which was slicked back with pomade, but light, shimmering strands fell over his eyes. Eyes of the purest, most stunning blue. Vivid and magnetic, they looked like a blue created by an artist, as if they could never be real.

He looked a great deal like Anthony. But the new earl was more grizzled, his features sharper and more intense. His nose had a bit of a kink to it, as if it had once been broken.

The entire room had gone silent, staring at him in shock and horror. As if a bear had wandered into the drawing room.

For a fleeting moment, Julia saw the American's expression change. The confident smile vanished and a look of hard anger came to his eyes.

Was this evidence of his bitterness? Or perhaps these were all the clothes he had and their shock had hurt him.

Julia helped the countess down to the settee, next to her grandmother.

Then she realized the silence had stretched from awkward to insulting.

No one seemed to know what to do with the earl—Cal—so she smiled at him and stepped forward. She curtsied. "How delightful to have you arrive and I do hope your journey was not too taxing. Shall I have one of the footmen show you to your bedchamber so you can change for dinner? Perhaps you would care to freshen up."

Stubble graced his jaw, as if he had not shaved for days. Up close, she saw how different he looked from Anthony. He looked too challenging, too bold.

At her small speech of welcome, his golden brows lifted. "My journey wasn't 'taxing' as you put it. I know you aren't the countess. Are you one of my cousins?"

"No, I am a friend of the family. We are neighbors. I am Julia Hazelton. I was engaged to be married to Anthony, who was your cousin, but Anthony was killed at the Somme." She rushed through that bit, giving herself no time to dwell on the words. "Allow me to do the introductions—and if there's a name you forget, don't hesitate to ask."

"Aren't you the sweetheart, Julia?"

The countess made a horrible pained sound. Julia heard her grandmother, the Dowager Duchess of Langford, sputter in outrage.

The mocking tone in his voice made her wary, but she made the introductions of all those in the room. The eligible bachelors had not yet arrived, so it was just the Carstairs family—the countess, Diana and the two other daughters, Cassia and Thalia. And Julia's family.

Zoe greeted Cal with open American charm, welcoming him. Nigel accepted his handshake. Her mother and Grandmama threw looks of sympathy toward the Countess of Worthington. Diana and her younger sisters curtsied.

Julia struggled to not stare at Diana's waist beneath her gold dress. She feared if she did, everyone would read her mind and know her friend's secret. It might be 1925, but to bear a child out of marriage meant a woman was ruined forever.

Would Diana really marry Cal and keep her secret? Julia turned her gaze to Cal. Would her friend really marry him on such an enormous lie?

Goodness, she had looked at him for far longer than was polite—and he was staring right back at her. With anger crackling in his blue eyes. She smiled calmly at him, though inside her stomach fluttered with shock.

She had grown up around Englishmen—they either showed no emotion at all or they clumsily displayed it. But the energy and emotion—and fury—that seemed to sizzle around this man stunned her.

Was Lady Worthington right? Did he mean to hurt them? Julia would never stand for that. She simply wouldn't.

He still held her gaze. "I'd better go and get dressed," he said.

Wiggins, the butler, moved close to him. "If you need to avail yourself of evening dress, I do believe there are clothes belonging to the late earl that would fit you—"

"I don't need them. I've got my own sets of fancy duds." The anger seemed to abate. His unhurried, naughty grin dazzled again. "I like dressing like this, because I don't need to impress anyone with what I wear. I don't judge a man by his suit. I judge him by his actions."

Julia saw her grandmother lift her lorgnette. "Appropriate dress is an action," the dowager pointed out haughtily.

"I suppose it is." Cal turned his stunning smile onto Grandmama. "But I know how to clean up when I want to."

Then he was gone. Julia's heart was pounding. For some reason, the man set her pulse racing.

"He is awful, isn't he?"

The whisper by her ear startled her. Diana stood at her side, and bit her lip. "He's so rough and uncouth and common. I don't want to marry him, but at the same time . . . I can't help wanting him."

"Wanting him?" Julia echoed, confused.

"You know . . . in bed."

"Diana!" Julia exclaimed in a horrified whisper.

2

The American's Revenge

As the butler led him to his bedroom, Calvin Urqhart Patrick Carstairs—now the 7th Earl of Worthington—remembered the shock on Lady Worthington's face when he walked into the drawing room and grinned.

A month ago, he had been woken from a hangover, hauled out of his bed in his apartment in Paris and told by a pale, nervous young lawyer named Smithson that he had inherited a title, three estates and the contents of four modestly invested bank accounts from the family who thought he wasn't good enough to lick their boots.

The lawyer who tracked him down had stammered and blushed throughout the meeting. Cal's latest model, Simone, had been walking around the room half-naked. She liked to feel sunlight pouring through the window on her bare breasts, and she liked to keep Cal looking at her. The lawyer had looked like his eyes were going to leap out of his head.

Cal had poured himself a glass of red wine to clear the hangover, then he'd let the lawyer explain his supposed good fortune—

"The master's apartments have been prepared, my lord."

The snooty tones of the Worthington butler brought Cal back to the present. The man had his hand on the doorknob of the room, but wasn't opening it. Maybe he hoped to learn it was all a joke before he let Cal across the threshold of the earl's bedroom.

It was a double door, so Cal shoved the other door open and walked in.

His trunk and his case were already in the room. The butler pointed out the bed, probably assuming he had no idea what a bed looked like if it wasn't a dirty mattress on the floor. The man opened the doors to the bathing room and the dressing room, as well as a small room with large windows where the earl would traditionally retire to prepare his correspondence.

"It'll do," Cal said indifferently.

Haughtily, the butler tried to look down his nose at Cal—though his eyes came up to Cal's shoulders. "Is your manservant traveling with you?"

"Don't have one," Cal replied, and he laughed at the look of smug satisfaction on the butler's face. "I'm bohemian. Wild and uncivilized. If you think you've been proven right about me because I don't have a valet, wait until I start holding orgies in the ballroom."

The butler turned several fascinating colors. His cheeks went vermilion, his forehead was puce and he developed an intriguing blend of violet and scarlet on his neck.

It gave Cal the itch to create a modernist portrait of an English butler, done in severe blocks of color. Red, purple, yellow-green and stark white.

"When should I tell the countess you will return downstairs?" the man asked, sounding as if his windpipe wasn't drawing air. "I will send a footman to unpack."

"I won't stay up here long. The footman can finish that job while I'm at dinner."

"Very good."

The butler turned away and stalked toward the door, but before he reached it, Cal called, "Wait."

The man turned, lifting his brow self-importantly.

"The dark-haired woman with the pretty blue eyes—Julia Hazelton. Was she really my cousin's fiancée? Anthony died at the Somme, isn't that so?"

"Yes. We lost Lord Anthony to that battle. Indeed, Lady Julia Hazelton was his intended. It was a tragedy, devastating to us all."

Yeah, Cal imagined it would be, since he was standing here now. "Why is she here?"

"Her family was invited to dine, and she is a close friend of the family."

"Did she find someone else—after my cousin died?"

"Lady Julia is still unmarried, my lord. If I may

ask, what is the purpose to these questions, my lord?"

"I'm curious," he answered easily. "And if you're going to ask a question anyway, don't waste time asking permission to do it."

The butler, whatever the hell his name was, glared snootily. "Very good, my lord." Bowing, he retreated.

The door closed behind the butler's stiff arse.

For the hell of it, Cal jumped on the bed, landing on his arse in his dusty trousers. He crossed his ankles, his boots on the bed.

He could just hear how his mother would berate him for that, so he slid off.

He went into the bathroom to wash and shave. Showing up scruffy had been his plan and it had served its purpose. The Countess of Worthington, his aunt, had looked like she was going to faint. She would expect him to show up at dinner looking equally bohemian and she would expect that he would have the table manners of an orangutan.

His family had stared at him with suspicion. He'd seen condescension on the countess's face, resentment on the faces of his cousins. His family had all glared at him, sullen, angry . . . and scared.

Lady Julia had been the only one to welcome him. She had been the perfect English lady to him, polite and unflustered.

Traits he should have hated, given how he knew

the aristocracy really behaved. She was likely no different than the rest of them. Masking her disdain behind a polite, reserved smile.

But she had been nice to him. And his mother would say that she didn't deserve to have him judge her—and dislike her—just because of who she was.

Cal opened the bag that contained his straight razor and he filled the small sink with some water—

Hell. That was freezing cold. He ran the other tap, but it didn't get any warmer. Cold-water shaving it would have to be.

He drew the sharp blade along his cheek, slicing off dark blond stubble. He had been looking forward to this ever since that morning when he'd been drinking while the lawyer was outlining the meaning of his new position.

At first he'd wanted to tell the young lawyer with the slicked-back hair to go back to the damned countess and tell her where she and her snobby family could stick their title.

They had disowned his father; they had rejected and vilified his mother for the sin of being an honest, decent woman from a poor family. His mother, Molly Brody, had gone into service to a rich family on Fifth Avenue; his father had been a guest. The usual story. Except his father, Lawrence Carstairs, had been idealistic. He'd fallen in love with the maid he seduced and married her.

Then his father had died. And his mother had gotten sick . . .

Cal had been fourteen years of age, with a younger brother who was eleven. That was the only reason he'd swallowed his pride and begged the damn Carstairs family for help. He'd been a desperate boy trying to save his mother's life. And they'd refused. To them, he and his mother and his brother, David, didn't exist.

Clearing his throat, the young lawyer had asked him when he would like to book passage back to England.

Cal had been ready to laugh in the face of Smithson Jr. of Smithson, Landers, Kendrick and Smithson. Go to England? He liked painting. He liked Paris. He'd finally found a place where he felt he belonged. He was happy in Paris whether he was sober or drunk, which he felt was a hell of an accomplishment.

"When you take up residence at Worthington Park, there is a dower house available for the countess," Smithson had explained, after pulling at his tie. Simone had come into the kitchen and stood in front of the window so the sunlight limned her naked breasts. Blushing, the lawyer had said, "Should I relay your instruction to have it made ready?"

"For what?" he'd asked.

"For the countess to move into, when you take up residence in your new home."

31

At that moment, Cal got it. He understood what he'd just been given.

Power.

Now, Cal sloshed the blade in the water and shaved the other side of his face. He patted his skin with a wet cloth, then slapped on some witch hazel. He got dressed in his tuxedo, tied the white bow tie, put on his best shined shoes.

From his trunk, he took out a faded snapshot. It was seven years old. He didn't know why he'd brought it with him. He should have burned it a long time ago. It was a picture of a pretty girl with yellow-blond hair and a sweet face. Her name was Alice and she had nursed him when his plane had been shot down in France. His brother, David, had ended up in the same hospital, three days after Cal got there.

Alice had taken care of David when both of his legs had to be amputated below the knee. Cal had fallen in love with her. The problem was David fell in love with her, too, but without his legs, he wouldn't propose to Alice. And with his brother being in love with her, Cal wouldn't propose, either.

Cal tucked Alice's photograph into the corner of the dressing table mirror.

David had wanted to come here, too. He supposed David had a right to see the house their father had grown up in. He would bring his brother over from America.

The problem was, David was a forgiving kind

of man. He was a stronger man than Cal. David wasn't going to like what he planned to do.

But Worthington Park was Cal's chance at revenge.

The Countess of Worthington was shaking. Julia had only seen the countess like this twice—when the telegram had come with its cold, direct message that Anthony had been killed, and the day John Carstairs, her second son, had died in an automobile accident.

"You must have a sherry. Or a brandy. You look very ill." She looked up to summon a drink, but Wiggins was already there. The butler must have almost run at undignified speed to return, and he now presented a delicate glass of sherry on his silver salver.

The countess stared blankly at it, as if she didn't know what to do. Julia took the drink and pressed it into Lady Worthington's hand. The countess's pallor terrified her. She looked more gray than white and quite severely ill.

Julia felt panicked—Lady Worthington had been very ill after Anthony's death. No one had known how to bring her out of grief. Julia had tried very hard to do it. She'd promised Anthony she'd be there for his mother and sisters should anything happen to him, and she always kept her promises.

"The boy is going to destroy us," Lady Worthington moaned.

"He is going to do no such thing," Julia said firmly. She would not allow it. Her mother, Zoe, Nigel and Isobel were conversing with Diana and her younger sisters. The younger ones kept glancing over, looking nervous and curious.

"Have the drink, Sophia," Grandmama insisted. "You will need it."

At Grandmama's firm words, Lady Worthington suddenly took a long sip. "I know what he is going to do," she whispered. "He wrote a letter."

"A letter? What did it say?" Julia asked.

"He threatened us. Simply because he had asked for money and we had the good sense to refuse him. His mother was a grasping, scheming creature. She is the reason my husband's younger brother is dead."

"Goodness, what happened?" Julia asked. "What did she do?"

The countess put her hand to her throat, to rest on the large diamond that sat there. At fifty, the countess wore a fashionable gown—blue silk with a loose, dropped waist, covered in thousands of tiny turquoise and indigo beads. The Worthington diamonds—huge, heavy and square-cut—glittered on her chest. "I can't speak about it. It is enough to know he is a danger." The countess grasped Julia's hand. "You must not listen to a word he says."

But the plea made Julia uneasy. She remembered Diana's words—that the countess had reason to feel guilty. But the look in the woman's eyes was pure terror. "What is it that you fear he will say?"

"He will tell you lies! Everything that boy says will be twisted and untrue. He will try to make you believe—" Lady Worthington stopped. Her hand clutched the center diamond of her necklace, as if clinging to it gave her strength. "That is not important. You, Julia, should have loyalty to us. Do not welcome him. Do not show him friendship. He will use you to destroy us. Do not forget that. You must be on our side."

"Of course I am." But the countess's words seemed so . . . extreme. Surely the countess was too upset to go into dinner. Excuses could be made. Julia leaned toward her grandmother. "Perhaps I could take her upstairs—"

"No," the countess cried. "I will not run and hide from Calvin Carstairs. I will protect my family from him. When you have children, you will understand . . . you would do anything on earth to keep them safe."

And Julia understood. The countess had lost both her sons. She would not allow anyone to hurt her daughters.

"As soon as the boy is downstairs, we will go in for dinner." The countess lifted her chin. Julia was amazed by the woman's strength and spirit.

Until the countess directed a sharp gaze at Diana, standing across the room. "Sometimes you must do something rather terrible to protect those you love."

Julia didn't understand. She had never seen the Countess of Worthington like this. Lady Worthington was usually so gracious, so kind. The tragedy she'd suffered in losing both her sons had broken the hearts of people on the estate, for she was so well loved. When Julia had lost her brother Will to the influenza outbreak and her own mother had sunk deeply into depression, Lady Worthington had been like a mother to her and Isobel.

She had never dreamed Lady Worthington would push anyone into marriage—despite Diana's warning that her mother would scheme to do it. She had thought Diana was exaggerating. Diana had always been dramatic. They had been such opposites—it was why they had always been great friends. "You can't mean to force Diana into marriage—"

"I will do what must be done."

"But not that. You cannot force Diana to be unhappy for the rest of her life—"

"Better that than poverty. Julia, this is not your concern."

The sharp words stung. But the raw fear in her ladyship's eyes startled her.

Yet it was wrong that both the countess and Diana wanted this marriage—it would be a disaster. It was something she felt she could not allow to happen, because it would only cause pain.

Yet, how did she stop it? It might be true that

she had no right to interfere, but she also couldn't stand aside and watch a disaster unfurl—

Wiggins's stentorian voice suddenly cut over all sound. "The Earl of Worthington."

From where she stood, Julia could see the entrance to the drawing room. The new earl stood in the doorway . . .

Tall and broad-shouldered, he wore an immaculate tuxedo jacket, black trousers and white tie. His hair was slicked back neatly with pomade, which darkened it to a rich amber-gold. The severe hair brought out the handsome shape of his jaw, the striking lines of cheekbones you could cut yourself on. Even from across the room, the brilliant blue of his eyes was arresting.

Beside her, a feminine voice drawled, "He was right—he *does* clean up rather well." Diana had moved beside her, perhaps sensing her mother's sharp glance. But Diana set down her empty glass then glided across the drawing room toward her cousin.

Julia had put out her hand instinctively to stop her friend. But she was too late. And what could she do?

She didn't know how to be there for Diana. To be pregnant and unmarried was a nightmare.

Diana's silvery laugh sliced through the room. She was right at the new earl's side, smiling into his eyes, running her strings of glittering jet beads through her fingers. Flirting for all she was worth.

"What's wrong, Julia?"

Zoe, looking lovely in a beaded dress of deep green with an emerald-and-diamond choker around her slim neck, came to her side.

She couldn't talk about Diana's secret, not even to Zoe. She smoothed her face into a look of ladylike placidity. "It's nothing."

"Do you really think Cal is the vengeful monster the countess paints him to be?"

"I don't know."

"It's not stopping the countess from pushing her daughters at him," Zoe observed.

Julia watched Diana move so close to Cal her bosom pressed to his bicep. Cassia, tall and blonde like Diana, but only twenty-one, had approached him, too. She smiled demurely at him— Cassia was always gentle and sweet. The youngest daughter was Thalia: eighteen and bookish. And when Thalia looked as if she wanted to escape, her mother propelled her to talk to Cal.

Then Julia realized Cal was watching Lady Worthington. Just for a moment, then Diana ran her finger along his sleeve and got his attention again.

But Julia had seen the cold, hard rage that seethed in that one fast look.

"I think the countess might be right," Julia said softly.

Zoe looked at her surprised.

Wiggins stepped in the drawing room and

cleared his throat. "May I announce His Grace, the Duke of Bradstock. His lordship, the Earl of Summerhay. His lordship, Viscount Yorkville."

Nigel immediately moved to greet his good friend Summerhay.

"Oh no." Julia swallowed hard. At least it would be easy to keep track of the three of them—Bradstock had black hair, Summerhay was blond, Yorkville had auburn waves. Other people arrived also—members of the local gentry, and an older gentleman to make appropriate numbers.

"Don't worry. I'm on your side," Zoe promised. "I don't think you should marry a man you don't love for his title."

It wasn't the right time to speak of it, but Julia suddenly felt she needed to take charge of something. "Zoe, I want to ask if you would consider lending me money."

Her sister-in-law stared in surprise. "Whatever for, Julia?"

"For war widows who have been left destitute. I would like to loan money to the women. They will pay me back over time. All they need is a few pounds to start them on the direction of a new and better life. I asked Nigel for a loan against my dowry, but he refused."

"Did he?"

"He thinks my work is too scandalous and it will ruin my marriage prospects." She couldn't help it—she glanced at Nigel, who was talking to the three peers who'd just arrived. For all she knew, he was pleading with them to propose to her.

"I would be happy to loan you the money, depending on the amount and the terms," Zoe said. "Is there a great chance these women will default?"

Zoe was never foolish. She was smart and shrewd. "I don't think so," Julia said honestly. "But I will start with modest amounts. If a woman defaults, I will be able to repay out of my pin money and my dress allowance."

"Your dress allowance." Zoe shook her head, obviously amused.

"Do you agree with Nigel?"

"I love my husband, but when it comes to what should be considered scandalous for a woman, we never agree. I am happy you are helping these women."

"You don't fear for my marriage prospects?"

"I already know who you should marry. Noble Dr. Dougal Campbell."

"Zoe . . ." Julia swallowed hard, aware of the sharp jolt of pain in her heart. "He just wrote to tell me he is engaged to someone else. I have lost him forever."

"Then it was not a great loss, Julia, my dear," the dowager duchess declared.

Julia jumped at the firm, autocratic tones of her grandmother. She turned to find the dowager duchess had walked up beside her and looked ready to deliver advice. Julia dearly loved her grandmother, but as Grandmama looked pointedly at the Duke of Bradstock, she swallowed hard.

"It is if Julia and Dr. Campbell were perfect for each other," Zoe pointed out, sipping her drink and toying with her long string of beads.

Her grandmother linked arms and swept her away from Zoe. "Bradstock keeps watching you," Grandmama said bluntly. "Why do you think he has never married? He is waiting for you. You could be a duchess with one simple word. And that word is *yes*. Julia, you must be settled. Where shall you live, if you end up a spinster?"

"Grandmama, I won't say yes to a man just to have his house. There's absolutely no reason I couldn't have a flat in London and have a job—"

She had to stop. Grandmama staggered back with her hand on her heart. "If I find you behind the counter at Selfridges, my dear, it would be th end of me. You wouldn't want that on your conscience, would you?"

"No, and I'm sure you wouldn't want my unhappy marriage on yours," Julia said.

The dowager's brows rose. "Touché."

Cal was seated between the Duchess of Langford and Lady Julia at the long, wide, polished dinner table. His cousin Diana sat near him, talking flirtatiously to the man beside her—another earl—but glancing at him. The dining table would have stuck out both sides of the narrow tenement

41

building he'd grown up in. The walls and floor of the dining room were covered in Italian marble shot with streaks of pink. On the table there was enough silverware and cut-glass crystal to pay a king's ransom, and half the room was covered in gold leaf.

So damned opulent it made anger boil inside him.

Lady Julia turned to him, a lovely smile on her face, and asked, "What do you think of Worthington Park?"

Up close, Lady Julia—sister to the tall, black-haired Duke of Langford—was even more stunning.

Smooth, alabaster skin. Thick, shining black hair. Huge blue eyes. Her cool, controlled expression fascinated him. Like nothing could ever upset her. Though once he saw her looking at Diana and she'd looked real worried. Maybe because Diana was flirting with him.

Once or twice, he'd seen a look of terror on Lady Worthington's face. That hadn't stopped her pushing her three daughters at him. His cousins, damn it. English royalty married their cousins, but it seemed like a strange thing to him.

The countess obviously hoped the backwater hick from America would be so bowled over by her pretty English daughters and their jewels and their manners and their titles—each one was "Lady" something—that he'd kiss the ground they walked on and jump down on one knee to propose marriage to one of them.

As if that would happen. He would never marry one of them—one of the aristocracy.

"Looking at this place," he said to Julia, "I can't believe no one ever chopped the heads off the English aristocracy."

He figured that would stop her trying to converse with him.

But it didn't. "I can assure you that many members of the aristocracy have been afraid of that very thing for quite a long time," she said smoothly. "But it is that fear that can lead to more justice for people, for better conditions and more decency— if it is pushed in the right direction."

That answer he hadn't expected. "You almost sound like a socialist."

"Are you one, Worthington?" At his look of surprise, she added, "That is how you are to be addressed now. By your title."

"I remember the lawyer telling me something like that. But having to hear that title is like having a bootheel ground into my heart. I'd prefer you call me Cal."

Her lips parted. God, she had full, luscious lips.

But then, why shouldn't she? She'd never slaved in a factory for fourteen hours a day. Or spent hours over a tub of steaming water, destroying her hands to scrub dishes.

A footman came by, holding a dish of oysters

toward him. When Cal had made his money—a fortune that this family knew nothing about—back in the States from bootlegging and other enterprises that he wouldn't talk about, he'd dined in a lot of nice restaurants. He'd liked knowing he could have whatever he wanted, whenever he wanted it. But the amount of food coming out— and going back—shocked him.

"How much food do you people eat at dinner?" This was the third course and they hadn't gotten to anything that looked like meat.

"There will be several courses, especially at a dinner party," Lady Julia said softly. She kept her voice discreet, he noticed. "I expect the Worthington cook, Mrs. Feathers, wants to impress you."

"Why? No one else around here does."

Lady Julia faced him seriously. "The servants all know that their livelihoods depend on you. On whether you are satisfied with them or not."

"They don't need to knock themselves out," he said. "I'm dissatisfied with this on principle."

Her lips parted—damn, he couldn't draw his eyes away from them. He wanted to hear what she would say, but then the duke sitting on the other side of her started talking to her. Not her brother, but the Duke of Bradstock. Black-haired and good-looking, Bradstock talked like he had a stick up his arse and couldn't find a comfortable place on his chair.

"Lady Julia, have you given up that shocking

hobby of yours?" the duke asked. "Or hasn't your brother taken you in hand?"

Julia turned from him to Bradstock.

For some reason Cal felt damned irritated to lose her attention. Julia was the type of snobbish woman he should avoid. But he liked talking to her. And that surprised him.

"I am not in need of being 'taken in hand,' " Julia said.

"He should forbid these forays into the sordid underbelly, Julia," Bradstock went on.

Cal had no idea what they were talking about, but he could tell Julia didn't like what the man was saying.

"I am over twenty-one, James," she said crisply. "If I choose to do charitable work, I do so. When I told you of my work, I did not think you would hold it against me."

"It shows you have a good heart, my dear." The duke laughed. "There's charity, my dear Julia, but surely this is beyond the pale. These women don't want help. They've found a métier that they enjoy."

"These women are starving and they have children to feed. I think what is beyond the pale is that there is no real help for these women. Their husbands were our heroes. And I don't believe they enjoy what they are doing," she said shortly.

Cal grinned. Not such a snob, then. He liked seeing Lady Julia with her blood running hot.

"My dear girl," Bradstock said condescendingly,

45

"we can't just hand out money *en masse*. Times are hard for all of us. This year, I could only put in half the order for the wine cellar at my hunting box. Austerity has hit us all."

"Hate to think you had to live without a bottle of wine," Cal said. "If Julia is helping the widows of servicemen, I think that is pretty damn admirable."

Bradstock glared at him. "A gentleman doesn't use language like that at the dinner table."

"Where I come from a 'gentleman' doesn't tell a woman what to do when she doesn't want him to."

"And I've heard where you came from was some kind of cesspool," sneered the duke. "You must be extremely grateful you were saved from whatever ditch you were in."

"James, please. And Worthington, I do appreciate your support, but there is no need for heated discussion."

So the duke got a "please" out of her and he got told off. "Get used to it, angel," Cal said. "I'm the earl now."

Her eyes widened in shock.

"If the man from the slums of New York agrees with you, my dear, isn't that a sign you are doing the wrong thing?" Bradstock asked, looking down his nose. Cal would sorely love to rearrange that nose on the handsome idiot's face.

"James, stop it. Let's speak of something else. And do remember Worthington is your host."

But Bradstock wouldn't give it up. "If I were your brother, Julia, I should give you a spanking for being so naughty."

Cal didn't like the hot, appraising look in the bastard's eyes. "If you don't leave her alone," he said heatedly, "I would be happy to beat you up."

"Please, Worthington. Don't. He is teasing." Julia's hand touched his wrist. Once, when he'd been working in a factory after the War, before he went back to life with the Five Points Gang, he'd gotten a shock from an electric outlet. The sizzle and tingle that had shot through his arm was nothing like the one that came from her touch.

Hell, she was everything he didn't want. Privileged. Ladylike. Superior.

Except she had a heart and was willing to defend her beliefs. He liked her—and he hadn't expected to like any of them.

All the men at the table—the Duke of Bad Manners, the Earl of Whatever, Viscount Something—watched Julia. They couldn't take their eyes off her. Which didn't seem to be making the Countess of Worthington too happy.

Just to piss them off, he said loudly to Julia, You asked me if I like Worthington. For one man to get all this by the accident of his birth is wrong. A man should earn what he gets."

She didn't look shocked. "I can assure you that an earl who runs his estate properly works extremely hard. A responsible earl ensures his

47

estate prospers, cares for his tenants and acts in a just manner. We are not frivolous and we don't spend money lavishly on ourselves off the backs of others."

He looked pointedly at the marble and gilt. "Don't you?"

"Worthington Park would no longer exist if the men before you did that. Anthony's father was one of the best landowners in the country. He was progressive, fair, compassionate. If he had not been, Worthington would have been destroyed by the harsh times that came both before and after the War."

"And you're telling me the tenants are happy to be poor while the earl is rich?"

"The tenants are happy with their treatment. On an estate like this, everyone knows the value of their place."

So damned arrogant. Cal saw red. "I bet that footman over there would rather be sitting at this table than serving it. In America, he could be—if he worked hard and fought for it."

His voice had dropped, low and angry. Lady Julia stiffened in shock.

"Maybe it would be better to keep the riffraff from inheriting," Bradstock sneered. "Stop bothering Julia. You're not fit to clean her boots. Wasn't your mother some servant?"

Damn you. "My mother was a maid who worked in a mansion on Fifth Avenue and my father met her, fell in love with her pretty face and seduced her."

He heard someone's fork clatter to the plate. Anger drove him on.

"My father didn't leave her high and dry when she became pregnant. He married her and got disowned for doing the right thing by her. But he loved her and she loved him. They spent their lives in squalor and as far as the Earl of Worthington was concerned, my mother, my brother and I didn't exist. We could rot in hell. Too bad for all of you that I didn't rot."

For the first time, the countess spoke to him. "Worthington, we do not discuss our private matters at the dinner table."

"Get used to it," he snapped, like he'd said to Julia. "I'm not ashamed to say where I came from. And truth is, I don't give a damn what you want."

The countess went white.

He knew his mother would have been shocked at his behavior. She had struggled to raise him to be honest and decent and good—then he'd had to throw all that away to survive and help his family after his father was killed.

A lot of good it had done. He'd had to do bad things to bring home money for her and his brother, to support them, to make sure his family survived. He'd had to work for the gang who . . . Hell, it was join them or be beaten to death

49

by them. After all that, Mam had died anyway—

Cal felt everyone's eyes on him. They all looked at him with disgust or anger. Good—there was no point making them like him before he ripped the estate apart and destroyed Worthington Park—destroyed everything they cared about.

After dinner, Lady Worthington approached her. "I am exhausted. Fear is a very draining thing. Julia, my dear, do help me upstairs."

Then Julia saw Lady Worthington look at Diana and frantically move her head to urge Diana to go to the group of gentlemen who were moving toward the drawing room—Cal, along with the duke and the viscount.

Julia knew what the countess was up to—getting her out of the room to give Diana a better chance to pursue the men.

Then Julia saw Nigel was heading toward her, leading the Earl of Summerhay.

And all she wanted to do was escape. She couldn't face making polite conversation with a man who might want to marry her, when she didn't want him. "I would be happy to take you up to your room, Lady Worthington."

But the countess didn't look pleased her plan had worked. She still looked afraid. Deeply afraid.

When they reached the door of the countess's bedroom, Julia knew she must speak her mind. "You must not force one of your daughters into an unhappy marriage. I will not let the new earl destroy Worthington. Or hurt you."

She was again reminded of the promise she'd made Anthony when he had gone away to war, a promise to look after his family if he didn't come back. His family desperately needed help now, and she must live up to that promise.

The countess laughed. A hard, mirthless laugh, just like Diana's, and it shocked Julia just as much. "What can you do, Julia? Accept that you are as powerless in this as I am."

With that, the countess opened the door to her bedroom and her lady's maid quickly came toward her.

When she returned downstairs, Julia did not go to the Oriental drawing room where everyone had gathered. Instead she slipped through the music room and went out to the terrace that looked over the east lawns and the woods.

The other drawing rooms overlooked the ornate gardens and decorative fountains. But Julia had always loved the view of the woods, which were wild and tangled. Ferns grew all around the edge of them, and the shadowy depths looked like a place where you could find faeries if you were very quiet and waited without moving. Julia used to do that with Diana, Cassia and Thalia when they were children.

Later, she would walk through the woods with Anthony. Looking at them brought that poignant mix of emotion, remembered happiness and pain.

Was she powerless to help? Or could she be like Zoe? Be courageous and grasp life. She believed the countess—who had been so kind to her when she was young and her own mother had fallen deeply into grieving—and Diana, her good friend, were worth fighting for.

"Lady Julia."

She knew who stood behind her from the husky male voice with its distinct American twang. She turned, rubbing her arms as a cool breeze rippled over her. "Good evening, Worthington. It's a lovely night."

He came out onto the terrace, his hair almost silver in the bluish moonlight. Shadows made his cheekbones look even more pronounced, revealed a slight cleft in his chin and curved around his full, sensual mouth. He definitely looked wilder, rougher than Anthony had done. Cal looked untamed and by comparison Anthony had looked gentle and domesticated.

Cal grinned at her around an unlit cigarette he had clamped in his teeth. "I saw you sneak past the drawing room to come out here. Escaping your suitors?"

So he'd noticed that. She was surprised. "I just needed a bit of air."

"You're shivering," he observed.

She turned from the balustrade, toward the

glass-paned door. "I should go back inside."

"Don't go back in. Here, have this—" In a quick movement, he pulled off his jacket and gallantly draped it around her shoulders. She was wrapped in his warmth, in his masculine scent—slightly smoky and earthy, and crisp with witch hazel.

He held it around her and stepped close to her. "You're different than the rest of them."

Caught in the embrace of his coat, she felt a shiver go down her spine. He looked so much like Anthony, yet he was so utterly different. It was confusing. Her heart raced, and she felt, strangely, on the verge of tears just from looking at him. She couldn't stop gazing at his face, thinking how familiar it was. But this was not Anthony. He wasn't Anthony come back to her. He was someone else.

"You're angry with me still," he said.

"No. I was just . . . just lost in thought. In memories." Then she thought: she must get to know this man. If she were to do battle with him, she must understand him. "How am I different?" she asked.

"You welcomed me and you don't talk to me like you hate the sight of me. I'm sorry I was rude to you at dinner. You didn't deserve that."

He looked so forlorn, her heart suddenly panged for him.

This didn't sound like an angry, vengeful man. How hard this must be for him, to suddenly become an earl, to be thrust into a position of responsibility, with a family he didn't know.

"You must understand Lady Worthington," she said impulsively. "Women in our situation know someone new will inherit and we could lose our homes. That is why the countess is so sharp. She really is a good person—she was always like a second mother to me. She is simply afraid. If you were to reassure them they have nothing to fear, I am sure it would help."

Cal looked at her thoughtfully. "What's she so afraid of?"

"She fears you will turn her and her daughters out of the house with nothing."

He stepped back from her. From a pocket, he drew out a silver-colored lighter and lit his cigarette. He leaned on the balustrade and smoked, his shoulders hunched and tense.

"The estate is mine now," he said. "I can do whatever I want with it. Maybe she's right to be afraid."

Julia's heart skipped a beat. "What do you mean? What do you mean to do?"

"Maybe exactly what she fears," he said softly.

"What did she do that deserves such a punishment?"

He blew smoke into the dark. Then he said, "I'm gonna sell the other estates—the hunting place, the house in Scotland. As for Worthington Park, I'm gonna sell it piece by piece."

Horror gripped Julia. She stumbled back, gripping his coat. "You can't do that! You can't destroy Worthington!"

"The countess was right. To say I'm bitter and vengeful would be an understatement. I want to torture the Carstairs family with the pain of watching something they love die."

"You cannot do this! Think of the tenants—all the people who live on this estate and rely upon it. What are you going to do with them? This house has been in the Worthington family for four hundred years." She began to tremble. Anthony had loved Worthington Park. He was devoted to keeping it strong and secure. She and Anthony would talk of future plans when they were married—improvements to the house, a new nursery, a garden in which children could play. New equipment for the farm, improvements to the school so all the children of the estate would be educated.

"You can't destroy the estate," she went on, trying to fight the shakiness of her voice. "It would be heartless. Senseless. If you really want revenge, be the most beloved Earl of Worthington there has ever been. Prove them wrong."

He laughed—a hard, bitter laugh. "No one here is ever going to love me. These estates should be ripped apart. They belong to the people. There should be no lords and masters."

Her heart thundered. "Well, there are even in

55

America. Can you tell me that in America, rich men believe poor men are equal to them? You can't, I'm sure." She leveled him with a firm gaze. "And I will stop you."

He looked amused. "How do you plan to do that, Lady Julia?"

"I will—" She didn't know what she would do but she had to think of something. She couldn't watch Worthington—the place Anthony had loved with all his heart—be destroyed. "I will make you understand you have a responsibility to the land, the house and the people who live on the estate. I won't stop until you love Worthington so deeply, you won't let it go because it is a part of your soul."

"That'll never happen."

"Yes, it will." She pulled his tailored tuxedo jacket off her shoulders and shoved it at him.

He caught it and straightened, towering over her. A roguish smile curved his lips. "We'd better go back inside, Lady Julia. Even I know that if we're away from the crowd long enough, people are gonna start talking about us."

He took out the cigarette. His mouth lowered toward hers.

She was literally shaking in her shoes. Shaking with fury. But also with something else. With heat and confusion and a sudden, intense . . . *whoosh*.

Dear God, she wanted to kiss him.

And he was awful. Cruel. The enemy.

She took a determined step back and glared at him. "If you think I would kiss you after you just announced you would destroy this beautiful place and ruin hundreds of people's lives, you are mad. Nothing is going to happen between us. Not *ever*."

She turned and walked toward the door, determined not to shiver in the cool night air.

"I think you're wrong," he called out behind her.

She turned. In clear, no-nonsense tones, she said, "The only thing that will happen between us is that I will make you see sense, Worthington."

She had no idea just how to do that at the moment, but it made a rather lovely exit line. Julia tipped up her chin and went inside, for once thankful she had been trained with a book on her head and could glide in victorious manner with aplomb.

3

Two Proposals of Marriage

Julia stormed back toward the drawing room.

How could she have felt a sudden, dizzying *whoosh* for *that* man?

The *whoosh* had been something she'd experienced with Anthony—that sudden feeling of the world stopping on its trajectory, while she looked into his eyes as if for the very first time.

She'd felt it with Dougal Campbell within minutes of meeting him. It had been when he had begun to describe the surgery he had performed to repair a child's leg and save it from amputation. Her head had swum a little at the thought of an operation, but she had fallen in love with him right then, right there, because he had been so passionate about what he'd done.

Dougal—well, she'd lost Dougal forever now. He was marrying the daughter of a doctor, a girl who would make the perfect doctor's wife. She was happy for him—he deserved the perfect wife.

But after caring so deeply for Dougal, how could she have had that devastating moment of—of something with Cal?

He actually thought he could kiss her *after* what

he'd threatened to do to Worthington. Well, really! And she now knew why she had been riveted to the spot, unable to move. She had been shocked. That was all.

The man was infuriating. Not because he was angry and hurting—she could understand that, if his family had been rejected by the previous earl. His father had been disowned after all.

No, he was infuriating because his mind was closed. This was the modern world—every breath you took was full of change. He must let the past go.

Destroying something never fixed anything. Heaping on more pain never made pain go away. She was certain of it. *Healing* was the most important thing in the world. Zoe had healed Nigel, helping him finally escape the way the War had hurt him. Her mother needed to heal more from the grief of losing Will—if Mother could, she could be happier.

Julia knew the power of healing. She had to make Cal see it.

"Julia."

She almost collided with the Duke of Bradstock as he stepped out of the shadows.

Frowning, he looked down at her. "You were outside with that American, Julia. I saw him follow you out onto the terrace. Did you invite him out there?" he demanded.

James had followed her. Why? Because Cal had?

"I went out on the terrace for some air," she said. "Then the new earl joined me."

"So he just followed you." James grasped her wrist and held it in the circle of his long, strong fingers, capturing her. He peered at her face in the darkness of the corridor—only two electric lights illuminated it. "You look upset. Did he try to force himself on you? Tell me and I'll grind him under my heel like the piece of dirt he is."

Most girls thought the Duke of Bradstock was more handsome than any movie star in the pictures. His features were striking and autocratic; his hair raven black, his eyes dark green and surrounded by thick, long lashes. He had a wicked allure, like Valentino.

Grandmama believed he was interested in Julia, since he had never married after he returned from the War. Grandmama's words haunted her: *you could be a duchess with one simple word.*

James was looking at her . . . as if he would slay a dragon if she asked.

For some reason, she did not feel like a heroine who wished to swoon into the muscular arms of a sheikh-costumed Valentino. She was angry with Cal, but she would not insult him. "He is not a piece of dirt—he is the Earl of Worthington, and we are in his house, James. It is most impolite to be rude. And we simply spoke out on the terrace. Worthington was the perfect gentleman."

"Was he? You were trembling when you came back inside."

"It was cold outdoors."

"I saw his face when he was looking at the countess across the dinner table. Pure hatred. What reason does he have to hate them?"

"That is the mystery, isn't it? I don't know. But I really must find out, if I am to fix this problem and put a stop to Cal's plans."

"Cal? You call him Cal? What plans?"

"He objects to Worthington," she said, not quite answering his questions.

"My God, Julia, you can't approve of this upstart and his lack of manners and breeding?"

What an odd question. She should disapprove of Cal—of everything he intended to do and the way in which he meant to do it. But she knew about grief and pain, how viciously it could hurt.

James moved closer. Suddenly, he clasped her hand in both of his large ones. "Julia—" His voice was husky. "Julia, you must know how I feel about you."

Oh . . . oh heavens. Grandmama was always right. It was an idiotic thought, but the very first one that leaped into her mind.

"I had no choice but to let you go to Anthony Carstairs," he continued. "You were so fond of him, and he was a friend of mine. Then, after his death, I waited patiently. It has been nine years.

Julia, I want to marry you. I must marry you."

Oh heavens. She did not love this man. She'd known him since he was a boy and he had only ever been interested in one thing—himself. And if she were his wife, she could never do anything unless he gave her permission. That was the kind of marriage that existed decades ago. It was one she would never accept.

Grandmama would faint when she learned what her granddaughter was going to do. Gently Julia said, "James, I am so very flattered by your proposal. I am so sorry you've waited for so long—"

"Don't go on," he said brusquely. "There is no need." He released her hand and stepped back. His face became a hard, emotionless mask. "But I would like to know why."

"It is not you. Truly, it isn't. I just—I just am filled with thoughts of Anthony still." But there had been Dougal, so she knew her heart could be touched. Just not by this man.

"Even after this long? Julia, I would treat you like a queen. You would reign over my four estates. I still have a considerable income. My God, Julia, I dream of you every night."

He grasped her wrist again, this time hard enough that she winced.

"James, you are hurting me."

"I'm sorry." He released her. "I've been a damned fool, haven't I?" he said harshly. "Hoping

62

you might realize how much I want you to be my duchess."

He looked at her with such hurt she felt guilty. But she'd never asked him to hope or wait. Never once had she been anything beyond polite and proper.

But this was going to turn messy and emotional and unpleasant, and all her training leaped to the fore. "Dear James, any woman would jump at your proposal. But you deserve a woman who can give you her entire heart. I can't."

"But if you could—" He left the sentence hanging.

What did she do? Lie? It was the ladylike thing to do. One simple statement had her facing the most stunning truth—did she want to be a lady and lie, or did she want to be bold and brave and tell the truth? "If I could . . . well, things would be quite different, I assure you."

That was a lady's response. It didn't insult and it said absolutely nothing. She felt rather guilty giving it. But her heart told her it was for the best.

"Julia, I can't wait any longer."

"I don't want you to wait, James. Please, do find someone else and be happy."

He straightened his dinner jacket. "I bid you good-night then."

He was gone.

Julia let out a deep, relieved breath.

Then she heard a soft movement. Smoke drifted

out from the doorway of the music room. She suspected Cal was in there. He must have come in from the terrace and heard everything. She stalked to the door. Cal was leaning against the fireplace mantel.

He looked up as she walked in. "Why did you refuse him?"

Julia felt her cheeks get hot. "That is none of your business."

"He's a duke, isn't it? Your family's gonna be disappointed."

"My family accepts that I will marry only for love."

"That's what you want? Love? Love can destroy you, you know. It can hurt you like nothing else can."

And he had been hurt. Very badly. By the loss of his parents? Or by something else? "I know that," she said softly. "I lost my fiancé. I know how much it can hurt to love someone and lose them."

"Do you think it's worth it?" he said suddenly.

"Of course it is."

"I disagree."

"Tell me why your heart is so badly broken," she said impulsively.

But he only grinned. "Angel, I have no heart to break." He threw the stub of his cigarette into the fireplace grate and, this time, he walked away from her.

Of course, it was because he was running away from her question.

In the kitchen of Worthington Park, early in the morning, Hannah Talbot let out a huffing breath as she lifted the porridge dish. This was the plain one, the one used for the servants' dinners and not one of the large gleaming silver dishes that was kept under lock and key. That one she never had to clean. As kitchen maid, she was too lowly. The butler, Mr. Wiggins, and the footmen tended to the silver.

With Tansy, the new girl, pretending to be sick this morning, Hannah had done the work of two maids. Her arms ached from polishing the range until it shone like a mirror. She'd had to lay the fires in all the rooms, make the morning tea, as well as stir three pots of sauce at once, since Tansy wasn't there to do any of it.

And she'd had to do it perfectly. With the new earl arriving, Mrs. Feathers, the cook, was in a state. She'd snapped at Hannah for making mistakes when Hannah had been doing the work of two women at once!

Then, while rushing through laying the fires, Hannah had gone to check on Tansy, only to find their room empty!

Tansy wasn't sick at all. She'd gone sneaking off somewhere.

Hannah could have told Mrs. Feathers. But

maybe there had been an emergency and Tansy had been too afraid to ask if she could have the morning off. Tansy had a large family and there was always someone sick or having a baby. Hannah had no family anymore. While Tansy complained about having a huge family who were always telling her what to do, Hannah envied her.

The other servants were already seated at the table as she hefted the pot into the servants' dining hall and set it on the table. Mrs. Feathers waited with the ladle and porcelain bowls. "What were you doing, girl? Harvesting the grain yourself?"

"I'm sorry," Hannah set the pot down as carefully as she could.

The maids and footmen, the valet, her ladyship's lady's maid, the daughters' lady's maid, the housekeeper and Mr. Wiggins sat around the table with their tea or coffee before them. Hannah always had to make tea for everyone else—it was hours after she awoke that she got anything. She was dying for a cuppa, but she had to fetch the other food first.

Finally she was able to slip into the only empty chair with a cup of tea for herself, just as Amy, the new parlor maid who came from London, asked, "What did ye think of him?"

"Who?" Stephen, the senior footman asked.

Hannah's heart gave a little flip-flop in her chest. Stephen had a delicious voice. And he was handsome enough to be a film star, she was sure.

"Rudolph Valentino," Amy said pertly. "His lordship, of course. The new earl."

"He's handsome," Miss White said. Pale and red-haired, she was lady's maid to Ladies Diana, Cassia and Thalia.

"Did you see what he was wearing when he arrived last night? My brother works on a farm and he's better dressed."

"That will be enough, Amy," warned Mrs. Rumpole, Worthington's housekeeper. She always wore a long black dress, and her graying hair was pulled back severely. The maids were terrified of her; Hannah was terrified of Mrs. Feathers, the cook.

"He's got no man of his own," said Mr. St. Germaine, the valet. "So it looks like I'll be dressing him. It's like trying to mold a diamond out of an unformed lump of coal."

Amy giggled at that, flashing her dark eyes at the valet, who was dapper and good-looking, but was apparently quite old because he never looked at the women, not even the young and pretty ones like Amy.

All the maids started talking about the new earl and what they thought of him. Then one asked her, "What do you think of him, Hannah?"

Her cheeks got hot. "I didn't see him. I didn't get lined up for him." She never was presented with the rest of the staff. And the new earl had shown up much later than expected—he'd telephoned to say he would be late. When Mr. Wiggins told him the staff would be presented to him and that the "lineup," as she called it, would delay dinner, the new earl had insisted they not do it. Mr. Wiggins had put it off until this morning.

"Hannah doesn't have time to think about anything but her work," said Mrs. Feathers sharply. "She has to get her breakfast finished. She's got pots to wash. Then we've got to start on the food for luncheon and on the desserts for tonight's dinner. And woe betide us if his lordship isn't pleased with the meals. We'll be out on our beam ends."

Dutifully Hannah finished her porridge. She wished just for once she could relax over a meal and not have to run about like a chicken with her head cut off. But Mrs. Feathers had been unusually worried and snappish ever since the new earl arrived.

She truly wanted to see the new earl—she hated being the only servant here who hadn't done so, due to her lowly rank. She'd hoped he might go into the study or the library while she was making the fires, so she could see him, but no such luck.

After breakfast, she had to plunge her sore hands into steaming hot water to clean the pots and dishes after breakfast. Then Tansy walked in.

"I was feeling much better, Mrs. Feathers, so I thought I would come and help."

"How sweet of you to volunteer your services, Your Highness," said the cook to Tansy. "One would never know that's what you're paid to do. Now hurry up and get to work. Hannah can't handle this lot on her own."

Hannah's cheeks burned. She thought she was doing a magnificent job in coping. When Mrs. Feathers left them, she looked at Tansy, who wasn't getting to work all that quickly. "Where were you? You weren't in bed when I looked."

Tansy, who had wavy black hair and huge blue eyes, paled. "Did you tell her?"

"No, but what happened to you?"

"I went for a drive, Hannah. My gentleman took me for a drive in his beautiful car."

"In the morning?"

"It was the only time he could come, and I knew I could slip out if I said I were sick."

"So you went alone with him in his car?"

Tansy gave a wicked smile. "I did. He drove us out to Lilac Farm and we parked under the trees. He kissed me!"

"Is that all he did?"

"He's a gentleman. A real gentleman. He said he knows he can't expect more unless he marries me. I can tell he wants me. He's going to propose. He's so much in love with me."

Hannah sighed. "But he's a gentleman and you're a kitchen maid."

"But I am pretty—I'm not being immodest. He

69

says I could be a film star. And he's got scads of money. He's got that lovely motor car, and he's been ever so generous with me. I don't think he cares that I'm only a scullery maid."

"All gentlemen care."

"That's not true. They do marry girls from trade."

"That's because those girls have enormous dowries."

Tansy folded her arms over her chest. "Look at the new earl. If a man who was nobody can become an earl, I believe it is possible to better yourself."

Hannah rolled her eyes. "He's the earl because his father was the old earl's brother, silly goose. Since girls can't inherit, and you don't have an earl in your family tree, you have no hope of joining those upstairs."

"I will if I marry a gentleman. And the earl's father married a maid—I heard the story."

"That's one story with a happy ending. Most of the time, gentlemen don't marry the likes of us."

"That they don't!" Mrs. Feathers's booming voice made both her and Tansy jump. "If I catch you flirting with any gentlemen, you'll be out of here without a reference. I'll not keep a girl around who's determined to get herself into trouble! Now, stop your woolgathering, the both of you, because if your sauces are not more than a charred coating on the bottom of a pot, you'll both be gone! And you'll have my boot in your backsides to send you on your way."

Tansy quickly grasped a spoon and stirred hurriedly.

Hannah stirred, too. She didn't say a word but tears stung her eyes. She had not done a thing wrong. Not one thing. Tansy was the one who caused trouble, but her trouble always seemed to include Hannah.

The youngest footman, Eustace, burst in, out of breath. He ran right into the table and Hannah had to sweep her bowl into her arms to keep it safe.

"What demon is chasing you?" Mrs. Feathers demanded.

"His lordship is downstairs," Eustace managed to gasp, between sucking in deep breaths. "Said he wants to talk to you, Mrs. Feathers."

"For pity's sake, what does he want? If he wants a proper dinner, he should be leaving me alone to get it ready."

But for all Mrs. Feathers spoke in her usual sharp, impatient tones, Hannah saw she looked dreadfully worried.

At Brideswell Abbey, Julia went down to breakfast early. In the dining room, the warming dishes were out on the sideboard and the coffee urn was set up, but the room was empty.

She'd feared Nigel would be waiting, ready to propel the Earl of Summerhay at her. Or her mother would have heard, somehow, that she'd refused a duke, and would be ready to lecture

71

her. Mother continually pointed out that one thing had not changed in the modern world—men still wanted young brides and Julia was going to end up on the shelf.

Julia filled her plate and carried it to the table, when a low, deep voice said, "G-good morning, Lady Julia."

She turned and faced the Earl of Summerhay. Who wore riding clothes. And a slight blush.

"Good morning. I take it you are riding today? It's the perfect day for it—not too hot yet," she said brightly. Weather was the safest and most mundane of topics.

Last night, she had spoken to him a little at Worthington Park, and then at Brideswell, after they'd returned and before they had gone up to bed.

Nigel had tried to encourage him to talk about the heroic things he'd done in the War. But he had been very modest about all that. Nigel told her Summerhay had saved many men's lives. He had captured a German machine gun nest single-handed. He was indeed a hero—a quiet and unassuming one.

She liked that about him.

But there hadn't been any moment with him when the world had halted on its axis. She didn't know why not—it simply hadn't.

In fact, she had rejoined the group after James's proposal. She had been talking to Summerhay when Cal had entered the drawing room. For a moment, she didn't hear anything poor Summerhay was saying.

Of course, that was because she'd been afraid of what Cal was going to do. Mysteriously, he hadn't done anything at all. He hadn't caused a scene or made any threats. He had played the perfect host. And she couldn't understand why—

"Yes, I'm going riding with Nigel," Summerhay said. "Care to join us?"

He looked so hopeful, her heart ached. "I would have loved to, but I have commitments for the morning. I rode earlier."

"I'm too late, then." He looked rueful. "I've heard you're a bally good rider. Nigel admits you've bested him at some fences. That's high praise since he never likes to admit he's been beaten."

She smiled. "Marriage changed my brother quite a lot." Then she could have bitten off her tongue. Talking about marriage was not a good idea.

"He's a lucky man to have found such a lovely wife. I hope to be as fortunate." Then suddenly, earnestly, he said, "Julia, I would like to see more of you. You are one of the most remarkable women I've ever met."

Oh dear. She was not on the shelf yet apparently.

Summerhay was a nice and charming man. For one moment, she thought: *This might be my last chance to marry. And he is a good man.*

"Julia—?" He was brilliant red now, the Earl of Summerhay. "I know we have barely spent time together but I am hoping . . . hoping that when we know each other better, you might consider doing me the honor of . . . No, I'm sorry. It must be too early for that for you. But I know my own heart."

Could love and desire grow? Did love have to be instantaneous?

But she thought of walking down the aisle and saying "I do" and not being in love with him. She couldn't do it. And it would be wrong to do it to a hero.

"I do enjoy your company, but my charitable work is taking up almost all of my time." That was too obviously an excuse. This man deserved honesty. For she could spend time with him, let him court her, but when she searched her heart, she didn't want to. It was wrong to judge so quickly, but she thought of being courted and she wanted to . . . to run, really.

"The truth is, I had already given my heart to a doctor," she explained, "but he has gone to London to work at a hospital. I know it takes me a long time to get over a lost love. I mean this as no slight against you. I am just not ready to move on."

"But you will be—someday?"

"I don't know," she said truthfully. "And so I can't ask you to wait."

"I want to wait."

"No, please. I can't make you any promises, Summerhay."

"I know that. If I wait, that's on my conscience, not yours. It's a chance I am willing to take." He stood, bowed. "I should go and prepare for riding. Until later."

Then he was gone.

She knew in her heart she had done the right thing. She wanted the *whoosh*. Even if it meant no marriage at all. Which meant she'd best be prepared to make a life without a wedding.

On the way out of the dining room, she encountered Zoe, who smiled and said, "I've decided that your plan to help your war widows is sound. You don't need to worry about taking a loan against your dowry. We'll be partners. I'll provide the financial backing and business advice, you will work with the widows to help them create businesses that are suitable."

She threw her arms around Zoe, who laughed. "I've never seen you look so bubbly, Julia."

"I don't know if I've ever been quite so happy. Except when you married Nigel. Good things will come of this, Zoe. I feel I am about to change the world." Or at least her precious corner of it.

4

Modern Art

Julia knew of one thing that could make a woman forget about marriage and love and all its associated problems.

Well, two things.

She left the house, walking briskly to Brideswell's garage. She had money thanks to Zoe. And a list of women whose lives she was about to change.

That was the first thing that was more important than suitors and marriage.

The second?

Her beloved automobile—a brand-new roadster from America with glossy paint and shiny chrome, leather seats, leather-wrapped steering wheel and an engine that roared with power.

She was driving past the house, toward the front gate, when a young footman ran out and stopped her.

Over the rumble of the idling engine, he shouted, "Lady Diana at Worthington Park asked if you might drive over there right away. She says they are in the midst of a disaster and only you can help, milady."

Julia's heart plunged. The new Earl of

Worthington—Cal—must have told them his plans. "Thank you, George." She put her motor into gear and pressed on the accelerator. Trixie, her motorcar, roared down the gravel drive and through the open main gates.

When Julia arrived, Diana met her on the drive. "Goodness, you look pale," Julia gasped. "Are you ill? Is this about Cal's—?"

"Not here." Diana dragged her to the music room. Sunlight flooded in on the grand piano, the harp, the cluster of gilt-and-silk chairs. A maid came in with a tray of coffee and before Julia could ask her question, the countess burst in. Her plucked brows flew up in surprise. "Why are you here, Julia—?"

"To see me, Mother," Diana said. "I asked her to come, since you are so upset. Julia will know what to do."

"Yes, I suppose Julia will." Lady Worthington sank into a chair. "Mrs. Feathers has quit! That *man* went down to the kitchens and questioned everything she did. Even suggested the servants should eat better and there should be less waste in the dining room. Apparently he cast some aspersion on her character—she believed he accused her of *theft*. She is packing her bags as we speak. He has done this deliberately to spite us, for where can one find a cook at short notice? He fired his valet, a hall boy and a footman this morning and he has driven away our cook."

Julia stared, dumbfounded. Heavens, Cal had already begun.

"This is wretched," she said. "How can he fire the staff when work is so hard to find?"

"*Servants* are hard to find," Lady Worthington said, holding out her hand gracefully for coffee.

Julia poured and gave the countess a cup, then handed one to Diana, who looked everywhere but at her mother and tapped her foot anxiously.

"The *earl* declared they should find real work and 'do better,'" the countess cried. "Do better than work at Worthington Park? Preposterous!"

Cal simply didn't understand. Many of the servants didn't want to "do better," which often meant long hours in gruesome conditions in factories and offices. They took pride in their work running a great house.

The countess tried to set down her cup, but her hand shook so badly the cup overturned, spilling coffee. "Blast!" the countess gasped. Then she began to sob, burying her face in her hands. Diana stared helplessly, in shock.

Julia quickly put her arm across the countess's shoulders. "I will see about this, I promise. I will stop him."

"Stop him?" The countess lifted her head from her hands. She had turned a terrible shade of light gray and looked deathly ill. "What do you mean?"

Julia swallowed hard. "Did Cal tell you he

intended to do this? Did he speak of any plans he has, now that he is the earl?"

"I do not care what he wants—" Lady Worthington broke off, putting her hands to her mouth. Through them, she cried, "I wish we could be rid of him! But we can't." She turned to Diana. "The only way I can see that we might have some protection is to have influence over him. As his wife, you would exert some control. Go and *find* him."

"Go and find him and do what with him?" Diana protested.

Lady Worthington had been on the verge of collapse. Now she became commanding and strong once more. "We are desperate, Diana. Go at once and make him fall in love with you. It is the only hope we have."

"Mummy, one doesn't just go up to a man, especially a horrible, obstinate, hate-filled man like that, snap her fingers and make him fall in love."

"You've always been a determined flirt, Diana. For heaven's sake, put it to good use for once!"

Diana burst into tears, turned and ran from the room.

"The girl is being an utter fool! Does she not see what will happen to us if she does not do this? She must marry the new earl."

Cal's arrival—and the fear of what he would do—had changed Lady Worthington completely. Julia had never seen her behave cruelly with her daughters. "Diana is just as afraid as you are," Julia said softly. Probably more, she thought. "Please don't be harsh with her."

"I must be harsh, or we're ruined. I suppose she is balking at her duty. She is behaving like a foolish modern girl who wants to marry for love. I suppose she has fallen in love with someone unsuitable, just to spite me."

"How—?"

"Aha! I thought as much." The countess fixed Julia with a penetrating gaze. Julia was astounded at the rapid change in the woman—she had been on the verge of collapse, now she was sharp and angry. This must be what sheer fear did to a person. And it appeared Cal hadn't told her of his plan. Lady Worthington did not know the worst of what Cal wanted to do.

"Who is she in love with?" the countess demanded.

Julia swallowed hard. She believed in honesty but she had to lie for Diana. "You are wrong. She is willing to marry him. For all your sakes."

"Do not sound so disapproving with me, Lady Julia Hazelton. I will protect my family at any cost. Remember that."

"But Cal is in pain, as well," Julia said. "I do not approve of what he is doing, but it comes from a place of great hurt. Was there a horrible thing that was done to him? If I knew what it was, I could—"

"It is none of your business!" The countess's voice crackled like ice. "Now go. Please."

"I will. I will go to see Cal and try to put a stop to this."

She must do so—just as she had promised Anthony she would look after his family. He couldn't have known such a disaster would strike, and it now seemed so sad and eerie that he had begged her so passionately to take care of them all.

She marched out of the room, but as she reached the hallway, she heard the countess erupt into violent sobs. Julia hesitated. Did the countess need her?

She paused just outside the door, her hand on the door frame.

"I will lose everything," the countess gasped, through choking sobs. "John, you wretched fool. I would have protected you. You didn't have to take your own life."

Julia was stunned. Lady Worthington had lost her eldest son, Anthony, at the Somme. And her youngest son, John, in a motorcar accident. But surely, John's accident had not been deliberate? It had been a foggy night. It was assumed John had taken a wrong turn—the gate to the lane leading to the quarry had been left open. In the poor light, he must have mistakenly gone that way, expecting the gate to be closed, as it usually was. He had gone over the edge—

Julia knew she should not go in now. The

countess would be appalled to think her words had been overheard. But if she had kept such a painful secret for years—one Julia wasn't sure how the countess could know—she had suffered greatly in silence. Julia wished to help.

She paused a moment, hoping to cover her eavesdropping, and knocked lightly on the door. Stepping back into the room, she saw Lady Worthington set down her cup. With a frightening calm, the countess said, "The curse is true. There is nothing left for me but tragedy."

"Lady Worthington, please don't say such a thing," Julia began.

"Why should you care about us? You could marry the new earl and become mistress of Worthington after all."

The woman spoke with such bitterness, Julia recoiled. "No. I don't want that at all. I want only the happiness that comes from love—"

"Happiness? What utter madness! Who would aspire to happiness? Who would chase such a fleeting and horrible thing? No one is happy, Julia. Life is about perseverance. I have to protect my girls. That is what is left for me. Protecting them. Settling them. Then nothing can touch them. Nothing."

"Let them find happiness. Please."

But the countess's eyes blazed. "I know what is best for them. Now please go. I wish to be alone."

Julia left, drawing the door closed firmly this

time. She was going to leave, but not without confronting Cal over what he was doing.

She knew the countess had spoken the truth in those unhappy moments. The countess believed the crash had been deliberate, not an accident.

But what had driven John to do it?

"Yes, milady," the Worthington maid replied, in answer to Julia's question. "His lordship has gone upstairs, to the attics."

"The attics? Are you sure?"

"Yes, milady." The girl tried to maintain a dutiful expression but then it failed, and her eyes were wide with excitement. "We've all been talking about it downstairs. Lord Worthington went belowstairs to speak with Mrs. Feathers. Then he wanted to know how to go up to the attics."

"Is it true he has let go his valet, a footman and a hall boy?" Julia asked.

The girl nodded. "It is true, milady. He said they are to find better employment. He told the valet that having a man button his shirt was demeaning to both of them. Mr. Wiggins was right shocked—oh, I didn't mean to be speaking out of turn, milady."

"I will not say a word to the housekeeper, I promise," Julia said.

As soon as she turned away from the maid, her patient smile died. She'd already heard Mrs. Feathers's account of events. To ensure the cook stayed, she needed Cal.

Who was in the attic. For what purpose, she couldn't imagine.

Julia hurried to the stairs that led to the upper story of the house—here were the servants' rooms and the nurseries. Sunlight spilled out into the hallway floor from a room at the end of the corridor and she smelled a strong odor, like potent alcohol.

Was Cal up here drinking?

Julia reached the doorway of the unused nursery—

And stopped in her tracks. A wooden easel stood in the middle of the room, a table set up beside it. A painting stood on the easel, but all Julia could see was Cal's back. He wore a white shirt with sleeves rolled up to bare his forearms. She'd never seen arms tanned to a dark copper on any man but a laborer or farmer. Wide shoulders filled out the linen shirt, and the tails hung out of his trousers. His feet were bare.

He balanced a flat board covered in blobs of oil paint and mixed it with a long, black-handled brush.

The muscles of his broad back moved under his shirt.

She was rooted to the spot—warm, breathless and feeling as if everything had fallen away.

Then Cal moved and she saw the picture.

"But that's me," she gasped.

It was a painting of the terrace where she had

stood last night. The picture was only partly finished. It was sketched with lead pencil and her face was filled in, as was some of the background of the night sky.

It was a wild, modernist painting—the sky was rendered in vivid slashes of black and indigo and violet, with gray layered upon it to show moonlit clouds. The sky truly looked as if the clouds were hurtling past the moon. And against all that darkness, she seemed to glow like a candle's flame.

Cal turned. "I don't let anyone look at my unfinished work."

"The door was open," she pointed out.

"I was told nobody comes up here in the daytime."

She looked past him at the intense, vibrant portrait. The woman's face was definitely hers, but more perfect. Her lips even looked as if moisture glistened on them. The blue eyes seemed to burn with inner fire.

"What do you think of it?" he asked.

"You've made me much more vivacious and interesting than I really am."

"I paint what I see, angel—but tempered with my feelings and my soul. I want to put raw emotion on my canvas. And that's what I see in you. Raw emotion. Fire and passion."

No one thought she was fiery or passionate. Everyone thought her cool and controlled. She felt passion, but she almost never showed it. How had he seen that inside her?

"You see something quite different to the person I am, Worthington."

"I don't think so." He mixed colors on his palette, looking at her from under his mussed blond hair. "I think I see the real Lady Julia behind the restrained exterior."

His gaze moved over her in the most shocking way. She should be outraged. Yet it wasn't a bold look. It was a raw, appreciative look, given to her by a stunningly handsome man—

She had better put a stop to it at once.

"I am a lady through and through, Worthington. You won't see anything beyond that."

He grinned. "It's too late, doll. I already do. And it's Cal, remember?"

His soft, deep voice sent a shiver through her. Then she thought of the countess sobbing with shock and terror. Julia crossed her arms over her chest. "Was losing the cook part of your plan to tear Worthington Park to pieces? As well as firing servants who are now out of work, with no place to stay?"

To her shock, he did not respond. He went back to his painting.

"It's rude to not answer," she said.

As he worked he said, "It's true that I would have waited to get rid of the cook. I like to eat. But it made me mad to see so much food thrown away. I know what it's like to be hungry. Have you ever lived a day on some broth and one piece of bread?"

That startled her. "Was that all you had?"

He slashed paint on the canvas and a stone balustrade began to appear. It looked real, as if she could feel the roughness of stone.

"No, I went without food by choice, Lady Julia, what do you think? My mother would feed my brother and me first and if there was nothing left, she didn't eat at all."

"I'm sorry." Of course, she didn't know what it was to be truly starving. Even when they had been in financial dire straits at Brideswell, there was always food. Instead, she had been trained to *not* eat, to do little more than nibble at all the dinner courses to keep her figure. "But I am familiar with hardship. There are many people in the village who are suffering after the War. And surely the food that is not eaten at meals is used."

"Not much of it." His voice was a low growl. "Why shouldn't it go to people who are needy? The dogs get more of the leftover food than people do. The cook didn't see anything wrong with that so I fired her."

For all he growled like a tiger, Julia felt hope. He cared about people who did not have enough. Once he understood the importance of Worthington Park to the tenants, he would never tear it apart.

Surely.

"Well, I have soothed Mrs. Feathers's wounded feelings," she said. "Cooks are accustomed to being the lords of their kitchens. She could be convinced to stay—if you apologize and tell her she may run her kitchen as she has always done—"

"Apologize? Isn't the idea of being the earl that I get to make the rules?"

"Large houses don't run quite that way," she explained patiently. "Servants work for a house for years—often decades. They outlast the peers. The houses run smoothly because servants know their duties and they take charge of them. Zoe—my sister-in-law—says they run like large American offices."

"I could hire another cook."

"A good cook can be difficult to find. All you have to do is tell Mrs. Feathers she can carry on as usual. Charm her. Then a plan must be made to change her to your way of thinking, but cleverly."

"Uh-huh," he said. He crossed his arms over his chest. "Have you ever cooked anything, Lady Julia?"

She felt a blush touch her cheeks. "My presence would not have been appreciated in Brideswell's kitchens. Our cook and kitchen maids would have been thoroughly shocked."

"So shock them," he said. "Or would you just starve to death if you were on your own?"

She would not give him the satisfaction of admitting she would be without a clue if she had to make her own meal. "I am sure I would survive. Can you cook?"

"I can. When my mother was sick, I cooked for all of us. When I paint landscapes, I travel out into the wilderness in a canoe. I camp and paint and cook over a campfire."

"You do?" That sounded so primitive.

He walked over to her. He held out the brush. "Would you like to try your hand at painting?"

"I have painted before in watercolors. And we really should speak to Mrs. Feathers."

"What if I'm not willing to grovel? After all, with all the food in the larders here, I'm capable of feeding myself."

He watched her as he spoke. Obviously, he was looking to get a rise out of her. "The servants must eat, as well as the family."

"I'd be willing to let them look after themselves. Or are you trying to tell me that the countess and her daughters would starve out of pride before they'd condescend to make their own meals?"

"I don't know about them but the servants would."

"The servants would what?"

"Starve before they would cook for themselves."

His brows lifted. "The servants think they're too good to make their own meals?"

"Exactly."

He laughed. "Is snobbery bred into all of you?"

"Everyone is aware of their own position. It's the way we are."

"So I'd have a mutiny on my hands if the cook

leaves and I don't replace her." His lazy, sensual grin unfurled. "That could be fun. But I have a better idea. I'll go and make nice with the cook, if you come here and paint."

"What about the footman and the boot boy? And your valet?"

"I'll help the young men find better work. And the valet was glad to leave. He said it was like dressing a performing bear. I told him a bear would be less dangerous, then he ran." Cal crooked his finger at her. "Come and paint with me, Julia. You'll like working with oil paint more than watercolors. It's more sensual."

That word made another shiver rush down her back.

"It's thick and tactile and you can build with it, play with it. I bet you were taught to paint timid little pictures. See what you can do with this." With a palette knife instead of a brush, he scooped up indigo and yellow and layered it thickly on the canvas as if to show her how very much unlike watercolors it was.

"I'm not dressed for painting and you do not have a smock or a coat," she said.

With infinite slowness, his smile lifted the right side of his mouth. That lopsided smile made her tingle deep inside.

He set down his palette, the knife, the brush. He undid the buttons of his shirt and shrugged it off.

Leaving his chest, his torso, completely bare.

Her jaw dropped.

He came toward her and she simply couldn't move. A lady shouldn't look, but she couldn't tear her gaze away from his beautiful, well-muscled form.

"Slide this on."

"Your *shirt?* I can't possibly."

He draped it around her. Staring at the shirt, she realized it was finely made. An expensive shirt. But he was supposed to be a poor, bohemian artist. It was like the beautiful dinner clothes he wore last night. Where had they come from?

She breathed in the scent of him on his warm, luxurious shirt. Heat uncoiled in her, like smoke spiraling from a burning candlewick.

He pressed the paintbrush against her hand and she clasped it. Then her good sense came back. "Cal, I can't wear your shirt. I cannot be in here with you in a state of undress."

"You're a grown woman, Julia." He put his hands on her shoulders, firm and strong. He turned her away from him and toward the canvas. "I've painted women in the nude."

"You were naked? Good heavens."

He laughed. "They were, not me. And I didn't sleep with . . . all of them."

She knew he was trying to shock her and she calmly said, "That is hardly reassuring."

"I suspect my honor is safe with you, Julia,"

he teased. He lifted her hand so the brush almost touched the canvas.

"What if I ruin it?"

"You won't. We can paint over anything you don't like."

"You can take your hands off my shoulders." She felt the warmth of his palms through his shirt and her frock.

"Not until you make your mark on your portrait, Julia." He picked up the palette.

"You are infuriating." She dipped the paintbrush into a mound of red paint. Then she made a small dab in the corner of the canvas. "There."

"You're not afraid to paint a canvas, are you? I thought you were going to be a tough adversary."

"Fine." She half turned and took the palette out of his hand. Using the kind of style he'd done—modernist dabs and slashes of paint—she tried to do the skirt of her dress. Tried to mimic the way it shimmered in the light. She all but threw paint at the picture. Then she stopped, her chest heaving. It was rather exciting—

She saw what she'd created. "It's awful. It isn't anything like what I wanted to do."

"But I got to prove I'm right and you're wrong." He leaned forward. The warmth of his breath caressed her ear. "You are passionate."

He moved, so his lips touched her cheek.

The *whoosh* came again, so startling and swift it almost knocked her back into the picture.

"You want to kiss me," he said huskily.

"I do not." But her heartbeat rushed up and down as if it was playing a piano scale.

She thought of Anthony, who she had loved with all her heart. And Dougal, who was so noble and admirable. She had *loved* those men. She didn't love this man. She barely knew him. And so far she'd learned he was brash and bold and infuriating.

But the temptation to kiss him was so strong she almost wanted him to just kiss her and take all the responsibility for it away.

No, she was *modern*. Modern women didn't act like weak waifs.

She turned, and smacked the paintbrush against his lips. "I do not want to kiss you." She looked straight into his blue eyes. "Now, if you intend to eat anything today, we had better speak to Mrs. Feathers."

She pulled away from him, and grabbed a rag from a small wooden table near the portrait. She tossed it to him so he could wipe the blue paint from his mouth. Then she held out his shirt.

Cal rubbed the rag over his lips, taking off the paint in one swipe. Grinning as he did.

If Julia were one of his models, he would put his now-clean mouth to her neck and kiss her until she melted. Until they ended up hot and sweaty in his bed, making love.

After the War, sex had become a hell of a lot

more available. Now women weren't willing to deny themselves pleasure until they got married. Everyone had seen that life could be a fleeting thing. One moment you were laughing, deep in love with someone, thinking of the future. The next you were in bits and pieces, strewn across some European field.

Could he coax Julia into his bed?

He threw down the rag, took his shirt from her hands and shrugged it on. After he buttoned it, tucked it into his trousers, he said, "Let's go and see the cook."

"All right." Julia walked ahead of him, her trim-fitting skirt swishing efficiently around her hips. It was a modest length, reaching her midcalves. But he liked the way it clung to the curves of her hips and hinted at the sweet voluptuousness of her backside.

He wanted Lady Julia Hazelton. He wanted to break through her ladylike reserve and release her passion.

Before he left Worthington for good, he was going to do it.

5

The Woman with Shell Shock

Cal followed Lady Julia through a green door. This part of the house looked different. The walls were plain white; the stairs narrow with worn treads. No need for beauty where the servants worked.

"Why you?" he asked. "Why didn't the countess go see the cook? Or Diana, the daughter who's being forced to flirt with me?"

Julia looked startled, but then said, in her cool, ladylike tones, "They are both too upset. The countess is living in terror. Diana is— She isn't well. You have not told them of your plans?"

"Not yet." He leaned against the banister, looking at her. God, she was a beauty. Ivory skin. Full lips lightly colored red with discreet lipstick. Stunning eyes with long, dark lashes.

"You deliberately want to draw it out and be cruel?" she accused.

"I've got my reasons."

Lady Julia had the most impressive poker face. She kept her expression serene but he could feel hot anger inside her under that controlled facade. For a moment, he thought about explaining himself. Telling her why he wanted to hurt the family.

Why should he have to justify himself to her?

"So you're trying to save the house by keeping the cook from walking out because the others don't have the courage."

She gave him a cool stare. "I believed I could convince Mrs. Feathers to stay, so I should try. Whether it is my house or not."

"And you thought I'd thank you for it?"

"You must not take your grievances out on innocent people."

"Her ladyship and the earl did." Cal had to struggle to speak as calmly as she did. "Don't speak to me like I must be scum because I was born poor. I was born to decent and honest parents who helped other people and were charitable, even when they had nothing."

He could see the flash of surprise and shock in her eyes. His heart pounded.

He wanted to kiss her. Wanted to push her back against the plain white plaster wall and devour her with his mouth until she was panting against him.

But that wasn't the way to do it with Lady Julia.

He raised her fingers to his lips. His father used to do this with his mother, and it always made Mam giggle, then melt and sigh and forget worry and despair.

Julia had soft skin. Pretty hands that smelled like flowers. His head told him to be angry that her hands obviously did no work, but lust shot through him at the idea of having such soft, pampered hands gripping his shoulders as he made love to her.

She pulled her hand back. "Stop this, Worthington."

He loved hearing her speak so primly. It entertained him. "I want to make amends."

"Then don't tear Worthington apart. Your father was disowned and that was *wrong*. But what others did to you should not dictate whether you behave nobly or not."

"You people would say a man can never rise above his birth."

"I would never say that." With that, she turned away from him and continued downstairs.

"You know what's funny?" he said. "When I took a tour of the house this morning and came down to the kitchen, the servants assumed I'd gotten lost. Every footman and maid I encountered, the butler, the cook, all thought I must have gotten lost to be down in the servants' basement."

"We refer to it as 'belowstairs.'"

He grabbed her arm, stopping her. "It's a cold, damp, stone basement without enough light. Don't give it a prim name so you people can pretend that the kitchen staff is happy to be trapped down there day and night, scouring pots."

Julia recoiled from his harsh, accusatory words and continued to the bottom of the stairs, but she paused before she opened the door.

"You want to sell Worthington. Whoever buys it will employ a kitchen maid. Count the number of servants next time you're at a house belonging to someone who is 'new money.' They will have more than us."

"New money." He scoffed at the term.

But Julia went on, "Inquire about the working conditions of those servants. Find out what their employers do when they can no longer work or become ill. All too often they are let go and replaced. There is no pension, no care, no compassion. We try to take care of our own. We truly do. You Americans champion capitalism, but it can be a harsh thing."

She pushed open the door and walked out.

He let her get the last word. This time.

Cal followed her through a stone-arched doorway, into a room with a long wooden table. A woman sat at it, sewing. Two footmen were having cups of tea. Two maids sat there, giggling together.

Their happy demeanor startled him. He'd expected to see girls who were exhausted, who looked like they were being crushed. He never dreamed a girl would sparkle when she was working her fingers to the bone as a maid.

Had his mother sparkled and laughed like that? He'd rarely seen her do it while they were struggling to survive.

"Good morning," Julia said. Every person at the

table pushed back their chairs and bolted to their feet to stand at attention.

"My lady?" The housekeeper hurried out of a room, keys jangling at her waist. "My lord."

"My lord. My lady." The snobby butler hurried in. "May I help you both?"

"We wish Mrs. Feathers to spare a moment of her time," Julia said. It wasn't a question. It was a command, but a sugarcoated one.

"Of course, my lady." The housekeeper disappeared into the kitchens.

A strident voice cried, "What does 'e want now?" Then it went quiet. A moment later, Mrs. Feathers showed up at the doorway. The pudgy woman wore a coat that strained over her ample figure, and a surprisingly stylish hat with a feather.

Cal was just about to capitulate and agree to a truce with the cook—just to see what would happen if he made nice with Lady Julia and to find out how she would coax Mrs. Feathers to change her way of thinking—when a loud crash sounded in the kitchen and Mrs. Feathers gasped, "Oh Lord, that was the sauce for the duck. Stupid, clumsy girl!"

Cal couldn't see why the cook would care since she was walking out the door, but then remembered Julia had led the cook to believe he would apologize. Maybe even grovel.

And the crash had interrupted them.

Face reddening with impatience and anger, the

cook whirled around and barked into the kitchen, "You daft twit, can't you be careful? That's ruined. And here's his lordship, concerned about waste. Well, we know who's to blame for most of the food that goes in the rubbish bin. You haven't got the wits of a dog."

Mrs. Feathers lunged into the kitchen with her hand raised as if ready to deliver a slap.

Cal had worked on the docks as a young boy. There he'd been hit and abused. No one was going to abuse anyone in his name. He stalked into the kitchen, sensing Lady Julia was close behind.

Mrs. Feathers gripped a young kitchen maid by the shoulders. Her face was contorted and red with fury. The girl, she'd been introduced as Hannah on his previous trip to the kitchens, was thin—skinny arms stuck out of the sleeves of a beige dress, and an apron was tied around a tiny waist. The cook shook Hannah, who had wide, frightened brown eyes and tears on her cheeks. "It was an accident. I was trying to be careful. But then I turned and the dog was there and I fell over him."

His late uncle's dog, a retriever, let out a whimpering sound and dropped to the floor, gazing up with pitiful eyes. The kitchen maid looked more scared than the dog.

Suddenly, Mrs. Feathers shook the girl, her face dark red with fury. She lifted her hand—

He grasped the woman's wrist and hauled her away from Hannah. "So you are responsible for the bruises on this girl," he said, his voice low and cold. He pushed up the girl's sleeve, revealing a row of fading bruises along her forearm. "I noticed them when I was downstairs earlier. But she didn't rat you out. She insisted she got them because she was clumsy. Now I see what's been happening." He dropped his voice lower, so it was nothing more than a growl. "No one hits anyone in my household."

The cook had turned white.

"Apologize to Hannah."

"What?" gasped Mrs. Feathers.

"You had no right to say what you did. No right to touch her. She's a person, not a whipping boy."

"She's not a person, she's a kitchen maid. I know how to keep my staff in line. I know what works with them and what doesn't, my lord—"

"And I know when I see behavior I refuse to condone," he said with lethal cool. "I was told to give you an apology to keep peace in this damn house. But you don't deserve one. I don't want a woman like you working here, taking out your anger on a defenseless girl. I don't care if you've quit or not, because you're fired. Now get out."

The woman's jaw dropped.

Lady Julia's jaw also dropped.

Hannah the kitchen maid stared at him with red-rimmed eyes. She was older than she looked, older than Mam had been when she had to start working as a maid in that Fifth Avenue house.

"Can you cook?" he said to her.

"Y-yes."

"Her? Cook?" cried Mrs. Feathers. "That's a laugh."

"She's going to cook from now on. Congratulations, Hannah. You've been promoted."

He turned to find Julia staring at him, in as much shock as the others. "I've solved the problem," he said. "I have a cook."

Julia pursued the infuriating Earl of Worthington along the downstairs corridor. "You simply cannot do that."

The earl stopped and faced her. He looked smug, of course, for he had no idea what he had just done. "It's my house. I can do what I want."

"What you have done is completely unkind to that girl."

His brows shot up. "I gave her a promotion."

"The poor kitchen maid has been just thrust into a terrible position, Worthington. She is too inexperienced, and she must be absolutely terrified."

He glared at her, his eyes a blue blaze. "I wasn't going to stand by and let her be abused. If you think I'm going to let my household be run by bullies, you are wrong, Julia. I don't give a rat's arse if that is the way things have always been done."

She supposed he had a point. "But Hannah has to face tonight's dinner without enough help."

"So she serves a bad dinner, so what?"

"I do not believe she is the sort who can easily ignore a failure. Not to mention she will be teased mercilessly by the other staff, who will not want her to get above herself."

"I'll make someone else help her. There are other kitchen maids. Some of the other staff can help. If they don't like it, they know I am more than willing to fire people who cross me."

"What are you going to do to me because I've crossed you? Forbid me from coming to the house?"

"I'd never do that." That slow, sizzling smile—like the path of a flame on a fuse—lifted his lips again. "I'd never get the chance to bring out your passionate side. When you're angry, you burn. You glow with an energy that crackles like lightning."

A mad thought hit her. "You did not just do all of that to make me angry."

"No, but I'll keep it in mind for the future."

He took two steps toward her. She had to tip her head back to meet his eyes. His arms bracketed the wall on either side of her, making her suck in a sharp breath.

"I figure the cook was stealing from the pantry, too, but I don't much care about that."

"That's a bold accusation to make. Don't Americans believe in a proper trial with evidence, just as the English do?"

"I'm not firing her for the theft, even though I'm sure she's guilty. She was offended right off the mark and I figured all that outrage and indignity was because she was hiding something. Also, she kept glancing at the pantry door. Her guilty conscience revealing itself."

"I—I had no idea this was going on."

"Why should you? It's not your house."

"Anthony—" She broke off.

His fingers gently touched her cheek, turning her to face him. Just the contact of his fingertips made her knees feel wobbly, as if she'd danced to jazz all night.

"What about my cousin Anthony?"

"He asked me to look after his family when he went away to war."

"Why would an earl and countess need you to look after them?"

She couldn't answer that. She'd never really understood why. "I did make him a promise and Lady Worthington needs my help now."

"Well, you'll have to excuse me. I have a painting to finish. I'm hot to get all this fire and fury in you down on canvas. But before I go—"

His lips lowered. They were in a shadowed downstairs corridor, but only feet away in the kitchens came the voices of the servants—all filled with vehement astonishment over what had just happened.

Anyone could walk in and see.

That thought alone should make her draw back at once.

But his lips seemed to have become the whole of Julia's universe. His lips were full and sensual and she wanted to touch them. The ache that shot through low in her belly made her gasp.

Now she knew what she felt for him. Lust. Pure and simple. And ladies with sense never let themselves be controlled by lust. Even in this modern age.

She had opened her heart twice and had been terribly hurt. She was almost twenty-seven and it was so hard to think she might never touch a man and be touched by him. She might never know passion or make love.

But she wouldn't do it without marriage. She couldn't . . .

She couldn't do it with this man who wanted only to destroy an estate and people she loved.

She jerked back. "You championed Hannah. What about the other people who live on this estate and who work hard? When you sell to the highest bidder, what will happen to them? You should meet the people who will lose everything when you sell. Or are you afraid to face them?"

He was breathing hard. "You're goading me."

"I'm pointing out the truth," she said sweetly.

"I challenge you to take a tour of the estate with me. To meet the people who are now putting their faith and their trust in you. Who are doing so with no idea that you want to destroy everything they've worked for. Some of those families have farmed for generations—"

"All right. I'll go."

"Fine. Why don't we go now? We could ride out from the house? Or do you ride—"

"Of course, I don't ride," he said brusquely. "The closest I'd gotten to a horse before the army were the ones pulling rag-and-bone carts in our neighborhood." His eyes narrowed. "My father did that at one time for the money. He drove a rag-and-bone cart. When do you think I should share that story with the countess?"

"Don't. It would kill her."

She'd spoken without thinking.

It was a mistake. His face tensed. His mouth went hard.

"It would be better to drive," she said quickly. "I have my motorcar."

He leaned closer and she forgot to breathe.

"You are the most beautiful woman I've seen, Julia. That's why I'm painting you. But the portrait can wait for today. I'd much prefer to spend the day having you try to teach me a lesson. Who knows, maybe you will heal my bitter heart and turn me into a changed man."

Oh no. He was mocking the very thing she hoped

to do. She hoped to heal his bitterness. She hoped to change him.

He knew it—and was making fun of it.

She gave him the smile all young ladies learned—polite, sweet, the butter-wouldn't-melt smile. "I believe I shall."

"You know," Cal said to Julia from the passenger seat as they rumbled down a country lane, "you're the only woman I've ever let drive me."

"I know my way around the estate and you do not. It is far more sensible for me to drive."

"Yeah, but someday I want to tempt the sensible right out of you." He grinned.

"I doubt that will happen," she said, her tone prim even when shouted over the roar of the engine.

He liked the way she looked while driving. She had put on goggles to keep out the wind and the dust, and they made her look sweetly adventurous. She had pulled on a cloche hat and wound a scarf around her neck that fluttered and snapped behind her like a crisp flag.

She was so determined to change his mind about Worthington. But what he had seen today had cut to his bone. He had felt for the girl Hannah. She was supposed to "know her place." What a load of damn crap.

Cal had returned to the kitchen and told Hannah she could give orders to any of the footmen to help her. The snooty butler, Wiggins, had sputtered, until Cal had told him he could follow Mrs. Feathers out the door if he wanted. Wiggins had drawn himself up and had claimed to have been in service to the family for five decades. "What a hell of a way to waste a life," Cal had said. Then he'd gone out. He'd found Julia in the drawing room with Diana, who looked strained and worried. The thing was—he'd looked at Diana's drawn expression and felt an unexpected jolt of guilt.

"So where did your brother get a beautiful American automobile like this?" he asked. "I'm surprised he lets you drive one of his cars."

"It's *my* motorcar. Not my brother's."

"You bought this fine automobile?" He had to admit he was surprised she knew how to drive and didn't just have a chauffeur take her around.

"It was a birthday present from Zoe, my sister-in-law. She had it sent from New York. She called it a symbol of my freedom. I do love to be able to say 'I shall go here' and I can take myself there. It does make you feel powerful."

"Does it?"

The car was a spiffy roadster. The chrome gleamed and the glossy cream paint shone in the sunlight. Julia was a surprisingly good driver, taking the winding turns with skill. She slowed and accelerated with confidence where she needed to. "I guess a duke's daughter is used to getting what she wants," he said.

"Hardly. I could have never bought a motor on my own. Until I marry, the only money I have comes from my pin money. That was how I was trying to fund my charitable work, at least when I was doing the work that no one approved of. Finally, I made up my mind to sell this car. She would have fetched a tremendous amount of money and I need it for the women I'm helping. It would have utterly broken my heart to do it, but I would have done it."

"Darling, I would never let you sell this car."

She glanced briefly at him. Then looked back to the narrow road. "The only money I can even call mine is my dowry and that is locked up as tight as Fort Knox in America. But my sister-in-law Zoe is going to provide the financial backing and I can use that to help women begin businesses or run their farms so they can feed their families. My brother and his wife take great care of the families on the Brideswell estate, but those on the Worthington estate have needed help."

"The Duke of Bad Manners didn't like the idea of mixing with the poor."

She giggled and it was a lovely sound. "You mustn't call him that. But too many people feel that way. It's rather frustrating."

"You still do it."

She turned, flashing a smile that made his heart stop beating. "I am a duke's daughter."

"You're not what I expected of an aristocrat.

Why do you do it, when you have to fight so hard?"

"Once, I would have followed duty and rules, but not now. People lost so much in the War. It is wrong to let children go hungry and women lose their homes! These men gave everything to protect our country, to protect our way of life. I lost Anthony to the Somme and I grieved him for a very long time. Then I realized I needed to find purpose in my life. I didn't want to go back to a life of dinner parties and presentation at court. I wanted to do something of value. It made the pain of losing Anthony go away."

"You're the bee's knees, sweetheart. A dame with a good heart, and a real Sheba."

Her eyes widened. "No one has ever said that to me before. What does it mean?"

"You know what a dame with a good heart is. A Sheba is a girl who oozes sex appeal."

The car jolted in a rut. It was the first time she'd hit anything. Good. It meant he was getting to her. Finding the ways to get under her skin.

Lady Julia turned off onto something that looked like a cart track. Apple trees stretched as far as he could see. "This is part of your orchards," she said.

"We're not on a road, Sheba."

"We are. This is the lane to one of your farms and it also passes several small cottages."

A cottage came into view and she drew off to the edge of the lane. "This is the first family I want you to meet. I was coming here when I received a message to see Diana." She turned off the engine and got out. Then she plucked a basket off the rumble seat behind her—filled with food, he saw—hooked it over her arm and firmly pushed open the small wooden gate in front of the stone building. It was tiny, with a short door flanked by two small windows. Roses budded all over the front.

"These are your tenants," she said. "Your estate encompasses about thirty thousand acres."

"Yeah. That's what the lawyer told me. It's a different thing when you actually see it." But there was something he didn't get. "Why are you looking out for the tenants and not Lady Worthington? Does the countess ignore the lowly peasants? Or is this another promise to my cousin?"

"The countess took very ill after her son John died in the car accident." She hesitated. She wasn't looking at him, which made him curious. "She has experienced so much loss. It was so hard on Lady Worthington. You must consider that—"

"Yeah, but she still hasn't developed an ounce of compassion. Couldn't she have sent her daughters to do what you're doing?"

Julia took a deep breath.

"What is it? What are you hiding from me, Julia?"

"This tenant—Ellen—has had to . . . to sell herself to men to earn money. That means all respectable women are supposed to shun her. They are not allowed to show kindness."

He knew exactly what she meant. "But not you. You aren't afraid of anything."

"That is not true. But some things are simply more important." She reached up to rap on the door. But it was yanked open.

A kid stood there—a kid in short pants and a cap, who looked as skinny as Cal had been as a boy. The child shouted, "I guessed it would be you, my lady!"

"You are very clever, Ben." Julia smiled.

The little boy looked captivated by her soft, melodic voice. Cal figured, from the boy's blush, he had a crush on Julia. He wasn't surprised.

Julia took something from the hamper. "This is from the village bakery. I bought some yesterday for you." She held out a sweet-looking strawberry tart with a shiny glaze.

The boy devoured it in two bites. "You should savor it!" Julia exclaimed.

Cal grinned. That was just what his mother would have said.

"I *did* sabor it. I could have eaten it in one bite," the boy declared with pride.

Julia shook her head. "That is just what my brother Sebastian would have done. Or my youngest brother, Will. Now, go and fetch your mother, young Ben."

As the boy ran off, Cal saw her brush away a tear.

Quickly she smoothed her features into serene, ladylike loveliness, but he asked gently, "What's wrong?"

"He reminds me so much of Will, and we lost Will to the influenza outbreak after the War. He was fifteen."

"I'm sorry." And he was. He'd assumed wealth insulated her from hardship. He could see he'd been wrong. "What about your brother Sebastian? I didn't meet him."

Her whole face glowed when she smiled—even the smallest, gentlest smile. It was sweeter than seeing Paris glitter with light, more breathtaking than dawn in the northern wilds. "He is an artist, like you," she said. "Sebastian went to Capri, but now he lives in Paris. As you did. He is rather like a bohemian, largely impoverished because he wants to support himself with his art, and he is very happy."

"I bet he is. I see the same streak of wildness in you."

She blushed. "Hardly." Then she frowned. "I'm surprised Ellen has not come out to see us." She lowered her voice. "Ben's mother, Ellen Lambert, never married. Ben was born six months after she came back from the War. She had been a VAD and worked as an ambulance driver."

"It was a hell of a job," he said. "A hard, terrifying job. There were a lot of intense romances in the heat of battle."

113

"You had one?"

"I had several. Only one that really mattered."

Her face shuttered, showing no emotion. "Really? I'm sure the others might have meant a lot to the women involved." Then she left him. She went through the living room to the rear of the cottage. He followed—as if he were tied to Lady Julia Hazelton by an invisible string. He just couldn't let her out of his sight. Every moment with her was proving to be something special.

He stayed behind Julia as she paused in the doorway to a tiny kitchen. A thin woman with short blond hair stood at a metal sink, scrubbing with ferocity at a pot. Her shoulders shook as if she were sobbing.

"Ellen, what's wrong?" Julia asked.

He heard Ellen Lambert take a shaky breath. Then she half looked over her shoulder. "Nothing, my lady. I'm sorry. I didn't hear you."

He figured there were aristocratic women who would be slighted because Ellen hadn't rushed to the door and curtsied. But Julia was not one. "There is something wrong, isn't there?" Julia asked.

"No—"

But Julia hurried forward, grasped Ellen's shoulder, forcing her to turn. The woman's right eye was surrounded by a large blue-and-purple bruise.

"How did that happen?" Julia cried. She urged Ellen to sit in a chair at a tiny, rickety table.

As she did, Ellen's fingers went to the large bruise. "The daftest thing. I woke up in the night and I walked right into the edge of the door."

"I doubt it," Cal said darkly. "That was done by a man's fist." His mother used to try to help women in their neighborhood who were beaten by their husbands. He knew all the excuses they'd used.

"What man?" Julia said, her lovely eyes widening. "Was it one of your—your—" For all she had spoken so derisively about propriety, Lady Julia was now—sweetly—at a loss for words.

But Ellen didn't need the word spoken. She paled, but insisted, "It wasn't. It was just a stupid accident."

"Now that I've seen it, why don't we sit down and have tea? You've nothing to hide anymore," Julia said firmly. "This is the Earl of Worthington."

Ellen stared at him. She stumbled to her feet. "My lord. Oh, I'm so sorry—"

"Don't apologize," he said.

The poor woman was white as a sheet. "I shall make tea," she said, but Julia insisted she sit down. Hell, Lady Julia went to the stove and put the kettle on. That stunned Cal.

While the water heated, Julia drew Ellen out of the kitchen into the small sitting room and gave her the basket and a small pouch.

Ellen gave it back. "I can't take this, my lady. And I don't need to, my lady. I've enough for the rent."

"But I don't want you to earn money as you have been doing," Julia said firmly.

"I would rather earn my money than be given charity."

That sounded just like his mother. Cal knew about a woman's pride and stubbornness. But then, his mother had not had any other choice. Just like Ellen.

"You do realize the house is supported by the money earned off the estate. Why then, should the house not support you?"

Ellen started in shock. "I never thought of it that way."

"Well, it is the correct way. The way it has always been and should be," Julia said.

"There are so many who thought we would go back to happy times after the War," Ellen said sadly. "I knew it wouldn't be so. But I never thought there would be such poverty, such helplessness. I've tried to get work. But with Ben—with everyone knowing my story—no one will give me a decent position."

"Well, you need not worry anymore. I have an idea." Julia outlined her plan to loan money for Ellen to open a business. "You may pay me back over time. First, we will find something for you to do. And Benjamin must go to school."

Cal leaned against the wall, watching Julia at work. Aware he was smiling.

Ellen looked worried though, not relieved. "A good school will look at me and refuse to take Ben." She lowered her voice to a mere whisper. "Perhaps I should give him away. He might have a better chance then. But I—I can't bear to give him up."

There were only two times Cal had seen so much pain on a woman's face. Once was in the War, when a village had been bombed and he had seen a woman who had thought she'd lost her children. He found them in the rubble of a collapsed house and brought them out to her. That moment alone had made his whole damned life worthwhile. The other time had been on his mother's face when he was young—and he hadn't understood back then that she'd feared losing him and David.

"You don't have to. You won't lose your son." Cal hadn't expected to say anything, but the words had just come out. The two women stared at him.

"But how can I have a business? Who would come to be served by the likes of me?"

"Don't say that," Julia admonished. "We can make this into a fresh start."

Lady Julia meant well, Cal knew, but she really did live a cloistered life. She had no idea of the reality—how hard it would be for Ellen.

But Ellen did. Glumly, she whispered, "Your

heart is in the right place, my lady. You are so kind. But this won't work—" The kettle let out a sharp whistle. Ellen went to it. Then Ben came into the sitting room. He gazed hopefully at Julia, but she said, "You cannot have another tart, dear. You must save them."

"Ah, give him another one," Cal said. "I'll bring him another treat later."

Julia frowned at him repressively. "Two tarts are rather a lot."

Suddenly Ben said, "Mummy is unhappy, isn't she? I know she's scared and worried. Is that why she doesn't sleep?"

"She does not sleep?" Julia echoed.

"Not very much," Ben said. "I know, because I wake up at night and she is awake. I get in trouble if I won't sleep. Mummy says it's important to sleep. Isn't it important for her, too?"

"Yes, Ben, it is." Cal took a tart from the picnic basket and made a show of sneakily giving it to the boy. Julia looked askance at him, but he asked her softly, "Did you know about this?"

"I had no idea."

When Ellen came back with a teapot and three chipped china cups, Julia asked right away, "Do you not sleep?"

"Of course I do, my lady. If I got no sleep, I'd collapse on the floor."

"Perhaps you only sleep fitfully."

"What woman with a house and a child doesn't

sleep in fits? And in a cottage, there are always things that need to be done. The fire needs stoking. More water might be needed. Often I've forgotten to do things in the day and I remember at night."

"You should try to sleep, Ellen. Exhaustion won't help."

"I will, my lady," Ellen mumbled.

But then Cal understood. "Lady Julia told me you drove an ambulance in the Great War, Ellen," he said. "I went to war in 1917, when America joined the fighting. I saw the women who drove the ambulances. It was terrifying, with shells going off around you. I saw many women killed."

"Don't, my lord," Ellen said sharply. Then she dropped her voice, wringing her hands. "I'm sorry, my lord. But I don't want Ben to hear about it."

"Do you have nightmares?" Cal asked softly.

Ellen hesitated. Shook her head. " 'Course not."

"You're not startled by loud noises? You don't always have a feeling of fear?"

"I— Of course not."

"But you do sometimes, Mum," Ben said, startling them all. "Remember when I knocked over the tin bathtub and you screamed so loud?"

"Ben, you have chores to do. Now be off with you." Ellen shooed him out of the room.

Once the boy had gone, Cal grasped Ellen's

hand. "Listen to me. You're suffering from shell shock."

She shook her head desperately. "I'm not. That would mean I'm mad. I am perfectly fine. Please—don't take Ben away."

"I won't," Cal said. "I promise I will help you. And I will not let you lose your son."

He felt a stare burning his neck. Julia was looking at him, her mouth open in surprise. Then her eyes softened and she looked at him like he was a hero—looked at him in a way that made him feel damn guilty. "Thank you," she whispered.

6

The Missing Girl at Lilac Farm

This was the most exhilarating and terrifying evening of Hannah's life.

As kitchen maid, she'd made all these dishes before, but tonight she felt like she'd forgotten *everything*. She checked the soup—not a cold soup as it was early June and not stifling hot yet. She'd made mulligatawny because the spice would cover up for any number of evils. The aspic was setting up properly, but it almost slid off the plate when she set it down and her heart just about stopped.

A pot boiled over and Hannah took off at a run, lifting it off the heat. The salmon! How long had it been since she'd last looked at it? She set down the pot, opened the oven. Not burned, thank heavens.

Hannah set to spooning the mustard sauce over the salmon. She looked over. Tansy was half-heartedly stirring the sauce for the Chicken Lyonnaise.

"Why am I running about like a chicken with my head cut off, Tansy?" she demanded. "I'm trying to do everything while you stir a spoon in a pot. You're supposed to be taking care of half of these things I'm doing."

"I *am* doing things. You've shouted at me and ordered me about all day!"

"I'm the cook now! That's what I'm supposed to do. When I was the kitchen maid, I took orders all the time. And I got an earful if I wasn't always rushing at full speed. You didn't finish cleaning the stove after lunch and you forgot to wash half the pots. I would have been sacked for that. You heard his lordship—you're all supposed to help. I am being nice to you."

"Well, thank you, Your Highness," Tansy said, her words dripping with sarcasm.

Hannah sighed. Why couldn't she be commanding? One word from Mrs. Feathers and they all used to quake. But Mrs. Feathers did it with words as sharp and wounding as her cleaving knife and Hannah couldn't do that.

Tansy started to hum a jazz song. She swayed back and forth while she stirred, which made the bowl tip precariously.

"Mind. You'll have it on the floor," Hannah declared. She hurried over and grabbed the bowl. Hannah hated to think badly of anyone, but she feared Tansy was deliberately trying to make her fall flat on her face tonight.

"I'm just happy. Do you want to know why?" Tansy dimpled.

Hannah hated the sour feeling that came over

her. She'd never really thought about how she looked until Tansy came. Her mum had always insisted she look "presentable." On her afternoon off once, she'd bought a lipstick and put some on, then forgot about it and had gone home to see her parents with her lips painted red. Mum had scrubbed so hard her lips had stung all day. Of course, now Mum and Father were gone and she had no one.

Hannah brushed back a stray hair with her flour-covered forearm. She had plain brown hair and brown eyes. Tansy's hair was blue-black and she was truly lovely enough to be a film star. Hannah hated the awful feeling of jealousy that now seemed to live in her heart. "Why are you happy then, Tansy?"

"My beau's going to take me out tonight in his motorcar. He's going to wait for me and take me for a quick spin when I'm supposed to go to bed. Says he has to see me tonight. He can't wait any longer. You know what that means?"

"Aye, it means he's going to expect you to give him something in return for these motorcar rides and gifts. You've let him think you're fast."

"I've not let him do anything more than kiss me! I think he's going to marry me."

Hannah's heart sank. "Oh, Tansy, I don't think so."

"He will." Tansy stuck out her lower lip.

"Who is he, anyway? You've never told me his name. Where'd you meet him?"

"Just outside the village. I was waiting for the

bus after visiting me family. It was raining something terrible and freezing cold. He offered to give me a ride back here. He's a gentleman, you know. I think he's the younger son of an earl. He doesn't like to talk about it much, but I can tell from his cut-glass accent that he's a toff. Gloriously handsome and he's mad about me."

"What's his name, Tansy?"

"I call him Geoff."

"He didn't tell you the rest, did he? Oh, Tansy, do be careful. An earl's son isn't going to propose marriage to a kitchen maid!"

"These days, gentlemen are a lot more interested in a girl with sex appeal than in marrying some dowdy lady who has a big dowry and a horsey face." Tansy stuck out her tongue. "You're jealous. That's why you're so hard on me."

"I'm hard on you because I know the standards of this house and you have to meet them. And I'm not jealous. I have your best interests at heart." Hannah wagged a spoon at Tansy. "There was a girl I knew. She was the daughter of the people at Lilac Farm. She went out in a car with a handsome gentleman one night. Maybe she ran off with him, or maybe he ruined her and she had to run away for the shame. Either way she disappeared. She was never seen again."

Hell, he found himself looking forward to seeing Julia again.

Rain spattered down as her car pulled up at the front door. Cal ran out so she wouldn't have to get out. He let himself in on the passenger side. Seeing her was like being hit in the gut—and that had happened to him a lot in the Hell's Kitchen neighborhood where he'd grown up.

Her lips were painted a darker red. A gray raincoat covered her, but revealed her stocking-clad legs below the knee. She had gorgeous legs. She smelled . . . probably the way heaven smelled.

"How was your dinner last night?" she asked.

"Great. Hannah did a good job. We had a dessert that I'll never forget. Fruit and cream and lady fingers soaked in liquor."

"English trifle." She smiled at him. "I'm so glad it was a success."

And off they drove. Along tree-lined lanes that swept up and down hills. Meadows and green fields stretched around them. In the distance he saw a soaring church spire, and buildings nestled among the hills. He had to admit it was pretty.

"This is Lilac Farm." Julia brought the car to a stop beside a low stone wall. Within the wall, a few stone buildings sat in a cluster with a muddy yard between them. The wall continued along a downhill slope, defining small square fields.

Julia pulled up the parking brake. She strode ahead, opening a wooden gate in the stone wall. Cal followed, and as they stepped into the yard, someone inside the largest stone building shouted, "Damn and blast!"

A stream of snorting pigs spilled out of a barn and headed toward them like an unstoppable wave. Pigs moved a hell of a lot faster than Cal expected.

They were going to be crushed against the stone wall. Planting his hands on Julia's small waist, Cal hoisted her up, over the wall. Then he jumped over himself.

The animals scurried everywhere, grunting and squealing. An elderly man stumbled out of the barn. Covered in mud, the white-haired man wheezed, "Stop 'em. They'll get away. Get two of 'em in the front and force 'em back."

Julia scrambled toward the rampaging pigs.

"Go back," Cal shouted. "Let me do this."

He got his hands on one of the pigs but his attention was on Julia. The animal pulled him off his feet. He fell as Julia cried, "Cal!"

Rolling over in the muck, he avoided the hooves and jumped to his feet. Hell, Julia had clambered back over the wall and was waving a scarf at the pigs like a Spanish bullfighter. This time he knew what to expect when he got his arms around one. He held on tight and dug in his heels. Julia flapped frantically and he managed to wrestle the pig so it was facing the barn. Spooked, it ran back toward home. He got a second animal running after the first. Sure enough, the rest began to follow.

A splashing sound came as the farmer dumped the contents of a pail into a wooden trough. Grunting, the pigs scrambled over each other for a spot, their desire to escape long gone.

Julia latched the gate, then ran up to him, laughing, gasping for breath. Her shoes sank in the mud. She stumbled forward, hands flailing because her feet were stuck tight. Cal leaped forward and caught her, wrapping his arms around her. It threw him off balance, and he staggered back so they wouldn't fall—

Their faces bumped. "Ow!" she said and he grunted as she dissolved into giggles. Something he never expected Julia to do, but the sound enchanted him. As he helped her stand up, he looked down.

"Your shoes are ruined," he said. "You should've stayed where I put you."

She laughed. Rain ran down her hat and coat. "Shoes can be cleaned. I knew it was more important that we herded the pigs. And you got the worst of it, Cal. It's ruined your rather nice suit."

He looked down. He looked like he used to in the New York slums. Covered in filth. "Damn it." He rubbed hard at the muck on his trousers, trying to brush it off.

Julia touched his arm. "You needn't worry about some mud on your pants. Anyway, I thought you rather liked to look bohemian."

Normally he didn't care what he looked like.

But in front of Julia, he suddenly felt like he was a poor kid in the slums again, with a dirty coat, torn breeches and a dirty face. "Maybe I just did that to shock the countess." He turned to the farmer and stuck out his hand for a handshake.

"I would like to introduce you to his lordship, the new earl," Julia said. "This is Mr. Brand, Worthington, and his family has farmed here for almost one hundred and fifty years."

Brand looked guilty. "Begging your pardon, yer lordship. Wouldn't have asked you to help with the pigs, if I'd known who ye were."

"You didn't object to Lady Julia helping," Cal observed. "Does she chase pigs often?"

He felt Julia dig him in his side. "Of course not," she said crisply. "But it is important to pitch in where needed."

"A right good sport is Lady Julia," Brand said. "Comes to see me and the missus all the time, she does."

"Harry!" A panicked woman's voice came from another stone building. An elderly woman hobbled out of what must be their cottage. "Sarah's gone. I don't know where she is."

Cal hoped Sarah was a pet pig who'd just been rescued. Then he saw tears streaking the woman's cheeks. He asked, "Who is Sarah? Are you sure she's missing?"

Julia's hand touched his shoulder. Just one look and he recognized she wanted to take charge. He might be the lord, but Julia knew these people and they knew her. He stepped aside. Julia soothed the woman and led her back to the small stone farmhouse. They had to step down some stone steps and duck to go through the doorway.

As Julia went in with Mrs. Brand, Cal turned to the farmer, who was sucking on his pipe. "Who is Sarah?"

"She were our daughter."

"And she's missing?"

"She went missing in the spring of 1916, before all the lads went to fight at the Somme. The missus gets confused. Some days she thinks Sarah is still here. Or she thinks Sarah has just gone missing. Then she gets upset all over again."

"Did you never find out where Sarah went?"

"I don't know what 'appened to 'er. She wasn't the sort to run off with a man. She was a good girl. Since she never came home, I think she's gone. Gone to a better place."

"You think she was killed?" He hated to be brutal, but it seemed to be what the man was saying.

"Even if she just ran away, she were on her own. Prey to the cutthroats on the roads and the scoundrels who ravish girls. If she were alive, she'd 'ave written to me and the missus. The lass never did. No, in my 'eart, I know my Sarah is gone." The old farmer put his pipe to his lips but tears welled in his bright blue eyes.

Cal pulled out a handkerchief, a fine soft square

of linen, handing it to the man. In New York, any woman of the slum neighborhoods knew about Jack the Ripper and the New York murder of a woman in 1891. Cal wouldn't have expected it here, on an English estate. Maybe the girl just ran away. Maybe she was ashamed to write home. She might have gotten pregnant.

"Is there any help I can give you?" he asked.

"We manage just fine, my lord. You may have heard some sorry tales from Mr. Pegg."

The farmer looked defensive, and Cal was thrown off by the shift in conversation. Who in hell was Pegg? Then he remembered the lawyer had told him Pegg was the land agent of Worthington Park. Pegg had left before Cal arrived, taking a job somewhere else. Apparently offended to work for the impoverished American heir.

"Pegg was gone before I got here. Is it just you and your wife on the farm? Do you have other children?"

"Another girl, but she's married. She married a lad from Stonebridge Farm. We lost our boy in the War. At Verdun, my lord."

"I'm sorry. Many good men were lost."

The farmer led him to the house. He ducked his head and went into a rough kitchen. A wooden sideboard held dishes. A teakettle whistled on the stove. Julia plucked it off.

Just as with Ellen Lambert, Lady Julia was

making tea for a farmer's wife. No airs and graces. No snobbery. Never once did she behave as if she were too good to make a cup of tea or too good to help these people.

Cal went to Julia and stood behind her as she poured tea in a pot. He had to ask her this privately, so he lowered his lips so they almost touched her ear. This close he could see the skin on her exposed neck looked satin-soft. "What's wrong with Mrs. Brand? Has she lost her mind?"

His warm breath. The closeness of his body. In the Brands' kitchen, Julia felt her knees go weak.

She was very close to crying—seeing the poor Brands always brought her to tears. For some mad reason, she wanted to press tight against Cal's broad chest. She wanted him to hold her.

But she had been raised to always be cool and composed. To never break down, except in private. And to never fling herself into a man's arms. She had never done that. Not even with Anthony or Dougal. She had been kissed but she'd never been comforted by a man.

She turned with the hot kettle of water, which forced Cal to step back.

Thank heaven. She could barely think with his hot breath on her neck. She hoped he thought it was the weight of the kettle that made her tremble.

"I do know the poor thing has been confused ever since her daughter's disappearance," Julia

131

murmured to him as she poured hot water into the teapot.

"Brand told me that some days she believes Sarah is at home. Or she relives the time when Sarah first went missing and she lives through the pain all over again."

"Yes." Julia could understand how such pain could make you go mad. When she had lost Anthony, it hurt dreadfully. Then there was loss upon loss. All the other young men she knew who never came back from war. Will's death. Her father's passing. Her heart broke and broke.

Oh, she had been strong and stoic. She never let anyone see how much her heart had been shattered. But all that was left of it was bits and pieces inside her.

The only difference between her and Mrs. Brand was that the poor woman's broken heart had broken her mind, too.

"Is there any way to make her understand what happened?" Cal asked.

"I explain it over and over, as gently as I can. But then she forgets what I've told her."

"She just can't face the fact her daughter might be dead. Maybe if she could be snapped into reality—"

"No!" Julia grabbed his arm. "What if that snapped her mind altogether? What if it made her so depressed she did something drastic? That would destroy Brand."

But Cal left her. Frightened, Julia watched him walk to Mrs. Brand.

He dropped to one knee and clasped her hand. "Do you know where Sarah is?"

"Don't do this," Julia hissed at him. "Please don't."

Slowly Cal told the woman who he was. "I'm so sorry to tell you that your daughter is missing. She might have gone away. That's what we hope. I'm going to find out what happened to her. For you. I promise."

He couldn't promise that. How could he find out now, so many years later?

He was gentler with Mrs. Brand than she expected. She had to admit that. He had been that way with Ellen and Ben. Kind. She could see they all liked him.

Of course, they had no idea what he planned.

She bustled forward and gave out cups of tea. "His lordship is worried about you trying to manage the farm," she said to Mr. Brand. "He wonders if you would be happier to leave it. You could be given a cottage—"

"Pensioned off?" Brand exclaimed. His cup rattled, spilling tea. "Nae, I'd not like that at all. This is our home. I won't leave until they carry me out. Brands have farmed this land for over a century. It should have gone on to me son—"

"We can't go." Mrs. Brand looked up suddenly. "We can't! We have to be here for when Sarah

133

comes home! We can't have her come home and we're not here. She'd never find us! If I leave here, she'll never come home to us!"

Julia saw Cal soothe the woman, a look of raw panic on his handsome face. She wanted him to see what it would do to these people to be forced out. Though she hated to make them upset.

"You won't have to leave," Cal said. "Don't worry about it."

Mrs. Brand stared at him, shaking. "Who are you?" she demanded. "I don't know you." The woman looked up helplessly. Then saw her. "Lady Julia! Good afternoon, your ladyship. Is the wedding to Lord Anthony going to be soon? I saw him yesterday. Driving his fancy horseless carriage, he was. All the silver on it shone in the sun. Brilliant red, it was, like a ripe apple. It'll be a lovely wedding, I'm sure."

Julia hated this moment. She didn't want to remind the woman that Anthony died in the War. That would lead Mrs. Brand to remember she'd lost her son, too. But she must be honest.

Then Cal said, "I'm afraid Lord Anthony was killed in the War. He was a brave young man. I am the Earl of Worthington now, Mrs. Brand."

"But you're Lord Anthony. I see it now. You've changed so much, but I do see—"

"No, Mrs. Brand. I'm not Lord Anthony." He gently squeezed her hand. "I'll find someone to help you here, with the farm. How does that sound?"

"We've got our son. And Laura and Sarah. We're just fine."

Cal flashed a helpless look. Julia mouthed: *You can't do anything.*

He stood and reiterated to Mr. Brand, "You need help around here. I'll see that you get it."

He was lying to Brand, surely. And she hated that. As they left, she whirled on Cal. "You aren't going to get them any help. Your plan is to sell their farm out from underneath them. It will probably kill them."

"And it's better to let them die there?"

"I look in on them almost every day. Though, I do agree they need help."

"I will look after them. I gave them my word. And, when I sell this place, I won't leave innocent victims."

"You were kind to Ellen and to the Brands. I can see you really do care about their welfare. You could be a good lord for Worthington Park."

He grimaced, as if in pain. "I couldn't live with myself, angel, if I stayed here and lived like an earl."

Rain came hard that night, slamming against the paned windows of his bedroom. Cal undid his right cuff link and tossed it into a silver dish on the dresser. By rights, he would be undressing Lady Julia right now, exposing her lush, creamy skin, kissing every delicious inch of her. But she kept taking him places where he had no right to be thinking about seduction.

He was going to have to fix that.

Removing his other cuff link, he tossed it, but it bounced out of the dish, landed on the polished floor and skidded beneath one of the wardrobes.

Cal squatted down, reached under the decorative wood skirting and found his cuff link. But his fingers touched something else and he pulled that out, too.

A small photograph, faded and curling.

He looked at it and almost dropped it in shock. Lady Julia gazed back at him with parted lips and enormous innocent eyes, and she was wearing almost nothing at all.

Cal rubbed his eyes. Sure enough, it was not Julia. It was a grainy photo of a black-haired young woman in a corset. The corset gave the woman a generous swell of bosom and the picture showed a stretch of fleshy bare thigh. Her hair was loose and thick. All that dark hair and the huge eyes made the woman look like Julia.

The photograph probably dated from the War, from the look of the corset.

Julia had said John Carstairs was just a boy during the War. So had this naughty photo belonged to Anthony? He flipped it over and there it was—written in careful handwriting. *A, with love.* No initial or name for the woman. Considering he'd sketched and painted dozens of naked women, Cal had to smile. He could imagine a repressed Englishman being titillated by the picture—

"My lord, when do you wish to begin a search for a new valet?"

Cal looked up. He held the photograph in his hand, and Wiggins stood in the doorway. "I told you I don't need one. I'm capable of taking off my own clothes." He held out the picture. "I found this under the wardrobe. Lady friend of Lord Anthony's?" He was teasing, expecting to make the butler blush.

He was surprised when Wiggins turned white. "I apologize, my lord. I did not realize the apartments had not been thoroughly cleaned. I shall have Mrs. Rumpole reprimand the maids for their carelessness." The butler yanked the picture out his hands. "Let me dispose of this, my lord."

Cal didn't want to see a maid getting in trouble. "It's not a problem."

"It is my duty to deal with the matter, my lord. If you will excuse me, I will take my leave."

Wiggins retreated so fast that the door slammed behind him. Lightning forked outside the window, illuminating the room in a flash of silver-blue, then thunder boomed.

It was then he realized that Anthony had never been earl, so had never slept in this room. So why was his picture under the earl's wardrobe?

7

The Gypsy Curse

"I'm to give cooking lessons to the kitchen maid of another house?" Mrs. Creedy, the cook at Brideswell cried, leaning rather fiercely on her rolling pin. Then she suddenly appeared to remember who she'd just barked at. "I mean, if that is what you wish, my lady, of course I would want to do so. But how would I fit it in with the tight schedule of Brideswell? What will Her Grace say?"

Julia smiled, moving back to let the kitchen maid scurry past with pot in hand. "We'll find a way, Mrs. Creedy. And Her Grace has already approved." Zoe was all for the idea, to help Hannah Talbot. "It might not be necessary at all. I shall speak to Mrs. Talbot today. She may not feel she needs help at the moment, but I want us to be there to support her."

"All right, but it seems a strange business to me. A kitchen maid elevated to cook in one afternoon? And I've heard the new earl wants simpler food and less of it."

Julia nodded. "Yes, his lordship is concerned about waste of food, which is quite admirable and noble."

Mrs. Creedy snorted. "His lordship has no idea what needs to be done in a kitchen."

"But he is in charge. And I want to ensure Hannah does not suffer as the new earl endeavors to bring American ways to his kitchens." In the depths of her heart, she did see why waste would appall him. After all, he had been starving. But she would not let him hurt or frighten the poor kitchen-maid-turned-cook, Hannah, even if he believed he was helping her. He had claimed she had produced excellent meals, but rumors had come to Brideswell from the other kitchen maid, Tansy, that poor Hannah was quite out of her depth.

Cal's anger at Mrs. Feathers was justified—Julia had been shocked by the bruises on Hannah's arm—but he had used Hannah as a pawn to score a point on Julia. And she intended to make that right.

"Thank you, Mrs. Creedy," Julia said. But as she walked away, she saw she was as bad as Cal. She was using Brideswell's cook to score her own point on him.

But she would ensure Mrs. Creedy was rewarded for helping, and it would make things much better for Hannah.

She had reached the bottom of the servants' staircase when Bartlet, Brideswell's butler, stepped out of his room and looked at her in surprise. "Lady Julia! I did not expect to see you here. There is a call on the telephone for you. The dowager duchess. I fear she believes she is already speaking to you, my lady. There appears to be sound emanating from the receiver."

Julia couldn't help but smile. "I will take it on one of the upstairs extensions."

Zoe had insisted Brideswell would have more than two telephones—it sported four. Most people were mystified. They all rang at once, for a start. And who needed so many? Their peers dismissed it as American vulgarity.

When Julia lifted up the telephone in the foyer, her grandmother was saying, "That is what I think, Julia. Of course you agree."

Julia rolled her eyes. "Grandmama, I just got to the phone. I haven't heard a word you said. But how are you?"

"Fine, fine, but let's not bother with that. If I shall have to say it all over again, I will."

Julia knew Zoe had given Grandmama a telephone to be cheeky, for the dowager duchess had first approached it as if touching the receiver would mean certain death. Now Grandmama was addicted to the thing. She'd realized its power. On any whim she could make a telephone call and disrupt the entire house.

"You have made a conquest, my dear!"

"A what?"

"A gentleman is smitten. Really, dear, do keep up. I invited the Earl of Summerhay to tea, and he would talk about nothing but you, Julia. All you must do is give a nudge in the right direction—"

"No nudging, Grandmama," Julia broke in. "I do know Summerhay is interested—"

"Then what on earth are you doing about it?"

"I told him I was not ready."

"Not ready? What are you waiting for, dear?"

Julia opened her mouth but the dowager rushed on, "If it's Dr. Campbell, I'm afraid he is out of the picture. If he isn't strong enough to defy all of us to pursue you, he isn't good enough for you."

Julia almost dropped the telephone. For she had not thought of Dougal when her grandmother asked the question. The first face that had come into her head had been Cal's.

But she *wasn't* in love with Cal.

"Grandmama, I must go. I am taking Cal—the new Earl of Worthington—around the estate so he can meet his tenants."

"You call him 'Cal,' do you? And what does he call you? Please tell me it's not 'Julie.' "

"I can safely assure you it is not that."

"Do not be too familiar with that man," the dowager declared, over the wires. "I think he's one who would need no encouragement. And since Nigel was overcome by madness and married an American, I dread to think what folly you might slip into if you are not properly guided."

"I'm rather old to be guided."

"That is often said by people who feel they are capable of living with their mistakes. The problem is that they have no idea how miserable that will be. Now I shall need to speak to Zoe. I think a dinner party is in order and I must convince my granddaughter-in-law to hold one."

Oh, she must stop this. "What of your romance, Grandmama?"

"What romance, dear? At my age, a woman barely remembers what romance was."

"That is not true. You can't deny Sir Raynard is courting you. Did he not invite you to a musical revue in London?"

"He invited me to a jazz club, my dear. Of course I said no. Next thing, he would be wanting me to dance the Black Bottom with him."

Julia had to clap her hand to her mouth. She had to smother the giggles that came from picturing her grandmother dancing a primitive-style dance with her bottom sticking out. "I'm sure he just wanted to introduce you to the new jazz music."

"I fear not. An older gentleman in love can be utterly exhausting. The first thing he wants to do is prove how young he is."

"Please don't discourage him. I think it would be rather lovely for you to have a gentleman in your life."

"I won't discourage Raynard, dear, if you don't discourage Summerhay. Now—to plan a dinner party. Toodle-oo, my dear."

She heard the dial tone. Grandmama was rushing off to scheme. Oh dear.

Julia set down the receiver, and someone cried, "There you are!" right behind her, making her jump. Before her heart slipped down from her throat, her mother grasped her hand and towed her into a drawing room.

Mother carried a letter. Her green eyes sparkled and she looked filled with life. She had not glowed with such happiness for a long time. Not since before Will had died. Losing her youngest son had devastated Mother. A Catholic, Mother prayed every day at the small chapel Father had built for her on the estate. Julia was happy that whatever news Mother had gotten was good.

"Bradstock writes to say how much he enjoyed seeing us again, Julia. Of course he mentions you. Of course he is too much of a gentleman to be blunt, but I know he's wrangling for an invitation. Viscount Yorkville is a disappointment—I heard he became engaged to an earl's daughter. I am going to speak to Zoe and Nigel about throwing a ball. That would be the perfect thing to place you in the path of the duke."

Now she knew why Mother was happy. "Mother, I am not interested in the duke."

Definitely not, after the things he'd said about her charity work. He had apologized but her entire life would be dictated by a man like that.

"Julia, you are almost seven and twenty. You *must* be interested in the duke, whether you like it or not. No woman wants to be a spinster. At this age, you should have an establishment of your own. You are restless—and you can't deny it. That is why you are dabbling in this rather scandalous work. Fallen women indeed!"

For years, after unhappiness in marriage, her mother had withdrawn from the world. For this, she had suddenly found strength. Julia wanted her mother to be strong. To no longer be trapped in mourning Will. But why did it have to be for something they were destined to fight about?

Zoe had confided how her American mama had wanted her to marry Nigel instead of Sebastian from the start. Now Julia found she was saying to her mother exactly what Zoe had said to hers: "Mother, I am not going to marry the duke."

For the first time in forever, Mother set her jaw resolutely. She folded her arms over her gray cashmere cardigan. "Then who will you marry? There were no dowries before, so there were no offers. Now there will not be many, my dear, because of your advanced age. You will never be content as a country doctor's wife. You were raised to be mistress of a grand estate. You would never be happy with anything less."

"As for men attracted by my dowry—what good are gentlemen who assess you only by your money?" Julia asked. "I don't want to be married to one. So many great estates are being sold. I could marry the duke and he could have to sell his home six months later. Nothing is certain in the world anymore."

"Julia, your dowry will be sufficient to keep an estate—"

"Not if he gambles his way through it. Or invests it badly." She spoke on instinct and pain flashed over Mother's face. Father had gambled through the money, and he'd had no sense of investment at all. "I'm sorry, but it is true. I do not want to have to turn over my money to a husband and have no say in how it is spent."

For she realized she didn't blindly trust a man to be cleverer than her. Ten years ago she might have believed it, but not anymore. She now knew marriage was not an achievement, but a beginning—and she didn't want it to be the beginning of a descent into hell.

She had no place in the world. She had been waiting for marriage to define her. She was not supposed to seek a career. And what would she do? Become a secretary? Build engines for locomotives? Take a job from a deserving man with a family to feed?

Her siblings seemed to have found their places. Nigel was the duke and he was a good, responsible one. Sebastian loved to paint. Isobel, her younger sister, wanted to become a doctor.

She needed to find her place.

Her mother touched her arm. "If you make a

ise choice, darling, you will have nothing to worry about."

"But that is not true! I do not want to hope and pray I marry a sensible man who doesn't make my life miserable. There must be more for me. Why could I not make money of my own? Buy my own house?"

"You are a duke's daughter. Dukes' daughters marry."

"And those who don't become spinsters. This is the 1920s! There has to be more. More than this constant worry about suitors and titles, dowries and estates."

"Those have been the reasons for marriage in our class for centuries."

"It's not good enough for me. I want love."

"Love and affection can develop."

And she knew that wasn't enough, either. "I want more. I want to be swept away by the person I marry. I want to feel a *whoosh*. I want *passion*."

Her mother's mouth dropped. She went white, then blushed scarlet. But what was wrong with a woman wanting to go to bed with the man she had married?

She'd had few kisses in her life, but Julia knew what she'd felt when Cal had draped his shirt around her. Hot, trembling, aching—and filled with a dizzying need.

She had seen the way Zoe and Nigel looked at

each other. Enough heat to ignite flames. She had seen Nigel sweep Zoe into his arms to carry her to bed—or Zoe lead Nigel by his necktie to his bedroom. Desire and joy had exuded from both of them.

How could a woman think of decades spent with anything less?

But Mother shook her head. "Passion is a terrible reason for marriage. It fades. It ends. And it leads to disaster."

Julia swallowed hard. "Maybe it doesn't have to. If both parties feel it."

"A gentleman is very ready to feel passion for any woman who catches his eye. He may still feel it for you, but I assure you that will extinguish anything you feel for him. You are much better to marry for sensible reasons. If you marry a man like the duke, he can never take away your happiness if you are happy to be a duchess."

"But your happiness was taken away—"

"Because I hoped for more, Julia." Her mother drew herself up, looking almost as fierce as Grandmama. "If I had not had that rather hopeless hope, I would have been happy."

Love would have made Mother happy. But what was the point of saying it?

She couldn't trade an estate for her heart and soul. She simply couldn't. Even if it meant eventually she ended up with nothing. For somehow she would survive. Wouldn't she?

"I must go, Mother. I must visit some families on the Worthington estate. And look in on some of the Brideswell families." She left the room and hurried upstairs. Julia threw on jodhpurs and a hacking jacket, along with her riding hat. The fashions had gone away from the old-fashioned riding habit. She went down to the stables and had a groom saddle Athena. Zoe and Nigel took care of the Brideswell families, but she still liked to visit them. And she had promised Anthony she would look after Worthington. Spurring on her horse, she galloped away to do this work she loved—leaving the problem of marriage behind her.

Being in the house made Cal feel like an animal trapped in a gilded cage.

He was walking down the drive when he saw an elegant white horse canter toward him. A woman was on top, wearing jodhpurs, a trim-fitting black coat, a black riding hat.

Julia. His heart rate accelerated and Cal felt nerves he hadn't felt since he was a boy of fifteen, trying to coax a girl to let him make love to her because he was tired of being the only virgin in the Five Points Juniors Gang.

"I wanted to take you to see more tenants but Athena needed exercise," she called to him. "And the chauffeur was fixing something on my motor. We can take one of your vehicles if you wish. Can I stable Athena here while we go?"

"I haven't been down to see the stables yet."

"You must go. The grooms will be wondering why you have not. I assumed you would have thoroughly explored the house and grounds. If I'd known, I would have taken you myself."

She spoke to him like a disappointed schoolteacher—not that he'd had much experience with one of those. Mam had wanted him to be educated but he didn't see much use for school. But his father bought books and pushed him to read, so they could debate, in the few hours his father was not working at some menial job.

"Worthington's stables are admired throughout the county," she went on. "There are some fierce horses, but there are gentler ones, too, so you could learn to ride."

Julia's smile entranced him, but it reminded him they were from two different worlds.

He had come to Worthington filled with defiance about his humble origins. Now, damn it, when he was with Julia he found himself wishing he had a better past.

Why should he damn well care? He wasn't going to be like the Duke of Bradstock or the Earl of Summerhay. He hadn't been to the right schools and he had the blood of simple, hardworking people in his veins.

He was never going to be good enough for Lady Julia. Not to marry her. But he could be good enough to seduce her.

What he wanted was to see her sparkling eyes filled with desire—for him—as he made love to her. That was all he wanted.

"It would be a good idea for you to learn how to ride. Most gentlemen ride. I would be delighted to teach you."

"I'm not a gentleman," he said, "and I don't have any intention of trying to act like I am one."

Hurt showed in her face.

He needed to remember that she was getting in the way of his plans. She was making him care about the people on the estate. Getting her to leave him alone would be a damn good idea.

But he wanted her. Wanted her badly.

"All right, doll," he said. "Teach me to ride."

Cal may not have ridden before, but he had a way with horses that surprised Julia. He went to the stables with her, dressed in his threadbare clothes, which shocked the grooms at first. But his engaging manner won them over. The head groom, Michaels, found a gentle mare for Cal.

As soon as Michaels gave him the reins, Cal stroked the mare's nose, fed her from the palm of his hand. The horse whinnied happily as he stroked her withers.

Cal could make any female melt, Julia realized.

He spoke in soft murmurs to his mount, Empress, then tried to swing up onto her. The first time, he fell back, landing hard on the ground.

Julia cringed, certain his pride would be hurt.

But Cal laughed. A rich, husky laugh that spoke of joy and wickedness. He tried again, and got into the saddle with stunning grace. He seemed happier, less angry than he had when she and he had herded the pigs.

Within an hour, he'd progressed to trotting around the fenced-in ring. Julia had seen many gentlemen ride and some looked magnificent in the saddle, but compared to Cal they all looked stiff. He had such sensual grace. Watching the loose-limbed movements of his arms and shoulders made her want to snatch off her hat and fan herself.

"You are a natural. Born to it," she called out.

"You're my teacher. The credit is all yours." He grinned. "Where did you intend to take me today? Can we ride there?"

"Lower Dale Farm. It's one of the most productive on your estate. Yes, we can ride."

She led him to a path that wound through the meadow below the stables. Wildflower blooms swayed in the late spring breeze. Bees buzzed around the flowers. The horses flicked their tails. The trail was wide enough for them to ride side by side. She could see Cal's inexperience in the jerky way he handled the reins, but Empress was a patient, placid horse.

"Do you realize everything on this estate needs modernization?" Cal asked. "I've driven around on my own, looking at the farms. I went out early this morning."

"You went to look at them?"

"Yeah. All of these farms would be improved with mechanization. They need tractors instead of horses and plows. They need to adopt some up-to-date methods of farming. New barns. New houses for the farmers. Those stone cottages are damp and cold. How does anyone survive the winter?"

Her heart lifted. For him to show such interest was a good sign. She was getting through to him. These were all the things she and Anthony had planned to do, but she knew she must take a different approach. "We use fires and once there is a good blaze going in the hearth, the houses do warm up. And the people of the estates are hardy. They are accustomed—"

"That's not good enough," he broke in. "What they need are—" He stopped and faced her with a stubborn look on his face. "Don't look so smug, Julia. These are just observations."

Bother. She had hoped to goad him into vowing to do all those improvements because she had "implied" the people did not need them. And it had been working, so it was *impossible* not to look victorious. "Of course. But I think the tenants are very happy as they are."

"And I say they are not." He frowned. Muttered, "Damn it." Then he said, stubbornly, "I have to examine the place before I figure out what it could sell for."

"I hadn't thought of that." She tried to sound disappointed. To sound as if she feared she had lost. But she was *certain* she was winning. So she asked, "What did you mean when you said you couldn't live with yourself if you stayed and lived like an earl?"

He rode in silence for a while. Silence that made her uneasy. She yearned to know the answer. She'd been awake most of last night wondering about it.

Suddenly he said, "I'm obsessed with painting you. I've tried painting you from memory, but I can't capture what I want. I need to have you sitting there so I can study you while I work. I need to paint you, Julia. It's eating at my soul. I need you to pose for me."

The fierce, vehement way he said it shocked her. But she didn't believe he *needed* to paint her. "You are trying to change the subject," she protested.

"I'm not, doll. I'm telling you the truth. For me, painting is like breathing air. I need it to live. And when I get obsessed over painting a woman, it drives me crazy. So will you pose?"

A searing image struck her. Cal in his white shirt with the sleeves rolled up, watching her with this fiery, intense yearning in his eyes. It took her breath away. But a lady would never reveal how unsettled she was. "You paint barely dressed as I remember."

He gave her a scorching look. "I need to be comfortable when I paint. Would it bother you?"

"I don't know," she said. "I don't know about having my portrait painted. I don't think I would like to sit for hours and hours."

"You don't want to spend hours with me?" he asked lightly.

"What if I said yes? Would you explain what you meant?"

He shrugged, holding the reins. "I meant what I said."

"Cal, you are a good man. A kind man. I saw that in the way you leaped to Hannah's defense, in the way you want to help Ellen, and how tender and gentle you were with Mrs. Brand. You don't seem like the kind of man to be vengeful or cruel."

"Every man has his breaking point, Julia," was all he said.

She wished she knew what exactly had happened when the old earl had disowned Cal's father.

"I asked around the village about Sarah Brand, Julia."

She jerked her head toward him. "You did?" He had been concerned about the Brands and that touched her heart.

"I heard she was seen driving with a man in a fancy automobile. How could she never have been found? Wouldn't it have been easy to find a man who drove a car back then? Or didn't they look for her all that hard?"

154

"What do you mean? I was quite young but I assure you that people scoured the estate in case she'd had an accident, Cal. Even I joined in to search—though my mother was shocked that I did."

He moved at her side, thighs rising and following with the motion of his horse. He seemed lost in thought for a while. Then he said, "People said there were only automobiles at the great houses at the time. Brideswell had a car. So did the earl at Worthington Park. I heard the old earl had bought an up-to-date motorcar for his eldest son."

Her horse reared beneath her. She had jerked abruptly on the reins, startling Athena. With a firm grip of her thighs, firm hands on the reins and soothing words she settled her horse. Was she just leaping to suspicions over what he was implying?

"Mrs. Brand said he had a flashy automobile," he went on. "Which means she must have seen it."

"Anthony loved it and drove it all over Worthington. Of course she would have seen it."

"The man who took Sarah out in his car could have been one of the men at Worthington or Brideswell."

"What are you saying?" she cried. "Brideswell's car at the time was a rather sedate vehicle. And I can assure you that none of my brothers was flirting with Sarah Brand. Nor could it have been Anthony or John."

"Why couldn't it have been one of them?"

155

"John was young. Only fifteen. And Anthony—Anthony was already courting me."

"You thought he was in love with you by then," Cal said. "I expect he was. But Sarah Brand wasn't a girl like you."

She knew he was implying she might be blind to the behavior of her former fiancé.

"I just wondered if the law believed the man in the car was a toff, a local one, if they really investigated."

"The magistrate did investigate, I assure you," she answered stiffly.

But he had put a horrible thought into her mind. One she had never, ever considered before. Could Anthony—?

What if he'd had his way with Sarah and didn't want to marry her?

No! No—Anthony was not that kind of gentleman. She was sure of it. "You are deliberately trying to poison my mind with awful thoughts so I'll stop fighting you."

She gave Athena a press with her heels and urged her horse ahead as they entered the woods. It was impossible to talk unless they shouted. Once they emerged from the woods into another meadow, Cal caught up to her. "Julia, that wasn't what I was trying to do. I didn't mean to hurt you. But there couldn't have been many men who could afford an automobile. And would Sarah Brand really have gotten justice if an earl's son was involved?"

——"Yes," she declared. "She would have done." But in her heart, she feared he was right. About justice, *not* about Anthony.

Cal glanced around, frowning. "I smell smoke."

"Cooking fires," she said. Her hands trembled around the reins.

Strains of music came to them from the other side of a meadow—the jaunty notes of a fiddle, the jingle of a tambourine. And laughter. A group of children exploded out of the tall meadow grass, chasing a young, barefoot girl who ran like wild.

Julia had gathered control of herself, and she turned to Cal. "There are several Roma families who come here to live in the summer and autumn. In return they work to pick fruit and to pick hops later on. Hop picking is grueling work and the hop juice stains your hands terribly."

"I would've thought the earl would have run them off his land."

"Not the old earl—Anthony's father. He appreciated their help with the work. They provided the labor he needed only when it was required, and they were quite content to camp and receive a stipend for their work. Though when John was the earl, briefly, he expressed dislike of the gypsies and did say he should not let them stay. Pegg, the land agent, talked him out of it." She dismounted and smiled at Cal. "Shall we go and say hello?"

● ● ●

Cal watched as the children spotted Julia and ran to her. She laughingly greeted them all and his heart gave a pang. Something he'd never felt. He never wanted to be tied down. Yet he watched Julia and felt yearning.

He also knew he'd frightened her with his speculation. Why else would she have jerked on the reins and made her horse shy?

"You have all grown so much!" she declared. She carried on as if nothing had happened to| disturb her. At first, that used to irritate him. He wanted to smash her sangfroid. Now—hell, now he found he admired it. Lady Julia Hazelton was tough and strong.

She motioned to Cal. "This is the Earl of Worthington."

The girls, all dark-haired and lovely, curtsied to him. The boys bowed.

He dismounted also and tied the reins of his horse to a tree, leaving Empress alongside Julia's mare, and he followed Julia into the camp.

Three caravans—wooden structures with domed roofs, all painted in bright colors—stood around a fire pit. Older men sat and smoked. A young man played a fiddle, all the while watching a young woman who worked with other women, preparing food. Others sat and sewed. The people treated him with deference, though they gave his clothing strange looks. Cal grinned at her. "Even to the gypsies, I guess I make a strange-looking earl."

"Isn't that what you wanted?" she responded teasingly. Then she left him to go and speak to the women of the camp.

Was she really teasing? Disapproving? That was the power of her controlled, ladylike expression. He couldn't tell what she meant. Couldn't see into her heart. And he wanted to know.

He wanted to break through that ladylike armor. Was she a mass of pain, passion and fear inside, and she'd never learned how to let it out? Was that why she'd been locked in grief for so long? That was another thing the villagers told him—that Lady Julia had spent too long grieving.

He stood, watching Julia, then felt someone staring at him and turned.

A woman with a grizzled, tanned face and white-streaked hair was seated in a chair by the fire. She motioned Cal to join her and handed him a drink—strong coffee. The gypsy woman smoked a pipe, and he had the sense she was someone of importance. Brightly patterned skirts spread around her. An embroidered vest and white blouse covered her upper body. Smoke wreathed her.

"I'm Genevra. So ye're the new lordship, are ye?" she asked. "Ye don't look all that happy to be in the role, milord, I would say."

"I never expected to be an earl," he said.

"Aye. I thought not. Ye look like a wild one." Genevra chuckled deeply. "I notice ye've barely taken your eyes off Lady Julia for all the time ye've been here."

His cheeks felt hot. "I like looking at her."

"I can see ye do." She wagged a finger at him. "She's not for you."

It was true, but her nosiness made him angry. "I don't see that's your business."

"Ye've got a hot head, too."

"I'm the earl around here. Did you pass personal observations on my uncle?"

"No. But then, he's not like you." She leaned toward him confidingly. "I'm happy Lady Julia did not marry Lord Anthony, the old earl's son. No good would have come of that. Not when the curse claimed her."

"You're saying there's a curse on Lady Julia?" There were gypsies in America, and they were driven away even there. People were suspicious of them, and many believed they could lay curses. He didn't.

"Does she have to cross your palm with silver to escape it?" he asked mockingly, remembering his dark-haired mother with her long-lashed Irish blue eyes, telling him of pixies, leprechauns, spirits. He had loved the stories as a boy, got impatient with them as a youth. He didn't believe in fortunes and fate.

Genevra shot him a haughty look. He'd offended her. "There is no curse on her. But if she had married Lord Anthony, there would have been. Have you not heard of it? You being the earl now, I thought someone would have told you. They're all afraid of it, up at the house. Oh, they deny it, but they are. If Lady Julia had married Lord Anthony, the curse would have been on her. That would have been a tragedy. She is good, kind and generous of spirit. Her soul is pure."

The gypsy blew a ring of smoke. It rose above her, lingered like a halo, then blew apart. "It will touch the woman you marry, milord."

"What is this curse?"

"The curse befalls whoever marries Lord Worthington, milord. A century past, the Countess of Worthington ran down one of our children with a carriage. The child's mother cursed whoever became the Worthington Wife. Callous and heartless, that countess was, and she paid the price. She lost six of her eight children to illnesses and accidents. Even the current countess has suffered much loss and much pain."

"I don't believe in curses. You can't say a few words and change someone's fate."

"But someone did with yours, milord, when they told you that you were the new earl."

He lifted his brow at her, and she laughed merrily. The sound was low and husky. "The funny thing about curses, milord, is that we make them

161

come true when we seek hardest to deny them. Or avoid them."

Then the fiddling music grew louder and faster. In the center of the camp, the children danced. Two girls clung to Julia, dancing with her. Julia twirled and laughed, nothing like a cool and austere lady.

And Cal couldn't take his eyes off her.

8

A Birth at Lower Dale Farm

"Do you believe in the Worthington Wife curse?"

Julia looked up, startled. "They told you about that?" They were riding down the lane to Lower Dale Farm. Cal looked magnificent in the saddle.

"The woman called Genevra did," he said.

"She told me not to marry Lord Anthony because of it—she read my palm and gave me a serious warning. She was so intense that I was quite frightened," she admitted. "In fact, I was—I was very angry with her. I thought the whole thing was a joke in poor taste. There was . . . quite a row over it. Anthony's father went to see her. Her words had made Anthony rethink our engagement. The whole story of the curse is rather terrible."

"Genevra told me that the Countess of Worthington was cursed one hundred years ago, after she ran over a gypsy child."

Julia nodded. "That is the story. Terrible things did happen to that countess, though I suspect that was due to the lack of medical knowledge and the countess's selfish character and not a curse. I don't believe in curses."

"The current countess has been through a hell of a lot of trouble," Cal said.

She frowned. "I don't believe the current Lady Worthington has suffered because of angry words spoken by a bereaved woman who had suffered unimaginable pain. But superstitions run deep in the country. Many tenants of the estate believe in it, especially with all of the tragedy that had befallen Lady Worthington. It has led to fear for the gypsies. Terrible, prejudicial fear."

Some villagers had said that the curse had touched her the minute Anthony proposed to her, the moment he intended for her to be his wife . . .

"What's wrong, Julia?" Cal asked gently. "You look so sad. Have I scared you?"

She could brush him off with a false smile, but she didn't. "Some said falling in love with me was what killed Anthony. That the curse took him away from me because I was to be a Worthington Wife."

"Who said that? Damn, that's a cruel thing to say."

"I knew it couldn't be true. But it did hurt."

"Sure it did. Tell me who said that."

His dark brows were drawn together in anger. Outrage—over someone saying something to her that hurt. He was noble. Julia knew she could do what she'd set out to do—make him care about Worthington. But what had he meant when he'd said he couldn't live with himself if he lived here as the earl? That was the key. If she could change his mind on that, she would win. She would save Worthington. And give it a master who was obviously worthy of it.

"Cal, it was nine years ago. You aren't intending to be angry with people over thoughtless words after so long. But I do appreciate you acting the knight in shining armor. For me."

"You don't have to tell me, Julia, but if I find out who hurt you that way, I'll make sure they regret it," he growled.

That was Cal—he was driven by vengeance. "There is a difference between revenge and justice. And I don't need either, Cal."

"There's not a lot of justice in this world, Julia. Sometimes a man has to help it along."

He said it so coolly, and a shiver rushed down her spine.

She slowed her horse to a walk, negotiating the narrow, rough lane that led down to the large, impressive farm. It was time to change the topic of conversation. Brightly, she said, "Lower Dale Farm is the most productive on the estate—the one Anthony was exceedingly proud of, for he and the farmer, Roger Toft, decided to start raising a new and hardier breed of pig and developed better ideas for the rotation of crops."

These had been her ideas, too, and Anthony had agreed, rather than tell her such areas were not for women. Some men would have rejected any-thing she'd said on principle.

Cal grinned, apparently forgetting his anger. "You're glowing, Lady Julia. I never thought any woman would find crops and pigs sexy."

He let the last word come out in his low, deep voice. She felt a pang of—of something intense that rushed right down to her toes.

He'd said that word to shock her. She lifted a brow at him. "Perhaps they have better sex appeal than some men."

He gave her his cocky grin. When he did, she could see his Irish side in the roguish nature of that smile.

"I have to admit I was impressed at you chasing the Brands' pigs," he said. "I didn't expect that of a duke's daughter."

"I am a rather unusual duke's daughter." She stopped. For a moment, there was silence. Muted baas of sheep. Clucking and honking from the birds. She locked gazes with Cal. "This farm is successful because this is more than the livelihood of this family—it's their life. Mrs. Toft is expecting another child—their fifth. Why should all their hard work be destroyed?"

Cal opened his mouth to answer, but a piercing cry drowned out his words. Julia stared at the house and Cal asked, "What in hell was that?"

It came from the farmhouse—Julia's favorite house on the Worthington estate. But now she looked at it as horror took a twisting grip on her heart. She knew what it was.

With legs trembling, Julia urged her horse to a canter. "It was a woman's scream."

It came again and quivers of terror shot down

Julia's spine as she neared the house. She'd heard cries like this before. Mrs. Toft was pregnant and had told Julia, last week, that she was very close to her time—

"I think a woman's in labor," Cal shouted as he caught up behind her.

She reined in and all but flung herself off the horse. Cal followed with a smooth flowing movement. He raced to the door with her—and Julia came to an abrupt halt.

Mary Toft—the oldest girl at age twelve—rushed out of the doorway and hugged Julia. "Me mum is poorly, they say. I'm so afraid."

No. Oh no. "Poorly" was an adult way to hide terrible news. Julia tried to hide the shaking that threatened to overtake her. She crouched down. "I don't know what's happening, my dear. But I think everything will be all right. Where are your brothers and your sister?"

"They're hiding in the kitchen. Father sent us outside, but we didn't want to go."

She must stay strong for the girl. She gently squeezed the child's hand. "Let me go inside and find out what is happening, Mary."

Her heart was in her throat. She remembered Zoe's cries of pain . . . then Zoe had lost the baby. Julia's strength was failing. Her legs wanted to collapse. But she propelled herself forward.

Cal's hand gripped her wrist before she could go through the door. "Julia, don't go in there."

"I have to. I—I am needed. I must *do* something."

"I'll bring the children out. Stay out here with them."

"No. I can't just sit by and not *help*." Pushing away from him, she ran in, but could feel him close behind her.

The cries and moans led her up the narrow wooden stairs to the largest bedroom. Julia walked into the heat and shouting and frantic activity of childbirth. Oh, heavens.

Mr. Toft was glued back against the wall, horror on his face. On the bed, Elsie Toft was half sitting, with women supporting her. Hair plastered with sweat, her face both white with shock and red with strain. She grunted and scrunched up her face, then screamed. "I can't do it no more."

The women eased Mrs. Toft back and she collapsed limply on the bed, her eyes shut.

"The babe is stuck. Wedged." That was Mrs. Thomas, the local midwife, speaking quietly. A broad, strong woman with a ruddy face. Her sleeves were rolled up, her apron wet and streaked with blood.

Such agony went across Mrs. Toft's face that Julia's heart broke.

"What about the doctor?" she asked. "We must bring him. He would know what to do."

"That fool with the clean sleeves? I doubt—" Turning around, the midwife stopped in mid-sentence. "My lady, whatever are you doing in here?"

"I've come to help. I could bring the doctor."

"Aye, he should be fetched. But I fear he won't know what to do."

One of the other women said softly, "How long has she got?"

"Not long, the poor thing. She hasn't got the strength anymore."

"And the baby?"

Roger Toft let out a sob. He was a huge, broad-shouldered man with a barrel chest and enormous arms. And it was awful to watch him break. Sobs racked him.

Julia didn't hear Mrs. Thomas's answer. The room seemed to swim around her. It shimmered, the way the air did on a hot day.

"I will get the doctor," she cried. She ran out of the room as if being chased by demons.

If only she had her car. She would have to ride back to Brideswell and drive from there.

But as she spun on her heel to rush to her motor, her legs buckled beneath her. A strong arm slipped around her waist and she was taken down the stairs and outside. She was deposited on an upturned bucket and she looked into concerned, sky blue eyes.

Cal.

"You almost passed out in there. I'll get the doctor."

"I can do it." She had to do something. That funny feeling—that dots were exploding in front of her eyes—was going away. "How can you be so calm?"

"I've done this before."

"You've helped a woman give birth before?"

"I helped my mother when I was a boy. *Her* mother had been a midwife in Ireland, and she'd learned a few things from her mother. When any woman was giving birth in the tenement, she would ask for my mam."

His mam. The word made her want to cry. This "Mam" might lose her battle—

Standing over her, he shook his head. "You're white as a sheet. You need a drink. Something strong, if they've got it."

"I am fine. I should be useful."

"Fainting won't be of any use."

"I am not going to faint. I wouldn't allow myself to."

"I don't think you'll have a choice, doll. Stay out here until I get back. Don't go back inside. My guess is that your snooty Society wouldn't approve of you helping at a birth."

"I don't care about that!"

"God, you are an amazing woman. You shouldn't have been born a duke's daughter. You're a real person."

That was the strangest thing anyone had ever said to her, yet it touched her heart like no flowery compliment had ever done. But then the worst agonized cry she'd ever heard came from the bedroom. "I must go," she said. When he shook his head again, she cried, "You are hardly in a position to dictate to me. I am tired of being told what I can and cannot do. I am a grown woman, capable of making choices. Capable of doing what is necessary to do! I absolutely must be the one to go. You don't know where the hospital is."

"I'm telling you what to do to protect you."

And she saw then, as she almost screamed with frustration, that she did not *want* to be protected. An English lady's life was all about being supposedly protected, but you were really not protected at all. You still knew loss and pain, heartbreak, desperation and desolation. All you were protected from was taking some control of your life.

"Don't. I refuse to allow anyone to protect me from life anymore." Courage and determination surged through her. She could do this—ride like the wind to Brideswell. She was going to do it. Julia leaped to her feet.

"I'm riding with you," Cal said. "Back to Worthington, and I'll drive to the hospital."

"You won't be able to gallop as I can. You'll fall."

"I'll take that risk," he said, his jaw set.

That was exactly the kind of person she wanted to be—willing to take risk.

She led Cal out to the road, where they could let their horses gallop. It was too far for a flat-out run. Julia had to admit she was amazed at how Cal stayed in his seat.

They reached Worthington with lathered horses, both coated in perspiration and breathing hard. Cal leaped down from his horse and shouted orders that her car be brought round. Julia wanted to drive, but he jumped into the driver's seat and refused to move, forcing her into the passenger side. Then he stomped the car's accelerator to the floor and took off with a spray of gravel.

Over the roar of the engine, she shouted directions. She couldn't believe Cal could drive so well on a road he barely knew. He slowed as they reached the village—just a moment before she was going to warn him to do so since there were bicycles on the road, and horses, and children.

Even though it was part of Nigel's land holdings, Brideswell's village hospital served much of the area, including the Worthington estate.

Inside the hospital and outside the office of Dr. Hamilton, a nurse tried to insist the doctor could not be disturbed. It was Cal who bellowed, "I am the Earl of Worthington and the doctor had better come with me right now. *Now*."

She and Cal burst into the doctor's office. The doctor dropped something very quickly into a drawer of his desk and gazed up at them calmly.

"What is all this, my lady? Is there an emergency? Or is this another woman with supposed shell shock?"

Julia gritted her teeth. She remembered the irritating debate she'd had with Dr. Hamilton about Ellen Lambert. He had insisted Ellen could not have shell shock, which only afflicted men. Obviously she had hysteria—it was obvious, he'd said, because her temperament had also *obviously* led her to her scandalous line of work. Julia had wanted to hit him with a bedpan.

Now she cried breathlessly, "You must come at once to Lower Dale Farm. We shall drive you. Hurry—you must hurry!"

She had never thrown away her composure like this with an outsider to her family, with anyone other than Cal.

"You must tell me what is going on," Hamilton said, unruffled. He wore a white coat, his graying hair and mustache elegantly styled with pomade.

"Oh bother! Just come with us," she cried.

But he was not moving, so she threw the story at him. He had a bland face that was somewhat handsome, but also had ferrety attributes. He was no substitute for Dougal Campbell. Not in the least.

He still was not moving. He should leap to his feet—but he did not.

"We must go now, Dr. Hamilton," she cried. Ladylike Lady Julia would never do what she did right then. She stalked around to his side and then she smelled the strong aroma of alcohol. Something snapped in her. "Are you drunk? Is that why you are not getting up? I will have my brother throw you out if you do not get up and come with us at once!"

He had the gall to look offended. "To Lower Dale Farm for a birth, my lady? That is the business of midwives. I'd come at once, of course, if it was a patient of mine at Brideswell. But these people prefer midwives who come from their own social stratum. They have no money to pay for a proper phys—"

"I will pay," Julia bit off. "Do remember my family is the reason this hospital operates. It is by the generosity of the duchy that you can even sit in this office and drink brandy, Dr. Hamilton. If you do not come, you will be removed from your position."

"And as Earl of Worthington, I will destroy your fat arse if you don't listen to Lady Julia," Cal growled. Then Cal made a fist and slammed it so hard on the desk she let out a gasp of shock. The force sent things flying and clattering to the floor. "Get the hell out of that chair and save a woman's life."

She'd never seen such rage on a man's face. Cal's anger wasn't even directed at her and it made her want to whimper. Dr. Hamilton stopped arguing. He did get off his bottom and grabbed his bag. Cal put his hand on the man's shoulder and pushed him all the way to her motorcar. Cal drove with Dr. Hamilton at his side. Against Cal's wishes, Julia chose to perch in the rumble seat.

Cal drove back with such speed the doctor turned green.

But it was all for nothing.

Hamilton examined Mrs. Toft, used forceps to take out the baby. Drenched in sweat, Mrs. Toft could no longer cry out. She sobbed, her breathing coming in small gasps.

The poor infant girl came out and Mrs. Toft gave out a terrible scream. The midwife quickly wrapped up the child. But Julia saw a small bluish face and her stomach churned. The baby was already dead. There had been no hope for the child.

Mr. Toft held his wife's hand. Told her it was all right. That she was not to worry. That she just had to get strong. He'd look after her. Their children would look after her.

But Mrs. Toft just simply closed her eyes, let out the softest sigh and slipped away.

Julia stood there, staring with horror and not quite believing that something so terrible could have happened. She knew what Zoe had suffered. Now this family had lost a child, and their mother, too.

Mr. Toft collapsed to his knees by the bed at his wife's side. He held his wife's hand. Clung to it. Julia hurried out of the bedroom and downstairs, knowing her own tears were going to come.

Then she saw them—four pale, frightened faces.

The children.

Watching Julia gather up the children to get them outside and away from their mother's room just about broke Cal's heart. Julia had brushed away the tears on her cheeks and she tried to herd them out briskly. But she hadn't told them their mother was gone. To spare them, he figured. But the children were going to find out—he realized he was going to be the one to tell them. He was not going to let Julia go through such a painful thing.

She was trying to urge them out the door that led outside from a surprisingly large kitchen, but he said, "Julia, let me talk to them."

Panic flared in Julia's large blue eyes. She had two little girls by the hand and she was trying to make the boys go outside. "Not yet."

"Now," he said firmly. "They're stronger than you think."

"But there is nothing to be done."

"They have to go in to see her. To say goodbye."

"No. I want to spare them the sight of—"

"Julia, I've been through this," he said softly. "When I was as young as some of them. The children need to see. They need to touch their mother. Give her a last kiss."

Cal got down on one knee in front of the children.

"Don't," Julia protested.

He had to. But suddenly he couldn't find the words. Christ, he just couldn't say it. All he could remember was the gut-destroying pain he'd felt when Mam died. And the anger. The white-hot rage.

The children were sniffling, looking at him. They had to know, but they needed to be told. And Christ, he was failing. "Help me with this, Julia. I need your help to do this."

She touched his shoulder. It was such a tender gesture it gave him a burst of strength. He told the children their mam was called back to heaven. That she loved them, but sometimes love was not enough—a person had to face something they weren't strong enough to battle.

"You have to honor her always," he said to them. "Be strong for her. Look after each other and your father. Your mother will watch you all the time from heaven. If you just think about her, it will be like having her with you."

He told them all the things he'd been told when he lost his mother.

The two girls began to cry and Julia hugged them both to her skirts. The boys sniffled. Cal remembered how he had been told to behave like a man. To hold in tears. But he said to the boys, "People will tell you to be tough. They'll say you have to behave like men. But I'm going to tell you to cry right now if you want to. Do it now, get it out of you. Then you'll be ready to help your father."

One of the boys flung his small body against Cal's chest. Cal embraced the lad. The other bigger boy staunchly held in his tears.

"It's not fair," the older boy said. "It's not fair."

"I know, lad," Cal said. "But even though life doesn't seem fair, we have to survive. You have to keep fighting. You have to get up and kick life in its crotch—"

"Cal!" Julia gasped.

But that was how he'd felt about life. He remembered what had kept him going—knowing he had to care for his brother. "You're the oldest and it's important you look after your siblings. They'll need you."

"Come, we must clean your faces," Julia said. She was using her crisp, lovely, ladylike tones and the children followed her. She herded the children into the kitchen and wiped small faces. She gave them coins for their savings, then she answered all their desperate questions as best as she could.

In that moment, Lady Julia reminded Cal of Alice. He had been deeply in love with Alice. He couldn't show it or act on it—he couldn't hurt his brother, David—but he'd never met another woman who compared to Nurse Alice Hayes.

Julia compared.

He saw her face. How pale she looked. She made tea as she had done before, with a big iron kettle. She poured a cup of tea for each child. Then one more. "Take this for your father. He might not want it now, but leave it close by. He should have something. I've put honey in to make it sweet."

With the tallest girl carrying the cup and saucer, the children went back into the other room to see their father.

Lady Julia leaned against the sink, her head bowed. She kept her back to the doorway, then she put her hands to her face.

She was crying. And she didn't want anyone to see.

His mother used to hide to cry, because she was so worried about where their next dollar would come from. But she always turned a bright and cheery face to him and David, no matter how scared, how hungry, how desperate she felt.

Cal used to wake up and hear her sobs, after his father's death. She would cross herself and touch the one picture she had of Cal's father.

Cal had been too young and too powerless to help his mother. He'd tried—he'd been young but the Five Points Gang had offered a way to make money. A lot of money . . .

Now he was an adult. An earl. A rich man. He could do anything he wanted.

Including soothe Lady Julia.

He wrapped his arms around her. Her dress was a summer dress, thin and soft. He drew her tight to his chest. She tried to push away, but he wouldn't let her.

"Cry against me," he said.

And she did.

She sobbed and sobbed. Then her crying began to ease. She looked up at him, her lips almost touching his chin.

She was the most beautiful woman he'd ever seen. A nice girl. He didn't know a lot of girls who were truly high-class. But Julia was.

Next thing he knew, he'd bent his head and his mouth touched hers.

"No," she whispered against his lips. "We shouldn't. That family has lost their mother. That tiny baby never had a chance to live. It will never be right . . . never. If only I could have helped them."

"You did everything you could, Julia. I'll help them. Don't cry and don't worry—the family will be cared for."

Her tongue swept over her lips, and his knees just about buckled. "You will do that?" she whispered.

"Yes."

He lifted her onto her toes to kiss her hard. To kiss her with his heart so full of longing and need he thought it was going to burst. He couldn't stop remembering his mother's death. How cold and empty he'd felt. He was kissing Julia, struggling to feel warm again.

Her arms wrapped around his neck, holding him tight. She broke away from the kiss. "You are truly an earl," she said, before pushing her lips against his again and kissing him back.

Cal felt a surge of heat like he'd never known.

Not sexual heat. Something deeper. Something more. Something that made him warm right through to his soul.

9

The 9:20 to Paddington

He was *kissing* her.

Cal's large, strong hands skimmed lightly down her back, caressing her. His palms went lower, following the curve of her bottom through her jodhpurs. He cupped one hand there and used it to pull her close. Shock hit her. Shock that his hand felt good there—that she liked the pressure of him holding her tight to his firm, warm body. His tongue traced her lips in a caress that made sparks burst and cascade through her with a hot sizzle.

Then his tongue slipped between her lips.

Panicked, Julia pulled back. Ladies didn't kiss like this. And they didn't do it in the kitchen of someone else's cottage. She'd needed to be held, but she couldn't do this. She gripped Cal's arms, feeling hard muscle through the sleeves of his worn sweater. "No. Don't. Please."

He let her go. "It's okay. We both needed comforting. Nothing more."

Nothing more. Of course, he was a wild artist who had love affairs with his models. A kiss didn't mean that much to him.

Embarrassment set her cheeks on fire. "I must go and see if I am needed."

He held out his hand for her. "You can't do anything more for them now. Let me take you home."

She wouldn't go until Mrs. Thomas said the same thing. Then she realized—because of her elevated social station, the midwife and the family felt awkward having her help them. She was causing them more distress by being there. When Mrs. Thomas urged her to go home, she finally agreed. Her heart hurt, her stomach hurt, and when she saw Mr. Toft, a most unsentimental man by nature, bend his head into the crook of the neck of his oldest daughter and let his back shake with sobs, she almost dissolved into tears.

Yet there was nothing she could do. Cal drove her home. They didn't speak in the car. Stars began to wink in the darkening sky, and just looking at them made her want to cry. The car rumbled up the gravel drive—a footman was coming out of the door before they had even stopped. As she was getting out, she said, "When you had to force the doctor to come, you used your title to convince him. I won't forget that, Cal."

"I'm sorry, doll. It doesn't mean anything. You aren't going to change my mind."

"I have to," she said. "I can't bear to lose anything more. Not even Worthington Park."

I can't bear to lose anything more.

Dawn light spilled in through the attic windows. It wasn't enough light to paint by, but Cal didn't care. He couldn't sleep. He would drift off, then wake up sweating and tangled in the sheets on his huge bed. He'd stalked up here about 3:00 a.m. First, he'd plundered a few bottles of good red wine out of the wine cellar—he couldn't find the key to the damn lock, so he'd picked it with the end of a kitchen knife.

Despite weaving on his feet from draining the wine to the last drop, he picked up the wooden board he was using as a palette. Squirted paint on it. He painted as hard and fast as he could, working out the frustration inside him.

He wanted to kiss Julia again. The heat she'd sent coursing through his body was like a drug. He wanted more.

His Irish mam had raised him to have a good sense of guilt, and a fear of paying for his sins that he never could quite shake out of his soul.

Both worked on him now, one kicking one side, and one kicking the other, like a couple of gang toughs working him over in an alley.

He'd planned to seduce Julia. Like an artistic challenge. Now he knew he couldn't do it. He couldn't pour on the temptation until she gave herself up to the adventure of sex. He couldn't do it to a woman who transcended the definition of "nice girl."

But that didn't stop him from wanting her. More than food. More than the clean, flower-scented country air that kept going into his lungs.

More than revenge?

Hell.

Voices buzzed downstairs. Cal could smell breakfast, even all the way up here in the attic. His gut growled, making him wonder when he'd last eaten. Not last night. He hadn't come ho— Come back to Worthington for dinner. He'd dropped Julia off at Brideswell, then he had driven down to the local pub.

The Worthington estate was huge, and bordered Brideswell's land. They were neighbors but miles apart. His lands encompassed several towns and villages, like that one of Chipping Worth, called that because it had been a market. The earldom received money from all the tenants and businesses within. Driving into a village and realizing that he was lord of it, that he owned his own tiny town, was crazy to him.

The beer was bitter and no one seemed to have discovered that the stuff tasted good when it was kept on a bed of ice, but he had to admit it wasn't half-bad.

Then, in the pub, he'd met a man whose sister had gone missing . . .

Cal dabbed green where it shouldn't have gone and stopped. Stepping back from Julia's portrait, he knew he'd done something damn stupid.

He'd destroyed the picture. Lost his focus and ruined it.

It wasn't the blob of green, but how he'd changed

her. Her face didn't glow with fiery passion any-more. The portrait was starting to capture her shielded, cool demeanor. It was like she was drawing away from him. There was no spark in her eyes that promised inside there was a lady who would go off like a firecracker.

He'd changed her face with strokes of paint here and there and now he was seeing the woman who had pulled away from his kiss yesterday. Who couldn't face losing one more thing.

He put more paint on the palette. He had to fix the damn picture.

He couldn't live with himself if he became part of the family that had left his mother to die. Couldn't face the guilt and pain of giving up this chance to make good on the promise he had made on Mam's deathbed—to make the Worthingtons, as he thought of them, pay.

It meant hurting Julia. Heaping pain on a woman who had known more than her fair share and who had done nothing but care for people and give her heart to them.

He couldn't do that. So how in hell did he get justice for his father, for Mam?

Someone was behind him. Quiet as a mouse, but he knew. Julia? He whirled around, hope, despair, desire, guilt, need and pure joy all fighting through his gut like an army.

Creeping daylight—like it was embarrassed to interject on British gloom—fell in through the window and slanted on a set of spectacles. Clutching a book to her chest, his youngest cousin stood there. Dark-haired, like Julia. Which one? Not the audacious flirt, Diana. Thalia.

"It's a beautiful picture," she breathed.

"It's not," he growled suddenly, hating the picture in front of him. Now he saw the emotion radiating out of Julia's eyes well enough to put a name on it. Sadness. Sadness that he'd put there—and not just with a brush. "It's a piece of damn crap."

He threw the brush, sending a slash of yellow across Julia's bare, color-dappled shoulders and her ethereal white dress. It felt good. Felt good destroying this thing that he'd tried to do and had failed at.

Rage flowed through his arteries and veins, pumped through his heart. He threw the palette at the top of the canvas, watching it slide partway down, covering unhappy Julia with a veil of yellow and ochre, cadmium red and cobalt blue. Halfway, the descent stopped. As if appalled at what it had done, the palette tipped backward and toppled off the painting, landing on the worn plank floor.

Thalia had stepped back, her stance a perfect mimic of a terrified deer. The rage, the act of violence had scared her. A heel—he felt just like that. And had scared himself. He thought he'd gotten the anger—the bitterness, along with the squeezing grip of having failed—under control. He let it fuel his rage but never command it. He could never hurt a woman physically, but Thalia was making little wheezing-sob sounds like she figured he would.

Then she exploded in a gush of tears and just as he said, "I'm sorry," and took a tentative step toward her, she bolted from the room on long colt legs.

In the morning, Julia wanted to hide in bed. Wanted to pretend that the Tofts were not waking up to a day of unimaginable pain.

But she could not hide under her counterpane. There was too much to be done.

It physically hurt to sit up. Her arms ached, feeling heavy as she pushed away the bedcovers. All over, she felt as if bruised. This was the toll of grief.

Imagine how those poor children felt!

Bustling footsteps sounded outside her door. It opened, and Sims glided in, carrying a warming dish and a coffee urn upon a tray. "You are awake, my lady. Her Grace instructed that you would want breakfast in your room this morning."

Zoe had done that. How good of her. But Julia doubted she could manage much food at all—still, she needed to eat something. Then she must get to work.

Sims set the tray across her lap and poured coffee.

"Sims, I will need a black armband." It was what was worn when mourning someone who was not an immediate family member, where the rules were most rigid about wearing black.

Sims arched her plucked brow. Folded her arms over her chest. Sims was rail-thin and managed to look astoundingly haughty when she wished. Even Grandmama had nothing on Sims when it came to pinched lips and disapproving looks. "That would not be appropriate, my lady."

"I wish to mourn a tragic loss. So yes, it is appropriate."

"But this woman was not a member of your family or your class, my lady. Perhaps you could keep a black handkerchief on your person. Where it would not be seen."

"I want an armband. Will you do it?"

"No, my lady, I could not. Your mother—"

"Do not tell me what my mother would want me to do," Julia snapped. She was just . . . angry and out of sorts today. And she was not going to be bullied by Sims, who acted as lady's maid to her and Isobel. Isobel delighted in irritating Sims, who could be tremendously snobby, by attempting to wear boys' clothing whenever possible and leaving her graphic medical books around her room. Julia had been too polite.

She just couldn't be polite anymore. "I am going to wear an armband even if I must make it myself. I will not be swayed on this. This is important to me."

Sims began to speak, then stopped, as if biting her tongue. "I shall prepare you an armband."

"Thank you. You may go," Julia said firmly.

As Sims left, she set down her coffee and sagged back against her headboard. She was exhausted—she had been awake through most of the night. Sobbing for the Tofts and for a sweet, small baby who would never know life.

Julia lifted the tray off her lap. Instead of summoning Sims again, she pulled on a simple skirt, blouse and cardigan. Thank heaven for modern brassieres—she could put one on herself. Dressed, she went in search of her brother. She could not do much for the Toft family, but she could do one good thing.

She couldn't find Nigel in his usual haunts—the study or the library. The dining room was empty. Frustrated, Julia poured a cup of coffee.

"What's wrong?" It was Zoe, walking in from the salon. "Is it about Mrs. Toft? That is such a tragedy." Zoe hugged her.

"It's also about Dr. Hamilton," Julia said. "He is a hopeless snob. He was going to refuse to help Mrs. Toft because she is not a highborn woman. I threatened him to force him to go."

"You threatened him?"

"I reminded him that our family is the donor for the hospital and Nigel could force him out.

Hamilton also drinks while he is working at the hospital."

"I think we must fire him," Zoe said firmly.

Here was her opportunity. "But we need a new doctor. Otherwise people will have no one."

"Better no one than a pickled quack," Zoe said. "You went with the Earl of Worthington, didn't you? You've been spending a lot of time with him. Are you falling in love with him?"

The warm tingle of his kiss sat guiltily on her lips. "Of course not," Julia protested quickly. "He wants to sell Worthington Park and I am fighting to convince him otherwise."

"Why would he do that?"

"He hates the family because they disowned his father. I understand his anger, but I don't want him to make the people of Worthington—the tenants, the servants—suffer."

"And it necessitates that you spend every day with him?"

"Well, yes, it does," she said, rather defensively.

Zoe smiled.

"Anyway," Julia went on, "what we need is a doctor."

"I agree. And I can think of one," Zoe said, casually playing with the long rope of her bead necklace, trying to sound as if this was an obvious, utterly natural decision. "There is Dr. Campbell of course."

"Impossible. He is at the London Hospital, and

very happy there. And he is to be married. To someone else."

It was easy to say that now. She no longer felt a stab of pain. When she said those words, she only thought of Cal's mouth coming down over hers and him kissing her slow and coaxingly, and it felt as if the world had tumbled over.

"Yes, he's said that. But is that certain?"

"Zoe, of course it is certain." She hesitated. "Of course, he would be an excellent doctor for the people of Brideswell, but I don't believe we could convince him—"

"We won't even try, Julia. I'm not having you see Dr. Campbell and his new bride here. It would break your heart every single day. For once, you're not going to make a sacrifice for the sake of everyone else. We will find someone else. I must go to London, to Harley Street. Why don't you come with me? You can help in the hunt for a doctor."

"Perhaps I should stay instead. For the Tofts . . ."

"We could be gone for only a day and a night. Enough time to make inquiries on Harley Street. I'm sure we could find recommendations easily. I'd say we need a new doctor with promise, or an older one looking to escape London's smoke-filled fog." Zoe picked up a plate and loaded it with selections from the warming dishes.

This was something she could do. "I will take up the task, while you go to your appointment."

Then she saw, with amazement, the food pile up on Zoe's plate—sausage, roast beef, ham.

Zoe looked up. "I am absolutely starving. I can't seem to eat enough and if I don't eat, I feel sick. No one knows yet but I suppose I have told you now."

"Told me what?"

"You must know, Julia! Why does a woman feel queasy?"

"She's ill?"

"Or she is pregnant," Zoe said, with American bluntness and honesty. An English lady would say "expecting" or "enceinte."

"How wonderful!" Julia cried. Her heart gave a pang. She was so happy, but there was that envy, deep inside. That wish she could have a child of her own. A home of her own. Then the image came again. Mrs. Toft closing her eyes and simply letting go, letting go of the world that her last child never saw—

"I'm sorry," Zoe said suddenly. "I shouldn't have talked about this now. Not after what you went through."

Had she looked so awful? One glance at her face and Zoe leaped to her feet and extended arms in comfort. "Zoe, I am happy you told me. Joyful news is exactly what I need. It gives hope. Little pieces of hope that all join together and become stronger than pain. It was just for a minute that I remembered . . . I don't want you to walk on eggshells around me. I think I am tough enough—"

"Don't become tough. People call it tough, but it really means they are trying not to feel anything. That never works. Trust me," Zoe said.

Julia hugged her sister by marriage. "You're right. I think—I think I'm going to go to Mother's chapel. I want to say a little prayer for the Tofts. And I shall probably have a good cry. Then I shall prepare for London."

She went out through the terrace doors off the gallery. A cool sting bit the air and clouds rumbled by, driven by a strong breeze that carried more threat of winter than promise of summer. She must go and see her war widows today, check on their progress before she went to London. On the days she hadn't seen Cal, she had begun arranging the loans. She had gone to see Ellen Lambert, urging her to take money and begin some sort of business. But Ellen continued to refuse.

Another figure walked ahead of her, a woman with her head bowed and a scarf fluttering around her head.

Her mother.

She knew where her mother was going—the same place she was. The chapel was a place Julia rarely went. But today she wanted to go there. Julia followed the path that led to the small stone chapel their father had built for their mother when they first married. When Julia was young, she'd thought it was a symbol of her father's devoted love for her mother. Then she'd discovered how unhappy they were. It was strange—one year a girl would have no awareness of her parents' strife, the next year she felt it in every breath she took.

Julia pushed open the low wooden door and stepped into the chapel. The air was almost cold. Her mother knelt at the altar and at the soft hush of the door closing, she turned around. "Julia? Is something wrong?"

She walked to the altar to join Mother. "I was at Lower Dale Farm last night. When Mrs. Toft passed away and her baby was lost."

To her surprise, her mother embraced her. Her mother had not hugged her . . . in years and years. "What a terrible tragedy," her mother said softly, but Julia didn't care about the words. It was nice to simply be held.

The largest stained glass window, with pride of place behind the altar, depicted the holy infant in the mother's arms.

"Why a baby?" Julia whispered. "A poor child who never knew life? Why?"

"The babe has gone to heaven," her mother said.

"You know as well as I do—any religious man would deny that was true for a baby who wasn't baptized." Tears leaked down.

"I cannot believe that—that an innocent soul would not be saved," Mother whispered.

Julia met her mother's large green eyes. Eyes

just like those of her brothers, Sebastian and Will.

"This has broken your heart, my dear," her mother said.

"I want to be strong. I want to be of use. But I'm not sad. Now I understand how I feel. So angry."

"I know, my dear. I was so angry when we lost Will. When Nigel came home to us wounded. I was so afraid to let out that anger that I couldn't let myself feel anything at all."

"It was anger, not sorrow?"

"Grief is many things," Mother said. "Oh, my dear, this has broken my heart, too. We must pray for them both."

Julia knelt at her mother's side. Her mother's soft voice flowed over her as she prayed. She wanted to believe in heaven—that Mrs. Toft could look down over her children and still watch them grow. That perhaps, in heaven, her baby wouldn't be lost and all alone.

After the prayers, Mother and she walked back to the house, their arms linked. Grief and sorrow had driven them apart for years. Yet now, it had brought them together.

"I will not push you to marry, Julia," her mother said.

"Thank you."

And with that, she felt she had put marriage behind her. She must look to a future without it.

Once she came back from London—having found a doctor for the Brideswell Hospital—she could move toward the real life she was going to have.

The next morning, as the mist scurried away from Brideswell's lawns, it was a flurry to get to the station for the early train.

Footmen hastened out of the front door with trunks and hatboxes. They stacked the luggage on the back of the Daimler and tied it in place, as the two lady's maids, in their traveling outfits, ensured no box or bag or case was missed.

Julia stood with Nigel, who held Nicholas in his arms, as Zoe came down, drawing on her gloves. Zoe wore a scarlet coat and matching cloche and her heeled black shoes clicked on the tiles. She kissed Nigel farewell—not on his cheek but full on his mouth. Then she lifted her son into her arms and rubbed her nose against his, until he giggled. "I'll miss both my men very much," Zoe whispered, her voice catching.

Julia certainly understood the catch in Zoe's voice, the tears shining in her eyes. Nicholas looked adorable in a blue sailor-style suit. His hair was dark as Nigel's, fine as silk, and his eyes were huge as he said, "Go wif Mama."

"Oh, darling, you can't come with me this time. Just a boring visit to the doctor for me."

"I should go with you," Nigel said.

Zoe gave him a wry, tough smile. "I'll be fine.

I'm sure this expensive Harley Street specialist will coddle me since I'm a duchess."

Then Julia was drawn into her brother's embrace. "Look after Zoe," he murmured by her ear. "You know how headstrong she is. I know you'll convince her to be responsible. You understand duty and responsibility."

When she heard it spoken that way, it sounded like a dreaded disease.

Zoe caught her eye and winked. "We will be the most responsible women in the country. I assure you that the prime minister will come calling by the end of our visit, to take notes on how to be properly cautious, responsible and dutiful."

"I know you won't," Nigel said. "But be careful."

"I will take care of her," Julia promised.

"And I'll take very good care of Julia," Zoe added.

When they reached the station, Julia was surprised to see Diana waiting on the platform. She looked lovely in a slim-fitting dress of black crepe with a short skirt, and a jacket of white silk, trimmed in black. Ropes of jet-black beads dangled over the curve of her bosom. Diana linked arms with her. "Do you mind if I go down to London with you?"

"Of course not." Then more quietly. "Why are you going? For shopping?"

"Why do you think? It's to see *him*. This is my last chance—" Diana broke off. "It's Cal."

And it was. The kiss tingled on her lips, as if it were still dancing there. For days, she had thrust herself into Cal's life whether he wanted it or not. Now she didn't know how to stand, or where to look.

He looked stunned to see her. "Julia? What are you doing here?"

She realized she really did not want to see him. She had kissed him. She had never dreamed of kissing a man she wasn't going to marry, even though women did that all the time now. They did just about everything you could do with a husband with men they desired but didn't want to marry. But she could never do that.

"We're going up to London," Diana said.

"So am I," he said.

Diana narrowed her eyes. "What for?" she asked, with bluntness that a lady was never supposed to use.

"To see a lawyer," he answered. "Worthington's man of business."

Julia jerked her head up. She looked at him, but Cal looked innocent, as if butter would not begin to melt on that warm tongue of his.

"Why are you doing that? You're not arranging the sale of anything, are you?" Fear gripped her. Her last words to him had been that she couldn't bear to lose one more thing—including Worthington. But she'd never thought it would change his mind and she supposed it hadn't. But she needed more time!

"Of course not," he answered, after a pause.

But the light way he spoke, with a touch of a lilting Irish accent he must have picked up from his mother, made her certain he was not telling the truth. He was trying too hard to sound innocent. Her heart raced. "You haven't even met all the tenants yet. You can't—"

"Not to worry, doll. I'm not going to pull the rug out from under you."

"Well . . . well, thank heavens for that at least. For then I would fall on my bottom."

"I would never do that after what you've just been through." He studied her and his voice was caress-soft. "But I'm thinking about making you a deal. If I keep going with you to meet the tenants, you have to sit for me."

"Sit for him? What do you mean?" asked Zoe. She asked it politely, but she watched Cal with a rapier-sharp gaze. Julia wondered if Zoe was worried about her safety with Cal. But she wasn't going to kiss him like that ever again.

"I'd like to paint a portrait of Julia."

"Oh," Zoe said. Then in a softer, but more intense tone, she said, *"Oh."*

"I need to paint you, Julia."

"I thought you already were. I saw the picture."

"I had to scrap it. Without you to model for me, I couldn't get it right. Say yes, Julia. This picture of you—it could be the best thing I ever do."

He'd moved close to her, holding her gaze, his

eyes full of hope and his voice full of urgency. It was as if it meant life and death to him.

She was going to say no—sit in front of him for hours? She'd yearn to kiss him.

Why couldn't she find out about passion with Cal? She couldn't do it without caring too much about him—she already did. And she couldn't lose one more thing—neither Cal, nor the very last unbroken piece of her heart.

"Please, Julia?" His voice was the softest rasp.

But *no* didn't come out. "Would you promise not to do a thing to Worthington while I sit for you?" she asked. She hadn't even consciously thought that.

He cocked his head. A train whistle blew and she heard the clatter of locomotive wheels on the tracks in the distance. "I'm almost willing to do that just to get you into my studio."

"But not willing to go that far?"

He grinned. "That's probably the first time I've said it. I'm not willing to go that far."

"Then what are you willing to do?"

"Keep an open mind. And give you another chance to convince me."

She was about to point out that she was not getting much in return when Diana, who had been standing there, broke in. "Julia, darling, he does paint women naked."

She had forgotten about that. "That's not what you want me to do, is it?"

"I never would have dreamed of asking. Unless you're willing."

She was about to say: *Of course I wouldn't.* Then she saw the wicked grin playing on his lips. He was expecting her to be shocked and outraged. So she gave him a serene smile. "The idea is more intriguing than I expected. I will be in London for three days. I'll give you my answer at the end of the trip."

He made a sputtering sound.

And despite the pain of yesterday, she felt a ray of hope blossom. She might just win the most important battle she'd ever waged.

The train chuffed in and smoke billowed out, wreathing them in its white mist. Julia felt a gaze on her, and turned to see Zoe staring at her with one brow raised.

People disembarked. Porters opened the doors of the first-class carriages. Farther down the platform, Julia saw all their luggage vanishing into the train, then Sims and Zoe's maid climbed the step into their compartment. As they got on board, Julia asked Cal, "Are you opening Worthington House in London for your stay?"

"Wor— What?" he said. He'd been staring at her. She managed to hide a smile of victory.

If he wanted this from her, surely she could use it to save the estate. And to help him heal. She could use the time with him while he was painting to do just that.

"The London house. Worthington House is just a block from our London house. In Mayfair. Near Hyde Park."

Then he said, "I plan to stay at a hotel. I don't think a man needs more than one house that's big enough to house a small village."

"Worthington House is *lovely,*" Diana declared. "Of course, you're going to stay there. Once we arrive, I will telephone and have it prepared. It's short notice, but it can be done. I will stay there with you."

"I'd rather stay in a hotel," Cal muttered.

"It is your house," Diana returned. "Get used to it."

Cal murmured something. Julia barely heard it. It sounded like, "Not for long." Her heart plunged. For a moment. Then stubborn determination kicked in as she followed Diana into one of the first-class carriages, and Zoe followed them as Cal held the door.

Maybe she would sit naked for him, if that's what it would take.

But she knew she couldn't. She couldn't do anything so intimate unless it was for a man she loved. And who loved her back.

Diana took a seat by the window and planted her hand on the cushion next to her. "Join me, Cal?"

Julia sat across, so she could sit by the window. A few whistles, much haste on the platform, then the whistle tooted once more and they set off.

She pressed close to the window as the wheels began to clack on the rails. She loved to see the steam billowing around them as the train started off, then to watch the scenery stream by.

"You look like a kid on her first train trip, Julia," Cal said. "All excited."

She looked away from the window. Cal was looking at her—only at her—as if they were the only two in the carriage. Zoe was reading a newspaper. Diana looked bored, as only a fashionable woman could, but she was watching Cal from under the fringe of blackened lashes.

"Travel does excite me," Julia admitted. "I love this sense of hurtling somewhere new."

"Hardly new, dearest," Diana drawled. "You've been to London thousands of times."

Diana partly slumped on the seat in a shockingly casual pose, extended one leg so it rested alongside Cal's long legs.

"Have you traveled farther than London?" he asked.

"We go north for shooting," Julia explained. "But that is the absolute farthest."

"Not Paris? Not Monte Carlo?"

She shook her head. "My mother has been very weak and troubled since after the War, when my youngest brother died. She couldn't travel and I didn't want to leave her. But now she's much better. Time seems to be healing her. And there is Zoe now, who watches out for her, too."

Zoe looked up and smiled, then returned to her newspaper. The *Wall Street Journal*—sent specially to her.

"So you're free now to go wherever you desire," Cal said. "Where would you like to go?"

"I don't know. I've never thought about it." She hadn't traveled very much. If she had married Dougal she wouldn't have traveled. If she married someone like Bradstock, she would be expected to travel to fashionable places—places deemed socially acceptable.

Before she could respond to that further, he said again, "You're free to go anywhere you like. Why don't you travel the world?"

Vivid images flooded her head. Of palm trees and the rippling water of the Nile, where pyramids could be seen from the deck of a steamer. Or the Eiffel Tower in Paris. Or the stunningly tall buildings of New York. Of course, her mental pictures were all from images in advertisements and magazines. "I couldn't afford to do that. Nor can I travel alone. Not as an unmarried woman. It would be much too scandalous and shocking."

"It's a modern world. You can be shocking."

"I'm not shocking at heart."

Zoe was not looking at her newspaper—she was discreetly watching them. But Diana piped up, "Oh no, Julia is not wild and adventurous at all. The most daring thing she's done is go to an underground jazz club. I've tried to coax her to do wild things in London with me. I mix with the most exciting crowd of young artists and bold young peers. They've taken to calling us the Bright Young Things."

Cal pulled out a black-bound book from a satchel and a pencil. He began to sketch. "Where would you like to go, Julia?"

"Paris."

His brow rose. "You're decisive. Why Paris?" Then he smiled. "Your brother lives there. Go visit him."

"I simply . . . can't. I could hardly get on a ship alone and voyage so far."

"Women do, doll. Or go with a friend. You know, I'd be happy to take you." He had his sketch-book open on his thigh, but his eyes held hers. "I'd be happy to take you to see the world."

She was aware of both Zoe and Diana taking in the whole conversation.

And her heart stuttered. He was gentle and teasing and deeply interested in her. She felt an impossible tug—a yearning to travel with him. To see the lights of Paris, the cafés, the galleries, the parks, and to do it with Cal, who was noble and exciting, naughty and sensitive—

But what did he mean? He must be teasing her.

She sat up in a straight-backed, ladylike way. "That's really not possible," she said briskly. "And I did want to talk to you about how women tenants at Worthington—women like Ellen Lambert—can be helped. I am still trying to push Ellen into starting a business. She is very adept with a needle and thread—and I believe she could readily learn to operate a sewing machine. That would open up many possibilities to her."

Cal looked taken aback. "She's going to struggle if she's suffering from shell shock."

Zoe frowned. "A woman with shell shock? I did not know such a thing was possible."

"It is," Julia said passionately. "Ellen Lambert was an ambulance driver in the War and I believe she is suffering the same symptoms as men. I spoke to Dr. Hamilton of course, but he just dismissed me. What she needs is help. Once she is able to deal with that issue, then she can begin a business."

"Oh, Julia, you are so dreadfully serious," Diana said. She leaned over toward Cal. "What are you doing, darling?" she trilled. "You keep looking at us, then down at your book. Are you sketching *us?* You devilish thing! Let me see."

Laughing, Diana motioned him to show the pictures. But Cal shook his head.

"I shall fight you for that book," Diana teased, batting her lashes.

"You can see them without doing that. But they're rough." He held out the book. Then he leaned back against the seat. His leg stretched along it. Julia realized he always sprawled over chairs in ways that looked defiant, not relaxed.

Propping the book on her skirted lap, Diana leafed through. "Julia . . . this is a good likeness. Here is Julia again. And—goodness, a figure without her clothing. But I can't see her face. Who *is* she? That isn't one of us, I hope. You aren't sitting there and imagining what we look like without any clothes."

"I hope not," Zoe said. "I'm here as the chaperone."

Cal gave Zoe a charming smile. "I hear you fly airplanes," he said.

"I do. I love it. When Nicholas is older, Nigel and I will take him up. Do you still fly?"

"I haven't done it since the War."

Julia saw the quick look of pain that showed in Cal's eyes. Then she glanced over at the picture. And swallowed hard. The woman was drawn with charcoal. Her hair was short and dark. She couldn't be sure . . . but the woman's figure looked like hers.

"That's not something a gentleman would do," Cal answered. "I admit I'm not a gentleman, but no, I wouldn't do that. Anyway, Diana, you're my cousin. That wouldn't be right."

Diana's smile vanished. She let the pages fall. "People like us marry cousins all the time."

But Cal just shook his head.

Diana put her hand to her mouth.

Julia realized Diana might be going to visit

the married man whom she loved, but she hadn't given up the idea of marrying Cal. Except Cal had just told her he would never do it.

Diana looked at the picture again, then up at Julia, her face sullen. It was as if the woman who had once been her best friend now hated her.

Julia looked at the picture again. Did it mean Cal had been looking at her and picturing what she looked like underneath her dress, her brassiere, her slip? He had said not, but she was not sure.

She felt hot, embarrassed. Uncertain.

Yet she looked at Cal and she remembered what he'd looked like without his shirt. What did *he* look like without any clothes?

"Behave yourselves," Zoe said, glancing over the top of her newspaper.

The first-class compartment suddenly felt too small. Julia stood abruptly. "I have to use the washing compartment."

But when she made her way back, bracing her hand against the swaying of the carriage, Cal stood in the corridor. His broad shoulders almost filled the space wall to wall.

Brilliant blue eyes gazed into hers. "Damn it, I want you, Julia Hazelton."

Julia's heart skipped several beats. Then she managed to give him a polite, restrained smile. "Cal, please don't. It's quite impossible. We kissed in a moment of intense emotion. But I cannot give myself to you in the way that you want."

His lower lip jutted out slightly, in a sensual pout. "You could. The only thing stopping you is the stupid rules of the aristocracy."

"It's not the only thing stopping me."

She moved to walk past him, but he stopped her. "I thought I could get over it. But I can't. I *dream* about you."

He dreamed about her? A forbidden image rushed in—Cal waking up in his bed, sitting up, sheets tumbling off him, revealing his naked torso. She swallowed hard. Cal made her have unladylike thoughts. Thoughts like she had never had in her whole life.

"I never thought this would happen," he said urgently. "Not with a duke's daughter. But you're different. You're special. I know you'd expect marriage. I know I can't give that to you. I don't know if I could even give you my heart. But I'd love to make you see what I already know—that you're passionate and alive, and you are ready to burst out of your ladylike shell."

"You wouldn't give me your heart," she repeated. She'd never expected him to be so blunt.

"I'd like to lay the world at your feet, Julia. I'd like to take you to Paris to drink wine in Montparnasse and dance to jazz. I'd take you to Santorini, where we could lie naked in the sun and eat figs and olives. I'd take you across a lake surrounded by vibrant autumn leaves in the Canadian north. I'd take you up close to the

Arctic Circle, where the northern lights would dance overhead like veils of brilliant color floating through the sky. I'd like to show you the African plains, the South American jungles."

If she never saw the world, and she did good works, and lived in the country that she knew, she could be content and happy. She was sure she would.

But deep inside, a voice whispered that she should have more. That she had waited and waited for life to begin, yet she had missed the point. She had to set her own life in motion.

What was she thinking? Cal had just told her he would never love her.

He moved toward her, bringing his lips close to hers.

On the brink of melting, she pulled away fast. "No. I can't do it without love, Cal. Without marriage."

"Julia is going to London, and will very likely see a man who was passionately in love with her." Zoe's husky voice startled. He jumped. So did Julia.

Zoe had come out into the corridor and leaned against the wall, smiling innocently.

"Who is it?" he asked. "One of those weak-chinned titled men who were chasing you at dinner? The Duke of Bradstock, a shallow, arrogant idiot who thinks he can rule over you?"

Julia was about to correct what Zoe had said,

but her sister-in-law cheekily added, "He's a doctor. A man who saves lives. He was absolutely perfect for Julia—a true hero who passionately believes in helping others, but he left Brideswell because the family objected and he listened, believing he shouldn't marry a duke's daughter."

"Zoe—" Julia began. For Zoe was leaving an impression that was not quite true.

"Of course," Zoe continued, "Julia would be willing to defy all her family . . . for the right man."

Cal's mouth was harsh, bracketed by lines. "He should have been willing to fight for you."

"He left me for what he thought was my own good." Julia felt she should leap to Dougal's defense. She had no idea what Zoe was doing, and she felt a bit guilty for leaving the impression that Dougal was still in love with her. But really, did it matter if Cal thought there was someone else? She could never be his mistress. It just felt wrong inside.

Zoe moved on down the corridor. Cal moved closer.

"If I wanted you to be my wife," he said huskily, "I'd fight heaven and earth to have you. I'd fight dirty to have you, Julia."

"But you don't want me to be your wife. And I'm not in love with you, Cal. Just as you are not in love with me. Now I really should return to our compartment. And you are blocking the corridor."

He moved so she could pass him. "If anyone asks, I'm going to the dining car," he growled.

"For lunch? They won't be serving it yet."

"For a stiff drink. Or ten."

10

London

At luncheon, after Zoe's appointment with a Harley Street specialist for pregnancy and "women's concerns," Julia dined with her sister by marriage in the elegant dining room of the Savoy. There had been a huge scandal at the hotel last summer when Ali Fahmy had been shot there by his wife, Marguerite. The trial was sensational, detailing sexual scandals in the style of *The Sheikh*. Despite the notoriety—or because of it— American film actors and royalty still flocked there.

Julia didn't know why that was what she thought of as they swept through the foyer and were escorted to a table, surrounded by London's Bright Young Things. Perhaps it was because it was in all the newspapers, or because she was worried about Diana, or because she was thinking of Sarah Brand—where had she vanished to? They passed a group of laughing women and Zoe murmured, "That one is the Prince of Wales's latest."

Julia recognized her. "She's married," Julia whispered back.

"He appears to like them that way."

Julia thought of Diana, in love and pregnant by

a man who was married. Her faith in modernity wobbled a bit. Was the frenetic pace of modern life simply a way to be too busy to be unhappy?

Zoe ordered champagne cocktails, but barely touched hers. "I was told it is not good for the baby. Dr. Haliwell does like to give orders. He also insisted the best man for Brideswell Hospital can be found at the London Hospital. Not Dr. Campbell, but another young, promising surgeon by the name of McLeod. Shall I go and interview him?"

Julia smiled. She knew Zoe was trying to spare her. But she could see Dougal without pain. "I inquired at a few of the other doctors' offices during your appointment. I was advised to talk to a doctor also at the London Hospital—Dr. Fenwick. So we'll both have to go and compare."

"What if you see Dr. Campbell?"

"Then I shall say hello."

Zoe lifted a brow. "You're remarkable, Julia. You look barely troubled at all."

"It's the breeding. Inside, I feel a mess of nerves."

"The Earl of Worthington said you're obviously very passionate on the inside." Zoe tapped a perfectly manicured nail—clear at the tip and the half-moon at the base, then red for the rest—against her lip. "I wonder how he knew."

Julia felt a blush creep up. "He claims he could tell just by looking at me. I am certain he was making that up. Simply to tease and unsettle me."

Zoe laughed. "The earl unsettles you?"

"We argue and debate constantly, Zoe. Hardly promise of a companionable marriage."

But Zoe's eyes sparkled. "But that isn't what you really want, is it? Nigel used to drive me crazy at first. We seemed to be on the opposite sides of everything. It made it all the more passionate. And the way Worthington looked at you in the corridor of the train, especially when I told him someone else is in love with you—"

"You shouldn't have fibbed. And there will never be anything between Worthington and I. I agree with my mother and grandmother—I think a companionable marriage, where a man and woman's passion hasn't turned to utter hatred, is a much more sensible arrangement."

But she was lying. Completely. Trying not to show that in her expression, she finished her champagne. What was the point in feeling desire for a man who blatantly said he would offer nothing more? Who didn't even bother wooing with pretty words? She admired honesty but she didn't think she could embark on an affair in such a cold-blooded way . . .

But as Zoe elegantly signed the check—"Zoe, Duchess of Langford"—Julia couldn't help imagining what it would be like to see the world. With Cal. To see all those exotic things he'd whispered about. See them at his side.

"Julia, you're blushing. What are you thinking

about?" Zoe asked. She was "Your Graced" by all the staff as they left, all the way to the doorman who opened the door to their car—the Daimler kept at the London house.

"Not a thing," Julia said as she slid into the car, and it took Zoe and her to the London Hospital, a charity hospital on Whitechapel High Street.

They halted on the road outside the front entry. The street was filled with carts pulled by ponies, even oxen. Julia looked up at the long brick facade, the arched entries, the people shuffling up the front steps. Would she see Dougal here? Her heart gave a quick, fast step, as if it was actually trembling with nerves.

With Zoe, she marched up the front steps and walked into the reception room of the hospital, crowded with patients. A nurse saw them and gaped in surprise. Their clothes and Zoe's announcement she was a duchess got them immediate attention. In moments, she and Zoe were being ushered to the ward where Dr. Fenwick was doing his rounds.

The ward was a large space with a surprisingly tall ceiling. Summer sunlight came in the arched windows and fell across the simple white cots that lined all the walls. Women lay on their beds. One young woman was sitting up and feeding her infant. A nurse in a skirt that swished low on her calves busily made her way from bed to bed with medicine.

Then she saw him as he straightened from the

bed of a patient. He wore a white coat with a stethoscope draped around his neck, and carried a chart in his hands.

Not Dr. Fenwick. It was Dougal.

For a moment, she couldn't speak. All she could do was watch him work.

Auburn-haired and handsome, Dougal was so at ease with his patients. He even drew a laugh from a woman who lay on her back and had been groaning in pain. It was as if just hearing his voice had made her feel better. The woman clasped his hand. "Bless ye, Dr. Campbell."

Julia had thought the same herself so many times when she watched him help people at the Brideswell Hospital.

After a few minutes she realized he was happy here. His patients adored him. He was surrounded by people recovering—by people he'd helped. And he discussed their illnesses with the interest of a man driven to find cures. Dougal Campbell's compassion and skill left her awestruck. This was a true modern man. He spent his days pushing his capabilities, his knowledge—the knowledge of medical science.

The hospital, with its nose-tingling scent of carbolic, with the life-and-death drama, was Dougal's place. This was his place in the world. His work here, in London, must be exciting.

He had found his place.

Her heart felt as if it had plummeted to her toes.

Watching him work, she realized how much good they could have done together. How she would have been in awe of what he did every day.

What was more important—being with a man you admired or a man who made the whole world stop, but in an unrequited way?

Or maybe the only solution was to have neither man.

She had been raised and trained to be the mistress of a great estate. But that was never going to happen. She could run off to Capri or Paris like Sebastian and become an artist. She was joking—or was she? She remembered the thrill she'd felt when Cal had forced her to put paint on his canvas.

"Lady Julia."

She knew the deep, husky voice, the trace of Scottish burr. She couldn't retreat now, even if she wanted to. Dougal looked startled at first. Then happy. Yes, definitely happy.

Seeing that glow in his dark eyes made her heart twist.

"Good afternoon, Dr. Campbell." She had never faced a man whom she had once loved and now must no longer love. It was an awkward sensation.

"What are you doing here?" he asked quickly. Then he corrected himself. "I mean, I'm surprised to see you at the hospital, Lady Julia. But it's an honor to have you here. A great pleasure." A blush touched his high cheekbones, and as he stumbled over his words, she smiled. But inside, she was remembering that they had kissed once. A polite kiss. At the time, it had been breathtaking. It had been sweet and it had set her heart soaring.

What a thing to think of. She must be serious. Not thinking of his sweet kiss. Or Cal's hot, melting kisses—that Cal gave just because he was bold and he was trying to shock her. Dougal had never tried to shock her. He had always . . . treated her as an equal. Not as a lady, not as a sexual plaything, but as someone with an intelligent mind.

"We are here to find a new doctor for Brideswell Hospital."

"We?"

"Dr. Campbell," Zoe acknowledged as she stepped forward—rather cautiously for exuberant Zoe.

He bowed to Zoe, fast and startled. "My apologies, Your Grace. I—I didn't see you there."

"No, I could see that," Zoe said, her eyes twinkling. Julia felt Zoe look at Dougal, then at her, and she knew Zoe was appraising them.

But there was nothing between them now. A past, but now only politeness.

"Your replacement at the hospital, Dr. Hamilton, has been a disaster," Julia explained. "He wants to be a fashionable physician. To force him to treat a farmwife on the estate who had trouble in her labor, I had to threaten to have my brother fire him. And he absolutely refused to recognize that women could suffer shell shock. Hysteria, he insisted, and he wouldn't recommend any—" She broke off. She was saying far too much. And not very coherently.

She knew she was blushing.

And Dougal couldn't seem to take his gaze away from her. Probably because she was making a fool of herself.

"We were given recommendations of doctors who work here," Zoe finished. "We were given two names, and assured either man would make an excellent head of the Brideswell Hospital."

Dougal nodded. "I see. You want to interview the men, Your Grace. You need a quiet place for that. Follow me."

That was Dougal—rather blunt in his conversation. Nothing flowery, as if he didn't have time to waste.

He took her and Zoe to the generously sized boardroom used by the directors of the hospital when they met. Portraits of austere gentlemen adorned the paneled walls and leather swiveling chairs were placed the length of a polished oak table. They took seats, Zoe turned things over to her and Julia explained their hope that either Dr. Fenwick or Dr. McLeod would prove to be good for Brideswell.

Dougal leaned back, steepling his fingers. "Both are excellent doctors. My recommendation is McLeod. Young but dedicated. Lives and breathes the work, eager to tackle any case. Good with the patients. He'd appreciate the opportunity to be the head of a hospital. I would be available to consult by telephone, if he needs an outside opinion or finds a problem that stumps him."

"That's very generous of you." Julia met his gaze. She still admired this man and her heart was warm with gratitude toward his offer. Impulsively she said, "You appear to be very happy here."

"Coming to London changed everything for me. My surgical skills and knowledge have expanded threefold. There are surgeries I have done here that I would have never dreamed of attempting at Brideswell Hospital."

"Oh. I am so very glad."

Her heart gave a sharp pang. In that moment, she knew how happy she could have been as Dougal's wife. She would have come to London with him. She would have kept his home for him, and been there to support him when he returned from the hospital, exhausted and carrying worries on his shoulders—

But then she thought of Cal casually draping his shirt around her, then standing behind her and holding her hand as she held the paintbrush. How much she had admired him when he promised to help Ellen Lambert, when he spoke to the Toft children.

Cal knocked her off her feet. He did something to her when she was with him. She felt—even when they were arguing—she felt she crackled with life.

But surely being happy and useful was much better. Companionship, as she'd said to Zoe.

Then Dougal took her and Zoe on a tour of the hospital, explaining the strengths of both men, and also their weaknesses, as they went through the wards. He stressed attributes that he believed would make each man suitable for a small country hospital, and their limitations. Truly, he did make McLeod sound the perfect candidate.

In that afternoon, she was transported into his world again. His world of medicine, and inquiry, and saving lives. She remembered how much she had wanted to be part of that world, to be of use, to do work of importance.

She had never felt so confused—so uncertain.

As he finished, Zoe said, "Dr. McLeod sounds perfect and your recommendation carries a lot of weight, as does your offer. Julia and I will interview both men. If Julia is in agreement, then we will make a decision."

That was Zoe. In matters of business, Zoe knew what to do and she would never simply take a man's advice. She would weigh it.

"Yes, I do agree."

Dougal took them back to the boardroom. "I'll fetch them then."

"Thank you," Zoe said.

"It is the least I can do, Your Grace."

Julia saw how awkward he looked. The only

moments he appeared to relax were when he was showing them the wards.

"Congratulations," she added quickly. She didn't want him to be uncomfortable. She didn't want awkwardness to be the last emotion between them. "I should have said before—I am so pleased you are to be married."

"You're very gracious," he said.

It was kind, so why did that word bother her so? Aging queens were gracious. Her *grandmother* could be gracious.

Cal had called her passionate. But he'd done it to tease her.

"I'll summon McLeod," Dougal said. He stood, gave a brief bow and left to find the two doctors.

Within the hour, the business was settled. After speaking with both men, Zoe concurred with Dr. Campbell's opinion. Julia agreed. Dr. Robert McLeod was to be Brideswell's new doctor. Julia felt something good had been accomplished. She and Zoe left, walking briskly down the steps toward the waiting car. Once in the rear seat, she looked back toward the hospital. Would she want that life—or did she want Cal? And did it matter, when she was to have neither man?

She had to decide. What did she want to do—?

She gasped. Dougal had come out onto the top of the steps. He lifted his hand in a brief wave and she waved back, startled he had come to watch her go.

• • •

The Earl of Worthington's London house stood on Berkeley Square. A four-story mansion of stone built in the early eighteenth century, it took up half the street. From the drawing room windows, one could see the square—the paths shaded beneath arching branches, the trimmed lawns that stretched within the wrought iron black fences. The park filled in the afternoon with strolling couples, elderly gentlemen taking their constitutional, and a veritable army of nannies and perambulators.

Cal was not in—he had sent word that he wouldn't come back for dinner. But Diana led Julia into the music room. By the window, with sunlight pouring in, Diana exclaimed, "You must come with me tonight. The Black Bottom is London's newest jazz club. It's modeled on a seraglio and most of the women go dressed in Turkish attire. I absolutely have to go."

"I can guess why. Diana, I wish you wouldn't."

"I must! I'm going to force him to make a decision, once and for all. He keeps telling me he yearns to be with me, that he wants to find a way to leave his wife. But then—then nothing happens. The days are ticking by and I know I don't have much longer. Just come with me and let me resolve it. Either I'll know he's going to divorce his wife for me, or I will know it is over."

With a sinking heart, Julia could guess what would happen. Diana would need a friend there for her. "All right. I'll go." Zoe knew Julia was going out to a jazz club, but she'd elected to go to bed early and rest. Pregnancy had made her tired, but she'd urged Julia to enjoy herself.

At the Black Bottom, Julia expected to finally see the heartless wretch who had used Diana so terribly. She didn't expect to see Cal—Cal seated at a table, talking to a black-haired man who dressed just like an American gangster.

She had walked in with Diana, drinking in the smoky atmosphere. The only lighting came from lamps made of metal with decorative cutouts, like those she had seen in pictures of Morocco. The tables were low, surrounded by cushions. The whole place looked like an opium den. Sultry, naughty-sounding jazz music wound silkily through the gloom.

Julia saw several women in embroidered jackets and voluminous harem pants, smoking cigars. She gasped at the sight of two girls, wearing only a strip of fabric over their breasts, along with diaphanous skirts that pooled on the ground. They wore veils, and black kohl rimmed their eyes. Their feet were bare. They looked exotic—except they both spoke with a London accent.

When she saw Cal, her heart gave a leap of surprise. When she looked at Cal, the band ceased to play. The girls serving drinks stopped in midmotion. A stream of champagne stopped in midpour.

The man sitting across from Cal leaned forward and spoke quietly. Cal's expression blackened into one of anger.

A lady shouldn't stare, but at the dramatic change in Cal's face, she did.

The man looked like one of the famed gangsters. She had seen pictures in the newspapers of them. Reputedly Al Capone insisted that there was no excuse not to be well dressed. This man wore clothes just like she had seen in a photograph of Al Capone—a white suit jacket over a black shirt, tie, but a white waistcoat. Gold flashed on his wrist as he lifted a cigar to his lips.

The man leaned close to Cal, muttered something, then straightened with a triumphant smirk. Cal's hand shook as he lit a cigarette—it took him two tries with his silver lighter. Cal's expression was positively thunderous for a moment, while he faced away from the man. Then Cal smoothed his face into a look of jaded boredom, and said something to the man, who didn't like what he heard. He shouted back at Cal. Julia caught two words right at the end. "I'll talk."

Talk about what? Was he threatening Cal?

"See you later, Julia," Diana said.

What? She jerked around, just in time to see Diana disappear behind a diaphanous curtain with a tall man. Damn! She'd hoped to find out who the gentleman was. Then she was going to tell him to stop stringing Diana along. She

227

feared he had no intention of doing right by Diana—and that would leave Diana with two choices.

Two heart-wrenching choices.

"Care to dance?"

Startled, she looked up—to find Cal beside her. He'd slicked his blond hair back and he wore a gorgeous evening suit that emphasized his broad shoulders. It was black, setting off his tanned face. Sultry music slithered through the smoky interior.

She looked to the table where the American had been sitting, but he was gone.

"All right," she said, and the moment she did, he put his hand to her lower back and drew her close. Right against his hard, lean body. Her head tucked into the space below his jaw, against the wide breadth of his shoulders.

But she felt a jerk of his arm muscles against her, as if his anger hadn't died away.

"Who was that man? And why did he make you angry, before you returned the favor?"

"I thought a lady didn't pry into someone else's business, angel."

"I do when I am concerned about the man doing business," she said, "and the person with whom he's doing that business."

"There's nothing to worry about. Now dance with me, Julia."

He danced divinely, moving her on the parquet

floor in a slow, sensuous rhythm. Julia barely felt the floor beneath her feet—she *forgot* there was one beneath her.

Cal had a way of moving his hands that set her skin on fire. It wasn't too scandalous—where a woman might have to resort to a slap. He didn't touch her anywhere naughty. His fingertips stroked in a sensual way, lightly on her back.

He bent to her. His lips grazed the line of her jaw, then moved lower, and on the dance floor of the Black Bottom, Cal kissed her neck.

Sensation shimmered down her spine. She felt hot all over. And that ignited panic. She wanted him to kiss her. She wanted him to keep kissing her until she couldn't think and that would be her ruin. She pushed away from him. "Don't."

She turned, desperately looking for Diana. Yanking her hand free of Cal's grip, she rushed through the dancers, darted around a young waiter who carried a tray of elegant cocktails.

She ran right into her friend who was hurrying from the opposite direction. "Let's go," Diana hissed. "His wretched wife is here."

"Diana, his wife isn't wretched. *He* is."

"He's trapped, Julia. He's trapped in a duty marriage."

"Diana, you must understand he's bad for you."

"But I love him! I love him desperately. I should go to his wife right now and tell her that he—"

"No!" She grasped Diana's arm. Rather harder than she intended. "He won't leave his wife."

"I don't believe that," Diana protested.

But she saw the fear in Diana's blue eyes. "Diana, he should never have put you in this position."

"Then what am I going to do, Julia? What can I possibly do?"

The music pounded and couples danced wildly on the floor. Julia moved close to Diana. She had to speak loudly over the racing jazz beat. "Switzerland." Then she moved Diana to the side of the room, where it was quieter.

Diana desperately shook her head. "No! This is about love. I don't just want to be hidden away on the Continent, Julia. This is the modern world and I want it all. I want my child, I want love, and I'm willing to go through a little scandal to get it."

"It's not the scandal, Diana—"

"You said you didn't care about scandal when it came to helping your widows. You should know how I feel."

She did. That was the problem—part of her was applauding Diana for wanting more than a lady-like life and a marriage without love. But she knew that Society would judge Diana ruthlessly. "I do. But men do not leave their wives."

"I can't go away anyway. I have no money and Cal won't give me any."

"Perhaps I can—"

"No! Don't tell him. He wants to hurt us all. What do you think he would do to me?"

In truth, Julia didn't know. She had seen him be so good, but he was also filled with anger. Anger that sizzled in him tonight. She felt someone watching her. She turned, expecting it to be Cal.

It was his American companion. Staring at her, and giving her a slow grin. A smile that made her shiver. It wasn't leering, but it looked . . . mean. She wanted to keep a large distance between her and that man. "We should go, Diana." She hastened Diana to the table, told her she was tired and hurried her to pick up her wrap.

Julia was exhausted, but she could barely sleep. For some reason, that man's smirking smile haunted her all night. So did Cal's kiss.

She lay in bed wondering what it would be like to fall into her bed with Cal. Have him on top of her, kissing her, caressing her, and then—

Oh! What was she doing to herself? Cal wouldn't offer her anything more than Diana's selfish lover had offered her.

Even if she were careful to avoid a disastrous pregnancy, would just sex be enough? Without love? Without a future?

No—because if she went to bed with Cal, it would be because she was in love with him, and was willing to accept that she was, and had stopped trying to fight it.

Right now, she was still fighting it.

But could she really spend the rest of her life as a virgin?

Julia awoke when the sun was streaming around her curtains. She hadn't slept in so late for years. Groggy, she sat up as Sims came in. "There is a telephone call for you, my lady. Lady Diana Carstairs. She insisted you must be woken and brought to the telephone."

Worry gripped Julia's heart.

"I warned it will take quite a while to dress you—"

Of course she had to be dressed as she did not have a telephone extension in her bedroom. "No. It won't." She wore a brassiere and pulled on a blouse and skirt. Sims fussed over her, especially her hair, but the truth was, with modern, simple clothes and bobbed hair, she could dress herself. Then she hurried downstairs and picked up the extension in the hallway. "Hel—"

"Oh, Julia, I can't stand it anymore. Cal knows my secret. I don't know *what* he will do when I return to Worthington Park. I fear he'll throw me out. He hates us, and ruining me would be just sport for him, and—"

"Diana, please calm down." Julia broke in on Diana's desperate, frightened, shrill words. "Let us face this calmly. I don't understand how he could know. I didn't speak a word of it to him. Not to anyone, I promise."

"He insisted you didn't say anything. He just—he just knew! I was having a drink when he returned from the Black Bottom. He came up to me, took the drink out of my hand. Then he asked me if I am expecting a child. He said he'd just . . . guessed. How could he do that? I was so shocked I almost passed out. I couldn't say a word, my throat was so tight. But I know—I know he would love to see me ruined. He would love it if I were starving on the street."

"He won't do that." But would he?

In that moment, Julia knew she had learned much about Cal, but she didn't really know him. She couldn't guess what he would do. Could he be kind to Ben and the Toft children, and then hurt Diana and her unborn child?

But Diana was a member of the aristocracy and of the family who had hurt him.

She must protect Diana. How could Cal have guessed? Then she remembered how he'd said his mother would deliver babies. Perhaps he knew the signs of pregnancy and had seen them in Diana. He must be incredibly perceptive—

He was an artist. And he had seen things inside her that she believed she kept completely hidden from the world. He saw things in her that no one else had.

"Julia, I must see *him* again. This will change everything. Now that Cal knows, *he* will know he must look after me. To protect me, he will do something. He wants to be with me. I know it."

Diana's voice rose in desperation.

It was confusing, but Julia knew which man Diana meant by "he" and "him."

"Diana, you must see it won't help to pursue this man—"

"No! He won't leave me at Cal's mercy."

But the man was married. How could he do the right thing? Was a divorce the right thing? It would give Diana marriage—it would save her reputation. But it would hurt another woman.

"I will talk to Cal. I'm sure I can appeal to his better nature."

"You can't."

"Diana, I have seen him be kind. Especially to children—"

"You can't because Cal left this morning. He bought a new motorcar in London and he drove back to Worthington. The butler said he was angry. Very angry. He oozed rage. And I don't know why—but I fear that anger will make him hurt me."

"Diana, no, don't do anything foolish—"

But the line went dead. Oh heavens, this was a disaster. What would Diana do?

"My lady? Is something wrong?"

She was standing, the receiver clutched in her hand. Their London butler wore a look of concern. "Everything is fine," she lied, adopting a bright smile.

"A Dr. Campbell has arrived for you. He is carrying flowers. He is waiting for you in the drawing room."

Dougal—here? And carrying flowers? It would make sense if Dougal had come to discuss Brideswell Hospital, but that didn't explain flowers.

He jumped to his feet as she walked into the south drawing room.

She had never seen Dougal look like this. He wore a simple but attractive suit. His hair was slicked neatly back with pomade. Before she'd managed to say "good morning" in its entirety, he thrust out the bouquet. Pale pink roses.

But she also saw his eyes were red rimmed and somewhat bleary. "Dougal, you look exhausted." She took the bouquet, and took his hand, led him to the brocade settee, then rang for tea.

"Sorry," he said gruffly. "I was up all night in surgery. A man struck by a motorcar."

"Is he all right?"

Dougal's mouth turned grim. "I lost him, Julia."

"I'm so sorry."

He lifted his hand as if to rake it through his hair, then stopped himself. His other hand rested against the sofa arm as if holding up his exhausted-to-the-bone body. "I fought for him. Fought for hours and I thought I was going to win. But in the end—I'm not God apparently. When I begin to think I can outdo our Lord with miracles, then I am brought down and humbled, but at the cost of a man's life."

Tea came, halting their conversation. Efficiently, she poured for him and herself. Dougal's leg was tapping, apparently with pent-up frustration, but it stopped as she handed him the cup.

"You remember exactly how I have it?"

"Of course I do."

"Julia, I have no right to be here when I'm dead tired. No right to be here at all. But I realized, when I lost that patient, that the person I needed to speak to was you. You were the one person I knew I could talk to."

"But your fiancée—"

"I care about Margaret a great deal, but she doesn't have your strength. It made me realize how much I loved being at the Brideswell Hospital."

That surprised her. "I thought you were happier here?"

"The truth is that here I have to answer to a board of governors. There are treatments I want to try but I've been refused. Too expensive. Too controversial. At Brideswell, when I went to the duke—your brother—I found him to be one of the most open-minded gentlemen I have met. He allowed me to do remarkable things. After his marriage, he was an extremely generous patron. He bought much-needed new equipment—gave me free rein in my purchasing and treatment plans—" He broke off, raking his hand through his auburn hair, but he stopped when he realized it was too pomaded to move. She smiled at the sweet gesture, but her heart seemed to have stopped beating.

"I know the duchess offered the job to McLeod, but he would be willing to take my place at the London Hospital, if you would consider allowing me to come back to Brideswell."

"But—but what about your fiancée?"

"I have to establish myself as a doctor before we can marry. I believe I could do that more quickly at Brideswell. Then I can have a house there and make her my wife. If you and the duchess—and the duke, of course—would consider giving me the chance."

Such fervent passion underlay his words.

She thought of the time she'd spent with him. Quiet walks across the village green. Dougal had discussed his cases with her. She'd loved listening to him. She would make suggestions, but he was always lost deep in thought, his brain considering the symptoms, the possible diagnosis, until he came to the right answer. He talked to her like an equal, not like a woman who should be protected from rational thought.

He would come back, but they could not do that anymore.

"Do you believe your family would consider it?"

He would be the perfect doctor for Brideswell. She could live with a little pain—the pain of seeing him, of being so close to him, but so distant.

He was waiting for her answer, hope in his eyes.

Two days after the dance with Julia that Cal couldn't forget, he stepped out of the small police station of Brideswell's village. He'd gone into the village to the local pub to get some information and that had led him to the police station, manned by a sergeant and two young police constables.

He walked out into a downpour. Sheets of gray rain swept in waves through the narrow streets. Cal lifted his collar. It was June, but bone-chilling today in the rain.

Ahead of him, a woman struggled with her black umbrella. She gasped as the wind caught it, turning it inside out and pulling her into the street, just as an automobile roared around the corner, headed toward her.

He ran out, gripped the woman around the waist and pulled her out of the path of the car.

"Goodness!" she gasped.

"Julia." He hadn't seen her since the Black Bottom Club. He hadn't seen her, but he'd thought about her every damn minute. And now he heard his breath hitch as he realized his hand was cupped around her small waist. He moved his hand.

"Thank you." She looked at him awkwardly. He felt damned awkward with her. What would

Julia think if she knew the things O'Brien had reminded him about that night in London? He'd heard she had gone to see the doctor she had been engaged to once. Maybe they'd rekindled their romance. Julia deserved a good man and he had to admire her for falling for a doctor, for being willing to marry a man who didn't have a title.

He took the umbrella and held it for her. As they walked together, they struggled to make conversation. She asked, "The gentleman you were speaking with at the Black Bottom, was he a friend from America?"

"Someone I knew in the States. Not a friend." He didn't want to talk about Kerry O'Brien of the Five Points Gang with Julia. He didn't want her to know anything about his past. Or what O'Brien had threatened him with.

"Julia, I have to talk to you," he said.

"I have to talk to you. About Diana."

"We can't talk out here in the rain," he said. "I have my car here. Where can I take you?"

"I'm finished in the village. You could take me home."

He stayed quiet until he got Julia into his automobile, out of the rain. It poured off her hat, dripped off his coat, as he went around to the driver's side, chucked in the umbrella and climbed in. Rain drummed against the windshield, and he couldn't see out.

"Diana hopes the man responsible for her condition will get a divorce from his wife and marry her. She tried to see him again the day after the Black Bottom, but he wouldn't respond. He didn't pick up the telephone, answer her notes. She even went to his house, only to find he and his wife had gone to the Continent. She was devastated. She—"

He heard her take a shuddering breath.

God, she was pale. She hadn't put on any makeup. She was lovely this way, but far too pale. "What did she do?" he asked slowly.

"She broke down into tears in her bedchamber and hammered her fists on her belly. She was trying to make herself miscarry. I stopped her, brought her back here, and promised to talk to you. To plead with you if necessary. She is so afraid, Cal. She fears you will throw her out."

"I wouldn't hurt her. Not when she's expecting a baby."

"What about afterward? If you throw her out because she is ruined, you would be condemning the child to poverty—"

"You mean how could I do that, when I lived through it? You're right. I couldn't. I'd look after Diana. Make sure she always has a roof over her head and enough to eat. I'd make sure the child stayed healthy, grew up happy, went to school. I vow I'd do that. Maybe the hypocrisy galls me. The old earl and countess condemned my mother while their daughter had an affair with a married man and their son—" He stopped. "But I wouldn't make the baby suffer. I'm a better man than that."

"I believed you were," she said softly.

The look on her face—

It made him feel ten feet tall. It made him feel like crap. He started the automobile.

"Cal, there is something you have to know. Women of our sort who get into trouble do not keep their babies. It ends any chance of marriage. Certainly a respectable one. Girls are taken away. They disappear on an extended holiday, where they discreetly have the baby. The child is given up for adoption. The girl comes back and she goes on with her life."

"That's the way it's done." He looked over his shoulder, through the rain, then pulled away from the curb. "Do you agree with it?"

"I don't know. If I had a child, I think it would break my heart to give up the baby. But maybe I would be so terrified, I would agree. Terrified because I would know I'd lost any hope of a future. That, as a ruined woman, I couldn't give my child a life anyway. But I admire the courage of women who keep their children, who struggle to raise them. I don't know if I would be so strong."

He was quiet, driving through the narrow High Street. He accelerated around a plodding horse-drawn cart. "What does Diana want?" he asked finally. "To keep the child? Or move on with her life so she can marry some gentleman and get a fancy title?"

At his side, Julia winced. "She has not thought that far ahead. She still believes she can have the child's father. She loves him. And she hasn't accepted yet that he doesn't love her in return."

"She's not gonna listen to me about that," he said gruffly.

"I know. I simply have to keep trying to make her understand that. At least I can now tell her she will be safe."

"Why you? Why do you have to take care of things?"

"I am her friend."

"And you always take care of everyone."

"You sound as if you don't approve. As if it is wrong for me to do so."

Doubt hit him. Could Julia, who worried about anything, really not have had suspicions about Anthony Carstairs? "There's something I have to know, Julia. Three young women went missing around 1916. Sarah Brand, a woman named Eileen Kilkenny, sister of the local blacksmith, and a maid, Gladys Burrows, who worked for the squire in the next village."

"Three women? All around the same time?" she whispered. "I—I don't understand. We searched for Sarah. We completely scoured the estate in case Sarah had met with an accident. We searched the woods for days. When no trace of her was

242

found, it was assumed she had run away. Then stories came out that she was seen riding with a man in a motorcar. Girls did run off to London. It was thought she might have had a secret love who was going to war and she ran off to London for a hasty marriage."

His hands tightened on the wheel. "I talked to the sergeant at the police station in the village. He confirmed that all three women were seen driving with a man in a flashy red car. They couldn't describe the man—he wore a hat pulled low and a scarf around his face. But I just found out the make of the car. It was a 1914 Rolls-Royce Silver Ghost, painted red. And I saw one this morning in the Worthington garage."

Julia gasped. "What are you saying? You think it was Anthony, don't you? Sarah may have vanished before Anthony went away, but he helped in the search, just before he left because he had enlisted."

"I don't know. All I'm saying is that a bright red Rolls touring car is in the Worthington garage. I'm going to take a better look at it."

"Could I—could I accompany you? I don't want to go to Brideswell now. I want—I want to see."

Her request startled him. Cal didn't want her to see. But he knew she would be able to face anything. She was so strong.

Julia felt sick with fear as Cal drove her to Worthington. It drove all thoughts of Dougal's return to Brideswell from her mind—she had spoken to Nigel and Zoe and they had all agreed to welcome Dougal back. She still did not believe Anthony could have done something to Sarah Brand and two other young women. She simply couldn't.

But as Cal's car turned in at Worthington Park's gates, a small figure rushed out from behind a thick lilac.

"Jesus Christ." Cal slammed on the brakes but the car skidded on the gravel. Right toward Ben Lambert. Julia reached her hand out toward the low windscreen as if she could push the boy out of the way. She shouted, "Run out of the way, Ben."

But the boy was paralyzed, frozen in place, afraid to move.

Cal jerked the wheel hard, cursing with words Julia had never heard before.

The car swerved so abruptly, it lifted onto two wheels and Julia's heart lodged in her throat. She couldn't scream.

As long as Ben wasn't hit, she didn't care what happened to her.

But she didn't want Cal to be killed, either.

The car fell back on all four wheels and skidded onto the lawn. Suddenly it came to a lurching stop and Cal's hand grabbed her shoulder and held her back. He had one hand on the steering wheel and his chest hit hard against it. But with his other hand securing her, she only fell forward a bit.

"Are you okay?" Cal's voice came tightly, and he was short of breath. He must have had all the wind knocked out of him.

"Yes. But what about—"

Cal got out of the car. She followed but he'd sprinted so fast he'd already reached Ben. Cal dropped to one knee in front of him and held Ben's slim shoulders. The boy shook his head then Cal pulled the child into a tight embrace.

Ben must have been telling him he wasn't hurt.

Julia reached them then. "Ben, you aren't hurt? Are you certain?"

"I'm not. But me mum is," the boy sobbed. "She's got hurt bad. I don't know what to do."

"Where is she?"

"At our cottage."

"How bad is she, Ben?" Cal asked, his voice cool and collected. Julia could barely think for the racing of her heart. They needed a doctor. And Dougal had just arrived today—that was why she'd gone into the village. To see him—

"She got knocked out," Ben said. "He hit her so hard she fell down. She won't wake up and she's bleeding. There's all this blood and I don't know what to do."

"Who hit her?" Julia demanded, shocked.

But Ben just mutely shook his head. He was too afraid.

Cal glanced back at the car. Then at the house. "Damn, I need to push the car out. Get behind the wheel, Julia. Put the boy in the car."

With Cal's direction, Julia put the car in gear and pressed gently on the gas while Cal pushed from behind. She turned, watching him. His face grimaced, his arms strained, but he made the car rock. She would let off on the gas and give it more, matching the rhythm he was creating.

Then Cal let out a roar and pushed hard. The car shot ahead and two of the wheels got traction on the drive. "Keep going!" he shouted.

She did. Mud sprayed out from behind her. But she kept going until the car was all the way out of the grass. Cal ran to the passenger side and he vaulted in, beside Ben.

"Drive as fast as you can, doll," he said.

Mud covered his jacket, trousers, shirt. Clumps of it clung to his face. But he obviously didn't care. And she drove as fast as she dared, her heart in her throat. It was only when they reached Ben's cottage that she realized they should have gotten the doctor first.

Cal was out of the car before she'd shut off the engine, running for the front door of the cottage. "Stay there," he shouted at her.

But she didn't. She reached the front door when she heard him curse again. "Ah hell," he muttered. "Who in hell could have done this?"

11

Suspicion

Through the haze of shock and fear, Julia watched Cal crouch beside Ellen and press his fingers to her throat. He bent so his cheek was close to her mouth. Julia knew he was listening for breath.

"Is she breathing?" This was her fault—she had pushed Ellen to stop letting that man hurt her and use her and pimp her, and he had no doubt reacted in pure rage.

Cal looked up. She'd never seen a man look so anguished—except Nigel, when Zoe lost her babies. "Julia, I told you to stay outside."

"What use would I be out there?" But she wanted to be sick and she was fighting to stay on her feet.

"You shouldn't see this. She's been beaten to a pulp." He surged to his feet. "She's breathing but unconscious. I need to stop the blood flow on the wound on her arm. What she needs is to get to a hospital where she can be stitched up properly. Her leg and arm are broken."

Now, without Cal's body blocking her view, she could fully see Ellen. At least, she thought it must be Ellen. Bruises had turned the woman's face into masses of black and blue. The nose—

heavens, it was a mess, and there was blood all over her face. There was blood on the floor and on the side of the stove.

Her knees wobbled. *Don't faint and be useless.* Isobel could look at medical illustrations while eating biscuits. She could cope with this. But Julia felt as if her head was full of nothing but air. Spots danced. She feared she would slither to the floor.

But then rage flooded her. Right now was the time to prove she was modern. And strong. She straightened her back; she regained control as Cal asked, "Can we get an ambulance of some kind?"

"There's the local doctor. I can get him and we can get a car from the hospital, Cal."

He looked up at her. His face softened. "Julia." Next thing she knew, he'd led her away, toward the door.

"No," she protested. "If you can face this with strength, I can. I'll fetch Dougal. He's come back to Brideswell and I know he can help her."

"I don't think you're fit to drive—"

"I am!" she cried. "I can do this."

She saw the doubt in his eyes and she wanted to scream. It was because she was a woman. Everyone thought she was so weak—

"Okay. Take the child with you," Cal said, surprising her by showing he believed her capable. "If I could get my hands on who did this, I'd tear him apart."

She nodded numbly, then stumbled to the door.

She believed she knew who had done this. But she didn't have his name. The man was a monster, but Cal couldn't tear him apart. The law would make this man pay. She grasped Ben's hand—he was in the hallway, white as a sheet. "Come and help me get the doctor, Ben—"

"I'm not leaving her!" Ben was going to pull away from her hand, but Cal was there, suddenly, at Ben's side.

"We'll get her to the hospital and the doctor will take care of her, Ben. Go with Lady Julia. She needs a strong man at her side."

She was going to protest—then saw, by the way Ben straightened and held her hand firmly, that Cal's words were to help the boy. He had known just the thing to say.

But as Cal turned to go back to Ellen, she heard him mutter, "God, don't let her die. Not like Mam." He stalked to the kitchen.

His mother had died . . . like this? Julia felt Ben's hand squeeze hers. They had to go. She hurried him outside, helped him into the car, putting him in the front seat next to her.

Having Ben beside her in the car made her aware she must hold herself together. Tears welled, blurring her vision, and she wiped the tears away viciously with her leather-clad hand, then drew her goggles down over her eyes. Ben said not a word.

She feared for Ellen Lambert, and young Ben,

and she feared she'd learned an awful truth about Cal's past. She pushed down the accelerator, hurrying to the hospital to fetch Dougal.

Once Julia had driven away—and he'd watched to ensure she wasn't weaving the car because she was about to faint—Cal went back in, ripped up some sheets and made the best tourniquets he could. Mam used to pray. He never did, but he was doing it now. Silently praying for Ellen.

Then Julia's voice called, "Cal, I'm back and I've brought Dougal—Dr. Campbell."

The sound of her voice . . . it did something to him. It went right to his soul. He couldn't even explain how he reacted. He'd been with a lot of women, but he'd never been through as much as he had with Julia, and he felt so close to her.

A tall, handsome man with auburn hair strode in, with Julia behind him.

Cal realized it was Campbell, the man Julia had intended to marry.

The doctor got on his knees beside Ellen's prostrate body. Nodded approval at the tourniquets Cal had made. Cal got to his feet and got out of the way so the doctor could work.

Dr. Campbell tended to Ellen with Julia at his side. And Cal saw the way Julia looked at the doctor. That look hit Cal right in the gut.

Campbell was a different kind of man to Hamilton. No snobbery, no drunkenness. Campbell got to business and concern for Ellen was obvious on his face. Campbell was different from him, too, Cal realized. The doctor's past included medical school, hard work and saving lives. Not like Cal's past of crimes and violence.

Campbell examined Ellen quickly, checking her heartbeat and for broken bones. He opened his Gladstone bag and gave Ellen an injection. "For the pain," he said in a Scottish burr. "The tourniquets are doing the trick for now. This lass needs to get to the hospital." He frowned. "Assaulted in her own cottage in front of her wee child. What ruffian carried out this misdeed?"

"I don't know," Julia said.

"Shouldn't the police be called in?" Campbell asked.

"I'll do that," Cal said. "But I doubt Ellen will be helpful."

"Surely she will now," Julia cried.

Cal shook his head. "She'll be more afraid. And afraid for Ben." Tires crunched then, and doors slammed.

"That's the car from the hospital," Julia said. "We left Ben there, under the care of nurses. He wanted to come back, but I told him to wait there, to be ready when his mother came."

Cal nodded, seeing how well she handled herself in a crisis. She was perfectly matched to the honorable Dr. Campbell.

The ambulance drove off with the doctor in the

back. Julia touched his arm. "I should go to the hospital to watch Ben," she said. "He'll need a familiar face."

"After, he can come and stay with me at Worthington."

She looked startled. "It would be better for him to come with me to Brideswell. The countess may not be welcoming. And Ben knows me."

"They're on my estate. They're my responsibility. That's what you wanted me to learn, wasn't it? I'm taking him to Worthington and the countess can keep her mouth shut."

Julia's eyes widened in surprise. "I will gather some of Ben's things."

She hurried away from him so fast, Cal knew something was wrong. He followed her. She stood in a tiny room by a small cot. She put her hands to her face.

She was crying. And she hadn't wanted him to see.

But he had comforted her after Mrs. Toft died . . .

Yeah, and he'd kissed her.

"Are you okay?" he asked. Of course she wasn't, but he didn't know what to say.

With her back to him, she wiped her eyes. She faced him looking collected, except for red rims to her eyelids. "I am fine."

She wasn't, but he guessed she didn't need him. He wanted to touch her, put his arm around her to take her to the car, but he didn't. He drove her to the hospital. Along the way, he stayed quiet. His gut was churning. Maybe his actions toward Ben made Julia believe he'd accepted his place as earl.

But he hadn't. He was angry about Ellen, but that had nothing to do with being an earl. He didn't need the title, the money, the estate. David, his brother, didn't need it, either. He'd sent a telegram, telling David he was now the earl. Temporarily. Because he had made a vow when Mam died. Julia didn't know that, but he'd made a promise, and he was going to carry it out—

"You look so angry," Julia said, breaking the silence as he drove on the rough road.

He could have told her exactly what was on his mind. But he just told her part of it. "I am. I guess you did a good job, Julia. You made me care about these people. I'm going to find that thug and make him pay. I'm going to make him suffer."

"What? You cannot. He must be arrested."

"Where I come from, he'd be found dead."

He heard her sharp, shocked gasp. "That is what they do in New York? I thought those stories of gangs and wars were all exaggerated."

"They're not. That's what the poorest neighborhoods are like. A constant war," he said bitterly. "That's the world that the Carstairs family condemned us to."

"Cal—"

"That's why I'm vengeful, Julia. Vengeance made the world go round where I grew up."

He shouldn't be doing this, shocking her when she was hurt. But the old anger was coiling in him. Then the look of horror on her face cut right down to his soul. She wanted to think he could be gentlemanly. But he never could. He'd never be the kind of man who came from her world.

He damn well didn't want to be. At that moment, he actually felt proud of his past. Proud of having survived poverty and fought his way out of the New York slums.

Then he remembered what he'd done to get out and that feeling of pride was replaced with cold, hard anger.

Meeting Kerry O'Brien in London had reminded him that he'd walked away from his past but hadn't escaped it. Most of New York had read about him in the newspapers. The headlines had screamed things like "American Artist Surprise Heir. The Earl of New York—found penniless in Paris." That was how O'Brien had tracked him down. He'd arranged to meet Kerry O'Brien in London to keep him away from Worthington Park. O'Brien wanted money—

"Cal, was your mother attacked like this?"

He hit a hole in the road because her question had stunned him. How had she known?

"I overheard what you said as I was leaving to fetch Dr. Campbell," she said softly.

He was going to say something hard and curt, something to end the conversation, but he opened his mouth and all that came out was a painful sound, like an abbreviated sob of grief.

All he could think of was the last night of his mam's life. How he had found her. The last words she'd said. After, he'd almost killed himself, he'd been so full of drunken rage and guilt. Painting had saved him. Painting and his responsibility to his brother.

He wasn't going to break down in front of Julia.

"Cal, I am so sorry. If that is what your life was like when you were young, I would like to summon the old earl's ghost and give it a damn good slap."

He'd never heard her swear. It made a laugh come up from deep in his chest. And he knew what he was going to do. Tell Julia Hazelton something that no one else knew. David didn't even know what had really happened to their mam. He'd kept the truth from his brother.

"I was fourteen," he said, a blunt beginning.

He'd had money then—nothing like he had now, but something. He'd earned it with the Five Points Juniors Gang. He'd been acting as lookout. Big for his age, he was being recruited to do more. Muscle was needed to threaten people who owed money, to act as protection. His money was supposed to rescue his mother—get her away from what she'd done when she was really desperate for money.

"Mam worked in a factory at a sewing machine in the day, washed dishes in a bar at night. She helped women deliver babies as well, helping those in our neighborhood. She didn't do that for money, but the families would give us food." He took a breath. "I was wild—angry. My father was dead and Mam had written to the Worthingtons, desperate for their help. They wrote a letter back that told her she wasn't good enough to lick their boots. I was so full of fury . . . I would come home drunk. I'd get into fights—I'd swing my fists at anyone, and half the time I got beaten senseless."

"Oh, Cal." Her voice was a soft, beautiful murmur beside him.

"That helped me learn how to survive the War, at least. But the night Mam died . . ."

He couldn't bring himself to tell her what else Mam had been forced to do. "I guess a ma broke into our room. He must have known Mam kept the money she had wrapped up in her underclothing drawer—" A lie. Mam had let the man into their tenement.

"She had sent David over to a neighbor's house for the night," he went on, "because she . . . worked so late at the bar. She was so tired, so thin, so worn to the bone, but Mam was still beautiful. Her eyes were pale blue, ice blue, and they looked like they could only have been made by magic."

Julia's fingers rested gently on his forearm as he drove. He knew it was pity for the damn wretch he'd been. He liked himself better as the angry man who'd arrived here determined to get revenge.

"I found her on the floor," he went on. "She was as badly beaten as Ellen. I thought she was dead. I threw up, standing in the doorway." He'd been scared and weak. "I knelt beside her, and she opened her eyes. Then her head rolled to the side and she coughed up blood. I ran for the doctor, clutching a fistful of money so the doc would know I could pay. But after I gave him money and he looked at her, he said nothing could be done. She was too weak to survive. The doctor left—probably to get a drink—and I stayed with her until she died."

Mam had wanted him to be decent and honorable and gentlemanly like his father. He'd sacrificed all of her dreams when he joined the gang. He'd done it for her, and then he'd been too late to save her.

Julia's hand was squeezing his. "I found the man who hurt her," he said coolly.

"What—what did you do?"

"I tried to beat him just as bad but I failed. I was big, but basically still just a fourteen-year-old kid."

"Dear heaven, that's terrible."

Her touch was gone. Startled, Cal looked down and realized she'd released his hand.

Yeah, he wasn't surprised she didn't want to touch him. He looked at her, saw the shock and horror on her face, and the same cold, hard anger that had lived inside him since he was a boy surged up.

"I've done bad things. I know you want to believe I'm a worthy noble descendent of the earl, but I keep telling you I'm not."

"That was not bad. It was misguided. But understandable."

She had no idea. But the hell of it was, even as he pushed her away, he wanted her. He itched to paint her. Ached to make love to her. He'd planned to seduce her, but now he knew the truth—he could never have Julia.

At the hospital, poor Ben was terrified, but Julia's heart wobbled as Cal lifted the boy into his arms so Ben could see his mother. Ben fought to look stoic and strong. "I'll look after you, Mum. I'm the man of the family."

"You'll need help with that," Cal said. "I'll help you both."

Julia's heart soared as he said that.

The local police constable arrived, a broad, burly man. He asked questions, but it became quickly apparent that the constable knew who Ellen was and what she did to earn money. His attitude was thoroughly unhelpful, until Cal loomed over him. "You will give this case all due attention," Cal growled. "You will find the man who did this. You will arrest him. I don't give a damn what this woman was forced to do to feed herself and her child. I'm the Earl of Worthington and the police had better give

258

Ellen Lambert's attack the attention it deserves."

"The constabulary will give this its due diligence," the policeman promised, chastised.

"See that is does," Cal said.

Julia could have applauded him. Cal truly did care—which meant she had done what she needed to. She had to wipe a tear that tracked down her cheek. A tear of hope.

Cal came to her. "I'm going to take Ben to Worthington. I'll have a warm bath drawn for him and a bedroom made up."

"In the nursery—"

"The hell with the nursery," he growled. "There's a room beside mine."

"Cal, children always sleep—"

"Ben is going to sleep where I say."

"I won't argue," she said softly. "I agree with you." She wanted to embrace him, but of course, she couldn't. She had to restrain her relief over his caring, responsible behavior.

Cal walked her outside. It was almost evening. "I'll take you home to Brideswell, if you like, Julia."

"I think I'll stay longer. With Ellen. I can have a car sent from Brideswell."

But later, when she left, Julia decided to go to Worthington Park to ensure Ben was settling in all right. As the Daimler pulled in front of the house, Julia saw Cal standing outside, drawing on a cigarette.

She got out, told him why she'd come.

He tossed the cigarette away. "Ben's already gone to sleep, Julia. I had to carry him up to bed. I figure he'll be out for a while, so I'm going to look at the car in the Worthington garage."

He hadn't gone yet. She felt exhausted, but she wanted to see it, too. She had to face the truth—whatever it was. "Let me come with you. And don't argue."

Cal shrugged. "Okay."

They reached the garage in silence. At Cal's side, Julia walked in through one of the open double doors. She smelled grease and oil, following him to the very back of the building. A cloth was draped over a car and was gray with dust, except where the corner had been pulled back, exposing the headlight and the red painted fender.

Cal pulled the dustcover completely away.

"This was Anthony's car," she said softly. "He adored it. The only other person who drove it was the earl."

"How old was the earl in 1916?" Cal asked.

Could it really have been Anthony's father who took young women for drives? "He was about forty-two."

"Good-looking? Could he have looked like a younger man?"

"I suppose. He rode religiously and kept himself trim. He was quite a handsome man." She stared at Cal. "Do you really believe he is the one who would meet Sarah and take her driving? And the other girls?"

Cal opened the door and climbed in. "Those girls would be flattered, wouldn't they, by the attentions of a lofty earl?"

Sarcasm made his voice hard. She watched him sit, holding the steering wheel for a moment. Then he bent to the passenger seat and the floor.

"What are you doing?"

"Checking," he said. She had no idea what he meant until he straightened, holding a ball of emerald green cloth. "It's a scarf," he said, and he straightened it out. It was wrinkled and a bit dirty. He looked closely at it. Then showed it to her. "See the dark hairs on it?"

Julia lifted the green silk. She coughed at the musty smell. By the light of the electric bulb, she could see a few long black hairs tangled in the fringe.

"Is it yours?" he asked. "Did you forget it in the car years ago?"

"It's not mine. It's a striking color, but it's a cheaply produced silk. Not the best quality." She frowned. "I doubt Sarah would have had a scarf like this, even so. It would be out of her means."

"But maybe it was a gift. To lower her defenses," he said.

"I don't think—"

"I do. Don't men like that think they can do anything they like to lower-class girls?"

261

"Not all of them," she said.

"It looks like it was my cousin Anthony or the old earl who picked up the girls in this fancy automobile."

She jerked her head up. "You have no real evidence to say such a thing."

"You just can't believe a gentleman you had dinner with could be a scoundrel."

"No," she said sharply. "I'm very aware of what men do. But I knew both men well. I was in love with Anthony and I was going to marry him. I know what kind of man he was. The earl was very much in love with his wife. She was so much softer and kinder then, before the tragedies happened."

"She wasn't kind to my family."

"I think you just desperately want the earl to have done something scandalous. But we have to know it's true. We need proof."

"That's what I want." Meeting her eyes with a grim gaze, he got out and went to the back of the car.

There was still no explanation for what had happened to the girls. Even if Anthony had flirted with them, where had they gone?

She walked to the boot just as Cal opened it, raising the lid. A spade sat in there, crusted with dried mud, and the floor of the boot was covered in dirt.

A spade? The electric light glittered on something

in the corner. Cal lifted up a tiepin, decorated with a sapphire.

"That belonged to Anthony," she whispered.

After Julia left to go home to Brideswell, Cal returned to the house to find Kerry O'Brien waiting for him in his study. Wiggins told him the American *gentleman* had pushed his way in, and had not given his name—had only said to tell Cal that a friend from the Five Points Gang wanted to see him.

Damn O'Brien. "Where are the countess and my cousins?" Cal asked.

"They have retired for the night."

The countess was avoiding him and eighty rooms made that easy to do. She hadn't even come down for dinner in the big dining room for the past few nights. She ate in her room, claiming she had headaches. His cousins ate with him, but they also stayed away from him as much as possible. He'd tried to apologize to Thalia for his outburst over the painting, but she had blinked at him like a baby owl, then scurried away. As if she was afraid that just speaking to him would unleash his rage. He found he felt like an idiot for making a young girl afraid of him.

But tonight, he was glad they weren't here to see O'Brien.

Wiggins cleared his throat. "My lord, if I may be so bold as to make the suggestion . . . I could return with a strong footman and propel this gentleman out of the house."

Cal tried to imagine the ancient butler trying to get rid of O'Brien, who carried both a gun and a blade. For once he felt a kinship with frosty Wiggins. And grinned. "Not necessary, but I appreciate the thought, Wiggins."

"Very good." The butler withdrew.

He stalked to his study. O'Brien was in his chair, his feet up on the desk. "You really are a goddamned earl," O'Brien said as Cal walked in and shut the door. Kerry waved his hand around at the books, paintings, furnishings. "You could fence this for a fortune."

"Why in hell are you here, O'Brien? We were supposed to meet again in London."

"I figured you might double-cross me." O'Brien took out a cigarette from a gold case. As he did, he let Cal see the butt grip of his pistol stuck in the waistband of his suit trousers. "That old stick-up-the-ass butler looked surprised when I mentioned the Five Points Gang. Just like I figured—your snooty family doesn't know about your past. They don't know what you did. I gave you my price for being quiet. I want to be paid. Now. If you don't got cash, I'll take some of your fancy goods."

"Maybe I don't give a damn if the family does find out."

Obviously that was something O'Brien had never

figured. "What in hell do you mean?"

In one fluid motion, Cal ground out his cigarette on the heel of his hand and grabbed O'Brien by the lapels of his shiny pale pink suit jacket. He lifted his former associate off the leather seat. "You can do whatever the hell you want with your story. I'm going to sell this place and take off. And I don't give a flying fuck," he said coarsely, "what Lady Worthington or this family thinks about me."

The truth was he didn't want them to know. He definitely didn't want Julia to know.

"You're bluffing."

"Try me."

O'Brien's face went red—his nose was always red, from a lifetime of hitting the Irish bars. "You owe me, Cal. I saved your life. You remember."

"You did. I've repaid that debt six times already. This time will make seven."

"What do ye mean 'this time'?"

Cal went to the desk drawers, pulled out a key and opened the top one. He pulled out all the ready cash he'd locked up in there—two thousand dollars in American bills. Tossed it on the desk blotter in front of Kerry. "That's all you're gonna get. Two grand."

O'Brien smirked at him, but his blue eyes were still wary. Watching. Ready to shoot to save his own life. O'Brien stuffed the money in the pocket of his pink jacket. "I need more."

"It's not worth it to me to pay you to keep your

mouth shut. That's because I had a debt to you. Now get the hell out."

O'Brien's hand moved toward the gun.

One quick breath later, Cal had O'Brien's arm pinned behind his back and his face shoved hard against the blotter. "Get out, O'Brien. I've got thirty thousand acres here. Easy enough for a body to end up in a shallow grave, never to be found."

As he spoke, he felt his gut churn. For three women, he figured that had already happened. He could be wrong, but his gut instinct told him those women were dead. He had no intention of even getting into a fist fight with O'Brien, so to make sure O'Brien believed his bluff, he leaned over the man and muttered, "I could break your damn neck before you even move. You know that, Kerry."

The War had taken all the brutal skills he'd learned growing up in the gang and perfected them. He eased off on the pressure and when Kerry didn't try to spring up and fight, Cal let go and stepped back completely.

"Let me escort you to the door," he said.

Kerry knew he was beaten, Cal figured. The gangster jerked up, straightened his suit and put his hat back on—it had fallen to the floor as Cal had shoved him down before.

He hauled O'Brien to the large double doors. Wiggins stood there, with a footman who was losing the battle to look like he was made of stone. Wiggins commanded the kid—a lad named Eustace—to open the door. Cal propelled Kerry out to the front step.

"Yeah, I'll go back to London," Kerry growled. "Right to the papers."

"I advise you to go back to the States," Cal said, low and soft. He had no idea what O'Brien was going to do, but he could smell the man's fear. His fear and his anger. Which one was going to win out? "I'm a rich man. I could offer the papers a lot more money to not print that story."

Kerry sneered, but he had a deflated look to him. "I need a drink," he muttered.

"You've got a couple grand on you. Don't spend it all at one bar," Cal said. After O'Brien left, he poured himself a drink. When he'd started painting in Paris, he'd sworn he would never do anything violent again. But to save his arse, he'd done that today.

And—damn it—he was imagining the horrified look that would have been on Julia's face if she'd witnessed it.

By the light of day the next morning, Julia still could not believe it was true. The horrible thing she'd been confronted with last night. That it might have been Anthony who had made Sarah Brand, Eileen Kilkenny and a maid disappear.

Anthony had been a good man. He'd loved Worthington Park with all his soul. If he had been warped, if he had been wrong in the head, surely she would have seen it.

Going down to breakfast was a nightmare. She could not eat. All she could manage was coffee. Black and strong.

"I've had a letter from the Earl of Summerhay," Mother announced. "He has to be in the area—he is purchasing a horse. He wondered, Nigel, if he might be able to stay. I have been corresponding quite regularly with that dear boy."

"The dear boy is almost thirty, Mother," Isobel pointed out. "And you've only been corresponding with him since Julia said she would never consider marrying the Duke of Bradstock."

Mother ignored that. "He is in need of a place to stay. He intends to stay at a public house, but I told him that is nonsense. He must stay with us. Are you in agreement, Nigel?"

"Mother, you promised not to push me to marry," Julia protested, for this was the last thing she wanted to think about.

"I would never push. But I see no reason why he cannot visit and you could not spend time with him." Mother looked happier than she had in years and Julia's heart twisted.

"Mother, I can't. Invite him if you wish, but don't try to push, or put, us together." She looked at the surprised faces—her mother's lovely pale face, Isobel's curious one, Nigel's startled one.

She couldn't tell them she feared Anthony had

committed terrible crimes. "Please. I just can't think of this right now."

"What is wrong?" Nigel asked.

"Nothing. I—I was thinking of Anthony. I'm simply not ready to think of marrying anyone."

She got up. "I must go out—I have things I must do." Julia left the room, the house. It was drizzling, so she threw on a mackintosh from a closet. She got her car and drove as fast as she could to Worthington.

There, she stopped in the drive. Her bare hands clutched the leather-wrapped steering wheel. She hadn't worn gloves. She usually did—Mother had said she could not drive if she didn't, or she would end up with a farm laborer's calluses. How unimportant such concerns were now.

The footman opened the door and Wiggins, walking past the foyer, saw her and hurried to her. "Good morning, Lady Julia."

It wasn't a good morning. It was a terrifying one. "Is the earl at home?"

"The earl has gone to Lilac Farm."

Lilac Farm. Yesterday, Cal had looked down at the shovel in the boot of the car. He had told her about a criminal case in America—a twelve-year-old schoolgirl from the State of New Jersey had been "criminally assaulted" and killed. He had stood there, the light casting the most ominous shadows under his sharp cheekbones, and told her that those three women might be dead. They might be buried somewhere. Even somewhere on the Worthington estate.

"Why has he gone to Lilac Farm?" He couldn't have gone to tell the family what he suspected, could he?

Cal hadn't voiced his thoughts but she'd seen it in the dark anger in his eyes. He thought a man from Worthington Park had done it. It could have been the old earl, or John, or even one of the men who worked on the estate—if he were bold enough to take the car. But she knew Cal was thinking it was Anthony. He'd said: *Likely a man got away with murder because of who he was.*

"My lady, I fear it is his lordship's intent to sell land to an American gentleman."

Wiggins's words broke through her thoughts. Julia felt as if the floor had suddenly tilted and she was going to slide off it. "What? What American?" The man from London, supplied her frantic mind.

"I did not eavesdrop, my lady. The gentleman bluntly asked Lord Worthington if the house was for sale. He also asked if I was for sale."

Her stomach lurched. But she hid her panic. "I am so sorry, Wiggins."

"The earl took this American with him. Should I be concerned for the future of the estate, my lady?"

Wiggins looked utterly composed, except for a twitch to his jaw, but Julia knew the poor man was terrified. Cal had been angry after they had found the shovel. He felt the Carstairs family had gotten away with murder.

She would have known, surely, if Anthony was so bad, so evil. And Cal had no proof. A shovel left in the boot of the car was not definitive evidence. Nor was the scarf.

Cal had been angry. But surely he wouldn't sell the farm away from the Brands because he was angry—without proof—at the Carstairs?

And even if—if Anthony was guilty, poor people like the Brands had suffered enough. Cal's rage must not hurt them, in any attempt to strike the Carstairs family. She had to stop Cal.

"This man was not the only American gentleman who came to the house in the past two days, my lady," Wiggins said. "Late yesterday an unsavory-looking man arrived by motorcar. He wore a suit of a pale pink, shiny material—" Wiggins sniffed "—and he had the mannerisms, accent and air of an American gangster."

That was the man in London. This then was a different man. What did that mean? "I must go. At once." Leaving Wiggins staring in astonishment, she turned from her heel and ran out of the house, as if pursued by hounds.

Was she already too late to save the Brands' farm?

12

The Arrival of Cal's Brother

Julia's shoes crunched on gravel as she rushed toward her car, her mackintosh flapping around her. She would drive like the wind to Lilac Farm—

She stopped abruptly, almost skidding on the drive. Walking away from the house toward the converted stable-garage were two men. One was Cal, wearing his rough sweater and trousers, the sweater spattered with paint. The shorter, portly man walking at his side wore a dapper suit. They hadn't gone yet—or were they returning?

Her heart lodged in her throat. Julia hurried up behind them as the man stuck out his hand to Cal. "If you change your mind about selling, give me a call, my lord. I want that piece of property. Several hundred acres. I could do a lot with that."

Cal shook the short man's large hand. "I'm sorry to have wasted your trip, but things have changed and I'm not planning to sell yet."

"These places can't survive and that's a fact. The future is in men like me," the large man crowed. "The self-made men. It was soap for me. Then locomotives. Love the iron horses and they've made me rich."

"I'm glad I could at least help your wife's charity."

"My Dora is a saint. Your contribution is very generous, my lord. As is your offer to sponsor me at your club. Damned hard to break into those places and my Dora is set on seeing our Annabelle married to a titled man. I don't suppose—"

"Sorry, Mr. Morgan, but I'm already promised to someone."

"Too bad. Annie comes with a dowry big enough to sink a ship." With that, the large man left.

Cal met her gaze. He looked guilty. She felt ready to spit fire. Yet the first thing that came out of her mouth: "I had no idea you're engaged."

"I'm not. I just wanted to make sure he didn't try to sell me Annabelle."

She smiled—just for a moment—then exclaimed, "Were you going to sell Lilac Farm to that man?"

He grimaced. "I'd made the arrangements before we went to London. I forgot to cancel the meeting."

"You changed your mind?" She barely dared to hope.

"Until I find out what happened to those women, until I get justice for them, I don't want to start carving up the estate." His blue eyes held hers. "And I promised you I'd wait if you posed for a portrait. I'm still waiting for your answer."

"I haven't even been able to think about that. A portrait doesn't seem so important now. But you are right to wait until we know the truth.

You do agree that we have no proof yet that anyone from Worthington was involved. Not real proof. Americans believe in justice, do they not? That is what you sought when you came here—justice for your parents, especially your mother. Don't condemn without proof. And what of the Brands—haven't they suffered enough? You can't throw them out of their home—"

"I'm not going to do that," he growled. "I'm going to look for evidence, find the truth. If someone on the estate murdered those girls, they must have buried—" He broke off. "Sorry, that's not something you discuss with a lady."

She lifted her chin, fighting to be strong. "I have had to face tragedy. And I'm not afraid of the truth. I would rather have that than have secrets. But how can evidence be found now, so many years later?"

"There are things that can be found. Even years later."

His face hardened as he said that. She knew what he meant—bodies. The spade in the boot of the car, encrusted with dirt. A man with a motor-car could have driven miles to find girls to flirt with, to lure into his vehicle. But why would that spade be left in the boot of Anthony's car?

He could have been helping with planting on the estate. He could have used it when they were searching for the girls. Or perhaps he had some other perfectly innocent reason for it.

Or perhaps someone else had put it there.

"You're pale. Let me take you back to the house, Julia. You don't need to worry about this."

"Cal, I can't just not think about this. I have to know!" She paced in a circle, feeling so tense she might burst. "I should see Ben, see how he is. I should be driving to the hospital to see Ellen. I should ensure the police constable is hunting for the man who hurt Ellen. But all I could do this morning was think of this—of whether Anthony had done this horrible thing."

"The photograph," Cal said suddenly.

She stared at him, confused. She saw the bristle of whiskers along his jaw. He hadn't bothered to shave.

"I found a photograph in my bedroom—it had fallen under the wardrobe. It was of a dark-haired girl wearing a corset. Signed 'to A.' "

"To Anthony? But why would that have been in your bedroom? Anthony never used that room. He was never the earl."

"I know. But the picture was there. And Sarah Brand had dark hair. Her mother confused you for Sarah."

"Sarah had black hair and blue eyes. We were of a similar height. I think her mind wants to believe I'm Sarah, when she sees me."

"Would you know if it was Sarah in the picture?"

"I suppose so."

Cal ran off, suddenly, sprinting to the house. She

275

followed, hurrying as fast as her low heels and trim-fitting tweed skirt would allow. By the time she reached the door, he was already coming back out. Frowning. "He burned the photo," he said.

"Who did?"

"Wiggins," he growled. "Maybe he knew the girl was Sarah Brand and he was protecting the family."

"Protecting them?"

"Maybe he knows Anthony Carstairs was driving Sarah around. Or maybe he knows what Anthony did to her—"

"We don't know Anthony did anything!" she cried. "It could have been someone else. Someone else could have used that motorcar and left the spade in it. There could have been some other reason. I want proof before I think of the man I loved as a—a murderer!"

She spun away from Cal, to go to her motorcar.

His hand wrapped firm around her arm—firm but gentle, forcing her to stop. "You aren't driving anywhere. Not upset like this."

"I am going to go to Lilac Farm. You can drive me there if you wish."

They reached the farm to find Brand finally making himself a breakfast of tea and toast after tending to the animals. Julia could see he was exhausted. Mrs. Brand had been awake most of the night, so she was sleeping now, even though it was midmorning.

"I have to watch her," he admitted. "She gets up and she wanders in the night. She tries to go outside. Once she got away and I couldn't find her for hours. I lock the place up now."

The poor man. She had to admit Cal was right—the farm was too much for them.

"I will help," she insisted. And she did, holding her umbrella up as she spread out seed for chickens. Cal helped, too, and when she attempted to carry buckets of water from the pump for the pigs' troughs, he stopped her. Brand looked shocked.

"Nae, ye shouldn't be working, milady," Brand said.

"I cannot stand by idle and not help," she said crisply. "But I wondered if Sarah ever told you she was frightened by a man. A man who might have tried to—to accost her."

She felt guilty as she asked the question. She knew, in her heart, she was trying to prove the man who had been driving Sarah wasn't Anthony.

"She never spoke of any such thing."

"Did Lord Anthony really take her driving in the car?"

"Mrs. Brand thinks Lord Anthony took her in his motorcar, but I don't believe it," Brand said. "Lord Anthony weren't like that. Neither were she. Sarah wanted to be married someday and she had no daft ideas about marrying above her station."

That was hope, at least. "Would you mind if I took a look in Sarah's room?"

Brand allowed it and Julia went to the house. Cal followed. She realized Cal was letting her take charge with this. The tiny room looked as it must have done nine years before. She looked in the one small wardrobe. Sarah's clothes still hung in it, smelling of lavender sachets. She found a diary, but there was no mention of any secret love. But Sarah did record times when she'd watched Anthony drive by in his lovely motorcar.

She had no choice but to let Cal look at it, too. Then she put it away, feeling sick. She left the Brands then. Told Cal, "I must go and see some of the women I'm helping today."

"I'll take you."

"It is not necessary. I am perfectly fine to drive." They argued—to her surprise, he finally relented. He took her back to Worthington, let her go off in her car.

She drove to the cottages and farms of several of the women. It made her feel better to see how they were surviving. One of the women, Mrs. Woddle, was in delight over the success of her sales of preserves. Now, after the War, with girls working in factories, they had to feed themselves and had no facilities to do so. Tea shops were booming.

She went to see the Tofts. Neighbors were helping—and Nigel had been sending baskets of food and treats from Brideswell's kitchens. It was almost heartbreaking, but she put on a brave face. If the family could, so could she. Seeing the eldest daughter, Mary, turned Julia's stomach upside down. The girl had dark hair in pigtails and large blue eyes.

Julia didn't remember any girl going missing after 1916. It seemed the disappearances had stopped then. Why?

Because Anthony went to war.

She did not know that for certain. And it was *not* proof.

Julia drove to see Ellen after that. In Brideswell's hospital ward, she told Ellen, "I will loan you the money to begin a business. A seamstress business, perhaps. Please accept this."

Tucked in her cot, Ellen shook her head. "I would only let you down, my lady. I could never pay you back."

"I believe you can. You must tell me who attacked you. He should be arrested and imprisoned for what he has done."

"I can't tell you his name. He would hurt Ben."

"Ben will be safe. I will ensure this man never comes near him. He almost killed you," Julia said, in a vehement whisper so as not to disturb the other women in the ward. "Help me and we will have him arrested."

But Ellen would not meet her gaze. "I can't do that, my lady."

Cal had been right. So painfully right. Ellen was willing to shield an evil man out of fear.

Julia stood. "I will find out who did this. I am not going to let him get away with it."

Panic flooded Ellen's face, turning her skin white where it wasn't bruised. "Don't, my lady. You have to keep out of it. You'll get yourself in trouble."

"Don't be ridiculous. I will be perfectly fine and I intend to help you."

Julia left, frustrated as she drove through the village. The dark, rainy weather matched her mood. But she was going to protect Ellen in some way—that was one thing she could do. She did not doubt the horrible wretch had taken money from Ellen when he had beaten her. It was the sort of thing a brute would do. And she knew where that money would be spent.

She drove to the village nearest Ellen's cottage, the small village of Worthington. Even in this tiny place, there were three pubs. Then she saw him. A large man leaving the Boar and Castle, the village public house. She was certain this was the man she had seen harassing Ellen on the street weeks ago.

Julia got out of her motor, stalked over to the man. But a few paces away, her courage failed her. But it was too late. He must have sensed her. He turned with surprising speed for such a large man and he strode back toward her.

She lifted her chin. It might be the middle of the day on the main street of the village of

Worthington, but the rain meant the street was almost deserted. She had made a terrible, terrible mistake. "Lay a hand on me and I will scream," she threatened, but her voice shook.

"Ye were the one coming after me, milady." His fleshy lips smirked.

"I want your name."

"Ye don't need it. Ye won't have any trouble from me if Ellen keeps doing as she's told." He puffed up his huge chest. "I'm looking after her. She doesn't need meddling from the likes of you, milady. Keep away from her."

"Ellen told me you have threatened her child to force her to—to sell herself and give the money to you. How small and pitiful you are. I will not allow this to continue. I will find out who you are and I will have you arrested."

He laughed cheerfully. "I doubt that. Ellen would be the only one who could back up yer wild tale and she won't grouse on me. Ye can't hurt me. But ye're fragile. I can hurt ye real easy. Ye go to see her one more time, and I'll really make ye pay."

Fury made her stand up to him. "I will have my brother destroy you. I will ensure you never hurt Ellen or her son again. I will move them away, to a place you will not find them. I am a duke's daughter and I have the power to crush you like the worm you are."

"Ye'll regret that," he snarled. "Don't ye dare

threaten me, ye cow." He loomed over her, lifting his fist. She was scared, using every ounce of strength not to melt in panic. But she had a weapon. She lifted her umbrella and poked the pointed end into his stomach.

He let out a howl of pain and doubled over. She spun and raced up the sidewalk.

A car was coming toward her.

It accelerated and as soon as it reached her, it screeched to a stop. The man behind the wheel leaned out to look at her.

Cal.

She wanted to throw her arms around him and hug him so tight he wouldn't be able to breathe. Of course she wouldn't do it.

He jumped out of the car. He ran right past her, down the sidewalk. Shaking, she turned to watch him, but she couldn't see any sign of the man who'd threatened her.

Cal came back to her. "Julia, who was that man?"

"I don't know." That much was the truth. She didn't have his name.

"Don't lie to me, Julia. I couldn't see exactly, but it looked like he was threatening you. I did see you drive your umbrella into his gut and I doubt you'd do that unless he asked for it."

Cal was looking at her as Nigel would. With the same autocratic, protective look.

She swallowed hard. "Perhaps I should return to my motorcar."

"You're trembling and you're pale. You need a drink, Julia. Something for the shock."

He hustled her into the Boar and Castle. He ordered a large brandy for her, an ale for himself. It was warm in the pub—despite being June, it was a cool, cloudy day and she felt cold through to her soul.

"That was the man who hurt Ellen Lambert," Cal said.

"Yes, that was her pimp. How did you know?"

Cal's brows shot up under his blond hair. "Lucky guess. But I'm kind of stunned you know that word."

"Well, I do. I'm not completely naive. But you mustn't tell my brother about this."

"I take it you mean you don't want me to mention some thug threatened to hurt you. If I were your brother, I'd like to know that."

"You can't. *Please.* He would use this as a reason to stop me continuing my work with women like Ellen. And Zoe might agree with him, if she thought I was in danger."

Their drinks came, served by Mr. Grey. As he set down Cal's pint, he asked, "I've been thinking about that business with those missing girls, milord. Did ye talk to old Brown, who used to work at the house? Did he help you?"

"Yeah, he did. Thanks." Cal was attempting to

sound offhand and casual. Then he asked about Ellen's pimp—about the man who had just been drinking in there.

"Aye. Don't know his name. He's only been in here twice for a drink. Usually drinks elsewhere, he said. I banned him for life this time—he wants to brawl and I don't need the trouble."

"If he comes in again, would you find out his name before you toss him out? I'll make it worth your trouble," Cal promised.

The man touched his forehead, a gesture of respect and agreement. "I will, milord."

After Grey left, Julia gasped. "Of course. I remember now. Brown is the former chauffeur at Worthington. When did you speak to him?" She had been hoping to get the name of Ellen's abuser and hadn't really thought about Brown until just now.

"After you left today," Cal said, "I drove over to the village where he lives with his daughter."

"What did you learn from him?"

Cal took a long swallow of beer.

Her heart dipped. He didn't want to tell her.

He set down the glass. "He said that he found Anthony in the garage one night. He was taking something out of the trunk, but when he heard Brown come in, he locked the trunk, then covered up the car with the white sheet. Brown said he looked upset, nervous. It was just the next day that Anthony volunteered and went to war."

"What are you saying? That he went to war to make up for—for taking those women?"

"Maybe."

"Why would he leave those things in the vehicle, where they could be found?"

"Maybe he thought no one would touch his car," Cal said. "Maybe he had no time."

Suddenly she realized the truth. Cal didn't just want justice. He wanted Anthony to be guilty. She believed she knew why—that would prove the Earl of Worthington had been utterly wrong to condemn Cal's family. That the wealthier, titled Carstairs had not been better or nobler people—since they had a criminal strain in their blood.

She wanted Anthony to be innocent. She wanted to believe in the man she had loved deeply.

They could not both get what they wanted.

Cal set down his drink. His hand rested close to hers. She moved hers away. She couldn't touch him.

"You need to go home and forget about all this," he said.

"I won't. I can't let you make Anthony guilty, if he wasn't. What will you do then—use that for justification to destroy Worthington? Hurt more innocent people?"

"I'm not going to say he's guilty if that's not true. But if he's guilty—"

Panic rose. "But if you stop searching for evidence, you can justify calling him guilty." She was sick with fear. "You can't do anything until you have actual evidence. Irrefutable evidence."

He didn't answer.

"What if I agreed to your bargain—that you won't touch Worthington if I let you paint me?"

"You were right, Julia. Portraits don't seem as important now."

Her heart sank. Then she thought of Cal's story. Of his mother dying and of him having to protect his younger brother and raise him—

"This is your brother's birthright also. How can you think of destroying his family home, when he has never even seen it? That is wrong, Cal. He should at least see his father's home. Wouldn't that be fair and just to him?"

"The way I see it, this isn't his father's home. This is where his father grew up, before being disowned by this family."

"But it was still his home when he was a child, and it was a part of him. Your brother should see it," she insisted.

Cal gave her an almost sulky look. She knew she'd scored a point. "Did your father ever talk about Worthington Park?"

"Yeah, he did."

"What did he say about it?"

"Said it was beautiful. That he was sorry we'd never get to see it. I knew we weren't considered good enough for this place—we were the dirt that had to be kept out. But David was younger than me and he didn't understand. He used to dream about seeing it."

"Then no matter what you do to Worthington, you must let your brother, David, see it first."

"You're right. And I did plan to do it. I'll send him a wire. Arrange his passage." He sighed heavily. "I wouldn't have sold the farm today because I know it would have hurt you. I couldn't do that to you now, after you've been through so much. You know I don't want to hurt you, Julia."

She knew the rest—the rest he left unsaid. That he feared he would have to. And inside she was in turmoil. To have a boy think he was dirt that should be kept out of a house . . . it made her blood boil in anger. But that was the past, and there had to be a way for Worthington and Cal to have a future together.

The day before Cal's brother was to arrive, Mother held a dinner party. Zoe was the duchess, but Mother had actually arranged everything for the party, something she had not done in many years. Not since grief over Will had consumed her. It showed her mother was healing and that was good. Mother insisted it was to help Julia get over her sorrow from the Tofts' losses.

But when she went down for cocktails before dinner, Julia discovered Mother had invited the Duke of Bradstock and the Earl of Summerhay.

Nigel had invited Dougal Campbell—he wanted to discuss some business about the hospital.

She wanted to turn and run—she was so worried about what Cal might learn about Anthony she couldn't bear to spend time fending off suitors.

Mother, of course, arranged for her to sit between James—the Duke of Bradstock—and Summerhay.

The electric chandeliers—installed by Zoe—sparkled on crystal and silver. Candlelight flickered on the table.

As they reached the savory after dessert, James leaned toward her. At the exact same moment, the Earl of Summerhay leaned to her also. Both men said, at once, "Would you ride with me tomorrow?"

They stared at each other as she said, "I am afraid I already have plans. But since you both want to ride, why don't you gentlemen go together?"

"We aren't courting each other," James said, lifting his brow in true ducal fashion. "Summerhay is courting you. And I want only to enjoy a ride with you."

But James was courting her, too, she saw. And she didn't want to be courted. Why didn't men listen? But then she felt guilty and softened the blow. "Though of course I am flattered and ordinarily I should love to . . ." She winced—she did not want to encourage either man, when she knew she couldn't love either one, but she had been trained to be so blasted polite. "But tomorrow I have plans to go to Worthington Park."

She could not wait to meet Cal's brother. He could be a valuable ally and she was going to be there, under any pretext, when he arrived.

"To see the American earl?" James growled. He gripped his wineglass so hard his knuckles went white. "You shouldn't go there. There are rumors—"

"Of an engagement," Summerhay finished.

"Not of an engagement. I knew that was rot," James insisted. "The man's behavior is notorious. I've heard stories about him in Paris, bedding all of his models."

"What is this? Are you speaking of bedding roses?" That was the dowager and Julia was quite sure she'd heard everything, and was stopping James before he said something even more shocking.

"I am going to see Ellen Lambert's son, who is staying there. And my good friend Diana."

"As long as it isn't to see him."

Obviously James did not like Cal, but she couldn't see how he had the right to dictate.

"He's also mentally unhinged," James said. "Apparently he goes around the estate, digging in random places, or so I've been told. Is he looking for buried treasure?"

She swallowed hard—she couldn't say he was looking for the three women, not if there was a chance Anthony had been involved. "This is the first I've heard of that," she hedged.

"He must be looking for something—"

Chairs scraped, interrupting James, signaling it was time to go to the drawing room. Julia sighed with relief. When the men joined the ladies, after having their port, Julia went over to Dougal. "I am concerned about Ellen Lambert."

His sensitive brown eyes showed surprise. "She is recovering well."

"Perhaps physically. I fear she is suffering from shell shock." She did love to be able to speak to Dougal as a partner, to have a meeting of minds.

"Shell shock?" he echoed. "Why do you think this?"

"It was Cal—the Earl of Worthington—who suggested it. She suffers nightmares. She can't sleep. Loud noises make her react in a panic."

"Some women who served at the front proved to be too delicate for the work—"

"It's not delicacy," she protested. "Women witnessed the same horrors as the men. Ellen drove an ambulance, where she saw victims of the worst injuries. According to Cal, the ambulances were shelled and shot at."

"Medical practitioners have diagnosed such women as suffering from hysteria. They proved unsuitable for the work and returned home."

"Unsuitable for the work? Who would be

suitable to drive a vehicle through a battlefield while being shelled?" She stared at him. "It is not hysteria. It's shell shock."

"Shell shock is a different thing entirely. The problems that men experienced were different from those that women did."

"How could they be? They experienced the very same things." She couldn't understand him.

"No male soldier would accept that his condition is like hysteria."

"Oh, that is it! You think the men would be ashamed to have the same problem as women. Well, they had best get over it. She has shell shock. And I fear she will not be able to improve her life until it is dealt with."

Dougal gave an awkward cough. "Julia, I would suspect Ellen Lambert's troubles are due to her current . . . profession."

She could not believe she had heard such a thing from Dougal. "Her current profession is a result of ignorance on the part of the government and society. We have turned our backs on people like her. I thought you would *champion* her cause. There has been help for men with shell shock. Why shouldn't women be helped? Really, Dougal, I cannot understand you."

"What do you want me to do, Julia? Even if I agreed, a diagnosis of shell shock would not be recognized—and would not help the woman in any way."

"But she could be cured."

"Not necessarily, and the forms of treatment are horrific, Julia. She would certainly be separated from her son."

She fumbled. She hadn't thought of that. And she was startled by the way Dougal smiled slightly, as though he were being patient with her, as though he knew, of course, he should win the argument. "There must be a solution."

"There's nothing more you can do, Julia."

"I thought we could work on this together. I have to help her—for her sake and for Ben's. She served her country, just as bravely as any man. How can there be no help for her now?" Even as she spoke, she saw from his face that he would not help. She had thought Dougal was a wonderful doctor, a progressive, modern man.

"The officials of her country would never call her condition 'shell shock.' And given what else she has done after the War, they would not help."

"But that's wrong!" she cried.

"What is wrong, Julia?" Grandmama asked, gazing at her with pursed lips.

"Apparently quite a lot with our country," she said. "But of course, nothing is ever solved at a dinner party."

She couldn't explain why—but she felt deeply discouraged that Dougal had turned out to be a different man than she'd believed. Cal had turned out different, too—but in good ways.

Without Dougal's support, what could she do for Ellen?

Julia was still without a solution as she rode over to Worthington Park the next day. The day Cal's brother was to arrive, being driven from the South Hampton docks.

She found Cal pacing outside the front door, a cigarette clenched between his teeth.

"You're waiting for your brother?" She dismounted—it was so deliciously easy to do so in jodhpurs rather than skirts.

Cal nodded, his face grim.

"I thought you would be happy to see him again. He's had a long journey. You will have to smile when he gets here," she teased.

"It's hard," he muttered.

"Why is it hard?" She stood at his side, holding Athena's reins.

"He was wounded badly in the War."

Badly? Heavens, how badly? "I didn't know that. Was the journey hard for him?"

"Yeah, I imagine it was very hard. But he made it—to see this damn house." Cal shook his head. "I told him not to join up. But once I went, there was no one to stop him. He followed me into battle, but I served as a pilot and he served on the ground. I didn't even know he was there until we were in the same hospital together—"

Cal had to stop talking. She saw tears in his

eyes. He blinked hard and the tears were gone.

"I am so sorry," she said. "It must have broken your heart to see him wounded."

"It did. He was eighteen. A shell exploded under him after he shoved two men out of the way to save them. They had to take off both of his legs below the knee. At home, when he was a kid, I protected him. Kept him out of—" He broke off. Drew on his cigarette. "Kept him out of trouble," he finished. "But he went to war and destroyed his life."

"He is still alive," she pointed out softly.

"He can't walk and has to spend his life in a wheeled chair."

How hurt Cal looked—he was feeling a huge weight of responsibility. For something that had not been his fault. He believed in protecting people—she knew it meant these wounds went very deep.

He kicked the gravel. "After the War, I hired a staff of nurses and servants to look after him. I went away to Paris. Sometimes I feel I was running away from my guilt. I tried painting it away, but it didn't work. I couldn't forget. So I tried to drink it away with good French wine and brandy. That didn't work, either."

"It is not your fault. He was of age and it was his choice to volunteer."

"But if you have someone you love, you want to protect them," he said.

"I didn't want Anthony to go to War, but I knew I couldn't ask him to stay. His father had not wanted him to go, since he was the heir. His father wanted him to wait until he was conscripted, but Anthony felt it was wrong to stay home when other men were doing their duty."

She expected him to dismiss what Anthony had done, but gently, he said, "You went through what I did. I wrote home and told David it was a living hell, but he ignored my letters. He thought I was trying to scare him away."

Cal's fingers brushed hers. Just that touch made her gasp. Then he moved abruptly away. "He's here." He threw his cigarette away on the drive.

The Worthington Daimler, large and black, drove into view on the drive.

"I shouldn't have brought him here," Cal said suddenly. "He doesn't need any of this. He has a home in America and people to care for him. The countess despises me. How is she going to react to my brother's condition?"

Cal was panicking, she saw. "It will be all right. I will not allow him to be hurt," she vowed.

The car stopped. Two footmen who stood on the front steps sprang forward. But Cal went forward, too, not acting like an earl, not waiting. He went to the boot of the vehicle where a wheeled chair had been folded and attached. After the footman took it off the motorcar, Cal took it from the young servant. With practiced motions he wheeled it to the passenger door on the far side, away from the house.

Wait—she realized what he had said. He had hired a staff of nurses and servants. She had thought he was an impoverished artist before he became earl. That he had still been poor.

But he could not have been impoverished to have spent so much money to look after his brother.

The front door of the house opened and the countess marched out. Julia saw her mouth held firmly, her eyes blazing. "It is my duty also to greet guests," the countess said to her. "Who is this man?"

Cal hadn't told her? "This is your nephew," Julia said. "He was wounded in the War. You must be kind and welcoming to him."

Julia saw how much Lady Worthington had changed. Once a warm, welcoming smile would have curved her lips. Now she looked tight-lipped, grim. Frightened.

From around the car came the wheeled chair. Cal pushed it smoothly from behind, even over the gravel. A young man—he must be about twenty-five—sat in the chair. He waved cheerfully. Julia had steeled herself to see no legs, or trousers pinned at the knees. But his trousers were filled out and he wore shoes. He must have artificial legs.

"You must be my aunt," said the young man. He held out his hand. His eyes were the same clear, vivid blue as Cal's but a shock of curly

296

black hair framed his handsome face. "Good to meet you. I'm David Carstairs, your younger nephew from the States. I'd get up but you'd be waiting a long time, I'm afraid." He grinned.

His greeting was so warm, so different from Cal's, Julia was stunned. The countess came forward. "I am the Countess of Worthington. Indeed, my husband was brother to your father, Mr. Carstairs."

"Please call me David . . . Aunt Sophia." He said it with a wistful expression.

Julia's heart tugged.

"You would address me as—"

Julia gave a soft cough, interrupting. The countess was trying to sound austere and Julia had to stop that. And she noticed how the countess's fingers plucked nervously at the beads draped around her neck.

Show kindness, Julia mouthed. *Please do.*

Did the countess read her lips? She didn't know, but the woman's tone softened. "Do call me Aunt Worthington. That is how we do things in this country."

"Aunt Worthington. I think Aunt Sophia sounds prettier but I want to do things right." David Carstairs's winning smile revealed dimples.

Rain spattered down. "I'd better get you inside," Cal said brusquely.

Julia watched Cal negotiate the chair around the house to one of the terrace doors where there was no step, and wheel his brother inside. She followed them in, but the countess went in through the front door.

David whistled as they entered the drawing room. "Whoa. What a beautiful place, Cal," David said. "So what's tea really like? Do they have cakes?"

"All they do here is eat, and have too much food," Cal said. "It's indulgent and disgusting."

"I'd like to have a meal of cakes," David said.

"It should take more than a tray of cakes to win you over, David," Cal muttered darkly.

His brother twisted to look at him. "We haven't got any other family left, Cal."

"David, I'm not here because they wanted to make peace and invited me. I'm here because I inherited the place and they're forced, by their precious English rules, to accept me."

"Yeah, but that doesn't mean things can't work out for the best," David said. "So have you gone riding? Did you fall off?"

They were very different, the two brothers. And David was on her side, thank heaven.

"I did go riding," Cal said. "Lady Julia taught me."

Julia lifted her head.

"I should have introduced you," Cal said. "David, this is Lady Julia, who lives at Brideswell, which is a neighboring estate."

She smiled brightly. "I am delighted to meet you, Mr. Carstairs."

"Cal me David. Could you stop a minute, Cal, so I can show some manners and shake her hand?"

Looking embarrassed, Cal did. She shook David Carstairs's warm, strong hand. "You taught my brother to ride." He looked down. "I'd like to learn, but I guess that's not possible."

"Perhaps it would be possible for you to sit on a horse and be led?"

"No. Too dangerous," Cal said shortly.

His brother rolled his blue eyes. "I think I've seen worse danger than falling off a horse. I'm game to try."

Julia felt Cal's glare. She thought Cal was wrong—overprotective. But fighting with him now was not sensible. She could arrange for David to ride. That might win him over to convincing Cal to keep Worthington intact. "I am sure we can think of something, together."

David gave her a smile that warmed her heart. "I'm glad to be here," he said. Then to his brother: "Cal, I've been thinking. I want to write a letter to Alice. Maybe we could pay for her to travel here. I'd like to see her. Nothing more, just see her. I know it's hopeless now to dream of more, but it would make my life complete just to see her smile again."

Julia was almost in tears. Alice must have been his sweetheart.

But Cal said abruptly, "No." Then he added, as if he knew he sounded unreasonable, "She's probably married by now. Let it go. It's only going to break your heart."

"Cal, I know there were a hundred soldiers in love with her, and each one had more to offer her than I do. But I'd just like to see her. Maybe she would come, if we invited her to something. Don't the English give fancy parties and balls? Just like they did at Mam's house, when she was a maid?"

Cal's face contorted with pain and Julia's heart contracted with it, too. He was behind his brother, who couldn't see his expression.

She said brightly, "I think it sounds like a very lovely idea."

Cal turned on her. "No, it's not." He whispered it, but so angrily, she was stunned. "I'm not having a ball here, David," he said more loudly.

"Of course you could not hold a ball," Lady Worthington declared as she approached, her heels clicking on the floor. "*You* would hardly know what to do."

It was as if she'd waved a red flag. "I know how to throw a party," Cal said sharply. "Forget what I said. If you want a ball, David, you'll get one."

13

David's Story

Cal carried David up the stairs to show him the bedroom he'd had prepared. He felt guilty and awkward as he put David back into his chair. Guilty because he hadn't been able to protect his younger brother. Awkward because he knew David hated to feel like a burden.

The countess had made him mad and he'd reacted. But having a ball now, when he was trying to find out whether three young women had been killed and whether Anthony Carstairs was responsible? Julia must believe he was a callous monster.

Maybe that was for the best. If Anthony was a killer, had been shielded from punishment, Julia would see Cal when he was full of rage.

"You're lost in thought."

David's voice jerked Cal back. "Do you like the room?" he asked fast. "I can have another fixed up for you, if you'd prefer. I thought you'd like the Oriental look in the place."

One wall was papered in scarlet, decorated with gold. The furnishings all looked like they had come from Japan or China. A rice-paper screen stood in the corner. This had been John Carstairs's room when John had been just the younger son to the earl. Before he'd become the earl and taken over the earl's bedroom.

Was John maybe the killer? He hadn't been popular with girls, Cal had been told.

"I like it," David said. He added wistfully, "Before the War, I always thought about traveling the world."

Cal's throat tightened. He'd tried to give his younger brother all the opportunity he never had. It was why he'd stayed in a gang. To make money to send David to school. He'd intended to send his younger brother to university. Then America had joined the War—

"I finally made it to England," David said. "I never did during the War."

David should be angry because fate had stolen his chance to travel the world. But his brother looked happy.

Cal stood uneasily beside David's chair. "Where do you want to go—to the window? If you want to rest before dinner, would you like me to put you on the bed?"

It was like he was asking his brother where he wanted to be stored. He'd fired nurses in the States after they just wheeled his brother to a corner and left him there.

"I can wheel myself you know," David said. And he did, taking himself to the window.

Cal went to the table that held a decanter of

the best damn brandy they had in this house. He poured two drinks and walked back, giving one to David.

If he'd been in David's position—missing both his legs—he would not be able to be alone with a decanter full of brandy. He likely would have drunk himself to death in despair and anger. Not David.

David sipped it. "Nice. Gosh, it's a beautiful view. Mam would have loved the gardens."

"Yeah, and she was never allowed to see them," Cal said darkly.

"Things can change," David said. "I know about how they can change in a heartbeat. I believe things can change for the better, too."

How did David stay so filled with hope? How did he look on the bright side?

Cal was the one filled with anger. Anger that ran in his blood, oozed through his pores. "There's something you need to know, David . . ."

His brother looked at him, trusting him. He should tell David about his plans to get rid of the place—but he couldn't do it yet.

"What is it?" David asked. "You look so serious."

"David, I don't want you to talk about my past . . . in New York."

"Your past?"

"The Five Points Gang. What I did. I don't want them to know. They already think I'm low-class scum."

"You aren't, Cal."

He didn't answer, so David had another sip of his drink. "Cal, I really want to find Alice—"

"No, David. I'm not going to let you do that."

"I'm a grown man. If I had two legs I could do what the hell I want."

For the first time since he got here, David lost his smile. Cal knew he was breaking his brother's heart, but he had to protect him. David was all he had left.

The next morning, Julia went to Worthington Park to talk to David Carstairs. Wiggins answered the door. Goodness, the butler looked as if he'd aged a decade in days. Pale, with dark circles under his eyes, he even appeared thinner than ever. "Is everything all right, Wiggins? You don't look well."

"I am quite all right, my lady," he answered. "If you are seeking his lordship, he has gone down to the kitchens I believe. His lordship tends to be eccentric in his behavior."

"They are his kitchens," Julia said. "And his lordship intends to hold a ball. I expect he wishes to speak to his cook directly about it."

"That should go through myself or Mrs. Rumpole."

"The earl does things in his own way." She realized she had said that with pride—at heart, Cal's independent ideas impressed her. She couldn't deny it.

"Indeed." But Wiggins looked more nervous than affronted.

"I am actually looking for his brother, Mr. David Carstairs."

"The earl's brother had indicated he wished to see the library."

"Thank you, Wiggins. But you do look ill. You should get more rest."

Was the butler really making himself physically ill over having Cal as the earl? What did he fear? Losing his job . . . or something more?

But as she left the foyer and walked into the wide receiving hall, Diana darted out of a doorway, grasped her hand and towed her into the music room. "Cal is going to help me," she breathed. "He's going to send me to Switzerland to have the baby, then I shall give it up over there and come home. Come home and pretend nothing ever happened."

"Yes. He and I talked about that." But Diana looked despairing and Julia whispered, "Diana, that will *save* you."

"Save my reputation. It won't save me. This will be done so I can make a discreet marriage—a lonely and cold marriage, because I can't stop my obsession with my baby's father. I know what you'll say—that he used me. But he was so passionate with me. I want that again."

"Diana—"

"He told me that I was the most beautiful woman

305

in the world to him. I don't care if it was lies. Mother always made me believe I wasn't good enough. Not as good as you—she always talked about how accomplished you are, Julia. It's rather a miracle I didn't scratch your eyes out. But when I was with *him,* I felt beautiful and exciting."

"Oh, my dear." Julia embraced her.

Diana nodded. "I was stupid. But I still *want* to love him."

There was so much pain in Diana's face, it scared Julia. "You must go away as Cal says. You do have to think of your future—"

Diana gave a sharp laugh. "An empty, loveless future. And Mother snaps at me all the time. Sometimes I fear she knows about the baby. She's upset and nervy and she finds fault with everything. Cal has told her she can stay here or go and live in the dower house. He has been . . . surprisingly nice. I guess we have you to thank for that, Julia."

"I think Cal is good by his nature, despite what he says."

"Mother still acts as if she's terrified of him. She keeps saying he is going to ruin us. I don't know what she means, but she says he is working to destroy us."

Julia blinked. She thought of Cal's investigation. Could the countess know about it? Was that what she feared? Cal learning the truth? But what *did* the countess know?

306

Heavens, could Cal's belief that the servants were covering up be true?

"Cal has been nice to me, but—but I don't want to give up my child." Diana gave a wobbly smile. "I know it's foolish, but I want to keep the baby. Cal has told me he would settle money on me. I would be ruined, but I could live with my child. I would be independent. Mother would disown me, of course. Society would shun me. But I am beginning to think I don't care. I was part of the Bright Young Things and I lived to be popular. I now understand there are more important things in the world." She sighed. "I always thought we would marry titled men and have children and live on grand estates."

"But we can still be happy," Julia said, "even if we don't."

"Yes. I suppose we can."

A sharp, sudden squeak came from the doorway. Julia looked up.

David Carstairs was there, in his chair, a blush coloring his cheeks. "I'm sorry. I was trying to find my way around and I came this way by mistake."

Using his hands to propel the wheels on his chair, he backed out of the room.

Diana was mortified that David had overheard. Julia calmed her—she sensed David would keep a secret as well as Cal. She found David in the library in his chair by the window. The library overlooked the rose gardens, and the woods, which made a dark green counterpoint to the sculpted hedges and the masses of pink, red and yellow roses.

Julia caught her breath. In the rose garden, Anthony had kissed her before he left for France. It felt like a lifetime ago. And was it a good memory now or not?

She pushed those thoughts away. Pasted on a cheery smile. "Good afternoon, David."

He turned in the chair, gave a boyish grin. "Hello, Lady Julia."

"And you must call me Julia." She was suddenly nervous about begging for his help, launching into such personal matters.

Then he said, "I guess you knew the family really well. Cal says you live at Brideswell Abbey, a big estate next door. What was it like for you, growing up here? I heard you had balls and went on hunts, and got presented at court."

She told him a little about that. He was an enthusiastic listener and appeared fascinated by everything. He wanted to know about the people who lived on the estate. Julia found she was telling him about Ellen—at first trying to avoid revealing Ellen's profession. But he was so concerned and so kind, she spilled out the whole story.

When she was done, he said, "I'm sorry to hear about it. But I'm sure she can be saved. She sounds like a good woman. Cal will help her. I know he will."

"I know he will, too, but she won't listen. She refuses to get any help. I believe—and Cal thinks so, too—that Ellen suffers from shell shock."

She could have bit her tongue—why remind him of the War?

"I'm not surprised it happened to the lass. I'd say what she needs is hope for a future. That's what is the hardest on those that came back. There wasn't hope. I felt sorry for them."

"You did?"

"I had hope."

She stared, realizing David Carstairs was like Cal—a remarkable, unexpected man.

"Cal had made money, you see. After the War, America was poised to succeed and Cal had real smarts when it came to investing money. He got out of the g—" David broke off. He coughed. "I mean, he had enough money to get a house for me and to hire people to look after me. He went to Paris to paint. He said he needed to forget things."

"Do you mean the War?" she asked gently.

"That didn't hit Cal as hard. He's tough. Keeps things inside. That's because it was tough for Cal when we were growing up."

"You were quite poor," she said.

"We were. Our father was a good man and he had an education. But you know that. When Cal and I were small, Da had a good job as overseer at the docks, but one night he was robbed on the way home. Beaten real bad, and it changed him. He couldn't think so well anymore. He got headaches. Lost his job because he couldn't do the work— there was a fire and he evacuated the warehouse. He saved everyone, but the goods inside were burned and destroyed. Father lost his job because the factory owner said he should have tried to put the fire out and save the building."

"That's terrible. Of course he could not have done that!" she gasped.

"I know. But that's the way it was. After he lost that job, Da couldn't get any other work. Mam went to work sewing clothes. Da ended up driving a rag-and-bone cart to earn some money. But he wouldn't pay protection to the local gangs. He was working to shut them down—to get poor people out of their control."

She remembered Cal telling her about the rag- and-bone cart, making it a challenge. Cal had a lot of pride. "Was he able to succeed?"

"He was murdered while he was on his rounds, collecting rags."

Murdered? "Oh—oh my goodness." It was all she could say, struck with horror.

"Two men grabbed him, pulled him down and kicked him to death. I was eight years old then. Cal was eleven. He'd gone out to find Da. He saw the attack."

Julia almost sobbed at the slash of pain that went through her heart. Cal saw his father die after a violent attack. A horrible, horrible thing. Then, three years later, he saw the same thing happen to his mother. "Were—were the men caught?"

David shook his head. "The police never found out who killed our father. Cal was tough. He looked after Mam and me. Said he was the man of the family. I never even saw Cal cry about it. I tried to be as tough as him, but losing Da broke my heart."

"I don't believe Cal was so tough at eleven years of age that he did not cry over his father."

"He's strong. He handled the things we saw in the War better than any man I knew."

Julia twisted her fingers in her lap. She knew Cal had been devastated by what had happened to his mother. Surely he must have felt the same about his father. He'd hid that from David. But he'd let her see it. It came out in his pain, his bitterness. She had been right—Cal needed to heal. How did she help him do that? She could make him care about Worthington, but how did she take away the pain of his past?

She felt a tear drop to her cheek.

"I'm sorry I've upset you," David said. He pulled at his pocket until he got a handkerchief out. He handed it to her. It was silk, of the highest quality.

"I'm glad Cal was able to get out of poverty at least," she said softly.

"He bought stocks in companies. They made money. He taught me to buy, to sell when you made some money and then invest it again. He got good at knowing how a company was run, and when to figure it might get in trouble."

Investing took money, though. "But where did he get the money that he started with?"

"He—uh, he started working. After Da was killed."

"But didn't he need to support you and your mother? Surely he wouldn't have had much money left over."

"I don't know how he did it, Lady Julia. Cal's just a smart man."

David looked embarrassed, and she knew she'd overstepped her bounds. "I'm sorry. That wasn't tactful at all." She gazed out the window, imagining how Cal felt the first time he saw it. All this wealth when he had lost both his parents . . . and lost them to the brutality of poverty. No wonder he had seethed with anger.

In retrospect, she realized he had been remarkably restrained.

"Has Cal told you about his plans for Worthington Park, David?" she asked.

"Plans? No. I hope he wants to stay. Having a home—a real home—will be good for him. He had a lot of pain in his past. And he could do a lot of good as an earl."

"You understand the situation completely," she said. "But do you think—do you think we can change his mind?" But could he ever accept this place? Could he ever heal, with Worthington reminding him constantly of his pain? Was she heartless to demand that of him?

No—she believed he could be happy here. If he healed.

"Change his mind?" David repeated. "What d'you mean?"

"Cal wants to sell Worthington Park, and turn out the countess and her daughters. He says now he'll look after them, but he wants to take their ancestral home away. He wants to put the farmers out of the farms, the tenants from their homes, carve it up and sell it."

David went pale. "I didn't know. I've got to find Cal and talk to him."

"I want to stop him. But he said he could never live with himself if he lived here as earl—"

"That doesn't matter. I've got to make him see that doesn't matter. Would you get him for me, Lady Julia?"

But when she went to the doorway, she saw Cal had found them. He came into the library. He wore his dirty sweater with the sleeves rolled up. Paint spattered his arms and hands. "I've got the food arranged for this swanky ball you want."

"Cal," David said, "I need to talk to you."

"You have to have your fancy tea first. Hannah's been working all day to make cakes, and they're gorgeous. Éclairs and a Victoria sponge—it's a cake but that's what she calls it. She made enough dainty little sandwiches to feed an army." Cal looked up at her. "Would you want to stay for tea, Julia?"

"David wants to talk to you about something important. I should go—" A lady would never say what she was about to. She would use subtlety. But Julia couldn't be bothered with ladylike skill. "David told me what happened to your father. I am so sorry."

For a moment, Cal was expressionless. Then he said, "David, I think your cousins Cassia and Thalia are going to have tea. Would you mind if I took you to the drawing room, then escorted Julia to her car? I need to talk to her."

David agreed. After taking him to the drawing room, she and Cal walked toward the garage.

They'd only gone a few steps when Cal said shortly, "So now you know about my father and my mother. Don't try to tell me I should turn the other cheek. I can't do it, Julia."

"I understand," she said softly. "I don't think I could, either. I think—I think you have been a remarkable man to even allow me to try to convince you. You saw both of your parents' tragic deaths and they were caused by—by the heartlessness of people who did not help you."

Cal heard the sympathy in her voice and he bristled.

David had promised he wouldn't tell her about

what Cal had done with the Five Points Gang. He knew his brother would keep his vow. Without knowing about that, Julia wouldn't completely understand.

"Don't feel sorry for me, Julia. But I need to talk to you about something else. Something about David."

He wanted to talk about Alice with Julia. He knew he was in the right—but somehow he needed Julia, the woman who cared so much about people, to agree with him. Then he'd know he wasn't being a bastard.

She was waiting for him to speak, all attentive.

"It's about Alice Hayes, the English girl my brother fell in love with. I know you'll understand without me having to draw you a picture." He raked his hand through his hair. "I never thought bringing him to England would mean he'd want to see her."

She looked surprised and confused, but she was Julia. She just said, "Tell me what happened."

"Alice worked as a nurse at the field hospital in France," he said. "After my plane was shot down and, by some miracle, didn't burst into flames, I was loaded on a stretcher and taken there. When I opened my eyes I was looking at the prettiest face I'd ever seen. She had huge blue eyes, and she took good care of me. I fell in love with her, of course. But, as fate would have it, David was brought to the same hospital."

"And you didn't know he had gone to war. It must have been a terrible shock."

"I was walking through the ward when I saw Alice tending to a man. She called him Private Carstairs and my heart stopped right at that moment. The sheets were off him, and I saw the bloody bandages around the stumps of his legs. There he was, my baby brother, lying on the bed. Nurse Alice was helping him eat because his right arm was in a plaster cast. I broke down and cried like a child. Actually, I'd never cried like that before. I learned early on not to cry—"

"I know."

"You know?"

"Your brother told me that you did not even cry when your father was killed."

He shrugged, shaking that off. "I watched how Alice took care of him. She was so gentle with him, and worked to lift his spirits. Some men would've wished they'd died. David is the type of man who felt he'd been blessed to live, even with both his legs gone and his arm hurt. The air force was going to ship me back to the front. I wasn't injured badly enough to go home. But I managed to get a few more days with my brother. He was so doped up for the pain that he didn't recognize me until two days before I was supposed to go back. The day he remembered me is the day I proposed to Nurse Alice. I had no right to do it. I had no money and no prospects and—well, I had no right. But she said yes, and we were going to wait until the end of the War."

"But you didn't marry her and your brother . . ."

"God, I wanted her. I was still in love with her after the War. She's the kind of woman who makes a man into something worthwhile because he's got to be worthy of her. But I couldn't marry her. David had fallen in love with her while she was taking care of him, too. Loving Alice was what kept him going, what kept him alive. I couldn't take that from him. He lost his legs and he lost his future. I couldn't take his sweetheart from him, too. So I wrote to her and broke off the engagement."

"But if you loved her—"

"It would have been too selfish to break my brother's heart."

"I am sure your brother would want you to be happy."

"No. It would have been impossible. I've come to terms with that." Funny—he hadn't thought of Alice since Julia had started taking him around to the tenants. "But David is still in love with her. Except he can't have her."

"Why not?"

Cal stared in disbelief. "What woman would marry a man who has lost his legs? It would break his heart if she turned him down to his face. I'm scared that he might do something bad if he was hurt like that."

"Do something bad?" Julia repeated.

"Take his life."

"But he isn't that kind of man, Cal. I've only just met him, and I know that. And he wishes to see her. Or is it that you can't face seeing her again?"

She wasn't agreeing with him. Hell, what was she thinking? She was wrong.

"I think he should see her. Perhaps—"

"No," he growled. "I know you believe you can help everyone, Julia. You can't fix this. David is strong and he looks on the bright side, but getting your heart broken is something else entirely."

"I know," she said.

She'd had her heart broken before, but he realized she was also having it broken by his suspicions about Anthony. Damn, he felt like a heel.

"I see no harm in inviting her," she said. "I could find her. They could talk and he would know—"

He stopped her by grasping her wrist. "Leave this alone, Lady Julia. You can rescue any family on the Worthington estate you want—but leave my family alone."

"Cal—"

Suddenly, he kissed her. Not a hard kiss, but a soft one, one that made his heart hurt as he did it.

She pulled back abruptly and he felt worse. She

didn't want his kisses. "Promise me you won't do this, Julia. Promise me," he said.

Cadmium red. Vermilion. Cobalt Blue. Sexual frustration made Cal paint harder and faster and wilder than he ever had in his life.

He painted until dawn blushed the sky through the high windows of the attic. He'd done this for three nights in a row, barely sleeping more than two hours. Tonight—or rather, in the early morning—the canvas swum before his eyes.

Yawning, he took his brushes to the table where he kept a basin of water, jars of turps—dirty and clean. He washed out the brush in one of the dirty jars, rinsed it in the clean. Blinking against the fumes, he carefully shaped the brush, wiped the excess solvent on a clean rag. He left the palette to dry. He didn't clean it, just wiped it and let the paint residue harden.

After that, he slugged down the rest of the brandy he'd poured earlier. Then stumbled downstairs to his room on the second floor. Christ, he was tired.

He'd argued with David after dinner. David had told him he loved the house; that he should keep Worthington Park. That it was tradition. *Hell.* Cal had said he wanted to go back to Paris. Give this life a chance, David had said.

He couldn't do that. Talking to Julia the other day about Alice had brought all his memories back.

Cal collapsed on his bed, fully dressed.

He was happy in Paris. It was the only place in the world he'd been happy . . .

Later that day, he was awoken by his curtains rattling open. Wiggins stood there—Wiggins was acting as his valet, whether Cal liked it or not, because he'd let St. Germaine go.

"My lord, you need a proper valet. Those trousers are creased beyond repair."

"I doubt that," Cal muttered.

"And the state of your shirt. Either you were stabbed with a letter opener while you slept or that is red paint on your shoulder."

"It's paint. I wanted to work on the portrait and I forgot to change my shirt."

"I fear it will never come out."

"Christ, Wiggins, that isn't something to be afraid of. I'll use it when I paint from now on. Don't you English people have more important things to worry about than clothing?"

"While you do not have a valet, it is my job to worry about your clothing, my lord."

Cal's head pounded. "Would you mind bringing me a cup of coffee? My throat feels like it's full of cotton."

"I shall have a footman do that." Wiggins sniffed and left.

Cal swung out of bed. He must have drunk more brandy that he remembered. He wanted to put on his own damn clothes, without someone fussing over him. He pulled open the drawers of his underclothes. Stuff made in Paris—made of silk and fine fabrics.

Something was sitting on top of one of the drawers. A lock of blue-black hair, tied with a pink ribbon.

"I found that in one of my drawers. There was an old Bible in there, and that was pressed between two pages."

Surprised by the voice behind him, Cal jerked around. His brother, seated in his wheeled chair, was at the doorway. "I put it in your room. I thought maybe Lady Julia gave it to you." David grinned.

"It's not Julia's. At least—she didn't give it to me." Cal fingered the hair. The Oriental bedroom had been John Carstairs's bedroom. Why had this been in a drawer, hidden in the Bible?

Then he knew. Sarah Brand, Eileen Kilkenny and the maid, Gladys Burrows, had hair as blue-black as Julia's.

Cal got dressed in his room fast, told David he would be back quick, drove out to the retired chauffeur's cottage. Found out that John Carstairs had gotten lessons from Anthony on how to drive before Anthony had gone away to War. John had been fifteen at the time—too young to enlist. But he'd been tall for his age, as tall as his brother, Anthony. Also awkward, spotty, pudgy and overlooked by girls who'd liked his brother better. For the rest of the day, and the next day, the day of the ball, Cal drove around the estate. After seeing the shovel in the trunk of that car, he knew, in his gut, the women were dead. But he needed to find the truth. Find the bodies. It would hurt their families, but it was better than clinging to false hope for a lifetime.

But Worthington Park had thirty thousand acres of land. How would he find where the bodies were buried? There had to be places on all this land that were pretty isolated.

John and Anthony could be innocent. He had to consider that. Someone else from the estate could have taken the car out secretly.

Either way, both Anthony and John were dead and beyond the grip of the law. So, if he found out one of them had been a killer, what was he going to do?

Smoking a cigarette, Cal looked out over the valley and Lower Dale Farm. Sheep rambled and bleated. A cow mooed from the depths of the stone barn.

He would know that the Countess of Worthington had had a killer for a son.

He thought of that photograph and how sick the butler now looked. How nervy the countess was. He ground his cigarette under his boot heel and got back into the car. He drove back to Worthington and went down to the kitchens to see how Hannah was coping with preparations for a ball and elaborate dinner.

Cal was pleased to find she had everything under control. The girl glowed with excitement—this was her first major event and she was attacking it with all the fervor and drive of a titan of American industry. That was one good thing—he'd made a good decision to promote her.

The housekeeper, Mrs. Rumpole, caught him as he was heading for his study.

She looked like she'd sucked on a toad. "My lord, the countess always attends to the details of balls and dinners. She has always overseen the invitations, the menu, the hiring of musicians, the preparation of the house. But this time, you have done all things traditionally carried out by the countess."

"Yeah, I have."

"It is most unorthodox. Do you intend to do this in the future?"

"I don't know. Maybe I won't be around in the future. Maybe I will."

She looked at him as if he were crazy.

"Delegation and position are the hallmarks of a successful household," she declared. "It is my job to ensure you are not troubled with staff problems, with the myriad decisions involved in running a household."

Position. Hierarchy. Just like a big business. Just as Julia had said. Julia was right—making them afraid for their positions wasn't proving anything, except what a bastard he could be.

"In the future, I'd like this place to run smart," he said. "I'll talk to you about what the jobs are, how they're done. Maybe I need to learn."

Mrs. Rumpole's brows shot up in surprise. "Very good, my lord." She turned and left.

He kept walking and went into his study. There, through the window, he saw the strangest sight.

David was outside. Diana, her skirts blowing around her legs in the breeze, had wheeled out his chair and she was pointing at things. He'd thought Diana selfish, vain, and he knew she was having an affair with a married man. To him Diana had represented the thing he hated about the aristocracy—they had no damn morals but they were happy to throw stones through their glass windows. They were happy to condemn his mother, who had done desperate things to keep her sons from starving, when they did immoral things just for fun.

But once he knew she was pregnant, he couldn't stand making her feel scared.

David, he saw, was smiling as if he was being given a personal tour of heaven by an angel.

14

The Worthington Ball

Fast-paced jazz music poured out of Worthington Park. Lights glittered in the gardens as if they were filled with fireflies. Silver trays covered in glasses of champagne were whisked by footmen. Julia had never seen this many people for any ball at Worthington before. There were hundreds and hundreds. An orchestra played outside and people laughed and danced wildly on the lawns.

The rest of her family walked up the steps, Nigel escorting their grandmother. Julia hung back, gaping at the scene around her. Zoe had let the others go on ahead, too.

Zoe observed, "It's like a wild American party thrown by a crazy millionaire," Zoe observed.

But would Cal have gone to those? Those parties were for the rich. "Goodness, it's rather stunning, isn't it?" Julia asked. This would be the first time she had seen Cal for days. She'd had to stay away—she'd been carrying out a search. One she didn't want Cal to know about. She hadn't seen him since he'd told her to leave his family alone, then kissed her. She—she was trembling at the thought of seeing him again. Filled with anticipation, joy, fear. She looked to

Zoe. "Is this really what you do in America?"

Zoe laughed. "Julia, I must take you on a tour of America."

Her heart pattered, then she shook her head. "I can't. I have Ellen to protect and people who depend upon my help. My days are busy. I'd have no time to go to America. I have too much to do. So I'll have to enjoy it by proxy tonight."

"We can have your widows looked after while you're gone," Zoe said. "I remember what you said on the train. You want to travel. I'll take you to America. When this little one is born, I want Nicholas to see America, and if I go to America, it means my mother won't stay for months at Brideswell."

"I like your mother."

"But that's because you are just one step away from being saintly, Julia."

"I would like to go to America sometime," Julia said. But strangely, the thought of going rather filled her with panic. This is the life she knew. This was her place in the world. But going away would only be for a visit. Why suddenly feel afraid to even spread her wings a little?

"Julia, I'm still surprised you tried so hard to convince Alice Hayes to come," Zoe said softly. They stood together on the steps, the rest of the family waiting at the door for them.

Alice was who she had searched for. "I thought she would come, but she changed her mind at the last minute. I must thank Nigel again for having the family solicitors locate her so quickly. Cal's brother very much wants to see her again."

"But if Cal is in love with her—"

"I am sure the two men would be able to work this out between them. It's ridiculous that they both have to give up on love."

"No." Zoe looked at her curiously. "I mean most women don't search for their competition."

"Cal loves Alice Hayes. I could see it in his eyes as he looked at me. That longing. I'm sure of it. And if he marries and is happy, he'll be far more willing to settle at Worthington."

She spoke calmly, but felt a sudden twist of pain inside. Cal loved someone else . . . Now she understood why he'd said he wouldn't marry.

"Julia, you'd do that to save the estate?" Zoe frowned. "Is your sense of duty more important than love?"

"Cal and I are not in love with each other," she said firmly. "I'm not about to fall in love with anyone in a situation that would be obviously hopeless."

"I know you think a lady must have everything under control, Julia. Love doesn't work that way."

For one foolish moment, she thought of that little kiss, that sweet but snappy touch of Cal's lips to hers. She'd pulled back because of Alice. That was why he'd told her honestly he couldn't marry.

He loved Alice. She'd found Alice, but at the last moment Alice had changed her mind, had decided not to come. Julia simply wouldn't breathe a word about it to David so he wouldn't be hurt.

She followed Zoe into the house and gasped in shock. It was impossible to move. People danced everywhere: girls with bobbed hair and short dresses; men in the fashionable baggy trousers and slouching-style jackets.

Julia followed Zoe's example, thrusting aside ladylike behavior to shove through the crowd.

She managed to reach the ballroom just after Zoe. The terrace doors stood open, curtains fluttering in the summer breeze. Another band played jazz in here, with a stylish woman singing with a throaty voice. Her deep brown complexion looked stunning against a gold beaded dress.

Champagne flutes were snatched quickly from the salvers. Crowds filled the stairs, attempting to dance on the steps. A woman tumbled down, but in the crowd, she landed on a dozen other people and didn't hurt herself.

Julia had never seen Worthington like this. A vase fell with a crash. A man shouted, "Watch this," and then slid down the banister. He knocked over a dozen people on his way down.

Julia felt overwhelmed. It was as if an amusement park had been stuffed inside the house.

Where was Cal? With his brother? But she couldn't find either of them as she fought through the crowd. One man grabbed her arm and pulled her into a wild version of a foxtrot. Another grabbed her after him.

"I don't want to dance," she cried, getting free.

The dining room was filled with a buffet—poor Hannah must have worked her fingers to the bone to produce so much food. Even though Cal had hired more kitchen maids, it was still the young cook's duty to oversee everything.

Julia didn't approve of this. It was too wild, too flamboyant, too wrong.

Searching for Cal, she ran into the Duke of Bradstock. "Dance with me?" James shouted.

She shook her head. "No, thank you, James. I must find Cal."

"He's probably having an orgy in a bedroom," James said sourly.

Maybe James was right. But she remembered that look of longing. For all Cal's reputation, she believed he was a man who loved deeply.

It was hard to escape the crowd. She encountered a man in a drawing room, looking at the items on the mantelpiece. So much like the Klipspringer character in *The Great Gatsby*—Zoe had had a copy sent from New York as soon as it was published—Julia felt she had walked into a fictional world. She expected him to observe that the books on the shelves were real.

"Have you seen the host? The Earl of Worthington?"

"The Earl of Worthington?" He looked blankly at her. "He's here?"

Julia plunged onward. She heard a soft musical sound at the end of the hallway. Another band? This was the study. She knocked on the door and opened it.

Cal sat there, his feet propped on the desk. A gramophone played a soft tune, sounding tinny compared to the vibrant music roaring from the ballroom.

"Do you know it's a madhouse out there? I'm afraid they will tear the house apart—" She broke off. "Was that your plan? To hurt the countess by forcing her to watch a madding crowd destroy things?"

He shrugged. "This is the kind of party I like— a thousand strangers all having a good time."

"That's not an answer."

He swung his legs down, got out of his chair. To Julia's surprise, he came right up to her, then he put her hand on his shoulder, her other at his waist. He waltzed with her, in a tight circle in the middle of his study.

"Stop this. Some of the paintings and porcelain are *priceless*. Something should be done."

He kept twirling her. "I've told the staff to stop the booze at ten o'clock. That will get rid of most of the crowd. And it's just stuff. There are things that matter a hell of a lot more." He stopped dancing. "I like waltzing with you. I like holding you close and moving slowly with you, like we're both suspended in time."

That was how she felt with him.

"No woman has ever gotten under my skin like you. You make me mad, you make me lust, you make me get angry at myself, and you make even the gloomiest day feel like it's radiant and beautiful."

Cal turned her, his feet moving them gracefully across the old Aubusson carpet.

When she looked up into his eyes, she saw so much yearning it took her breath away. But he'd told her he couldn't love her—and she knew why. He'd told her he loved Alice, the woman he couldn't have and he must still love Alice. Perhaps he was dedicated to revenge because he thought he couldn't have love.

"I know you lost your mother and father, and I understand your anger, but is it truly making you happy to turn everything into a battle?" she asked softly. Even the missing women were a fight between them—a fight between her belief in Anthony and Cal's hatred of the family.

He let her go. Backed away. "Don't pity me. I prefer your contempt."

"That's ridiculous. And I don't pity you. I want you to heal. You must make a new life and be happy."

"Some things don't heal, Julia. And what's the point of struggling and fighting to survive if you don't put the things right that hurt you badly?" He took a step away from her. "I should go to my party. Play the host. And remember—don't pity me. I'd rather have you hate me."

Then he was gone.

Julia's heart trembled, like a large rose bloom on a slender stalk. "It's not pity," she said softly, because he couldn't hear. "It's love."

It was true. Zoe had known—Zoe had seen it. But Julia was like Cal with David . . . she only wanted his happiness. She had to remember he'd told her he loved Alice Hayes.

She hurried out, with no idea where to go or what to do, wanting to escape the raucous party. She spied David sitting in his wheeled chair along the wall, near an open door. He grinned at her. "When I said I wanted a ball, I didn't expect this. It's like Grand Central Terminal in here."

"Yes, but unfortunately nobody leaves," she muttered.

"Pardon me?" David shouted.

"David Carstairs? Is that you, David?" A rich and clear voice struggled to be heard over the crowd. Julia looked up at the same moment David did, and she heard him say, "Oh Lord. It's Alice."

Julia straightened. "She came after all."

The crowd had one of those moments where it parted, revealing the woman who stood there. A young woman who seemed to glow because her hair was pure gold, and her dress was a soft shade of pink that spoke of summer gardens. She was older than her midtwenties, beautiful with an oval face, high cheekbones, a small nose and large eyes.

David gulped. "God, I didn't really think . . . What's she going to think . . . ? What am I gonna do?"

Julia touched David's shoulder. "Don't worry. You are going to talk to her, that's what you are going to do."

Then Cal would, of course. Julia would probably love Cal forever—but he would be happy with Alice.

Cal looked out the window. Hanging lights gave the garden a surreal glow. He saw a rotating glint that caught his eye. It was David's wheeled chair, the wheel spokes reflecting the lights. Someone was pushing him. Someone with light blond hair.

Then he saw *her*.

He stalked out, confronting Julia who was walking back up the stone steps to the terrace. "That's Alice Hayes pushing David's chair."

"I know," Julia said softly. "I found her, wrote to her, and she came tonight to see David after all. I've offered to let her stay at Brideswell for a few days."

"You brought Alice here? I told you I didn't want that. You had no right."

"Your brother wished to see her, and in her letter answering mine, she expressed a strong desire to see him."

"Goddamn it," he snapped, "he's going to get hurt."

Julia flinched. But insisted, "She seems genuinely happy to see David."

"That doesn't mean she can find it in her heart to love a man who can't provide for her, who needs her protection rather than the other way around."

"But she came here, knowing that he did not have legs. That has to mean something, Cal. Perhaps you should give Alice more credit. Cal, you told me how much you love her. It's obvious why you are notorious for love affairs with models and such scandalous things. You believe you can't have the woman you love. But I think you would be happy if—"

"I don't want to be damn well happy. I want to protect my brother. Look at them," he snapped.

Alice and his brother were talking. David held Alice's hand, but she was shaking her head. He could read her sadness in the way her head was bowed, and he saw pain on his brother's face.

"I'm watching my brother get his heart broken. Why couldn't you have left it alone? Neither David nor I belong here. I'm not going to fight to belong in a world that doesn't want me. I'm not going to put my brother through it, either."

"But Alice—"

"I could never damn well have Alice. Not without telling her a bunch of lies. I want you to keep away, Julia. Keep away from David. Stay at Brideswell. I'll help the families on this estate from now on. Not you."

The pain on her face made him feel like crap. |But she'd pushed too hard. She wanted too much. She was never going to make him happy— she was the thing making him crazy.

"I won't stop doing that, Cal. Not for anyone."

"There's someone who can stop you. I'm going to tell your brother that Ellen's pimp almost attacked you, and that I'm forbidding you from dealing with my estate to keep you safe. He won't let you out of his sight."

She recoiled, white as meringue frosting. "How could you do that? This is so important to me—it is the only thing that I have."

And he knew this was his chance to push her away completely. To take the thing that mattered most away from her. Then she'd leave him the hell alone. Leave him to his revenge, and stop tempting him with what he couldn't have.

15

Attack on Julia

For days after the party, Julia's heart was in turmoil. She had wanted to give David Carstairs his chance to see his beloved Alice again. She had hoped to save Worthington by giving Cal the chance to be happy. How much of his anger was driven by having to walk away from the woman he loved for his brother's sake?

Finally, Cal had admitted to her he wouldn't "rat out" to her brother as he'd put it. But he was hurt, angry, protective as a bear. He'd cut off the liquor and shut down the party after that. David had coerced him to let Alice Hayes stay at Worthington. Would Cal surrender to love with Alice so close?

Ellen had been sent home from the hospital yesterday, having improved a great deal. She'd only just learned Cal had taken Ellen back to the cottage, and had taken Ben, too. Ellen's pimp was still at large and Ellen still refused to give his name. She had admitted the man had beaten her badly because she had refused to prostitute herself anymore.

What had happened to Ellen—and Cal's anger—made Julia question herself. Was she making things better for people—was she truly helping, or making things worse?

Now, carrying her umbrella—it had proved invaluable—she knocked on the door of Ellen's cottage, rather startled when a burly-looking man answered it. "Who are you?" she asked. This was not the man who she had confronted in the village about Ellen. This specimen stood even larger.

Off went his cap and he bowed. "Makepeace Jones, my lady," he answered. "Hired by his lordship to keep watch over Miss Lambert and her lad."

So Cal had thought of that. "I have food for Miss Lambert." She saw Ellen, and shared the special sticky buns between Ben and Makepeace. She did not launch into a plea for Ellen to give the name of her attacker. Instead she ensured Ellen was eating well, and she took a look at the bandages—Dougal had shown her how. It had been awkward dealing with Dougal. Julia could not forget how he had dismissed the possibility Ellen had shell shock. His stubborn acceptance of the prevailing *male* point of view had shocked her. And even now, she could see Ellen tremble. She had seen Nigel do that, even though he used to hide it well.

But when she left the cottage, at least she knew Ellen would be safe, with Makepeace to watch over her.

Julia walked back to her car. She'd had to leave it down the lane as there was an enormous muddy hole between her motorcar and Ellen's gate. After the hot night of the ball, the weather had been stormy. Many places had flooded, creeks had spilled over their banks, and it made for a wet, mucky trudge on the lane. At least the rain had stopped today.

Ahead of her sat her car, the cream-painted sides and chrome spattered with mud. She had to turn it around. But that put her at risk of getting stuck in the quagmire of mud in front of her car.

"I'm going to have to reverse," she murmured aloud.

She did, twisting around and moving slowly to ensure she didn't drive off the track and get stuck. Then, as she put her foot on the accelerator, a large figure jumped out from a laurel bush behind her. Julia slammed down on the brake. In her shock, she jerked the wheel and the car shot sideways, off the track. She lurched to a stop and had to swallow hard for her heart was in her throat.

"Are you all right?" she cried, her hand on the door handle.

Suddenly the man was at the side of her car. Her door was ripped open. He grabbed her wrist and jerked her toward him—fast enough to pull her right off the seat—and she went down on her knees on the muddy track. Stones bit into her knees. She cried out in pain.

Julia saw mud-encrusted, battered brown boots, then looked upward. His face—it was covered by a black mask from his hairline to his lips. "Who are you?" she demanded. "What are you doing?"

Was it Ellen's pimp? He towered over her as that man had done. He wore the same clothing as most laboring men of the village—checked cap, heavy brown coat, worn trousers.

Why was he wearing the mask?

So she couldn't bear witness against him? So no one else could?

Fear swamped her, running through her veins like ice water. She must fight. She thought of what Ellen had been through. She lashed out with her leg, trying to kick him.

The slap he gave her sent her head snapping to the side.

"Who are you?" she demanded again, trying to sound like the angry daughter of a duke and not a terrified woman, while her face throbbed with pain. "You would be a fool to hurt me. You will end up in prison."

Apparently he didn't fear her threat for he pulled her to her feet as if she had the weight of a pillow. He started down the lane away from her motor, dragging her with him. Without saying a word. She tried to dig in her heels, grabbed at branches. Desperately, she screamed, hoping sound would travel past the bushes to the cottage. He jerked her to him and slammed his gloved hand over her mouth.

She bit his hand and he pulled it away. "You let me go or you will suffer the consequences. My brother is a duke. Hurt me and he will see you—"

He put his hand back to silence her, cursing low under his breath. And he raised his other hand to hit her again.

She kicked at his legs and her shoe connected with his shin. He stumbled. In rage, his other hand shot forward and wrapped around her neck He was throttling her. All she could see was the triumph in his dark eyes in the eyeholes.

His fingers tightened and she tried in vain to pull them away from her throat.

Julia struggled. Her lungs oddly felt like exploding when nothing was going into them. Like the sound of a hundred mocking crows, his laughter filled her ear.

Wildly she swung her arm and tried to drive her finger into the eyehole on the right side. At the same moment she drove her knee up and hit as hard as she could into the front of his trousers.

She missed his eyes. He gave a grunt of pain, but it wasn't enough. It was like poking a bull with a sewing needle. She'd only provoked him.

He pulled out a knife. A horrible, wicked-looking dagger-type thing.

Was this what had happened to Sarah, Eileen, Gladys? It wasn't Anthony or John, but some brute who had surprised them and dragged them away? She had no weapon. She had nothing but her *social* position and that was hardly going to stop this man—

A large shape suddenly appeared behind the fiend and she cried out before she realized who it was. Her attacker jerked, started to turn, but before he could, Cal grabbed the knife out of the man's hand and pressed the blade to her assailant's neck.

"I would suggest you let Lady Julia go. Let her go gently and I won't be forced to draw this blade in a quick slice across your throat."

He said it in a ruthless tone that made even her blood run cold—and he was saving her.

Pressing the blade harder against the man's throat, Cal forced the man to release her. Then Cal gripped the man's muscular arm, twisted it, bent it behind the man's back. She was stunned at his strength and the way the simple maneuver immobilized the brute. Her attacker stood about the same height as Cal.

"What's your name?" Cal snapped. But he didn't say it quite like that—he spoke in a low, ruthless tone that made her shudder. And he threw in a very shocking, naughty word.

Then Cal's gaze met hers and he jerked. It was as if he'd forgotten she was there.

The man didn't answer.

Cal twisted the man's arm and the cry of pain made her wince. "Oh, don't—" she began.

"Julia, he was going to hurt you. Don't waste your good heart on this scum. We have to get him to the local jail," Cal said. "I'm going to get some rope to tie up his hands." To the man, he growled, "Get walking."

She followed. This all seemed so unreal. Cal shoved the brute along the lane back toward the cottage. Her neck was so tender. She touched it. Then the full miracle of her escape hit her. "You saved my life. If you hadn't come— But what are you doing here?"

"I was keeping an eye on you. I didn't like the idea of you going around alone after Ellen was attacked."

"You were protecting me. Even after you were so angry with me at the ball."

"I was mad, but I'd never forgive myself if anything happened to you."

Cal's prisoner made a grunting sound of disgust. Julia stumbled on the rough track in her heeled shoes. She regained her balance, but Cal turned to her. His attention was on her, not on her attacker. In that moment the man jerked around and he managed to pull the knife from Cal's grip. Snarling in rage, he slashed it at Cal.

"Look out!" she cried.

Off balance, Cal stumbled as he avoided the slicing arc. The man took off running. He left the lane and sprinted down a slope into a valley.

Cal ran after him, his tweed jacket open and flapping. He almost lost his balance on the ground. He threw himself forward and grabbed the man by the legs. They both went down, rolling over and over. They slapped into the stream, which was a bubbling rush of water after the rain. And the attacker had a knife.

Oh God. Julia couldn't breathe—her heart pounded in her throat. She had to run to the cottage and fetch Makepeace and a weapon of some kind.

But at that moment, Cal slammed his fist into the man's jaw, water spraying around him. She heard him shout. "That's for hurting Lady Julia."

He hit the man again and again. Violence had erupted in him. If the attacker still held the knife, he was given no chance to use it.

The man slammed his fist into the side of Cal's face. The knife must have been dropped when they fell. Huge, heavy, the man managed to shove Cal over and Cal landed with a splash. He kicked Cal with his heavy boots.

She shouted, "Help! Help us!" and she ran for the cottage. Alerted by her cries, tall, powerful Makepeace Jones was coming out of the cottage. "Have you got a weapon?" she cried. "A shotgun? A man is attacking Worthington!"

"I do!" Ellen cried. "I'll fetch it."

That took precious moments and Julia shouted for Ellen to stay with Ben. She dragged Jones up the lane. They reached the place where the man and Cal had run down, just as Cal was making his way back up, panting hard. His clothes and hair were soaked. Blood tinted the water that streamed down his face. "You're hurt," she gasped.

"Flesh wound," he said. "But the bastard got away. Damn—beg your pardon, Julia." Then he asked, "Who was he?"

"I don't know. With the mask, I have no idea."

"Are ye all right, milord?" Makepeace asked.

"Yes. I'm going to get you back to Brideswell, Julia, then do a sketch of the bas— The man," Cal said.

"But I didn't see him."

"It has to be the man who attacked Ellen and you've seen him before. He must have been waiting for you to come here, to get revenge. I'll take the sketch around the village. Someone has to know who he is. Maybe the sketch is what will make the difference and someone will finally be able to identify him. And you are not to come out alone again. Do you understand?"

Julia nodded. The insulation of shock was wearing off. She felt sick and cold. "I won't. I promise I won't."

"He's frightened you a hell of a lot."

She winced again at his harsh words. "He threatened to kill me."

"Hell, he tried to do it," Cal said. His voice was half growl, half thunder.

Ellen joined them, her face white.

"He didn't seem to care that such a thing was against the law," Julia said primly. "This might be the modern world where there are laws, rights and civilization, but there are still men who believe violence can get them what they want."

"That, sweetheart, is the brutal truth. And something I don't think you understood."

"I do now," she whispered.

"I'm sorry," Cal said. "I'm being too harsh."

"You're bleeding," she pointed out. "Are you all right?"

"No, I'm not all right, because for a damned moment there, I thought I was going to lose you. But I'm going to find him. I'm going to hunt him down."

"You absolutely cannot! It's too dangerous."

"Hunt down a goon like him? That isn't dangerous. I've done worse."

Ellen said suddenly, "No. I'll tell you who he is. I'll tell you, my lord. I don't want Lady Julia hurt again. I didn't mean to cause this. I'm so sorry."

Ellen hurried to Cal, whispered something, then Cal told Makepeace to take her back to the cottage, warning the man to keep the weapon on hand and to watch over Ellen and Ben.

With that, Cal carried Julia down the lane to his car. "What did Ellen tell you?"

"Precious little," he growled. "She only had his first name—Jack. Doesn't know his surname. She doesn't even know where he lives. Unless she's still lying—"

"I don't think she would now. Cal, what did you mean you've done worse? In war?"

Cal set her on her feet at his vehicle. "I'll get men from the local garage to get your car out, Julia." He didn't answer her question or say another word as he drove her to Brideswell. There, he carried her to the front door.

"Cal, I am fine. I am capable of walking."

His hand lingered at her waist as he set her on her feet. Then he took her inside and told Nigel and Zoe what had happened to her—even though she begged him not to.

"Not this time, Sheba," was all he said. And she knew—everything she loved to do would be over now.

Zoe put her arm around Julia's shoulders. Next thing Julia knew, she was in her dressing room and Sims had drawn a steaming bath for her.

The warm water was lovely—she hadn't realized her teeth were chattering until she sank into the steamy water in the deep tub. Plumbing was a marvelous thing. She was glad Zoe had insisted on it. But even the warmth didn't melt fear—she knew what was to come.

After she'd dried, put on fresh clothes, a knock sounded and Nigel called out, "May I talk to you, Julia?"

"Of course." She swallowed hard.

Her brother closed the door behind him. He was pale, his mouth tight with fear. He looked a dozen years older suddenly. "I'm so sorry," she whispered. "You look terrible, Nigel."

"I'm just thanking God you are all right." He bent and hugged her. And Nigel was not a demonstrative man. He was very much a cool, aloof Englishman. But he bent and kissed the top of her head.

Then it began, of course.

"Julia, I will not allow you to do this work anymore," he stated. "It's too dangerous. It is putting you in the path of dangerous, ruthless people."

Panic flared. "I'm twenty-seven. You can't forbid me."

"You live in my house and you are dependent on me. So that does give me the ability—and I believe the right—to tell you what you can do."

Her heart sank. "Nigel, I need to help these women."

"No, Julia. This has become too dangerous. You are not to continue. *That* is the final word on the matter."

She tried to make him see how important this was. It was who she was! The thing of value she could do in the world. But Nigel was unmoved.

All the rest of the day, Mother fussed over her. And urged her to consider marriage as a much safer and happier thing to do. Grandmama arrived and laid down the law with Nigel. Julia could hear them in the drawing room. "She is your sister—how could you condone this behavior? Rough laborers. Women of the night. You are to protect her until she is married!"

Julia hurried into the room to protest. "Nigel is not my jailer."

"No, he is your guardian. And you must obey him."

"Grandmama, this is 1925!"

"And a woman is still vulnerable and at risk, Julia."

It was true—she knew that so very well now—but it made her so thoroughly angry.

She'd frightened them all. It made her feel guilty, but she couldn't simply be packed away in a closet until she decided to marry.

By the next morning, Julia couldn't cope with being treated like an invalid for another moment. When her sister-in-law came to her room, she cried, "Zoe, I'm going to go mad. Nigel insists that I continue to rest. It has been a whole day. I am quite recovered. And nothing really terrible happened to me. Cal got there in time."

"He did. But it was still a frightening experience," Zoe said. "And you know Nigel—perhaps you've recovered, but he hasn't."

In her vanity mirror, Julia glimpsed her reflection. She had covered the bruises on her neck with foundation powder, but she could see them faintly. The imprint of the man's fingers. But what was worse was she was realizing what Nigel said was true. She lived under his roof. She was dependent on him. In that circumstance, she was expected to obey him.

"Dr. Campbell has come to see you," Zoe said.

"Dougal? Heavens, I'm not wounded, I assure you. Just bruised."

Zoe waved her hand. "Nigel didn't send for him. He came himself."

Sunlight spilled through the drawing room windows onto Dougal's auburn hair as he paced, making it glint like copper. She assumed he'd come in a professional capacity. The moment he saw her, he blushed and he hurried to her. He grasped her hands. She'd never seen him so . . . passionate. "Julia, I heard you were badly hurt. Of all people, I do understand your desire to help people, especially the less fortunate. You know, as I do, how those people can end up ignored. But, Julia, you must not do this any longer."

She blinked. "Dougal?"

"This woman consorted with dangerous men and brought you into danger. You say she has resisted your every attempt to help her. You must leave this alone."

"How can you say that? You save lives—you know how important this is. I can't just give up, Dougal. This is not like you," she said desperately. "I don't understand. And you certainly can't tell me what to do."

"I haven't done this well. I haven't expressed it properly. I mean to say, that I will help her, Julia.

I will study her condition, determine if she has shell shock and treat her."

"Thank you. What has changed your mind?"

To her surprise, Dougal dropped to one knee. "Julia, being here has made me realize I need you at my side."

He couldn't be . . . that was impossible. "But you are engaged—"

"It's not a formal engagement yet. I tried to throw myself into work, into research, but I can no longer focus, no longer think. All I can think of is you, Julia. I knew I couldn't have you, and I knew Margaret, as a doctor's daughter, would make me a good wife. I care very deeply for her. But being here, with you again . . . I was a damn fool to ever leave Brideswell. Julia, would you ever consider marrying me? I know I have no right to ask, but I knew, after I saw you in London, that I could not live without you."

"You would end your . . . not formal engagement?"

"How can I make Margaret happy when I am in love with you?"

In love with her. She had longed for this moment before—to find out Dougal loved her deeply and would surmount the obstacles for her, overcome the bridge of their class difference. But—

He was waiting for her answer, hope in his eyes. This man who fought to save lives every day had told her he needed her. "Julia, I know there is no other woman in the world for me but you."

She could be a doctor's wife, and have a family of her own. She would have purpose. She could do good things. But—

"Dougal, I can't. I admire you. I did love you very much. But I—I can't marry you now."

"Because of my engagement?"

"Because I fear I have fallen in love with someone else."

"Are you engaged?"

"No and I won't be, because he has no intention of marrying, and even if he did, I think he would marry someone else. I believed I wouldn't marry and I thought I had found my place—helping women like Ellen. Now, all the men in my life insist I can't do it. So I no longer have a purpose and I am supposed to . . . do nothing but wait for marriage. But I can't do that. Not anymore. And I can't make you happy if I'm not deeply in love with you. I want you to find happiness with your fiancée. If you believe you can't, you shouldn't marry her. Don't marry her to simply have a wife."

The pain on his face sliced to her heart. "Julia, are you certain?" he begged.

She could change her mind. She could embrace everything she'd always wanted . . . No, she could not. "I'm so sorry, Dougal. I hope I haven't hurt you."

"And I am sorry if I ever hurt you," he said gruffly. He bowed stiffly, then took his leave. From the doorway, she watched him walk away through Brideswell's salon, out through the front door, holding his hat in his hand.

She never dreamed Dougal would propose. Two years ago, she would have happily accepted. But that was before she'd met Cal.

She glanced up to find Bartlet, Brideswell's butler, standing in the doorway. "Mr. David Carstairs to see you, my lady. I have taken him to the south drawing room. The doors are open, the breeze is pleasant today and Mr. Carstairs should be able to maneuver in the room as it is more spacious."

"Thank you. That should be perfect."

She was tremendously worried about why David Carstairs had come—until she reached the drawing room and he smiled at her. He reached out. Warmed by the gesture, she went to him and clasped his hands.

"I had to come—forcing a lot of footmen to carry me downstairs and put me in my chair," he said, wearing that endearing, self-effacing smile. "I had to come and thank you. I heard Cal was angry with you at the ball. He was afraid I was going to be hurt when Alice told me she is in love with someone else. I'm actually happy. When you really love someone, you just want them to be happy."

Her heart stuttered. Was Cal the person Alice loved? "I was afraid I had meddled and hurt both you and Cal," she admitted.

"I know Cal told you not to do it. I'm really glad you didn't listen. It was good to see her again."

"But didn't it hurt?"

"Yeah, there was some pain. But that's how I know I'm alive—because I can still feel some pain in my heart. Cal was trying to spare me pain. But he's wrong. I can take it." He squeezed her hand gently. "I know you understand. You survived losing your fiancé."

"I managed to get through it. *Survived* is probably too generous a word."

"I told Cal he has to apologize to you, Julia. For his outburst. When he returns, he will come and tell you."

"Returns? Where is he?"

"He's found the man who beat up Miss Lambert. I guess that's the same man who attacked you."

16

Fight at the Sawmill

"Who is this man?" Julia gasped.

"A gypsy woman named Genevra came to the house," David explained. "Wiggins tried to tell her to run off, but Cal saw her and insisted she come in. She read my palm, told me I had a long life line, and that I would find great love. Then she talked to Cal and he took off in his automobile. I thought he should go to the police, but he said he wanted to take care of things himself."

David looked satisfied about that, not in the least worried. And she was pleased Genevra had read such a wonderful future for David, but her heart slammed against her chest. What had Cal been thinking? What did he plan to do? "Where did he go?"

At her frantic tone, David's blue eyes stared at her in shock. "Genevra told him that the man he was looking for works for the Worthington sawmill. She told him to beware, but Cal thought that was funny. I didn't know the estate owned a sawmill."

"The estate owns everything upon it," she said distractedly. Cal was going to confront that brute of a man. She stood abruptly. "I must go to the

354

police station in the village, to tell them where Cal has gone. They can arrest him."

David touched her arm. "Cal doesn't want the police involved."

"Cal will have to have the police involved." She couldn't imagine why he would not. That simply made no sense. "I must go." Her heartbeat, hard and frantic, filled her head. "It's impolite, but I must leave you here. I'll tell Zoe—the duchess—she'll look after you."

"Lady Julia, wait!"

She hesitated at the door.

"Cal can take care of himself," David promised.

"That's what I fear."

Leaving the house caused a flurry of panic. Zoe agreed to stay with David, to play hostess after Julia was racing off rudely, but Nigel stepped in front of her and refused to let her go. "He'll be killed because of me if I do nothing." Or worse, he would kill. And then what? Cal might think earls were above the law but they really weren't. His American belief that titled men could do whatever they wanted might get him in terrible trouble.

Nigel tried to take charge. "I'll take care of this, Julia. You stay—"

"No! We must get the police constable. You can do that, and I shall try to stop Cal." She raced out through the front door, not caring about a coat, or gloves.

Nigel took the front steps in one leap, which

gave him the advantage and he caught her. "I don't want you going anywhere alone, Julia."

He insisted they go together to the police. She was about to go mad but Nigel drove faster than she'd ever seen him. He drove rather like Zoe for once—like a race car driver. At the tiny stone building used as the police station, complete with small cells in the basement, he pulled ducal privilege when the police sergeant refused to see why he should rush to the sawmill. If a duke demanded the sergeant go, the man was not going to refuse, and the balding, craggy-faced sergeant traveled with them in the Daimler. The constable followed on his bicycle.

Dust and a smoky, sweet smell filled the air as Nigel raced down the lane to the large stone building used as the Worthington sawmill. Lumber was stacked all around and carts stood, carrying logs. The air was filled with the screech of saws.

Julia had the door open before the motor stopped and Nigel stomped on the brake, halting them with a lurch.

Men milled about, forming a circular crowd, catcalling and shouting, and she knew at once Cal must be in the middle of it.

"Julia, wait," Nigel called, but she tried to push her way between two of the men—bulky, barrel-chested specimens with bulging biceps, who smelled of sweat. One lifted his huge arm, yelling something, and she was almost knocked back, but she ducked in time.

Her slender size was an advantage—she slipped between the men, stopping on the inside of the rough circle. Ellen's pimp stood there, his pock-marked face red with fury, his fists doubled up. His cap was gone, revealing thinning brown hair, and his biceps strained at his sleeves. He was even bigger than she remembered.

Then she saw Cal. Blood ran down from his temple. Sweat soaked his hair to amber. The pimp lunged and threw his fists with intense speed. Cal ducked the blow to his head but took a punch in the gut that made her want to be sick. The brute was fast and powerful. Cal landed blows, but the pimp's fists were hard, as huge rocks, and were damaging Cal in a horrible way.

But Cal bounced lightly on his feet, seeming able to take the horrifying punishment. Truly, he should be unconscious.

Ellen's pimp—the men were shouting, calling him "Lowry"—grinned. The smug grin of confidence. He lunged again, ready to fell Cal.

Fists flew, but they were Cal's fists. Cal moved so fast, she could barely tell what was happening. She was almost swaying from lack of breath, from her heart forgetting to beat, when Cal slammed his fist into the man's gut, and as the fiend doubled over, Cal's blow to his jaw sent him sprawling.

Cal towered over the fallen man. His mouth

357

twisted into a snarl. His eyes blazed. Pure rage flashed across his face—the heat and rage seemed to glow from him, so hot and different than the cool, controlled anger she'd seen before.

She remembered how he said he'd done far worse than fighting a goon like this man. She could believe it. He looked . . . lethal.

Cal lunged down and clamped his hand around the man's throat. For all the man had a huge neck, Cal's powerful hand spanned it. "I've broken men's necks before. Hand to hand. In battle."

Lowry blubbered. He was pleading for his life. This vicious man who hadn't listened to any of Ellen's pleas or screams . . .

"No! Stop!" She hurried forward, into the center of the circle on the muddy ground, aware of murmurs halting, men staring.

"Break this up now. Move out," commanded the police sergeant. He pushed the men aside with aplomb.

"This man, Jack Lowry, attacked Ellen Lambert in her cottage and almost beat her to death. He also assaulted Lady Julia Hazleton," Cal declared.

"It was an attempt at an assault," Julia said to the sergeant, "thwarted by the earl. But this man has been abusing Miss Lambert. He's stolen money from her, forced her into prostitution."

The sergeant's eyes bulged in shock as she declared that. Lowry snarled, "I didn't force her into nothin'."

"You did, and you took money from her. Then you almost beat her to death," Julia cried, glaring down at the fallen brute. She realized she'd drawn back her shoe. She wanted to kick him, and she had to stop herself.

The constable, a young, strong lad, came up, puffing. Between the constable and sergeant, they got Lowry to his feet. "I'm innocent," he growled. "Never touched 'er ladyship."

"You assaulted her outside Ellen Lambert's cottage and tried to drag her away with you. What was your damned intent?" Cal stalked up, glaring down at the man, even though Lowry was two inches taller.

"What're you talking about? You're trying to pin somethin' on me. I never touched her."

"You touched her outside the Boar and Castle in the village," Cal barked. "Then, because Lady Julia stood up to you, you went after her again."

"I talked to her at the village, but she came up to me. I never saw her near the cottage. That's a lie. I swear."

"There are other women missing from this estate," Cal said. "Maybe you know something about that."

Lowry stared with panic.

The sergeant pulled Lowry's thick arms behind his back and snapped on metal shackles with a swift, careful motion. "You're coming back to the station. You're going to be charged with assault, Lowry, likely attempted murder."

"You can take him in my car," Cal said.

As they hauled Lowry away, she stepped toward Cal. There was blood all over his face, but he held up his hand. "Listen up," he shouted to the workers. "I want you to see I don't allow this kind of behavior. No one working for me beats up a woman, hurts his wife, hits his kids. No one bullies or hits anyone weaker than he. You want to work off some anger, we'll set up a ring and you can do it with some boxing. As for the conditions in that mill—things are going to be changing around here. Starting with the fact I need a new foreman. I'd appreciate applications dropped off with— Who's in charge of keeping the accounts here?"

The smallest man, a slim one in an old suit, lifted his hand. "Stevens, my lord."

"Give them to Stevens."

"There are good men who cannot write," Stevens pointed out.

"Hell," said Cal. "Then you take down the information about who they are and what qualities they've got for the job. Can you take charge for today, step in for Lowry?"

"Yes, my lord."

"Now go back to work, all of you. Stevens is acting as foreman until I hire a new one."

The men began moving back to the mill, all murmuring, realizing any of them could apply to be foreman. From the lighter expressions she saw on faces, she had no doubt Lowry bullied men here, too. Pleased, she fished out a handkerchief and briskly went to Cal. "We must clean you up. Thank you—thank you for capturing the man who hurt Ellen. But still, you shouldn't have put yourself in such danger."

"Julia, you shouldn't have come forward. You could have gotten hurt," Cal said.

"I was afraid—" She broke off. How did she politely say what she'd feared?

Cal's expression darkened. "I saw it in your face. You thought I would kill him. You thought the wild, violent American would murder a man in cold blood."

"I've never seen you angry like that."

"I thought you've always seen me angry."

"Not like *that*. That was hot and wild and for a moment, I thought it was out of your control. All the other times, your anger has been cold and obviously controlled. I don't understand why you were fighting. You should have telephoned the police. You are the earl. You had no need—"

"This isn't entirely for Ellen Lambert. Lowry, as foreman of this mill, was cutting corners on safety, endangering men. When I told him things would be run differently, he thought he could scare me with the threat of physical violence. I gave him the chance to show me what he could do."

Cal tried to make his blue eyes look guileless, but he failed.

"So you let him beat you up, then you took control and pounded him into the ground—" She broke off. She saw respect in the eyes of the other men round, and they were all large, muscled specimens. They all respected Cal, the Earl of Worthington. He wasn't a weak man given power by the accident of birth. He was a man who believed in their rights and safety, and who could fight as rough as any of them. He had shown them he was an honorable man and a tough one.

"I'm going to clean this place up," Cal said. "Improve conditions. Then I guess I'd better take a look at the other industries on this estate— Stop smiling, Julia. This doesn't mean anything."

But it did.

"But if Lowry was the foreman of the mill," Julia mused, "why did no one identify him?"

"I guess he hasn't lived here long. Came from Yorkshire originally. Most people were afraid to get on his bad side."

"And you have stopped his reign of terror."

He grinned at her, one of those slow grins that made her ache, and melt, and yearn.

Nigel came forward. She realized he had been unable to get through the crowd and stop her, and she'd never seen him look so worried over her. "Don't do that again," he said, as he escorted her back to their car.

"I had to ensure Cal didn't hurt that man badly," she said softly, trying to recover from—and hide—the devastating desire Cal's smile had evoked. "I had to ensure there could be no charges against him. We must take Cal back with us."

Nigel frowned, then nodded. The three of them traveled back to Worthington Park.

"How did you know I was there?" Cal asked.

"David told me. He told me Genevra had looked at the sketch, told you the man worked at the sawmill." She shivered as she thought of Lowry fighting Cal. Lowry might have hit her like that, if Cal had not rescued her.

Her stomach felt rather strange. Oddly weightless and funny.

"I asked Genevra if she thought he was responsible for the other girls' disappearances," Cal said.

He had done that. He had looked into a different possibility than Anthony.

"Disappearances?" Nigel asked, at the wheel.

Cal explained. But he did not tell Nigel what they had found in the car, what he suspected.

"Genevra pointed out the women must have been laid to rest somewhere or else they would have been found. I've been searching the estate. Driving around where the women were likely taken from. Now I'm expanding the search."

"I could—" Julia began.

"No." Both men said it at once.

"Genevra suggested I ask you," Cal said. "She said there is no one who knows Worthington Park as well as you. I told her no. I'm not putting you through that."

"I want to help. And both of you cannot dictate to me." Her head did feel oddly dizzy. It must be from seeing the force and violence in that fight and fearing Cal might lose control.

"Genevra said that Lady Worthington is suffering, just as the curse decreed. But this has nothing to do with a curse. This is human evil. And for that reason, I'm not asking you to help, Julia. I asked Genevra why she thought it stopped. She told me a hunter might search for prey farther away. Or he might have a reason to stop. She told me to look farther away to see if any girls with black hair and blue eyes had disappeared. Genevra has more brains than the police sergeant—"

"Those women look like you, Julia," Nigel said suddenly. His hands gripped the wheel. His face went white. "And you were attacked outside Ellen Lambert's cottage. Julia, you will have to stop your work. You cannot be putting yourself in danger."

"But that must have been Lowry and he has been arrested."

"No, Julia, I'm putting my foot down," Nigel said, in his ducal tones. "You are to stay close to home."

"No—" she began.

"You are under my roof and this time you will listen to me."

She knew he was scared, but he was going

beyond unreasonable. "But there is no danger now." Even as she said that, she had to admit, she didn't feel completely sure. There was something wrong. She remembered her attacker gripping her throat. He'd been so strong—

But had he really been that big? She struggled to remember. Thought of the horror. Thought of how Cal had been covered in blood and now in cuts and bruises. She had thought the attacker was the same height as Cal, but that was when Cal had his arm captured behind his back. Could that have made him seem shorter?

Her attacker hadn't spoken. He had dragged her, struck her in terrifying, creepy silence. If he had spoken she would have known for certain if Lowry had been that man. Still, she wasn't going to point out that her memory of her attacker didn't quite match Lowry. Instead, she protested, "You can't forbid me from doing the one thing I can do." But they'd arrived at Worthington.

Cal got out. Julia wanted to move to the front seat to argue with Nigel all the way back to Brideswell. But as she stepped out of the car, her legs seemed to disappear and the ground rushed up toward her.

She opened her eyes to a darkened room, the flutter of pale ivory drapes and a gentle breeze that eased the too-hot feeling of the air.

"Are you all right? I've never seen you faint,

Julia. Not even when— I mean, you have always been so remarkably strong."

Julia recognized Diana's voice. Wearing a loose dress with many layers of tulle, Diana sat down on the edge of the settee Julia lay on. She also recognized the pale pink decor—this was the most feminine drawing room at Worthington.

Julia sat up. "What happened? Did I really faint?"

"You did. Cal fears it was his fault, because you saw him fight. He fears you have been through so much. Both he and your brother feel you need rest."

"Oh no. That means I'll be essentially locked up at Brideswell. They'll never let me out."

"Between men and mothers, we women never get to have any lives at all." Diana smiled, but then Julia saw there was sadness in Diana's eyes.

"What's wrong?" she asked. "It's not something with— I mean, all is all right, isn't it?"

Diana let out a deep sigh. "I really shouldn't trouble you now—"

"Diana, you can tell me. I'm not a piece of porcelain. I imagine it was just the heat that felled me. The sun was scorching and of course there were no shade trees around the sawmill. So tell me!"

"I've made my decision. I've realized I can't keep my baby. I have been thinking of how much Ellen Lambert has suffered. It would be condemning the baby and me to hardship. I don't think I'm that strong."

"Diana, you are strong."

"Julia, don't lie. I am too used to being an earl's daughter, one with position, privilege and very few real cares in the world. Even if Cal sells Worthington, the one thing protected is my dowry. I could marry."

"Cal promised to help you."

"He can't help me if everyone is judging me for being a fallen woman."

Which was wrong. So wrong. Julia was getting more and more fed up with societal rules. "There must be a way."

"This is the best way. And I'd probably make a wretched mother. Too selfish." Diana tried to smile.

Julia didn't believe Diana was. She had changed—she was more thoughtful, less wild. But to protest that Diana would make a good mother would make this hurt more.

"This week I'll leave for Switzerland," Diana declared. "I didn't think I would show yet, but in the past few days, I've suddenly developed a little bulge. Cal will take me to Paris. He knows a widow there that he wants to hire as my companion in Switzerland. She's Parisian but speaks excellent English. She's titled and respectable, but in need of money. He'll turn me over to her. We'll claim she's a distant relative of his, so it makes it look like I'm just traveling to Switzerland to see the sights. I'm sure there will be gossip but no one will be able to prove any-thing. So after it's all over, I can marry." She sighed. "I wish I'd have a friend with me, not a stranger."

"I could go with you."

It came out impulsively. But Julia saw she could go. She was forbidden from working with her widows. What she could do was go away, give Nigel instructions on all the work to be done for the women—and he would have to do it since he was pigheadedly stopping her. By the time she returned, Nigel would beg her to take over. And by then, surely he would see sense about the risk of danger. She would also be able to see Sebastian in Paris.

"Will you come? Are you certain?" Diana bit her lip. "I would so love to have you with me. It's going to be hard, when I have to give my child away," she whispered.

"I'll be there," Julia promised, "to support you."

"You are the very best friend in the world, Julia."

Julia stood. "I should go back to Brideswell. I have to prepare for going away."

"Pack?"

"Well, that. But I must send a telegram to Sebastian in Paris, telling him I'm coming. Then I have to write a very large list of instructions for my other brother."

Diana looked mystified, but stood and hugged

her. Diana then went to fetch Nigel. Julia went to the terrace and looked out over the lawns. Soon she would see Paris, a lifelong dream—

"We could marry now."

Julia started. She heard the voice from around the corner of the house. It sounded like Alice Hayes.

"I know why you broke it off all those years ago. I did marry after the War, but my husband had wounds—he died of them."

"I'm sorry, Alice."

Cal's voice. When Alice had told David she loved someone else . . . she must have meant Cal. Cal said huskily, "I can't marry you, Alice. Even if David had never been in love with you, I couldn't do it."

"Because you are an earl now?"

"No. You think I'm turning you down because of social position? God, no. I don't deserve a woman like you, Alice. Being an earl doesn't change who I was. What I was."

A lady would not listen in. A lady— Oh, forget being a lady. Her heart ached. Of course she could never have him, but she hated to know how much this must hurt him.

Alice said, "I know how you grew up in New York—"

"No, you don't. David would never tell you the full story."

"It doesn't matter. I've always loved you, Cal Brody."

369

"My name is actually Carstairs. I loved you, too, Alice. I'm sorry to hurt you."

"I do think your brother would accept your marriage. David is a good man. And I would be happy to help take care of him."

"There can't be anything between us, Alice. I'm not planning to marry anyone. I'm going back to Paris. I could turn this place over to David. He'd make a better earl than me."

Julia's heart plunged. It thrilled her to think Worthington Park wouldn't be destroyed, but she realized how little that mattered, if Cal never healed, never found happiness.

"Cal, I think you will be a smashing earl," Alice said. "It was so good to see you again. I don't regret coming. And I wanted to see David. But I guess this is goodbye."

"My lady?" Wiggins stood in the terrace doorway and Julia almost leaped out of her shoes with guilt. "His Grace is out on the drive with the motor."

"Th-thank you." She hurried out. No doubt Wiggins knew she'd listened in, and there was no way she could gracefully explain that.

All the way home, she bit her lip and fought tears. Cal had been in love. Cal, who deserved love more than anyone, could not have the person he adored. Because he loved his brother so much.

And he might leave Worthington forever.

She arrived at Brideswell to find her maid, Sims, standing in the foyer, with a carpetbag beside her. Zoe was there, holding Nicholas. "Sims has found a new position with Grandmama. Apparently, Grandmama's maid has left her and—well, you know the dowager. She wanted someone at once."

"I can work my notice, my lady, if that's what you want."

"Oh, Sims, that is fine," Julia said. "I can brush my own hair, and I don't need anyone putting me in a corset anymore. I wish you the best of luck with Her Grace. This will be a great step up for you and I am happy."

"Are you certain you will be all right without a lady's maid?" Zoe asked. "I can have my maid help you and Isobel as needed."

Julia watched Sims get into the Daimler and drive away. "I'm going to Paris, Zoe. And I intend to pack my own trunk."

"Paris?"

Julia hastily explained as they walked back to the drawing room, the one used in the late afternoon.

"I will help Nigel with the widows," Zoe said. "I think it's a rather good idea to let him take charge for a while. You've dreamed of seeing Paris—you should see it. It will be a wonderful adventure."

"Yes. It's been my lifelong dream. Perhaps I'll find my heart's desire there. I'll stay in Paris with Sebastian and become an artist."

"Why not?" said Zoe. "It's time you did something just for you—to make you happy."

17

Paris

Paris had been the first big city outside of New York that Cal had ever seen, when he'd arrived there in 1917. It had been wild in the War. When you could die any day, you fit in a lot of living.

In Paris, he drank a lot of red wine. He gambled. He seduced a few bold French girls. They liked the Americans—their money, the treats they brought, their bravado and their bold, cocksure attitude.

Cal had gone back to Paris after the War, after he made money bootlegging and in other . . . illegal enterprises. Paris always made him feel like he could be something more. Made him forget what he'd done. When he argued about art in the cafés, he felt like he was more than a rough kid from the slums.

He wanted to show Paris to Julia—Julia who had never traveled but always dreamed of it. Maybe he wanted to do it so badly because it was a gift he could give her before he left.

Once he'd started talking about changes for the sawmill he'd seen the hope in Julia's eyes. She thought she'd won. And for a moment, she almost had. When he was talking to Alice, he'd got a crazy idea. He'd looked out over the green lawns of Worthington and he'd thought about getting married, having a family, staying there. Julia had almost made him forget the promise he'd made to Mam.

He would take care of Diana—he would never turn his back on an innocent child. And he would lay Paris at Julia's feet.

From Brideswell's station, he traveled with Julia, Diana and David by train to London's Victoria Station. They took a ferry to cross the Channel to Calais, and were now on a train steaming across the French countryside to Paris.

Cal knew Julia was worried about her brother Sebastian. Something about a telegram she'd received just before she left Brideswell—days after she'd telegrammed her brother to let him know she was coming. But when Cal asked what was wrong, she told him she didn't know. He could tell she was hiding something. Why?

Right now, the troubled look had left her eyes. She glowed with excitement. The train to Paris clacked along the tracks. Following Julia's gaze, Cal looked out at the blur of scenery. It was strange to see leaves on the trees and fertile fields following the tracks. He remembered blackened trees, bombed villages, fields that were wet, muddy mires. Or frozen with ice.

"Are you remembering the War?" Julia asked gently. She sat across from him.

He glanced up. "How did you know?"

Her hand brushed his wrist. He forgot all his memories and got hard at once. The more he was with her, the less of her touch it took to arouse him. But he knew he couldn't have her.

"I can see it in your face."

He'd been a flyer. There was no need to tell her what it had felt like to look at the charred remains of men pulled from wrecked planes—fuel consumed those bits of wood, paint, cable and fabric and burned the men down into wizened statues of charcoal.

She touched his knee as if soothing him.

But her light touch was like a jolt of lightning.

"Are the memories troubling?" she asked.

He met her large, concerned blue eyes, and—and hell, he wanted to be alone with her. He wanted to lay her back on the velvet first-class seat and make her scream with ecstasy. He wanted to be thinking about nothing but pleasuring Julia.

"They do trouble you, don't they?"

"They aren't sunshine and roses, but I don't have shell shock, Julia. I'm fine." He sounded abrupt, fighting to hide the raw need coursing through him. Anyway, war memories weren't the ones that haunted him. It was the memories of what he'd done before that.

"I learned you are hiring a special doctor to come from London to heal Ellen's shell shock. Dougal told me, before we left. Thank you." She smiled.

And he knew that was why he'd done it. Not just for Ellen, but to see Julia glow. "You're welcome. Tell me, what's the first thing you're going to do when you reach Paris?"

"I'd like to go to a dressmaker," Diana said. Then bit her lip. "If I have a clothing allowance."

"You do. Get the bills sent to me," Cal said. "What about you, Julia? Are you going straight to the House of Worth and Coco Chanel's establishment?"

She looked surprised he would know fashion designers. Then an adorable frown puckered her brow. One day he would paint her like that. He loved her expressions when she forgot the rules about ladies hiding emotion and let the real woman peek out.

Hell, he wasn't going to paint her. He should leave before that.

"I should like to see the Eiffel Tower. But I would love to visit a café. Or go to one of the clubs. Seeing Josephine Baker perform would be thrilling. I would also love to see the Left Bank and see where you would paint." Words bubbled out of her, like she was made of champagne. "Paris is filled with painters, writers, dancers, musicians. I'm so excited to see that world. Since I'm going to give up on marriage, perhaps I could become an artist or novelist. Though I fear that artistic talent begins and ends with my brother."

"You'll never know unless you try. I never

thought I could really paint until I came to Paris," he admitted. But her words had hit him hard. She was giving up on marriage.

This was Paris, where he'd reveled in a bohemian artist's life. He'd get drunk and engage in wild sexual activity—love affairs with married women, multiple partners in one bed. But he didn't want that now.

He wanted Julia.

When he desired a woman, he would paint her, make love to her, and once the painting was finished, his ardor was spent. He always chose experienced women who wanted no more of him than a wild affair.

Damn it, he couldn't have Julia.

Alice had told him she was in love with him and he'd pictured marriage. But it had been Julia's laughter he'd heard in his imagination. Julia playing with their children on the Worthington lawn. It was a fantasy he would never have—not with his past. He couldn't marry a lady like Julia without lying to her about his past, or keeping it hidden. And he couldn't seduce her.

The train chuffed into the station. "I'm here. I'm finally here," Julia breathed, and her delight almost broke his heart.

Cal summoned a cab. The car made its way through the ancient streets and took them to their hotel—the Hotel Le Meurice. Julia's sister-in-law, Zoe, had suggested it. Old and beautiful, it had majestic rooms. The largest suite had a terrace that gave a complete circular view of Paris.

He hadn't wanted to spoil Julia's chance to stay in Paris's most beautiful hotel, or his brother's chance to savor the luxury and the views. So Cal had agreed. It had been a long time since he'd been at Le Meurice and he figured no one would remember him.

"Do you like it?" he asked Julia as they drew up in front of the classic stone facade, the archways decorated with ivy, and the French flags snapping in the wind.

"It's beautiful."

Then he saw the surprise in Julia's eyes as the doorman's face lit up in recognition.

He was wrong. They remembered him.

Julia received a message from the concierge, left by Sebastian, to meet her brother at a Parisian café at two o'clock that day. Just before they moved from the desk, Julia heard the concierge say to Cal, "So delightful to have you with us again, Monsieur—Monsieur Le Comte."

She turned to Cal to ask him about it, but he put his hand on her lower back and led her through the lobby.

Her heels clicked on tiles polished to a mirror finish. Cal was recognized here and the Hotel Le Meurice was one of the most fashionable hotels in Paris. The cream of Parisian society dined at the beautiful Roof Garden. Picasso and his wife had selected the hotel to host their wedding dinner.

"You've stayed here before," she said as he took her to the lift. She spoke casually, but she *ached* with curiosity about his past.

Cal shrugged. "When I sold a few paintings I brought a model here to celebrate. We dined on the rooftop. That's how I know the hotel. And that's where I would like to have dinner tonight. All four of us. Surrounded by the lights of Paris."

But the staff wouldn't remember him from that. No, he had been important to them. But a lady couldn't pry. "It sounds lovely."

"It is. And I want to see you, silhouetted by Paris."

Her heart pattered. But Cal loved Alice Hayes— and she wanted him to find happiness with Alice. She had no right to be dazzled by the idea of dining with him with the lights of Paris spread around them.

Cal helped David roll his chair into the lift, while a porter brought the luggage and trunks. She and Diana followed and when she stepped into the suite she was sharing with Diana, Julia ran across the thick carpet, pulled open the glass doors and stepped out onto the balcony.

Paris spread out around her, trees rich with foliage, the streets in the complex circular pattern of an ancient city. The Eiffel Tower rose against the sky. Boat and traffic horns blared, and out there, all around her, adventure waited.

Behind her, Diana laughed. "Julia, I've never seen you like this. Bouncing like a child."

Julia spun. "I'm being thoughtless. This isn't such a happy time for you."

"No, I don't think I shall enjoy the wildness of Paris this time," Diana said ruefully. "But I should be relieved—that's a good enough substitute for happy, isn't it? And at least my mother never found out I'm pregnant."

Julia knew relieved wasn't as good as happy, but someone rapped on their door and she went to answer it. Cal lounged there, looking gorgeous in a summer-weight suit of pale gray. It made his hair look utterly gold. "I'll escort you to meet your brother," he said. "Since I know my way around."

She hesitated. Sebastian had warned her something devastating had happened. He could be awfully dramatic, but his terse words in the telegram made her realize this was the truth. Sebastian had secrets he wouldn't want a stranger—Cal—to know. "I don't know—"

"I'll leave you to meet him alone. But I don't want you getting lost in Paris."

She agreed and Diana offered to stay with David. As they exited the hotel, Cal commanded a car—a gleaming blue four-seater Citroën. The driver wound his way through streets crowded with cars, motorized streetcars and horse carts. Everything was thrilling to see.

Cal smiled at her excitement. Then he pointed

out the window. "Here's the café from your brother's message."

Heavenly yeasty scents of bread wrapped around Julia, along with another rich scent of coffee roasting. Small tables sat on a cobblestone terrace. Across the road from them, a railing followed the Seine, and beyond the railing the water rippled.

Julia looked in the café. Inside sat old men and young women with lipsticked mouths. But no Sebastian. "He's not yet here. I am early, of course."

"Have some coffee. I'll sit with you and leave when he comes." Cal pulled out a seat for her.

A waiter wearing a long white apron came to them and took orders. Her café au lait arrived in an enormous bowl-like cup. Frothy milk defied gravity to sit upon her cup, already melting away into the hot drink. She cradled the cup and sipped.

She was here. In Paris with Cal. Except there could be no romance in it. She had to make him see he should be with Alice. "Cal, you should bring someone special to Paris," she began.

He set down his coffee. Slowly, gently, he drawled, "Sheba, I already have—"

"Julia!"

She looked up and saw golden hair beneath a white hat—brilliant and gleaming in the sunlight. "Sebastian!"

Her brother looked utterly stylish in a white boater, white trousers and a white jacket over a shirt of pale pink and a tie of the same color. As

380

she stood, he embraced her, kissing her cheek. "Julia, my angel. My savior. My dearest one."

She lifted her brow. "I know you too well. When you slather on compliments like marmalade on toast, you are up to something." For example, there was his engagement to Zoe, when he needed a marriage and had tried to make Zoe believe he loved her. But then Julia saw the shadows under her brother's eyes and knew he was truly troubled.

Sebastian looked toward Cal, then leaned close to her ear. "This one looks wilder and more interesting than Dr. Campbell."

"Behave," she whispered.

"If that is what you wish, then behaving is all that I will do, my dear."

"This is the Earl of Worthington." She inclined her head toward her brother. "My brother, Lord Sebastian Hazelton."

Cal held out his hand. Sebastian took it and they shook hands as Cal said, "Call me Cal. I don't believe in titles. I'm an American."

Sebastian cocked his handsome head. "I recognize you. I think I've met you before. At Bricktop's place. Don't think we had a formal introduction." And under his breath, to her, "More intriguing all the time."

"Cal lived in Paris to paint," Julia explained.

Sebastian murmured by her ear, "A wild, artistic American. Have you brought him here—" He broke off. He coughed. "Wait. You are my sister. No love affairs for you."

"Sebastian," she whispered fiercely. Of course she couldn't have a love affair with Cal. But deep inside, she felt an astonishing pang of regret.

And despite Sebastian's lightheartedness, his eyes bore sadness.

Cal stood. "I should leave the two of you to speak of your private business. I think I'll go to my favorite bookstore. Shakespeare and Company. A gathering spot of Americans in Paris. When should I return for you, Julia?"

"I know the store. I'll bring her to you," Sebastian said.

As soon as they were alone, she asked, "What is wrong, Sebastian?"

Coffee arrived for Sebastian—the waiter didn't even have to ask his order. Sebastian took it with thanks. He swirled it. "Just seeing you, having you here, is a blessing for me, beloved sister."

"You look so thin and pale, Sebastian. I am terribly worried about you."

She had always admired Sebastian's courage. He had fallen in love with a handsome young man, Captain Ransome. It was still forbidden in England. She knew of the trial of Oscar Wilde. She knew Sebastian could be arrested and imprisoned. Yet she knew Sebastian was a good man who was only seeking love. He truly cared for John Ransome. And to be together, both men had left England to live in Capri, and now in Paris.

"John left me," he said bluntly.

Her heart broke at the pain on her brother's handsome face. He looked a lot like Nigel except his hair was gold and his eyes a stunning green. "I thought you were both happy."

"We were," he said darkly. "But John's family issued him an ultimatum. He had to return or he'll be dead to them forever. I told him there's nothing for him there. How can he be happy trying to live a lie, living a life without love? I didn't see how he could go back, after we'd been living together in Capri, then Paris, but his parents have told their friends he went on a tour of Europe with me— that we are friends from school. They believe that if he 'quells his disgusting proclivities' as they put it, he can return to the army. They actually want him to marry 'for appearances.'"

"You were considering marriage for appearances, once," she reminded him. "It was Zoe who realized that was a foolish idea. You can't condemn Captain Ransome if he does the same things you thought you must do."

He grimaced. "I know. I didn't feel like getting beaten to a pulp by English louts trying to prove their manliness. It's why I came here. But did John leave for his family, or did he leave because he no longer cares for me?"

"Didn't he give you his reasons?"

"We fought, I got roaring drunk, and when I woke, he was gone and only a note remained."

He drew a folded paper out of his pocket. "You want too much from me," it read.

"Do I chase him, Julia, or do I accept defeat? I'm happy to live in exile as long as I have John. Yes, once I was engaged to Zoe, but only because she needed a hasty wedding herself. I've changed. Love is too important to toy with, too important to cast aside. John is willing to give me up to return to England and live a lie, rather than accept exile. Perhaps there's no hope for us."

"I think—I think you should fight for love."

"What if I fail? Having a broken heart hurts."

"I know. But you do heal."

"As you have. Admirably, Julia. But why are you with the wild American?"

She explained about Cal and Worthington Park. She could not reveal Diana's secret—Diana had not given her permission, but Sebastian believed she'd come to Paris only for him, and she couldn't bring herself to disabuse him of that.

"So you're going to marry the wild American?"

"No! He has no interest in marriage. And neither do I. I've decided that instead I should grasp life on my own terms. I won't marry without love. And I won't marry a man who wishes to put me in a box or a gilded cage."

"Julia, there will eventually be a man who loves you enough, who does not see your desire for freedom and autonomy, your desire to be equal to him, as a price to pay but rather an asset."

Her heart ached, but she smiled to hide it. "That is rather lovely."

"I agree. I surprise myself. Perhaps I should have taken to writing prose instead of painting." He winked at her. "Do you want me to take you to the most shocking Parisian clubs?"

She knew he was teasing. But she called his bluff. "I came to Paris to experience adventure." And to see what she really wanted in her life. "Tonight I am definitely going to wild clubs."

She finished her coffee with a flourish. It was lush and strong and gave her a jolt that shot to her fingertips and toes. "I have spent twenty-seven years being dutiful and ladylike. It hasn't brought me anything I wanted—love, a home, a family. Now I am going to begin my life all over again. I am going to try being wild. Then, I am going to help you heal your rift with John Ransome. You deserve to have love, Sebastian."

Julia quickly saw Paris was a place one must go with someone one loved.

With Sebastian, she met Cal at the bookstore, Shakespeare and Company, where she bought a travel guide to Paris and met sparrowlike Sylvia Beach. Then the two men together took her everywhere. On a boat on the Seine. To view the monuments—L'Arc de Triomphe, the Eiffel Tower.

Her day was a whirl of cafés and flowers and many glasses of wine. Then they returned to the hotel, having dinner with Diana and David on the roof-top of Le Meurice.

At night, lights glittered all around, reflecting on the Seine to make the river appear to be full of diamonds. Julia changed into a sheath of a dress, pale blue with silver beads. Her dress glittered and sparkled every time she drew breath, but it was nowhere near as brilliant as the lights of Paris.

She had been to jazz clubs. Before Nigel married Zoe, she and Zoe had gone to a secret downstairs club in London where—to Julia's shock—a dancer had taken her clothes off.

She was rather nervous. Paris must be even wilder than London. She had boldly told Sebastian she wanted an adventure. But did she?

The five of them made their way to the neighborhood of Montparnasse, past cafés with lights that gleamed on cobblestones and wrought iron fencing and on the faces of chic women. Cal pushed David's chair and she had linked arms with Sebastian. Diana walked at David's side.

As they reached the famous Café de la Rotonde, Cal clasped her hand. Threaded his fingers through hers and she felt it. A *whoosh*. All of Paris stopped in its tracks—and if a man could stop Paris, that man had to be truly something.

She had to release his hand so he could steer David inside, into a room filled with cigarette smoke, crammed with people—women in brief dresses or plain trousers, men dressed in either immaculate dinner jackets or threadbare sweaters. There appeared to be an understanding that the young man in the chair must have been wounded in war, because a path was cleared for them all.

"Cal!" someone called. Cal sat her at a table, and greeted many friends, introducing her.

As Cal fell into conversation with fellow artists, a young gentleman smiled at her from another table. He asked if he could break off the end of the baguette in the basket on their table.

She handed him the whole thing. He waved his hands. "Not all that. I'd be asked to pay."

Another man joined him. "Still nursing that one cup of coffee?"

The first man smiled. He was young, tanned, with curling black hair. "Ten centimes for the cup and I can sit for the day and sketch."

The other man laughed. "I would like to sketch that lovely one."

Julia blushed and looked up as Cal returned with a bottle of red wine and five glasses that he held adroitly by their stems.

The noise grew louder—she could hear the debate of the two men beside her better than she could the conversation at her table. The man with the black hair insisted the new art would be found in the objects used by the masses—automobiles, the newfangled toaster, furniture. "Mass production allows us to bring great art—to bring beautiful but practical form—to all people," he declared. "We must educate people so they learn to throw off Victorian fuss and frippery. And see the beauty of simple form—of a form that follows from its function."

They argued vehemently. Then the second man left and the black-haired man leaned to her and pointed to the walls. "Those sketches are mine." He grinned. "People come to Montparnasse to sin disgracefully. How unfortunate I didn't get to do it with you. Unless you wish to come to my studio and I will paint you. Then make love to you."

"The lady is with me," Cal growled.

"Actually I am not . . . exactly. But as delightful as your offer is, I must decline. My time in Paris is limited and my schedule is already thoroughly booked," she said politely.

That was how it would be done in the drawing room. But the man put his hand on her knee, bent to her and kissed her neck. She was shocked into immobility.

Until Cal hauled the man off. He helped her to her feet. "We're going. There's a fight about to break out."

"Between you and he?" she inquired. The dark-haired man was cursing eloquently in French.

"It might, but that wasn't the one I was thinking about. That intellectual debate in the corner over there is about to erupt into a brawl."

And it did, just as Cal whisked her out, followed by Diana and Sebastian, pushing David's chair.

Julia tried not to look shocked. "Did you paint in places like that? That man wouldn't accept bread from me in case he had to pay for it. Are they really so impoverished?"

Cal grinned. "We all were. The proprietor, Libion, would let me stay there and drink his coffee if I gave him a picture or two to keep up until I could pay."

That didn't make sense. She was certain he had done more than have one dinner at the exclusive Le Meurice, so how could he not have afforded to pay for coffee? But ladylike training would not allow her to say he was lying—questioning him would imply that. David had told her Cal had made money, but she had thought it was enough to care for David.

"What would you like to do with all of Paris here for your pleasure?" Cal teased.

"Sebastian has promised to take me to a jazz club," she said. "Let's go together."

Sebastian and Cal then traded names of clubs back and forth—names that didn't mean anything to her. Cal suggested one that made Sebastian's brow shoot up and Julia said quickly, "That one. I want to try that one."

David and Diana decided to return to the hotel, and Cal acquired a taxicab to take them, helping David out of his chair.

It was strange—she was eager to be shocked, and terrified of it at the same time. It made for a rather intoxicating mix of emotions as they made their way through the steamy streets of Montparnasse. Finally, Cal led her beneath an awning that read Dingo American Bar and Restaurant. He held the door for her and murmured, "One of the favorite bars of the ex-pat American painters and writers. A lot of my friends are here."

A long wooden bar stretched before her, crowded with patrons. Simple stools of bent wood gathered around small tables. Here was more hazy smoke. Sensuous music drifted out, much more mournful and aching than any jazz she'd yet heard. It called to her. The whole night felt like a surge of electricity—and she was thrilled by the glow but also afraid of the shock. It was so crowded, noisy, wild. She was used to crushes at balls, but this was a world she didn't know.

However, everyone seemed to know Cal. Especially the women. Women wanted to talk to him, touch him, slip away into a dark, quiet corner of the bar with him.

Cal was invited to a table. A good-looking man with dark hair and a bourbon in front of him pulled out a chair for her. Julia sat as Cal made introductions. On her left, the handsome man who had pulled out her chair was named Ernest Hemingway. "The writer," Cal added. "And his wife, Hadley Richardson."

On her other side sat Zelda Fitzgerald, famous in America, the embodiment of the "flapper." And wife to F. Scott, who had written the rather stunning novel *The Great Gatsby*. Julia felt awed to be there—she had never run with the artistic set or the Bright Young Things.

Zelda had bobbed blond hair and compelling, emotive eyes. Mrs. Fitzgerald burst out with the most intriguing and unusual comments. "Why do they call you 'ladies'?" she asked pointedly. "Isn't it rather obvious that is what you are? And for those who aren't called ladies, what is that supposed to imply?"

Julia was taken aback. "Do you know," she answered finally. "I truly don't know. It was really a way of distinguishing those who wanted an elevated position. It goes back centuries."

"Are you slavishly devoted to having a title?" Zelda demanded.

Julia knew how to be polite in awkward situations. "I've never thought about it, since I keep mine no matter what."

"Do you?" Zelda drank the rest of her cocktail. "How positively open-minded of your country. Marriage is the ruin of any woman, you know. I haven't any idea why we rush to do it. It's all we girls are brought up to hope for, isn't it? You build your whole life on the idea of landing a man who's worthwhile. Then, once you've done it, it doesn't take long before you realize there's not much to it. It can stifle a woman. Once you're married, you're not interesting. Unless you are really good at something."

Julia managed to follow the swift, dramatic speed of her words. She asked, "Do you write?"

"A little. I was trained as a dancer. I'm quite good. If I were dedicated, I could really be something, you know. Something really dazzling."

"Well, you are, aren't you?" Julia's heart panged. There was something a little desperate about Mrs. Fitzgerald. Beneath the beauty, the perfect brazen flapper loveliness, she looked haunted. "You are both quite famous in America. The predominant couple of the Jazz Age."

Zelda shrugged. As if it was of no consequence. As if it wasn't enough. Then her gaze went to her husband and became a little wilder. "You see the woman he's talking to? That creature in the man's tuxedo? She's the kind of woman who entices a man until he just can't look away."

Julia saw a kind of anguish in Zelda's eyes. She, like Zelda, had been raised to plan for marriage. Now she was going to have to build an entirely different future. And she could see Zelda was searching as she was—and maybe was as lost, for all she was lovely and famous.

Hemingway was talking to Cal. Leaning over to hear Zelda, Julia couldn't hear much of the men's conversation. She heard the term "bullfighting," then talk of Italy and Spain. She gathered

Hemingway admired Cal for having been a pilot in the War.

Zelda leaned close.

"I have a daughter, you know," she said. "Just the most precious thing. When she was born, I was coming out from the ether and I said the most unrelated things. He wrote them down, you know. Scott. And he used them. The words that came right out of my mouth when I didn't even know where I was. It would be so much easier to be a beautiful fool, wouldn't it?"

Zelda liked to say shocking things, Julia felt. She answered thoughtfully, "I don't know. I was raised to expect to marry, manage a house, and let my life be directed and shaped by my family and by circumstances. And yes, it would have been best if I had been nothing more than a beautiful fool. Now I realize it's frightening to want more. But I'm ready to face being afraid."

"The Lost Generation," Hemingway said then, his voice carrying over the table. "It's a name for us all. Gertrude gave it to me. She had work done on her car. The young mechanic didn't impress her. She asked the garage owner where the man had been trained. The owner said the man had been through the War and they were all *une génération perdue*."

"The Lost Generation. It suits us, doesn't it?" said Fitzgerald.

They looked at her.

Julia said, "It does. I feel quite lost some-times. As though there is something of great importance I could do, but I don't quite know what it is."

She felt Zelda Fitzgerald staring at her.

Couples got up to dance then. Not wives with husbands—the couples split apart and paired up with others. Julia was left at the table with Cal, Hadley Richardson and a female author—the woman in the man's tuxedo.

"What do you do?" The question came from the author. She smoked a cigarette in a long holder. Her dark hair was cropped short and slicked back with pomade. "You must do something."

What did she do? She thought of Ellen. Of the Brands. Of the people on the estate like Mrs. Billings, who had lost all her sons to the War. "The work that I do that truly inspires me is my charity work. Though I have rather shocked Society with what I do."

"Darling, you look as if butter wouldn't melt in your mouth. How could you shock anyone?"

"I work with women who lost their husbands and have to turn to drastic measures to support their families. Fallen women."

"You, darling? Work with prostitutes?" The woman's hand stroked down her arm.

The woman blew a smoke ring. Julia found the woman's kohl-ringed eyes rather magnetic. They were huge and pale blue. She had a strong nose and high cheekbones. Almost masculine features, but she was strikingly beautiful.

"You're really lovely, Lady Julia. I've been on a man kick for the last few months. About every six months, I change my mind. My last really serious love affair was with a woman. She was married, but I adored her. Then, I decided it was time for men. But you've tempted me to change my mind tonight."

The woman's hand settled on her leg. And squeezed.

And in that moment, Julia knew she hadn't wanted quite this much adventure. Paris was wild and she wasn't. Not desperately, determinedly wild, anyway. She loved art and literature and beauty—but she loved her work at Brideswell, her home, country life.

But suddenly, a strong hand gripped hers and she was lifted to her feet. "Julia isn't available." To her, Cal said, "We should get you back to the hotel. We'll tell your brother that you're leaving."

They were almost at the door—the crowd had magically parted for Cal. She gripped the door frame to stop him. "I don't want to run away. I know I'm not wild. I wasn't going to slip off with her into a corner and do—do Sapphic things, you know."

Cal groaned loudly. "That is an image I didn't need right now, Julia."

"Well, I don't need a man rushing me away from

something a little scandalous." In truth, she was rather glad to get away—but she didn't want to be hastened away as if she were a young virgin who mustn't see anything.

"That's not what I'm doing. I'm rushing you to the hotel because I need to paint you."

"Paint me?"

"I've watched you all night, falling more and more under your spell. The only thing that's going to save me is to paint you. I thought I wasn't going to do it. But I have to."

"You mean our bargain. The one we hadn't actually made yet." She was confused. She thought that hadn't mattered anymore. And she thought it didn't need to matter—not after he'd talked about future changes for the estate. Not after he'd chosen to take care of Diana and Ellen. "Where you said you'd be willing to leave Worthington untouched while you painted me?"

"I'm willing to give you anything you want for it, Julia."

18

Painting in Paris

A lady should not be alone with a man in a hotel room.

Julia stood in the middle of the living area, on the elegant Turkish carpet. She was surrounded by furnishings of royal blue silk and gilt in the style of Louis XIV. A canvas was set up near the window. The deep blue and gold curtains were tied back, and Paris glittered below them. Cal was pouring champagne.

Julia could just imagine Mother falling into a swoon at the thought of her doing such a scandalous thing. In England, if a rumor began to spread that she had been in Cal's room her reputation would be in shreds.

Of course, nothing would happen. This was for her to sit for a portrait. She knew he loved Alice and she believed Cal would not try to seduce her. He'd teased her with that before, but he'd proven himself honorable.

"You aren't going to want me to take off my clothes, are you?" She had wanted adventure in Paris. And for art, why would she be so nervous about doing that? Could she do it?

397

The champagne bottle jerked in his hand and the stream flew clear of the glass.

"I'm not sure if I can do it," she admitted. "Tonight, I met the most exciting, artistic people of our times and—and I was shocked. By what they said, how they live, the fact some of them take both men and women as lovers." She sighed ruefully. "I'm simply not modern. I don't belong in this world. Even if you asked me to pose naked to save Worthington, I now know I couldn't do it. I'm not daring and brave. I'm dull and boring. A true English lady."

Champagne dripped off his hand and Cal grabbed one of his painting rags to clean up. "You are anything but dull and boring. Just because you were shocked doesn't mean you don't belong here. I'm not going to ask you to take off your clothes. You're something special, Julia. Something remarkable and unique. You are really the perfect lady."

Strangely, she wasn't so sure she liked that. She didn't know quite what he meant. She thought Cal disliked perfect ladies.

He handed her the flute of champagne. She sipped and the bubbles tickled her nose.

"I'll show you how I want you to pose. Fully clothed." He pulled a stool over so it stood in front of the window and the view of Paris. "First, I want you to sit there. Talk to me."

As she settled down delicately, Cal took off his

dress jacket and his tie. Watching his shoulders and back move and his muscles bunch made her feel giddy. He kicked off shoes and socks so he was barefoot. Even in his fine shirt and tailored trousers, he looked bohemian. Wild.

But his heart was Alice's.

He began to squirt paint onto his palette.

"Why do you need to paint me?"

"Because you're the most beautiful thing I've ever seen in my life and an artist gets an obsession to record something like that," he said.

The champagne was loosening her inhibitions—on top of the cocktails she'd drunk. He gave instructions and she sat as he wanted. As he sketched on the canvas, he kept looking at her so intensely. With a hot, penetrating gaze. She knew it was just to get the detail, but she felt her cheeks grow warm.

Giggling a little, she said, "You told me that the staff of the hotel knew you because you came here to celebrate after you sold a painting. I don't believe that. They know you too well."

"What I told you was true. Whenever I sold a painting, I always came here. I tipped well, which guarantees they'll look after you and remember you." He shrugged. "I always took the viewpoint that money would come from somewhere, so I spent it when I had it."

"Truly? Even though you had been poor?" The English aristocracy used to take it for granted they would be the upper tier of society, with grand houses and grand lives. They feared losing everything now. Brideswell was safe, but she remembered how terrifying it was to fear losing her home and having the tenants lose theirs. That was why she sympathized with Lady Worthington, Diana and her sisters.

"Having been poor once meant I wasn't scared of being poor again," he said. "After the War, everything felt like heaven. Even camping out and sleeping beneath the stars felt like luxury after catching a few minutes' sleep standing up in a trench that was ankle-deep in sloppy, stinking cold water."

"You camped under the stars?" Goodness, had he not been able to afford a roof over his head?

He laughed. "*That* shocks you, doll? I went to paint the north—the wilds in the north of Canada, just below the Arctic Circle. There are artists painting landscapes not as dainty places tamed by men, but as wild and untamed land. I joined them, canoeing into the north, then camping and sketching."

"But didn't you get wet and cold?"

"I set up a canvas tent. I had to fit what I took in a canoe." He grinned. "I had a sleeping sack made of waterproof cloth and sheep's wool. I cooked food over a campfire. I learned I could live with very few belongings."

She stared at him, amazed. He was so intriguing—he knew so much, had done so much.

He sketched, looking at her, then at the easel.

She loved to watch him draw, with all his focus on the picture. He brushed his hair back as he worked, as the pencil flew over the canvas. He frowned, smiled, grimaced, as if experiencing all the emotions possible in the minutes while he sketched.

She couldn't stop watching him. She wanted to touch him.

All of him.

Suddenly the room felt hotter than even on the most baking summer's day. But she couldn't touch him. She couldn't have a love affair with a man who truly loved someone else.

"I would be scared of being poor," she admitted. "I don't have that much courage."

"I think you have a lot of courage," he said.

She was about to shake her head, then remembered models were not supposed to move. "I don't really. I just hide things very well. Ladies do. For a long time, we had no money and we thought we would have to lose Brideswell. But the aristocracy wants to 'keep up appearances.' We threw dinner parties we could not afford and ate tiny meals as a family. We burned fewer fires and shivered more in the winters. We shut up much of the house."

"What would you have done if you'd lost the house?"

"I guess we would have found somewhere smaller to live. We would have had much less, but we would have still tried to carry on as if nothing changed. That is what people like us do."

He shook his head. "You come from a world I'm never going to understand."

"It doesn't make sense to me anymore, either. Our world has value and meaning but it needs new ideas—it needs men like you. You truly were born to be an earl," she insisted. "To be a true self-made man, you are obviously quite brilliant at business. And you truly care about people. You are probably more qualified to be an earl than most men who have the title."

He didn't answer.

She went on, in a voluble rush, "You could make Worthington into a great place. You could marry Alice Hayes and have a family. You could be happy."

"Marry Alice?"

"I—I overheard her tell you that she is in love with you. I am sorry. That was most unladylike of me. I know you don't want to hurt your brother—"

"Julia, there are a hell of a lot of reasons I wouldn't marry Alice. David is only one of them."

He looked past her at the city beyond, and she was sure he was drawing in the background. She knew she mustn't stop now. "I understand why you hate Worthington. How could you ever forgive the old earl and the countess? But it was *their* mistake and it's wrong for innocent people to suffer—"

"They forced my mother into committing a sin—at least she believed it was a sin. Mam apologized to me. She said she was already damned forever. She said she was better dead than alive to poison us. Don't you see I can't forgive that? *Goddamn* them. I hope there is a damn curse."

Julia jumped at his rage. She almost fell off the stool. "A sin? I don't understand—"

"It was my fault, don't you see? My fault . . . Christ." He threw the palette to the floor.

She was shocked. His head was bowed. His shoulders were tense, his hands fisted. She got off the stool. "Whatever it was, whatever this sin was, it was not your fault."

"It was. It— Damn, you don't know."

She kept trying to reassure him.

Tears glittered in his eyes and she thought of a fourteen-year-old, too late to save his mother, blaming himself for her death. It was so wrong.

"Maybe you are right," she whispered. "Maybe Worthington has been poisoned by pride and arrogance. If there was a way to ensure the people who live on the estate are safe, I guess I would say—destroy it."

"Julia—"

She jumped off the stool, hurried to him. She kissed him. A passionate kiss.

He pulled away, cupping her face. Then he

403

groaned with such frustration and pain, she felt it shiver down her spine.

Cal braced his hand against the top of the canvas. He tossed the pencil to the small ornate table beside him. "I'm going crazy, Julia. Crazy with wanting you." His blue eyes blazed at her. "You're the real reason I wouldn't marry Alice. I thought I loved her—until I met you." He kissed her again, trailed kisses down her neck and she was turning to steam.

She should stop him. She was still a lady. Years of training told her that she must not do this. She had been taught five words: *wait until your wedding night.*

But she wanted Cal.

His arms went around her and he swept her up off her feet. He lifted her so high that an instinct kicked in and she wrapped her legs around his hips so she didn't fall.

She didn't want him to stop and she knew, with a lady's intuition, that they were perilously close to the point she *must* stop him.

His lips trailed over her jawline. Teasing sensations made her whimper.

His mouth skimmed down, and he eased the straps down her shoulder—the straps of her dress and her brassiere.

She knew he would kiss her nipple. He couldn't—he mustn't—but she ached for it. Her nipple puckered and poked against the firm fabric of her lingerie. Her back arched, lifting her bosom toward him. His lips trailed over her skin, above the lacy trimming of her undergarment.

Julia never dreamed she would physically hurt with the wanting.

His hand cupped the top of her thigh and she gasped. She'd never had anyone touch her so close to her private place. His rough palm slid up her bare thigh, above her rolled-down stockings. Oh, the touch of fingers on her skin—

He pulled something out of the back waistband of his trousers. His paintbrush. A clean one. He brushed the soft bristles across her lower lip. Then down, across her collarbones, into the low neckline of her dress to caress the swells of her breasts held up by her brassiere.

With his paintbrush he teased her all over. He drew up the skirt of her dress, revealing her girdle and her panties. Up went the brush, making her tremble. The soft bristles tickled her inner thighs.

She moaned with the sheer need.

Cal got onto his knees in front of her. He took hold of her girdle, unfastened it and drew it down. She stared at him, but she didn't want to stop. Then she stood in front of him in her filmy underpants. He leaned forward and kissed her. There, right between her legs, against her silk undies.

She almost died of shock.

He swept her up into his arms and carried her easily to the bedroom. Julia gasped as she saw the huge ornate bed, festooned with silk and gilt, and large enough to fit the entire court of Louis XIV on top of it.

She wanted Cal. But this was disaster. Every lady knew that. Panic took her. Panic she couldn't stop or control. "No!"

He set her down on her feet.

"I *can't*. I want to, but I don't dare. I know you have no intention of marrying me. I desire you like I have never desired any other man. But I can't have a love affair."

Cal panted hard, his brain full of hot desire. One promise would be all it took. One question.

He'd come to Worthington full of rage. Being in Paris with Julia had been the sweetest time of his life. He'd loved seeing her delight, her shock. She made him laugh, made his heart glow. She made him want something more than anger and revenge.

He wanted to laugh with her, make love to her. Wanted to watch her eyes go wide and flash with pleasure when she came beneath him. Or on top of him. He was more than happy to bow to a woman's desire for equal control in sex.

He wanted it so much his every breath hurt.

"I won't ruin you, Julia. I wouldn't do that to you."

Yet even as he made that promise, he knew he needed her. "I was thinking of asking you to marry me."

"Just so you could sleep with me? Cal, that's a terrible reason."

He laughed; a raw, hoarse laugh from deep inside him. She had no idea what a damn hellish thing he was doing—proposing to her when she didn't know the truth about him. "A better reason than an aristocratic one like marrying you to get your dowry or a tract of land. At least marrying you for lust would be all about you, doll."

"That is rid—" She broke off. "I suppose it is true. But it's not a very wise reason."

He stroked her hair. "Marrying me would be a dangerous thing for you. I wouldn't accept separate bedrooms and discreet visits for the purpose of making an heir." He didn't know what he was doing—trying to scare her into saying no? To ease his conscience. When he ached for her.

"I don't believe that is what I want."

He took her hand, led her to the bed. He sat on the end of it, pulling her with him. He pulled her onto his lap. Felt her rounded bottom settle on him, smelled her light rosy perfume, gazed at her perfect profile. And something happened to him. He threw aside any noble part of him.

"I'd want to take you around the world while I paint," he said, keeping his voice low and seductive. "I'd want to sleep under a lean-to with you in the north, cuddled tight together against the cold of frost."

She caught her breath. And he was holding his. Expecting her to turn him down flat. Giving her every reason why she shouldn't want him—except the real one.

"I wouldn't mind that," she breathed. "Being with you—every moment I've spent with you—has made me see there's something I couldn't live without in marriage."

"What's that?" he asked, all innocence, even as he trailed his lips down her neck, then nipped the very base of it.

She moaned and he felt a jolt of lust and pain. "What can't you live without?" he asked again.

"Passion," she squeaked.

The way she said it, all wrapped up in ladylike nerves, only served to make him want her more. Wanting her was a feeling more powerful than the beat of his heart.

"You could marry me," he said, "if you were willing to live a nomadic life with me."

"But I want you to find a home. To build a family and be happy. What if there are children? They can't live in a tent or be taken all over the world."

"Worthington will never be my home."

"I haven't changed you at all, have I?" she asked softly. "It's not you selling Worthington that frightens me now. Doing so will not give you peace from the past or change anything that happened. It won't make your past go away. It won't heal your pain."

"If I gave you the choice, Julia, would you choose Worthington over me?"

"It doesn't have to be a choice."

"Yes." His voice was cool and low. "It does."

"No, it doesn't." She moved away from him.

"If you don't marry me, I'd sell the damn place in a heartbeat."

Her eyes went wide. "You can't blackmail me into marriage."

"I can."

"No, you cannot. This is a mistake. A terrible mistake." She jumped off the bed to her feet. "I'm going back to my room." She pushed her skirt back down so it covered her thighs. Hiking up her straps, she hurried to the door. Cal followed her and saw her snatch up her girdle. He almost smiled as she clutched it to her chest and ran out into the hall.

He stalked over to the champagne bottle in the bucket. The hell with a glass. He lifted it to his lips and drank straight from the fancy bottle.

He knew loss and he knew pain. He'd lost his father and mother. Both deaths—in a way—had been his fault. He had witnessed hell in the War. He'd seen David wounded. He knew what it was like to have your heart broken by grief and pain.

But right now, it felt like his heart had shattered. Into pieces too small to ever fix.

He couldn't lose Julia.

Every moment he'd spent with her flashed before his eyes, like a moving picture. The first night he saw her on the terrace, sparkling as if all the stars in the world surrounded her. Her determined vow to make him love Worthington. Her glowing smiles for young Ben. Her strength when she helped Ellen. How she'd gamely herded the pigs.

He loved her. More deeply, more intensely than he'd loved anyone.

He shouldn't marry her. Not a girl like Julia. He had no right to her, but he was going to make her his. And he would sell his soul to do it—that's what Mam would say, wasn't it? That keeping the truth from Julia was as good as lying to her. Marrying her that way had to be a sin.

Julia knew a lady should probably throw herself on the bed and cry. But she jumped on her bed and pummeled it with her fists.

Inside, she was all wound up. And all mixed-up. Had he seriously offered marriage—or was it a joke? Or was he just trying to get her into his bed?

A knock sounded at her door. "Julia, it's Cal. I want to ask you to marry me. Seriously this time. Honest."

His words answered her unspoken question so clearly, it stunned her. Sometimes she'd imagined a proposal from Cal—imaginings she wouldn't even admit to herself. She never dreamed she would feel as if walking across clouds to receive it. As if she could fly, as if she were lighter than air, but tentative and full of nerves, too.

The instant she opened her door, Cal dropped down on one knee and took her hand. "You've changed me, Julia. I know Worthington means so much to you. You don't know how much it touched me to have you say you agreed with me—that maybe the place is poisoned and should be destroyed."

She was about to speak, but he rushed on. "Julia, I'd rather live with you at Worthington than live in pain and anger for the rest of my life. I need you. A life without you would be too empty for me to bear. I love you. You've changed me because I love you. Would you do me the honor of marrying me?"

"I *didn't* change you," she whispered. Her throat was so tight. "You've always been a loyal, loving, good man. I know that from everything you have done for your brother, for Ellen and the Brands."

Cal got to his feet. What did it mean when a man got off his knee during a proposal, before she'd answered? Had she ruined the moment? Julia struggled to find a rule of polite behavior to deal with such a thing—

411

He drew her out to the terrace, holding her hand. He walked with her to the railing. Lights sparkled all around her, streamed up the Eiffel Tower and shimmered at the dizzying top.

"In front of all Paris, Julia, tell me—do you care for me enough to marry me?"

She sucked in a breath. She saw the vulnerability in his eyes. The hope.

"You're the most wonderful woman I've ever met," he said softly. "You're ladylike and elegant—"

"I thought you didn't like such things."

"I adore them about you. But you also have all the kindness my mother always had. You truly care about people. You are too good for me. I've no right to ask you to become my wife—"

"Stop that. I love you—" She hesitated. "And you are really willing to keep Worthington?"

"Yes, Julia."

"Then, yes, I will marry you. Yes! Very much yes! But we should be modern about this. Are you, Cal Carstairs, willing to become my husband?"

He grinned, dazzling her. "With all my heart, Julia."

19

Wedding at Worthington

"Silly twit. I'm right worried about her," Hannah muttered as she worked on the preparations for the wedding feast. Tansy had vanished again, just when Hannah desperately needed her help. The food for the earl's wedding must be perfect.

"Worried about whom?" Eustace the footman asked. He was clearing the luncheon dishes, bringing them down from upstairs.

"I'm just wondering where Tansy has got herself to."

"Maybe she's lying down. She's kind of delicate," Eustace said.

"She's kind of lazy," Hannah said sourly. "I expect she's snuck out to see that man."

At first Eustace had looked affronted by her comment, then he looked panicked. "What man?" He was in love with Tansy—that was written all over his face. But Tansy didn't even know the poor lad was alive.

If it were Hannah that he admired, she'd be thrilled. And she hated the way flighty Tansy was making her growl and snap—everyone thought it was her new position going to her head. But she had so much responsibility, and no one seemed to understand.

She hated to break Eustace's heart. And she knew he wouldn't thank her for giving him the truth, but she was tired of covering up. She was also scared. "Tansy is chasing after a toff who takes her for rides in his motorcar. It will end badly. I just know it."

"What do you mean?"

"He'll seduce her, use her and then leave her hanging."

"But Tansy's lovely and any man could fall in love with her."

Hannah wished it would all work out for the best. But she had a country-bred mother—the sort who always saw disasters and dangers looming. She sighed. "Anyway, I have bigger problems to worry about. I have to make a wedding cake and I have no idea what to do!"

"Don't you just bake it?"

Hannah shook her head. "Wedding cakes are fashionable, so I must make something grand and dazzling. I tried one already and—" She went to the larder and took out her first attempt. She'd found some little decorative columns stored away in the kitchen and she'd used them to stack two layers of cake. The upper one had crushed the columns right through the lower one.

Eustace frowned. "You can't stack something on a cake. Of course it won't hold it up."

414

"Then how do they do it?"

"I don't know. You're the cook. Can't you read a book?"

Hannah bit her lip. She could read a little, but she hadn't found any recipes for wedding cakes. And she couldn't really read most of the recipe books that Mrs. Feathers had kept.

If she failed at this, she would be out on her rump. What was she going to do?

"Mrs. Talbot? May I speak to you for a moment?"

Hannah jerked her head up. She gazed into concerned blue eyes and gasped, "My lady, I didn't see you there. Of course you can speak with me." She bobbed a quick curtsy to lovely Lady Julia of Brideswell Abbey, the woman about to become Countess of Worthington.

"I wished to speak to you about the menu for the wedding reception, Mrs. Talbot. I wish to know if you can cope. Do you need extra help?"

Oh God, her soon-to-be mistress doubted she could do it. "Of course I can, my lady," Hannah said defensively. "You've nothing to worry about." She thought of the horrible squashed cake. Her cheeks got hot. She swallowed hard.

"How many kitchen maids do you have?"

Hannah saw Lady Julia was not going to be easily bamboozled. "There's two." Did she defend Tansy? Did she reveal the truth—that she was trying to do most of the work herself? She hated to admit that she couldn't control Tansy. That she

415

gave orders and Tansy did whatever she wanted. She might get the sack for Tansy's disobedience.

Lady Julia looked over to Pru, the new kitchen maid, who was scrubbing the breakfast pots. "You seem to have only one helper today. Where is the other maid?"

Hannah gulped. Why risk her job for Tansy? But she couldn't bring herself to tattle. Tansy would be fired without a character. She wouldn't do that to her worst enemy.

"I think she's under the weather," Hannah began.

Then they all heard feminine squealing and Tansy rushed into the kitchen. She called over her shoulder, "You can be a naughty thing, can't you, Stephen?"

The first footman came in, grinning. He saw Lady Julia and froze. Eustace glowered at Stephen.

"Hurry up and get to work, Tansy," Hannah snapped. "There's to be no fooling around in my kitchen." She tried to sound as forceful as Mrs. Feathers. Especially in front of her future mistress. She just wasn't good at it and she feared Lady Julia would think her inadequate. "You don't want her ladyship to think we will let her down over the wedding meal," she said briskly.

Tansy gushed over Lady Julia, giving all kinds of promises. Tansy could lay it on thicker and gooier than treacle when she wanted. Then, Hannah almost fainted in shock when Tansy said, "Everything will be just perfect, my lady. Except for the wedding cake. Hannah has no idea how to make a wedding cake."

"That's not true," Hannah declared, panicking.

Lady Julia lifted a brow. "Could we speak privately, Mrs. Talbot?"

Hannah saw Tansy's tiny smirk as she followed her ladyship. And she knew—Tansy wanted to become cook.

They went into the housekeeper's sitting room, which was empty. Hannah was impressed—her ladyship was sparing her embarrassment—but also terrified.

Lady Julia closed the door quietly, then said, "A wedding cake is a very difficult thing. We could have it made in London."

And she'd look like a failure. "I can do it, my lady."

"Have you ever made one before?"

"I—" She could lie, but she'd be caught. She shook her head. "No. I have no idea how to make a wedding cake." She winced. "Are you going to tell his lordship to let me go?"

"Of course not." Lady Julia tapped her finger against her chin. "What we must do is find someone to teach you. We have a few days yet. Perhaps we can find a chef in London to assist you. That way, you will learn how to do it."

"But, my lady—" She broke off. No doubt she would lose her place—to the chef!

"What is it, Mrs. Talbot?"

417

"I feel I've failed you."

"You have not. But I will be disappointed if you do not take this opportunity."

"You'd be disappointed if I don't let him help me?" She didn't understand.

"I want you to learn. I don't expect you to magically know how to do things."

"I will learn, my lady," Hannah said quickly. If she wasn't so afraid, she'd be over the moon to be getting lessons. But she was a simple girl from a simple family. What if she couldn't learn how to make a fancy cake? What then?

It was the morning of her wedding and she was in her wedding gown.

Julia took a deep breath and turned in front of her mirror. The white silk dress skimmed over her breasts and hips to a dropped waist accented with a band of pearls. The skirt flowed to midcalf, so it showed off quite a bit of her legs in silk stockings. An overskirt of tulle billowed behind her, tumbling over her train of satin. Light and airy, the dress seemed to float on its own and she felt as though if she lifted her arms, she'd take flight.

After all, she was floating on air. Though trembling with anticipation.

"There, my lady."

Zoe's maid, Callie, sat back on her heels, and let out a big puff of breath. She'd had to fix a small tear in the hem and she'd done it quickly but admitted, "It's not as well done as I'd like, my lady. But it will last for today."

"It's wonderful." Julia was grateful and did think it was wonderful. "You've done miracles."

"Thank you, milady," Callie said.

After all, with help from one of the upstairs maids, Callie had managed to dress Isobel and Zoe, and then she had tackled Julia's wedding gown. It had been made in London, rushed to be prepared in days because Cal had wanted to marry quickly.

She didn't understand why, but after they'd returned from Paris, she'd barely seen Cal. He went out all day in his motorcar, touring around the estate. He had been invited for several dinners at Brideswell and she saw him then, but in the crowded dining room and drawing rooms. He had never tried to get her alone. He had spent more time with Nigel than with her—he'd gone to Nigel not to ask permission but to say they were getting married.

If Cal was trying to build anticipation . . . well, she was ready to explode.

But strangely it was as if he was avoiding her. Nerves? What was he doing? She was going to marry him. She should trust him. She knew it was wrong to doubt, to wonder: Was he breaking apart Worthington and not telling her?

Julia took a deep breath. She would not think of things like that.

Callie fussed a bit with her hair. Then said, worriedly, "But we don't yet have something old, something new, something borrowed and something blue."

Zoe breezed into her bedroom. She wore a beautiful dress of white and blue that set off her golden hair. "Oh my gosh, you look beautiful." Zoe laughed, brushed a tear and embraced her.

"Oh dear." Julia broke from the hug, laughing too and waving her hands. "You'll make me cry."

Callie held a mass of tulle. "It's time for your veil, my lady."

Zoe stepped back. Julia turned to face the mirror and stood utterly still as Callie secured the veil and diamond-encrusted circlet in place. Grandmama had worn it for her wedding and while it was old-fashioned and Victorian, Julia had been touched when her grandmother gave it to her to use. It was her borrowed item.

Grandmama had done nothing more than raise a brow and say, "Oh, you're marrying the *American*. I can't say I'm surprised. But I can't say I approve, my dear. You barely know him—and while I grew up in a time when it was best to know as little as possible about one's husband when marrying him, I fear it will cause trouble between you."

Julia had smiled. "I intend to find out everything about him now, Grandmama."

"You'll only learn as much as he wants you to

know," the dowager had replied. "At least until you fight. Then you'll learn everything."

"There, my lady," Callie said, bringing her back to the present as she smoothed the tulle.

Zoe sat on the edge of the bed. "Now that you're leaving Brideswell, you'll need a lady's maid."

Julia jerked up her head. "I hadn't thought of that."

"You hadn't? Julia, you always think of everything when it comes to running a household."

"I know, but since coming back from Paris, all I could think of was Cal. Being in b— I mean, marrying him. I suppose I will have to advertise. And quickly."

"It is a shame there is no one local who could do it. That makes it so much faster. You'll need someone responsible, someone with excellent sewing skills, someone you can trust."

Julia's heart soared. "Of course. Ellen Lambert."

"The woman with the small boy? The one who—"

"That one."

"Do you really see her working as a lady's maid at Worthington?"

"Zoe, you are an American. You can't turn snobbish on me now."

Zoe waved her hand. "Lots of Americans are terrible snobs. We're worse than the English because we don't have our social structure all laid out." Then Zoe winked. "But I agree with you—it would be perfect. I just wanted you to know you'll have to fight prejudice to do this. Not from me—from other people."

"I'm willing to fight. Ellen needs a second chance. This would give her references. And Ben loves Worthington," Julia said. "It's perfect."

This whole day would be perfect. Diana was to be her maid of honor and would go to Switzerland after the wedding. Cal had wanted her to go on from Paris with the companion, but Diana had pleaded to come back for the wedding. Cal relented to make Diana happy. Sebastian had come home to England to pursue Captain Ransome.

Julia smoothed down her skirts, aware of Zoe gazing at her thoughtfully.

"What?" she asked.

"You left for Paris determined to strike out on your own. You came back engaged to Cal—and ready to be mistress of Worthington Park. How did he convince you to give up your plan?"

Julia frowned. She hadn't really thought about "giving up" anything. "He proposed—and I realized I wanted to marry him. I realized this is where I belong."

"Callie, would you check on Lady Isobel?" Zoe said. Then when they were alone, Zoe stood and clasped her hands. "You went with him to Paris and came back engaged. You aren't marrying him because you think you have to, are you? Because something happened in Paris?"

"Something came very close to happening in Paris, but didn't quite."

Zoe looked grave. "You don't have to marry him just because you want to make love with him. He's bold, wild, and he's angry—and brooding anger is gosh-darn sexy in some men."

"There's more to Cal than just that," Julia declared. "That's why I love him. And why I'm marrying him."

"That's good enough for me." Zoe pulled out a handkerchief. "Now I'm going to cry. Because when I first came to Brideswell, I wanted to see you become happy. And here you are—about to be happy for the rest of your life."

Julia hugged Zoe and together they left her room. She took one last look—this was not to be her room any longer. Then she walked down the hall.

Did all brides feel this strange mixture of emotion—half anticipation and half poignant sorrow at leaving their homes?

Here was the little niche in the wall where she used to hide and jump out at Nigel to scare him. Here was the landing where she and Sebastian had dropped peas onto the heads of guests—they'd gotten in enormous trouble for that.

She was going to Worthington, which was full of memories, too. But she was going to make new memories. New and happy ones with Cal.

She'd reached the top of the stairs when her

mother caught up to her. Zoe was ahead on the stairs.

Mother looked nervy and pale and Julia worried, until mother said, "Now I must tell you what you must expect for your wifely duties."

"Oh no," she said hastily. "Don't worry. I know what to expect."

"You know?" Mother gasped. "Has the earl compromised you? He seemed so gentlemanly."

Julia was rather delighted Mother thought so. And Cal, for all his insistence he wasn't a gentleman, had always been one with her. He had kissed her with her skirt up . . . but he'd still been quite a gentleman. "I haven't done anything. But I have an idea what is involved."

"Well . . . it is the most intimate you will ever be with another person," her mother said.

"It's not necessary for you to explain, Mother—"

"It can be the most wonderful thing—shocking but special," her mother continued, regardless. "Or it can be the most dreadful thing. I shall not say more. I just want you to be happy, but I have no advice to give you about a happy marriage, I fear."

"I will be happy. I don't need advice. It is just wonderful to know you want me to be happy and that you are here."

"I am always here for you. I was so sad for such a long time. Your husband-to-be said you feel you failed me because I was grieving for so long."

"Cal told you that?" Julia was shocked. She'd never said that to him.

"He came to my little chapel to introduce himself. I had no idea, Julia. My unhappiness was not your fault. I am sorry my pain pushed you away."

Julia felt her mother kiss her forehead and her heart wanted to break. Tears came, but they were happy ones. "I love you, Mother," she whispered.

"Now we must get to the church or your groom will think you're not coming."

She hadn't heard Mother be joking and firm for ages. It made her so happy, even as she scrambled to gather up her train and hurry downstairs to where Nigel waited in the foyer. Her mother was going to follow in a second car with Zoe and Isobel.

Nigel smiled. "You are so beautiful." But he scrubbed his hand over his jaw. "You are marrying Cal for love, aren't you, Julia? I wouldn't accept this union for any other reason."

"Nigel, only you could drive me mad and touch my heart in one statement. It would not matter if I had your acceptance or not. But I am moved that you want me to marry for love. It shows that marriage to Zoe has been the making of you."

He cleared his throat. "I can see many good traits in Worthington. But I cannot see what you have in common with him. People are often attracted to opposites, but it might not be the strongest foundation for a marriage—"

"I think we have many things in common—he cares about people as I do. I also love him for all the things about him that are different. Cal put a paintbrush in my hand and showed me how thrilling it is to paint. He showed me Paris. Each time I am with him, I feel like I am having a whole new world unfurled for me."

"I was worried you were marrying him for Worthington Park."

"That's ridiculous. Nigel, I am marrying him for love."

"Julia!" Sebastian waved from the top of the stairs, ran down and jumped the last four steps.

His jaw dropped as he saw her. "You look like a star plucked from the heavens and brought to earth. That Earl of Worthington is an attractive man. Full of sex appeal, I have to say. But will he make you happy?"

"Not you, too! Nigel has already been through this with me. I *know* Cal will make me happy."

Sebastian pouted. "We love you and are doing our protective brotherly duty."

"And I love both of you for it," she said, and hugged them both.

Cal stood at the altar. How had he got here—to a four-hundred-year-old church in the English countryside, a title attached to his damn name and a beautiful English lady about to marry him innocently, without knowing the truth about him?

He could give her the whole world—could give her anything she wanted.

But without Worthington Park, he knew he wouldn't be enough for her.

A week ago, he'd been in the study of the Duke of Langford, telling the man he intended to marry Julia. Langford had asked about his past and Cal had said bluntly, "I grew up in a seedy tenement in Hell's Kitchen. My father was working as a rag-and-bone man and was murdered on the street, likely by members of a gang. My mother was beaten to death. And if that hadn't killed her, she would have worked herself to death, because she worked so hard to support my brother and me. So that's my inglorious past. I've got an earl's blood in me, but you would never know it."

He'd said it carelessly, casually, making it sound like the whole truth. But he'd left out a few important things.

Langford had studied him. "Julia told me that you had devised a plan of revenge when you learned you had inherited Worthington Park. She told me what she has done to make you change your mind."

And Cal knew, then, he'd carried off the bluff. "She tried to make me love Worthington Park with the same passion and fire as she does," he'd said.

"She believes you intend to keep the estate intact and live there. But I understood that you agreed because if you'd said no, she wouldn't

427

have married you," the duke had said. "I want you to understand something, Cal. Worthington was a second home to her when she was growing up. A refuge from our parents' unhappy marriage. It represents her first great love in Anthony Carstairs. It would destroy Julia to watch it go, especially if she was mistress of it."

"I know how much it means to her."

"It would destroy her if you went back on your word. It would destroy your marriage. I'd be damn tempted to destroy you," Langford had said.

Cal respected a man who was direct. "I love her and would never hurt her. I know what the estate means to her."

"Good. Then you have my blessing."

He knew he didn't need approval. He and Julia were both adults. But what surprised him—scared him—was that he wanted Langford's approval. Langford, he'd learned, was a man who helped his tenants. Who, since his marriage, embraced new technologies and industries. Langford was a duke born and bred, but one who apparently enjoyed tinkering on airplane engines with his wife. For a moment, Cal had thought: *I'd like to be worthy of the approval . . .*

But if Langford knew the truth, he wouldn't have let Julia within a mile of Cal.

"You okay, Cal?" David's voice, at his side, brought him back to the present—to the interior of the church, filled with women wearing fancy

428

hats, and men in funny coats with tails. Morning coats, they were called. Like the one Langford had insisted Cal had to wear.

David was his best man. To Cal's surprise, his cousins had thought that idea brilliant. Thalia had added flowers to his brother's chair, and David had been happy to let her do it.

He couldn't tell David why he was so damn nervous. That guilt had kept him away from Julia for the past few days. But before he could give his brother a lie for an answer, the wedding march burst out, soaring in the church. Sunlight filled the arched doorway like a curtain of gold. Into all that gold stepped Julia, her arm linked with her brother's. Right then, Cal didn't give a damn about their differences. Or that he'd lied to her. It was worth it for this moment. To know she was coming down the aisle to him.

Even down the length of the aisle, she glowed with happiness. Her lips parted and her tongue swept them.

His knees almost buckled.

Love didn't conquer all. He knew that. His parents had loved each other but poverty, fear and violence had destroyed them. But he was still going into this marriage hoping that he could make love—and lust—work for him. Hoping he could keep Julia happy and keep her from learning the truth about him.

Then she was there, at his side, and her brilliant

smile was for him. Her radiance almost knocked him on his heels. Flowers and people filled the church, but the only thing that existed for him was Julia.

He was supposed to take her hand. He did it gently. The significance of it almost floored him. They were to go through life hand-in-hand now.

They'd practiced the vows but now he couldn't remember a word. Somehow he managed to repeat the words after the reverend, so dazzled by Julia that he forgot each one as it came out.

"I do," he said. In his head, he thought, guiltily: *I do agree to lie to you, to keep my past hidden from you because I want you so much.*

Clearing his throat, the reverend read Julia's vows. She got through his name—Calvin Urqhart Patrick Carstairs—without even a look of surprise. She recited each word with clear precision.

Then the reverend reached the words "to love, honor and . . ." and the man hesitated. Cal heard a hushed gasp ripple over the assembly. There was something going on.

Or maybe the reverend could see Julia had changed her mind . . . Maybe she'd found out the truth and she'd let him cling to a dream until this point, when she'd confront him over his past, over what he'd done, tell him she didn't love him . . . she hated him—

No, the man kept going.

Then they got to the question that really mattered.

Cal couldn't breathe. No man, he realized, knew for sure what his bride was going to say until those two words came out.

"I do," Julia said, her lovely voice rising in the sunlight-filled church.

The usual stuff came next. About any man who knew of a reason why they should not be joined, etc. He was the only one who knew of a reason and he kept his peace.

"You may now kiss the bride."

One kiss and it was official. Lady Julia Hazelton was his.

She gasped as he lifted her off her feet into his kiss. His lips caressed hers. A surge of desire— the most damned inappropriate thing—swelled in him. He almost let her go in case a bolt of heaven-sent lightning fried him to a crisp because he was lusting in church. Mam would have been shocked. But after all, he was bad.

He broke away from the kiss. He wanted to paint Julia at this moment and capture the flush of her ivory cheeks, the sheer radiance of her. He had two unfinished paintings of her. Now he had a lifetime with her to complete them.

But first, he wanted to carry her off to bed.

"Now, we have to sign the marriage registry. Then we are to go outside," she reminded him. She tightened the link of their hands. "I want to make you happy, Cal."

He wanted to believe it. But in his gut, he knew

what she meant: *I want to make you happy to be an earl, to be a gentleman, to have Worthington Park.*

A slow grin lifted his mouth. "Remember I want to make you happy, too."

He swept her into his arms and he kissed her again, even though they were supposed to be leaving the church. His desire felt like what happened when you tossed airplane fuel on a bonfire.

Minutes later, he was signing the names he'd hated—Carstairs and Worthington—to a paper that was intended to represent the happiest moment of his life.

It stunned him to realize those names didn't represent the old earl to him anymore. It felt like they represented him. He was so stunned Julia had to lead him out of the church.

Rice showered them. People rushed forward with hugs, kisses, congratulations. Flashbulbs popped. A photographer with a camera mounted on a tripod took photos of Julia and him, then commanded, cheerfully, "Now the family of the Earl of Worthington. All together."

Cal grasped the handles of David's chair and wheeled him. Diana and her sisters took their places. Then, Cal offered his arm to the countess. In a low voice he said, "The dower house is ready for you to move, whenever you want, like I promised."

"Thank you," she whispered. "I shall go this afternoon. I am ready to go."

He caught Julia looking at him with surprise. Then she smiled again and he saw the hope in her eyes.

When he'd told the countess he was marrying Julia, he'd asked her about her sons and the three missing women. She had insisted Anthony had looked at no one but Julia, and that John was too young for driving motorcars and flirting with women. Then she'd apologized, profusely, for not helping his mother. She'd broken down in tears. He'd tried to harden his heart, but Julia had gotten to him.

He was tired of hatred, tired of anger. That fantasy of a happy home—it had wrapped around his heart, and that afternoon, he'd made peace with the countess.

Glowing, Julia brought her brothers, her sister and Zoe over for photographs. Then she fetched her frail-looking mother and her autocratic, tough-looking grandmother.

After the photos were done, Julia tossed the bouquet. A chubby girl tried to push Isobel aside, but his new sister-in-law caught the flowers. Then tossed them quickly away, where young women jumped for them like cats on a mouse.

Ignoring the melee, Isobel came up to him. "I am happy to have you as my brother by marriage."

"I'm happy to have you as a new sister."

Together they looked over to Julia, who stood with her mother and grandmother and chatted with guests.

"Did you like her dress?" Isobel asked. "It's all anyone has talked about since she got back from Paris. What she would wear and how long it should be."

"She was wearing a dress?"

"Of course! She would have looked pretty shocking in the church without one." Then she grinned. "You were teasing."

"Sure I was."

"Did you hear Reverend Wesley pause? He looked at me as if he was going to smite me."

"The reverend can't smite you, Isobel. Only God can do that—and he's not going to do it to innocent young girls."

"You don't know what happened last time, when Nigel got married. I scratched out the word *obey* in his sermon book. Zoe didn't want to say it, and the reverend wouldn't omit it to please her. So I took it out."

Cal had to laugh.

"I got caught out at the ceremony. Anyway, if a woman has to obey her husband, why shouldn't he also agree to obey her?"

"Maybe because two people can't be masters in one house. It's better if they're equals." But he and Julia could never be that. They were from different worlds.

"I suppose that is true." Isobel frowned. "There's a man standing there, smoking a cigar. I've never seen him before. He looks like one of the pictures in the newspapers of Al Capone."

Cal turned. The man, standing beneath an oak, had his hat pulled low. It was like the feeling of having his fighter plane engine cut out on him. Kerry O'Brien was here. At Worthington. On his wedding day. What the hell—?

"Is he a friend of yours?" Isobel asked. She must have seen the recognition on his face.

His blood felt colder than ice coating a northern lake. "Not exactly. Why don't you go and see how Julia is feeling? Would you do that for me?"

It took some coaxing, but Isobel left him and he went over to O'Brien.

The bastard grinned. "Congratulations, Cal. But I bet your new wife doesn't know where you come from."

Cal didn't answer. Julia knew—but not the things O'Brien could tell her. But he knew to never show fear.

"I need more cash, Cal."

"Or you tell my wife?"

"I figured you might care what she knows about you."

"We had this discussion before. You were supposed to go back to New York."

"I hung around. Then heard you were getting hitched to a real fancy lady. That means things have changed, Cal. You've got something to lose now."

He did. But coolly he said, "I need time to think about it."

"Two days. Or I tell your precious wife everything about you."

"A week, damn it." His heart thundered. If O'Brien did it, he'd lose Julia forever. His hands shook and he fisted them by his side.

The man shrugged. "Okay. But I ain't going nowhere. And don't think you're gonna get me bumped off quietly and buried somewhere. I'm too careful."

O'Brien walked away then, toward the woods and the path that led down to the village.

Cal looked up toward the church. Only Zoe, Nigel and Julia were left, waiting to leave. Julia was going to wonder where in hell he was, why he was not with her. He started walking toward his new wife, when a hand touched his arm. He swung around, ready to slam his fist into O'Brien's mug—

He was face-to-face with piercing black eyes. It was the older woman from the gypsy's encampment. He forced himself to calm down. "Morning, Genevra. Are you coming to our wedding reception?"

Genevra cackled. " 'Course not, yer lordship. I wouldn't be welcome at the big house."

"Why not?" he said stubbornly. "You live on the estate like anyone else."

When she laughed again, he said, awkwardly, "If you'd like to take some food, there will be plenty. I could have the cook put together a basket for you to take back to the camp."

"Ye're kind, milord." She was swathed in a black shawl and her eyes were unblinking, like a crow's. "You shouldn't have married her ladyship. You've condemned her to the curse."

"I told you I don't believe in curses. I'm going to take care of Lady Julia."

"It might be your life that's in danger, milord. For what would be a greater tragedy to the new countess than to lose the husband she loves?"

"If you've come to spread fear, you can leave my family alone."

Genevra backed away.

Then he felt like a heel for scaring her. It was O'Brien he was mad at, not Genevra. Suddenly Cal realized when he'd said *family* he hadn't only meant Julia and him. He'd meant his cousins and even the countess. Julia really had gotten under his skin.

"I'm sorry, Genevra," he said. "But I don't like threats."

"There's something you should know, milord. I were out walking yesterday and a fancy motorcar drove past me. Driving it was a man with a fedora pulled low. The girl beside him had blue-black hair."

"Who was the man?"

Genevra shook her head. "I don't know either of them and the man was driving fast. But it was near the road by Miss Lambert's cottage, where a man attacked Lady Julia. And now you've married her." With that, the gypsy turned and ran off.

He scowled, his mind racing at the possibility of the brute still out there, targeting young women.

"Cal?" Julia was walking toward him, puzzlement on her face.

He pushed aside the threats from O'Brien, his own lies and Genevra's warning. This was his first day married to Julia, the only nice girl he'd known. If O'Brien talked, she would be gone, but this day was precious—he wanted this day, and he was committing a sin to have it. He tried to push aside the threats from O'Brien, his own lies and Genevra's warning. But he couldn't help looking at Julia's neatly bobbed, shining blue-black hair.

In the center of a long table, the wedding cake stood.

Hannah had slipped up the servants' stairs. She peeked through the rear doorway into the ballroom. No guests were inside, but footmen rushed in and out and Mr. Wiggins was overseeing.

Biting her lip, she studied the cake.

It was made of octagonal shapes. The wine-soaked fruitcake had been carefully measured, then shaved with a knife to make the shape even. Dowels had been used within to support the structure. Pure white royal icing covered each layer, decorated with fanciful icing shapes that were tinted rose, pale blue and mint green. Edible silver balls reflected the sunlight pouring into the room. The cake stood elevated on pillars, and real white- and cream-colored roses were heaped at the base.

Hannah felt a glow of pride. Mrs. Feathers had always accused her of being clumsy. Obviously she wasn't. She truly had the skill to be a fine cook. She was glad she had made something beautiful for the earl and Lady Julia.

She no longer felt terrible jealousy for Tansy, who was so much prettier than she would ever be and who had Eustace wrapped around her—

A flurry of noise startled Hannah and she stepped back, closing the door until it was open just an inch. She peeped through. The earl's family came in, the young ladies elegant in their hats with feathers and their flowing summer dresses. Lady Julia's family also walked in, the gentlemen startlingly handsome in tailcoats. Then the earl came in himself with his new bride.

Holding her breath, Hannah watched the new Lady Worthington approach the cake. "Cal, look! It's exquisite."

"It's a work of art, that's for sure," he agreed.

Then, in front of them all, the earl swept his wife into a kiss. A kiss that could have melted all the ice in the icehouse, it was so wonderfully romantic.

20

Wedding Night at Worthington

With Cal at her side, Julia cut into the beautiful wedding cake. Laughter surrounded them, and cheers rang up as she made the first slice. Wishes flowed for their happiness, for a fruitful marriage. A string orchestra played and Cal put his hand on her lower back and led her into a waltz.

She was gloriously in love. It made her heart ache with the sheer joy of it.

Cal danced with her toward the terrace windows. They slipped outside—where they were alone. Cal led her into the shade. He held her hand, fingers entwined with hers. "Suddenly I have good memories of this place."

"I'm so glad." Worthington had been filled with poignant memories for her. The joy of having been in love with Anthony; the sorrow of losing him to the War. For her, those memories were as imbued into the estate as wax was worked into the woodwork. But now this would be the house where she had married. Where she built a future with Cal.

She had saved Worthington. But that mattered far less than the fact Cal must be healing. "I always loved it here." Her voice wobbled. "But now it

440

seems so much more precious—because I am here with you."

"Julia—no one's ever said anything like that to me before. And I feel like you mean it."

"Of course I do." He was the confident man who painted naked models, yet sometimes he was so vulnerable.

He grinned—more shyly than she'd ever seen. "I can't wait for tonight," he said softly.

Tonight. Their wedding night.

He drew her into his arms. Cal kissed her neck, right at the join with her shoulders. The day was warm, but this set her on fire. She was ready to dissolve . . .

"We should go back," she said briskly. At least she tried to sound brisk. It came out rather croaky. "The guests will think we've slipped away . . . to do things."

"We can do things now, Sheba. Any wicked thing you want. I bet you've fantasized but made sure no one ever found out about it. Or do ladies not allow themselves to have erotic fantasies?"

She blushed fiercely. "Don't tease me."

"I'm sorry. Just don't ever forget how much I love you."

"Of course, I won't," she promised. "And Paris opened my eyes to naughty ideas."

He drew in a sharp breath. "We'll go back to the crowd for now," he said, his voice more hoarse. "But tonight I'm going to make you mine."

"I already am yours."

"I want to make sure I can never lose you."

Julia caught her breath. Why would he fear losing her? Because he had lost people he loved? His smile had faded and he led her back to the glass terrace doors.

Later, as she was preparing for bed—for her wedding night!—Julia gazed in her mirror and she hurt for him as she remembered how nervous he'd sounded about losing her. She wanted this night to be special. Perfect. Ellen was behind her, brushing out her hair. "You do not need to do one hundred strokes tonight." Cal, being sweet, had arranged for Ellen and Ben to move into the house that afternoon. His specialist was already helping Ellen, who had told Julia she was having fewer nightmares.

"It's my wedding night. My husband will be here any minute," she added.

Ellen smiled. "And you'll bowl him over, I'm sure. You look lovely, my lady."

Julia gazed at her reflection. Did she? She wore a new nightgown from her trousseau. There was barely anything to it. It looked like what a moving picture star would wear. Silk with tiny straps, a bodice of lace shaped to curve around each breast, so it was almost like having them bare. Although it was pure, pale white, she knew it certainly did not look virginal.

Cal was going to see her in this. And he might want to see her in much less.

"I will go, my lady."

"Wait—"

Ellen stopped. "Yes, my lady?"

She'd realized that once Ellen left her, Cal could come in. Nerves gripped her. But this was the 1920s, not Victorian England. She was supposed to be brave about this.

But that was also what scared her. People talked about sex all the time—women and men. Everyone wanted passion and if it wasn't to be had in marriage, they got it elsewhere. The women in the Parisian nightclub talked openly about sex, but she—she didn't really know anything about it. For all she'd told Mother she did.

"What's wrong, my lady?"

Really, she couldn't stall all night. Or night after night. "Nothing at all. Thank you."

"Yes, my lady," Ellen said, and left.

Once she was alone, Julia got up from the vanity, pulled on her robe and tied it tight. She started to pace. She was in the countess's room. Cal had vowed to hire an army of decorators to change it however she wished. The countess had gone to the dower house on the estate. And now the wedding was over, Diana must soon go to Switzerland to have her baby.

At the wedding reception, the Earl of Summerhay had been a true gentleman about losing her to

Cal, wishing them happiness. The Duke of Bradstock, however, had said, "Julia, I am afraid he's going to make you unhappy. He's not one of us. But I will be there for you. I promise. I won't let him break your heart."

"How considerate of you to worry about me," she had said, secretly rolling her eyes.

What was taking Cal so long?

On the other hand, was she ready for him? How did one go from being too ladylike, embarrassed and restrained to even address the subject, to actually doing it in a way that would please a man?

What if this part of their marriage didn't work? Would he stray?

"Stop," she said to her reflection. It was crazy to worry about losing him before they'd even started. She ached for his touch. Didn't that promise it would be wonderful?

The door opened and Cal stepped into her room.

"Oh, er," she said. Eloquently.

He wore a robe of indigo silk, belted at the waist. His feet were bare. His tousled blond hair fell over his brow.

A lady took charge of all situations—she greeted visitors, knew how to engage in polite conversation, knew how to address the myriad details that went into running a house.

How on earth did one greet a man before getting into bed with him? Julia tried what any social hostess would do—bright and innocuous remarks. "The wedding was lovely, wasn't it?"

"All I needed was to hear you say, 'I do,' doll. The rest of it just got in the way."

"In the way of what?"

"Making love to you."

The intense way he looked at her—all blue eyes and heat—made her feel she was melting. There was such naughtiness in his gaze. She focused on his wrists, of all things. Bare under the sleeves of his robe. He had elegant, long fingers.

"Perhaps we should slip into the bed. Which side would you prefer?" she asked politely.

That ignited one of his naughtiest grins.

He came to her, tipped up her chin, slanted his mouth over hers. His tongue teased hers. He tasted of brandy, but mostly of Cal—the warm, sensuous flavor she knew from kissing him.

He slipped his hand in her robe, cupped her breast through the filmy bodice of her scandalous nightdress.

"Oh," she gasped.

His palm caressed her nipple, then his fingers lightly closed around it. He gently pinched.

"Oh!" It came out much louder.

His fingers did wicked things to her nipple and, through the satin of her nightdress, to the private place between her legs.

She felt the familiar flare of nerves over doing

something naughty. But she could now be as wicked with Cal as she wanted to be.

"I want to watch you come, Julia. I want to see you in ecstasy, hear you scream my name."

She stared, not comprehending a thing.

"You're the most beautiful woman in the world, Julia. I used to dream I could escape New York's slums and touch the stars. Holding you in my arms is as magical as touching all the stars in the universe."

Hands trembling, she undid his robe. He murmured, "Yes, Julia," as the dark blue silk parted, revealing his lean body. She'd never seen a whole naked male body. Statues always had fig leaves; illustrations in books had some kind of demure covering added.

She giggled.

Cal stopped kissing her and his hands stopped caressing. "I look funny?"

Oh goodness, he was pouting. "No. You're just so lean and firm. And then there's that part that sticks out. Like a baton. I just didn't know it looked like that." Her cheeks burned.

Cal grinned. "You're more than lovely. You're like a drug I can't get enough of." He opened her robe. She knew it was going to happen but she felt nervous, standing before him in her skimpy gown. His eyes went wide, met hers, glowing a fiery blue. "Julia—you aren't just as lovely as a star, you're the sexiest Sheba I've ever seen."

She blushed. A lady should be shocked to be described so, but she felt a thrill. She moved to close the robe again, but he pushed it off her shoulders. It fell to the floor. Cal lifted her up, her silk skirts spilling over his arms. He carried her to her bed. Then he whisked up the skirt of her nightgown and—to her absolute shock—buried his face between her bare legs, kissing her in that most intimate place.

"Cal! What are you doing?"

He couldn't answer, of course—

Oooh. His tongue moved over her private place, caressing her. This was stunningly wonderful. Julia closed her eyes, too ladylike to look as he did things to her. He tasted her in such an intimate way that she was blushing. He didn't seem to mind. Or be shocked.

Oh!

She'd never dreamed Cal would put his mouth to her sex and would caress her, nibble her. Or that it would feel so good. Julia stretched her arms over her head. Pleasure made her want to moan. She felt so sensuous. So thoroughly feminine.

His hands pressed to her naked bottom, making her gasp as he lifted her.

She opened her eyes and saw Cal's heavy-lidded blue eyes watching her. A bit of blond stubble graced his jaw and cheeks. She couldn't resist—she reached out and rubbed her palm against it.

It tickled and the light stab sent a shot of desire right between her legs.

"Oh!"

He was hers now. She could touch him in any way she liked. She couldn't quite believe it.

He bent to her sex again and caressed with his tongue. He flicked a place that sent a bolt of lightning through her.

Pleasure grew and grew. She rocked her hips, driven to satisfy this need building in her. A need that made her hands curl into the bed. That made her moan his name. She'd never known anything like it.

"Oooooh!"

The most unladylike things happened. Her hips launched up and smacked him. Her arms flailed on the bed. She cried out. She was in a maelstrom of pulsing muscles and pleasure.

She reached a peak, almost flying off the bed. It began to loosen its grip and she flopped back to the mattress feeling as if she was floating, as if she weighed nothing at all.

Cal moved up and kissed her. She tasted ripeness and blushed. Perspiration prickled on her and she was panting for breath.

"Good?" he asked.

"The bee's knees. I had no idea. I mean—I've felt desire for you that is so strong it made me rather desperate. But I had no idea it made one feel *this* wonderful."

His grin would have melted icebergs. "Once you've had an explosive climax, Julia, you're driven to seek it again. Now, let me give you another."

Julia looked down and saw he was still erect. "Oh yes. Of course. That is my duty—"

"The hell with duty," he said roughly. He moved over her, naked. His legs were spread to rest on either side of hers. "I just want to make you feel good."

He kissed her and she ached inside. She felt empty and wanted—needed—him to fill her. Was this what she'd been missing all her life? She'd thought dancing wildly to jazz was thrilling, but this was the most special dance of all.

Then he touched the tip of his erection to her most private place. She held her breath. Held his gaze—his vivid blue gaze. The way he looked at her . . . it was the most intimate thing. She'd never had any man look so deeply into her eyes.

He touched her down there, opening her. Something thick and warm pressed against her. She had never dreamed it would be like this. Primitive. Hot. Sweaty. Earthy and real.

Daringly, she let her hands move over his back. She shivered at the flex of his big, powerful muscles. He was so different than her—broad back and narrow hips. Her hands went down low enough to feel the hard curves of his naked buttocks.

Beautiful. He was so beautiful.

She let her hand drift around his hip. Her

fingers brushed the hair that grew thickly between his legs. It tickled her fingertips.

Then she touched it. The thick shaft of his erection. Her fingers skimmed over velvet skin, the ridges of veins, and touched a soft full shape at the end. Wetness stuck to her fingertips.

Cal groaned. "I like that, Julia." His eyes glowed. "I knew you would be like this. Here, in bed, I knew you wouldn't be ladylike at all."

His fingers touched her as she stroked him. He opened her and she gasped at the flood of wetness he released.

"Do you want me?" he asked.

"So much it hurts." She giggled shyly, but it was true.

The world hadn't stopped this time. It still raced on all around them. But nothing else mattered other than this moment. Nothing except showing Cal how much she truly loved him.

She arched her hips against him. Gasped as his hardness slipped inside a little.

"Let me do it," he murmured. "I'll be gentle."

He was. Slow, gentle, moving himself into her with restrained power. She felt a twinge of pain, dug her fingernails into his bare arms.

He stopped. "Are you okay?"

The pain eased. "I am now."

Then he was inside her. Completely. Deeply. His body lay along hers, touching hers, though he supported his weight on his arms.

"You're so lovely. So hot. Like silk." His words came out jerky. "I can't hold on."

"Hold on to what?" she breathed.

"Sanity," he muttered. He moved inside her, drawing back. Slowly, he thrust forward again. Sensation exploded in her brain like a band bursting into frantic jazz music.

Over and over, he thrust. She—she liked it. Moans escaped her. She made all kinds of funny little sounds because she had to let them out or she'd explode.

He shifted, so his shaft rubbed the place he'd touched with his mouth—

She squealed. A wave of sheer joy hit her. Her whole body erupted all at once. All her muscles pulsed. Pleasure rushed all over her again.

She clung to him. Felt him go stiff against her. He shuddered. "Julia."

She'd never had her name said like that. As though she was the most powerful thing in the whole world.

His hips moved against her. He was having his pleasure, too. She held him, loving that she could share this with him.

After, Cal rolled off her and wrapped his arms around her. He covered them both with the sheets and counterpane. He kissed the top of her head. "I love you so much. I'm a lucky man."

She closed her eyes. "Not half as lucky as me," she breathed.

He gave a soft laugh. "Oh, Julia. God—" He broke off and kissed her passionately.

Sapped of strength, still delirious with pleasure, she cuddled in his arms.

Just before she fell asleep, she knew she'd found her place in the world.

Julia woke in the morning, cradled by Cal's muscular arm. It was the second most thrilling moment she'd ever known. Most aristocratic couples did not share a bed. After last night, she would not accept anything less.

He stirred at her side. She gazed up at him, and he kissed her forehead gently. "Good morning, my lovely wife."

She giggled. "Good morning, my gorgeous husband." Wild ideas filled her head. She wanted to make love again—but it wasn't nighttime, of course.

"I knew when I broke through that ladylike shell I'd find a woman inside who was all fire and passion. I want you like this always, Julia. I don't want you hiding who you really are anymore. Promise me you'll never hide the fire inside you again."

"Cal, I can't be like this at dinner parties and in the drawing room."

"Sheba, you're not going to have time for dinner parties and drawing rooms. I'm going to keep you in here." Then he looked serious. "Except for today. I have to go out this morning. I have some business to attend to."

That startled her. "You do? What sort of business?"

"Some private business."

She realized he was not going to say any more than that.

"I don't want you to worry your pretty head about things," he said. "That's what I do as your husband. I take care of you. I have to leave right after breakfast. I don't know how long I'll be."

"Pretty head!" She frowned teasingly. "Cal, I expect to share burdens with you as your wife. But you don't know when you will return?"

"No." He hesitated. "I might be out tonight."

"Tonight? But it is the night after our wedding."

"Sorry, Julia. I have to do this. I'll make it up to you. And, Julia, you can't go anywhere on your own. Genevra saw a man in a fancy automobile driving a dark-haired girl on the estate."

She wanted to ask him more, but he was gone then, out of their shared bed. He wrapped his robe around him, but left his belt untied, as if he didn't want to linger long enough to do it up. He went through the connecting door to his room with the parting words, "See you later."

She didn't quite understand. She thought they were beginning their lives together. Being alone wasn't what she'd planned for the first day after their marriage.

Minutes later, her door opened and her heart leaped with hope he'd changed his mind—

Ellen came in with a tray. She placed it across Julia's hips. A married woman had breakfast in her bed. "His lordship said you were ready for your tray." Ellen poured her a cup of tea. "What will you be doing today, my lady? What clothing should I put out?"

"I will do what I always do. Put out my light tweeds. I suppose I will go and see the various women who have accounts with me. But first I have work to do—review the menus, arrange to meet with the housekeeper."

She knew what it was to be mistress of a great house. This was what her mother and grandmother had groomed her to do. It would not worry them in the least to have their husbands disappear. They would have expected it. She had thought, long ago, she would be mistress of Worthington. And now she was here, in the house she loved, that had been so special to her.

But Julia felt empty. She felt as if a huge part of her would be missing, if Cal was not here.

That was nonsense. She drank her tea. There was so much to be done. She could now fulfill all the plans she and Anthony had made for Worthington.

She should be happy. She had purpose. And much to do.

21

An Automobile Accident

After breakfast, the lady of the house always took care of the business of the house in the morning room. At Worthington Park, the morning room was painted pale lavender, the furnishings in the same pale purple and gilt. A walled garden lay outside its windows, with small paths and fountains and statues of slender Grecian ladies.

Julia took her seat at the desk. For years, she had been prepared for this day. She drew out the day's menu. She telephoned the housekeeper on the house telephone and relayed changes she'd made to the menu. "I have to go out this morning," she said, "but this afternoon we shall review the rooms, the linens and the household accounts."

"Very good, my lady." The housekeeper rang off.

After that, Julia set out in her motorcar. Cal was not here to go with her, but this was her place, her work, and she would not be kept from it.

Her morning spent with the various women of Brideswell and Worthington, the women who had accounts with her, cheered her immensely. Her loans had started a tea shop in the village and a millinery, had sent a woman for medical training and saved a widow's farm, allowing two war veterans to be employed as farmhands. Julia drove to Lower Dale Farm with treats and books for the children. Everyone congratulated her on her marriage, wished her well.

But as she was walking back to her car at Lower Dale Farm she spotted Genevra.

The elder woman wagged a finger at her. "You be careful, my lady. Now that you're wed, you'll be in danger."

"From the curse? Genevra, I don't believe in such things."

"You'd best heed my warning," the gypsy woman said. "Look out for yourself." With that, she retreated into the woods and disappeared between the fluttering leaves.

Julia did drive back to Worthington very carefully. Foolish to be even a little superstitious, but she was. She left her car outside the garage and started up toward the house.

She was halfway, passing a large grove of leafy laurels, when a branch snapped behind her. She heard a sharp breath drawn from someone who was close to her. She fought panic and turned—

The Duke of Bradstock stood on the path behind her. He wore breeches and a riding jacket of black. His hat was tucked beneath his arm.

"You startled me." But she smiled in great relief. It was no mystery man here to attack her.

"I apologize. I came down from London. Just

456

bought a horse from your brother's stables today. Took my new gelding for a run. I decided to ride over and see you, Julia. I was riding up from the path through the woods when I saw your car. I left my mount at the stables. I wondered if you would care to come for a ride with me this afternoon."

She had not been riding in a long time—since she had ridden with Cal. Athena had been brought to the Worthington stables. "I would love to, James. Just allow me a moment to change."

She did so quickly, eager to ride. Soon, hooves clopped as their horses trotted along a dirt track that wound through a meadow and led to fields. Then James sent his horse racing off. She did the same. He soared over a stone wall. She followed. After taking the jump, she leaned against her horse's extended neck, laughing.

James reined in, brought his horse to a walk, patting the animal's lathered withers. She joined him. His dark eyes glittered. "I guess you do not do this with your American husband."

"Cal does ride, though he is just learning."

"If you yearn for a good gallop, Julia, you need only make a telephone call to me. I'll be more than happy to join you. In fact, I see it as my duty."

"And why would it be your duty to accompany me when I'm riding?" she asked.

"It is my duty to ensure you are not denied the activities an English lady enjoys. I should be more than happy to join you on a ride, take you to

London, escort you to the opera. I've heard your husband regularly travels to the wilds of Canada to paint. I assume he will still do it. I think it's a crime for him to leave you alone while he lives in the bush like a savage. It would be a privilege to ensure you are never lonely, my dear."

"James, perhaps I am misinterpreting but I thought this was to be a ride of two friends. You aren't flirting with me, are you?"

"Of course I am."

"But I'm married."

"Married women have love affairs, Julia. I would be an escape from your uncouth husband."

"I love my husband," she protested.

"Rubbish. Your father hoped to marry you to the Earl of Worthington years ago. I can only assume your brother continued the family ambition and pushed you into the marriage."

"He certainly did not. I made my own choice."

"You chose a man who dresses in rags and possesses no manners?"

"He dressed that way deliberately to shock people. In truth, Cal is very gentlemanly."

James scowled. "His ignorance of our rules will frustrate you and his cocky attitude will grow tiresome."

"James, I would never betray my husband. The fact you believe I'm that sort of woman hurts me deeply. I am going to return to the house." She turned Athena around.

But Bradstock had his horse canter beside her, and positioned himself to block her path.

"What about when he's unfaithful to you? Are you going to allow him to paint nude women? He's been notorious for love affairs. Men don't change."

She'd struggled not to blush at the word *nude*. Now she felt her blood turn to ice. "I believe people can change. I've seen evidence of it again and again." Cal *had* changed.

"I'm not giving up, Julia. At some point you will despise that rough diamond you married. And I will be there for you."

"Forget about me, James. Marry someone for love and devote yourself to them."

He reached out and grasped her reins, startling her. Suddenly, his arrogant mask had dropped. She'd never seen him look so vulnerable. "I'm in love with you, Julia. I've been in love with you for a long time. That has never changed. I'm hoping, someday, you might finally see what you've overlooked all these years."

"James—"

"I paid one of those private investigators in New York, a former policeman, to find out something of your husband's past."

"You didn't—"

"I did it for *your* sake. Some of the things I learned about your husband would shock you. He associated with those mobsters involved in prohibition. He's a thug, Julia."

"I don't believe that."

"Ask him about it. I can give you evidence if you want it. The investigator has photographs, statements. Your husband is a rich man, Julia, and he made his fortune illegally in the trade of selling bootleg liquor. Men who crossed him were beaten up. There were men who accused him of being involved with murders. He is a ruthless criminal, Julia."

Murders? Assaulting people? How could Cal do that—after what he'd seen happen to his father? Her heart raced, but she hid the cold fear in her veins. "I will talk to Cal about this, James. For now, I think I had better return to the house. Good afternoon." She skirted Athena around him and took off at a gallop. She arrived at the Worthington stable alone—James had not followed her. She supposed she had offended him, but she refused to worry about that.

Cal did not return for dinner.

Julia ate with David and her new cousins by marriage, but she couldn't get James's words out of her mind. David asked where Cal was—so she knew he hadn't confided his plans with his brother. She retired early, her heart pounding. Was Cal really a criminal in America? Had he behaved with violence? Had James made up the awful story?

For her whole life, she'd slept alone in a bed. Now it felt strange to do it. After just one night sleeping with Cal, she found her bed empty and cold. She turned off the light, rolled on her side.

Her door opened with a soft whisper and Cal walked in. Light spilled in through the connecting door. He wasn't changed for bed—he wore trousers, suspenders and a white undershirt that molded to the muscles in his arms and stretched over his broad chest. "Sorry I had to miss dinner, doll. Let me make it up to you."

She sat up. "Where were you? What was it you had to do?"

She should ask: *Did you really do criminal things in America?* But she couldn't.

Cal didn't answer. Instead, he casually stripped naked. The sight stole any further words out of her mouth. He got on the bed, sitting beside her. He leaned over and kissed her.

Cal didn't just kiss. His hands did the naughtiest things. Caressing her breasts through her night-dress and hiking up the skirt to stroke between her legs.

She should talk to him—but she wanted him too much.

"I've been thinking about this all day," he rasped. "I'm going to make love to you all night."

And he did. She had no idea she could reach her peak so many times. Finally, she was an exhausted puddle on her bed, but he took her one last time, giving her a long, languorous wave of pleasure.

She cried out in sheer joy. Then Cal arched against her, driving his hips tight to hers. He shuddered and gasped her name. "Julia, my love. My beautiful love."

She thought of James's words as Cal slumped against her, but carefully so he didn't press his weight on her. She stroked his damp back, dizzy with pleasure.

And she knew what she was doing. She was afraid to find out the truth.

He rolled off her and she stiffened, expecting him to leave her bed. But he snuggled against her, caressing her shoulder. "What did you do today, love?"

"I went to see the women who have business with me." She wished she could relax under his touch. But she kept *thinking*. The illegal things—that must have been where he'd made the money to stay at Le Meurice.

Cal sat up. Moonlight outlined his wide shoulders and his strong muscled arms with silver. "Alone? Julia, it's not safe."

"I had no other choice."

"Julia, this house is crawling with servants. Take some of them with you. Do that or you can't go."

She blinked. "Cal, this is important to me." It was her place in the world.

"There's something you have to know, Julia. The police sergeant telephoned for me—that's why I missed dinner. I had to go back out, down to the station. Lowry has an alibi for the time you were attacked. He's charged with assaulting Ellen

Lambert, but he couldn't have been the man who attacked you."

She stared in shock, but then Cal's strong arms went around her. His lips closed over hers and she couldn't be afraid. Not with him kissing her. Not with him making love to her. And she went to sleep in his arms.

After breakfast, Cal left again. Julia watched him go out to his motorcar from the drawing room window. She'd promised Cal she wouldn't leave the house alone. His words had chilled her. If Lowry hadn't been the man who attacked her, then who was it?

How could it be possible there was a man who had once lured and killed women with dark hair back in 1916, and now, nine years later, was doing it again? She had asked Cal that very question and Cal had given her terrifying answers. That maybe the man had gone to the War, and had only just returned here. Or maybe innocent women had disappeared in other places over the years and no one knew it was the same man behind them all.

As a new bride, Julia had correspondence to attend to. But she sat, pen in hand, unable to do the duty she'd been trained for. The housekeeper had to telephone her to ask about the menu. Flustered, she made no changes and as she set down the receiver, Wiggins came in.

"There is a—a gentleman caller to see you, your ladyship."

From the sour face on Wiggins, Julia knew the man was not what the butler considered a gentleman. "Did he give his name?"

"His name is O'Brien, my lady. He visited his lordship before. He is an American. I believe they exchanged heated words." Wiggins sniffed. "This gentleman was also seen on the grounds two mornings ago, at the wedding reception, but he did not enter the house as a guest. However, he has insisted on speaking to you. He claims he has something to tell you that you would wish to hear about his lordship."

She frowned. Curiosity ate at her.

"I put him in the library until I could speak to you, my lady. Not one of the finer drawing rooms, however there are still objects that may take his fancy and thus disappear."

"Wiggins, that is most prejudiced."

"He has the look about him of an American criminal, my lady. A 'mobster,' as they are termed in colloquial American. I obtained the impression his lordship is not pleased with this man."

A mobster? Could it be the man arguing with Cal in London? She was even more curious, but pointed out, "Americans speak English."

"Not by my definition, my lady."

She had to smile. But she asked, "Wiggins, before you go—his lordship mentioned a photograph that he found. I believe you destroyed it. Why did you do that?" She watched Wiggins's face carefully.

Saw the flicker of fear behind the correct facade.

"I believed it would spare her ladyship—the dowager, now—a great deal of pain, my lady." He bowed. "I must return to the wine cellar, my lady. The delivery will soon arrive."

She watched him go. What did that mean? But if she'd been attacked by the same man, Anthony and John were innocent. There was no reason for Wiggins to protect them, then.

She wanted to speak to this man, find out why Cal had been angry with him. Cal had been mysterious—keeping quiet about where he went, about the business he had to do. Was this man involved? What was going on with Cal?

Cal slowly walked along the lane behind Lilac Farm. Above him, a bird cawed, and a breeze sent tree branches shivering.

He crept along, moving as stealthily as he would have when he'd had to land his plane behind German lines. War had taught him a lot of things about killing and survival—he never expected to use any of that knowledge in the rarified world of the aristocracy.

But he had to use every skill he had to keep Julia safe. Julia had been attacked here. This was where Genevra had seen a man and a dark-haired woman in a car.

If he hadn't been here that morning, that bastard would have pulled Julia into a waiting car—

Christ, he couldn't think about that. He couldn't think about what would have happened if he'd been too late.

He scanned the ground for some kind of clue. Desperate and crazy, likely enough, but he knew a lot of the criminal element wasn't all that smart in covering tracks.

But he kept thinking of Julia. Couldn't stop his thoughts from going to their wedding night. Which got him hot under the collar. He'd had to leave her the day after their wedding. Gone to see O'Brien and warned the gangster not to reveal the truth of his past to Julia. Warned Kerry that he'd get hurt if he did it. But he saw the smirking appraisal in O'Brien's eyes and knew the bastard wouldn't give up so easily. He must figure he had a plum mark in Cal now. He had to know Cal was desperate to keep his wife in the dark about his past. That was the "private business" he'd had to take care of.

He'd intended to keep Julia happy in bed. Never dreamed it would feel like . . . like he'd gotten a chance to have real heavenly bliss. Making love to Julia had seared him to his soul. It wasn't just sex, it was like a special painting that was more than just a canvas—it was a revelation.

Ahead, Cal spotted the pattern of automobile tires in the dried mud. On the edge, branches were broken down. He walked up to the spot. Someone had parked a car there, hiding it from sight. Why?

Had it been to spy on Julia? Sunlight reflected off

something that glinted. Stooping, he picked it up. A button of onyx rimmed in silver. Not likely from the clothing of the laborer who'd grabbed Julia. Nor had a man like that likely had a car.

So who had been there?

Julia hurried to the library, her skirts swishing around her calves, her heels clicking. Cigar smoke floated from the open door. From the doorway, all she could see was the back of the man's head. He lounged on the settee, his arm stretched along the back of it. The electric light gleamed on his hair, slicked down and neatly parted in the middle.

Julia walked in, saying briskly, "Good morning, Mr. O'Brien. I am Julia, Lady Worthington."

The man clamped the cigar between his teeth and held out his hand to her. She recognized him—he was indeed the man Cal had been speaking to in the Black Bottom Club in London.

He shook her hand firmly, startling her. He definitely did have the look of an American mobster. The newssheets carried pictures of famed American criminals such as Al Capone and Charles Luciano. This man was dressed in the same manner—a pinstripe suit, with matching waistcoat, a white hat on the seat beside him.

"Hello, Julia." He grinned, a smug, arrogant grin.

"I would prefer Lady Worthington," she said. That smile had put her back up. "Would you care for tea?"

"Don't mind if I do, Julia."

She could reprimand him over the use of her name again, but she didn't. He exuded edgy nervousness. His gaze flicked all around the library, and he kept grinning until tea came. Then he pulled out a flask and took a long swallow before taking his cup of tea. She noticed the scar running from his ear to his throat. A war wound, perhaps?

"I have to say, Julia, sitting down to tea with you is a lot more pleasant than looking at Cal's mug."

"You are a friend of my husband's, from America?"

"Cal and I go way back." He leaned back. "Grew up together. There ain't nothing I don't know about Cal. I hear he didn't tell you much about his past. There are a lot of stories I could tell you . . . but Cal wouldn't like that. He wouldn't want me talking about that stuff with his pretty new bride."

She thought of James's words, but she said politely, "I am sure Cal has just not had time to tell me many stories about his youth."

"I don't think he'd like to talk about that to a nice girl like you."

"Mr. O'Brien, I feel you have something you want to say to me."

"I could be willing to give away some of Cal's secrets. For the right price. Wouldn't you want to know all about Cal's dirty past?"

He smirked. A look that made her shiver in apprehension. She was so curious, but she wouldn't give this man the satisfaction of letting him talk. "I am afraid you have made a wasted trip. Cal has been nothing but honest with me." She stood.

"Wouldn't you wanna hear about what he did as a bootlegger? Wouldn't you wanna hear about the Five Points Gang?"

"Mr. O'Brien, I suggest you leave. I shall summon my butler, Wiggins, to escort you to the door. This house can be quite confusing, when one is in a hurry to depart."

She hadn't even reached the bell when two of the Worthington footmen walked in. "Mr. Wiggins sent us to help the gentleman out."

Mr. O'Brien's expression was livid. "There's other people who'd be interested in knowing the real truth about the Earl of Worthington. You tell Cal I said that, Julia. How about that? And tell him I'm staying at the Boar and Castle hotel in the little hick village."

"The public house," she corrected automatically.

He stood, straightened his tie and plopped his hat on his head. "I'll follow the penguins outside. But you give my message to Cal."

She watched him exit the room. After he left, Julia sank to the chair, shaking. What James had told her—it must be true. It explained why Cal had money. It explained . . . why he was ashamed of that money.

But Cal had needed money to take care of David. Cal would have been desperate to protect his brother, desperate because of what the earl and countess had done.

She was still in the library, staring out the window, when footsteps stormed into the room. "I've torn a strip off Wiggins. He should have thrown O'Brien out. He should never have let you speak to him—"

"Why not?" She turned around to confront a white-faced, angry Cal. Then she saw dirt was streaked over his face and his hands were covered in mud. She wanted to tackle Cal about his past, but horror filled his eyes. "What have you been doing?"

"Doing my lordly duty and traveling around my estate, greeting my tenants."

She didn't believe him. It was the way he kept his blue-eyed gaze right on her as he said it. "You look exhausted," she said crisply. "I shall ring for tea."

"Julia, what did O'Brien say to you?"

"Very little, since I was not willing to pay him."

"Did he frighten you? Threaten you?"

"Do your friends always behave like that?"

"He's not a friend, Julia. And I need you to tell me the truth."

"He told me he would be willing to give away some of your secrets for the right price. He asked if I would like to know about what he termed your dirty past. Cal, were you a bootlegger? Did you commit . . . crimes to make money . . . to support David?"

"O'Brien was trying to con money out of you. I was never arrested for doing anything illegal. He probably figured you'd be shocked to know I was poor. But you know all about that."

She did. They were married and the future was what mattered now. Impetuously, she said, "Cal, whatever was in the past is behind us. We have both had sorrow in the past and I believe we must focus on the future. We'll have tea, then I must go out. I want to bring food for the Tofts."

"Forget tea, Julia. There's something I need to do. Upstairs."

Mystified, she followed Cal up the sweeping stairs to their connecting bedrooms. He closed his bedroom door behind them and turned the key.

"Cal—" She broke off as he lifted her off her feet and into his arms.

"Wrap your legs around my waist, doll."

"Around your waist?"

He set her back on her feet, skimmed her skirt up to bare her legs. She squealed—then prayed it wasn't loud enough to startle the upstairs maids. He lifted her up, put his hand under her round bottom to carry her.

She gasped as her husband balanced her on the marble surface of the vanity table on her bottom. Sensually he kissed her neck, his tongue running along her sensitive skin.

She clung to his shoulders. "Cal, it isn't night-time."

He laughed, low and gruff. Deeply, he made love to her, rocking her with him as pleasure built. Her nails dug into his broad, strong shoulders. Heavens, she could see them in her mirror, doing this intimate thing.

"I'd like to paint you like this. The way you look when I'm making love to you. You're the most beautiful creation on earth, Julia."

She gasped at the glorious peak. She cried his name, which ended on a moan. Then he cried out her name.

He held her in his powerful arms and she pressed her cheek over his heart. She loved hearing the fast beat, knowing she'd done that to him.

"I'd like to keep you in bed day and night."

She flushed. "Cal, I have things I must do." Then she regretted the prim words.

"I'll go with you." He nibbled her ear as he said it, and she almost melted. "Cal, I have pies for their dinner. I simply can't wait or I'll be too late."

He smoothed down her skirt, held out his hand.

Cal's automobile was still sitting in Worthington's front drive. He walked around to the right-hand side of the car without thinking. Then growled, "Forgot again."

"Could I drive?" she asked, as she went to the driver's door. "I've never driven your motor."

He winked at her, and she blushed. But he tossed her the keys. "Sure," he said.

It was almost as delightful a vehicle as her Trixie.

The engine purred and the car clung to every turn, rumbling with the promise of decadent power—if she dared. But on the winding road, she just didn't dare.

They'd crested a hill and were heading down toward the road that led to Lilac Farm. From there, she would turn off to Lower Dale Farm. Like the other roads, this was narrow, winding around rocks, trees, following stone walls that bordered fields.

She pressed the brake pedal but nothing seemed to happen. The car was going fast—too fast.

Cal's hand braced against the mother-of-pearl inlay on the dashboard. "Julia, doll, you have to slow down on this road. You don't have to prove to me you're a fast driver."

She pushed desperately down on the brake pedal. But it simply sank to the floor, with all the resistance of a dry sponge. She released her foot and tried again, pushing it down. Nothing happened. "Cal, I'm not trying to prove anything. The brakes don't work!"

Zoe had taught her how to drive, but she didn't really know how one of these automobiles worked, and right now, she rather wished she did. "I will try again. Harder. So this motorcar knows I mean business."

"Try it, doll. Push down hard."

She did, but the brake simply refused to work.

A stone wall was coming up—one that bordered

a farm. The rutted road made a sharp turn in front of it. What if she couldn't make the turn? They'd crash. Cal, in the passenger seat, would be plowed into the stone wall. The motorcar was filled with fuel. Could it explode?

She had to make this corner.

Julia held her breath and stiffened like a board. She thought she'd known fear before. It was nothing like this. She couldn't even feel her heartbeat—which might mean it had stopped.

Cal reached over her and planted his hand on the wheel. "Hang on to it. I'll help you steer."

Even from the passenger side, he was steering with aplomb.

But they were hurtling toward the wall at the bottom of this hill.

"Stay calm, Julia. We can stop this car. I want you to downshift to a lower gear. But do it slowly. I'm going to steer to the side here and use the rougher grass to slow us down."

He moved the wheel firmly and the car rattled toward the edge of the track. She felt the jerk as the wheels left the firm track of the lane.

"Now gear down."

"What will that do?"

"It slows the engine. We're going to put on the handbrake."

But with the hill they just seemed to go faster. Cal said a very rude word. She didn't blame him. She was thinking it herself.

"We're going to have to do a controlled crash."

"*Controlled* and *crash* are two words that can't possibly belong together."

He grinned—a wild, confident grin in the face of danger. "See that bunch of bushes over there? I'm going to steer us into them. I want you to duck down. Cover your face."

"Those are *laurels*. You can't mean you deliberately intend to—"

Cal put his hand on her shoulder and pushed her down. She had one last view of leafy branches coming at the windscreen at high speed. Snapping sounds came from all around her. Something scratched her cheek and she made sure her hands covered as much of her face as possible. The car lurched and there came more sickening breaking and grinding sounds.

The car stopped. The sound of the engine ceased.

Julia parted her gloved fingers and looked between them. Leaves seemed to fill the car. Cal was no longer forcing her down so she straightened. He grabbed broken branches and threw them away. The car and a scrawny laurel brush seemed to have merged in some kind of unholy alliance.

"Are you okay, Julia?"

"Yes. Much better than your motorcar." The glossy front end was crumpled inward. The car had mown over the shrubs with smaller trunks, leaving a trail of destruction.

Cal was fighting with a branch that jutted into

the car on the passenger side and prevented him from opening the door.

"Goodness, this is my very first motorcar crash."

Cal broke the branch with a loud crack and threw it out of the car. "I'd like to think it's going to be your only car crash."

She looked back toward the road. If he hadn't forced them to crash, they would have gone hurtling down the treacherous hill with the right-angle turn at the end and the stone wall at the bottom. If he hadn't forced a crash, they would have been . . . killed.

"Well, thanks to you, I survived it. I think you deserve a reward."

To Cal's surprise, Julia flung her arms around his neck. Her mouth met his in a searing kiss and knocked him back against his seat. At once, he felt the rush of blood to his groin, hardening and thickening him.

They could have been killed. Julia should have been terrified and fainting. But she was talking with toughness. And all he wanted to do was open his trousers and pull her on top of him and take advantage of all this hot passion she was giving him.

So he did that.

With laurel branches tangled in the car, he held Julia on his lap. And he pushed her short skirt out of the way. With his fingers, he teased her, gazing deep into her eyes. He could have lost her. The thought speared him.

She moaned. "Oh yes."

He pulled open his trousers and she wrapped her hand around his shaft, making him groan in sensual agony. To his shock, Julia took him inside and began moving on him. He grasped her hips and met her thrust for thrust. He was driving to take her to her peak when he heard a loud bleating. A voice called, "Hello there? Are you all right?"

"We're okay," Cal called casually, as if he wasn't making love to his wife in a crashed car.

A flock of sheep wandered up to inspect the car. Then Cal saw a gnarled man with a walking stick making his way toward them. The farmer, Brand. He quickly lifted Julia off him and set her back beside him. He heard her giggle behind her palm.

"I can bring me plow horses and pull the car back to the big house for ye, if it will roll," Brand said as he approached.

"I'd appreciate it, Brand," Cal said, fighting to discreetly fasten his trousers. "The brakes failed and we had to crash."

"Newfangled things." Brand shook his head and went to get the horses.

"What happened to the brakes?" Julia asked. "When I put my foot on the pedal, it sank to the floor without doing a thing."

"There was no hydraulic pressure in the line."

"What does that mean?"

He explained quickly how brakes worked. "There's got to be a break in the line." He would be able to figure out what happened if he could get under the car and check the line. But there were too many broken branches snagged beneath the car, and the rutted ground was too high for him to crawl underneath.

Then he saw Julia was shaking. Cal swung out of the vehicle, lifted her out and led her to the farmhouse. Mrs. Brand was upstairs, asleep. Cal made tea.

After a few sips, Brand said, "You'd best be careful. We don't want any harm to fall upon her ladyship, my lord. She's most beloved around here."

"I know she is. And I won't let anything hurt her."

"There's the curse, you know."

"There's no such thing as curses," Cal muttered.

"The curse came true for the dowager countess. Old Lady Worthington has known nothing but pain. Her eldest lad was killed at the Somme and the youngest died in a motorcar accident."

Cal's mam was Irish and believed in pixies, fairies and evil sprites. But he had grown up in a world where he'd fought to get out—and he'd won. Airplanes and motorcars were possible, and they were based on the principles of physics, on chemical reactions and combustion and gears.

"I don't believe it, Brand. No one can utter a few

words and cause accidents to happen, or create illness, or cause people to die. A man can cause harm to other men—but he's got to use something physical to do it. Like a machine gun or an artillery shell."

But when he got the car back to Worthington, after giving Brand some money for his trouble and sending the chauffeur to deliver the pies for the Tofts—which had survived the accident—he took a look under the automobile to see what had gone wrong with the brakes. What he saw gave him the shock of his life.

Cal went to Julia's bedroom. He didn't knock. Julia was his wife, and he didn't see that a husband and wife should be asking permission to see each other. But when he opened the door, Ellen Lambert stood there, arms crossed over her chest.

"Her ladyship is not well tonight."

"What's wrong?" Fear gripped him.

"Your automobile crashed into a tree. My poor lady was shaking. She certainly does not need . . . attentions from a husband tonight."

"I crashed the car to save her life. Is she all right? Does she need a doctor?"

"She needs her rest."

He was going to push past, but then Ellen added, "Her ladyship has not looked well since the day after the wedding, when you went away."

Guilt hit him. He couldn't admit he'd gone to

tell O'Brien to get the hell away from his family. And his anger had only made O'Brien realize he was afraid of Julia learning the truth.

Retreating to his room, Cal undid his robe. He was naked underneath, hadn't bothered to put on pajamas. It almost physically hurt not to be with Julia.

He was stepping into trousers when his door opened.

Julia stood there. "Ellen told me she sent you away. But I wanted you to come to me tonight." She shut the door. "Then I realized I could come to you."

"Then I should be a good host. Do you want a drink?" Cal pulled out a flask. He was tired of brandy and cognac, snooty drinks consumed by pompous men. He needed a stiff drink right now.

"What is it?"

"A drink I would have drunk at home."

"Moonshine?"

He laughed. "I've never had moonshine. Some of it could make you blind. So could bathtub gin, but I admit I've drank that. But this I bought in London. Good Irish whiskey."

"I've never had whiskey. Women don't."

He poured a finger of the liquor in a tumbler. Handed it to her where she sat on the edge of the bed. "But you aren't controlled by rules and tradition, Julia." He held his glass in the air as if toasting her, and took a drink.

She took a swallow. Pulled the glass from her lips. Coughed. "It's like fire in a glass—if fire tasted bitter and awful."

He grinned, though he was troubled. "That is fine ten-year-old whiskey."

"Then I think it has gone bad. Unlike wine, aging didn't seem to help."

He swung away from the bedpost and sat down beside her. She looked a bit shocked, then, to his delight, she pressed against him.

"I know you looked at the motorcar. What had gone wrong?" she asked. "It wasn't the chauffeur's fault, was it?"

"No, it wasn't his fault."

"What is it?" He didn't answer and she pressed, "There's something wrong, isn't there?"

"The brake line had been cut. Deliberately." Had he been too blunt?

"I don't know a lot about automobiles," she said, looking direct and determined. "But if someone cut the brake, doesn't that mean that person meant us to have a car accident?"

God, he admired her. She had incredible strength. "Yeah, I think so."

"That means someone wishes us ill."

"It was my car. It looks like it was intended for me. There have to be a lot of people who'd like me dead," he said. O'Brien, possibly. The dowager countess—maybe her apology had been false.

"Why do you think that?" she protested. "All

the tenants believe they have no better champion."

The idea of someone wanting him dead didn't surprise him. He'd run the risk of getting killed in a gang. At war, he'd escaped death more times than he could remember. In the prohibition world, he'd almost been snuffed several times. Death had been a part of his life for as long as he could remember.

What made him angry this time was that Julia had been in danger.

"What about Lowry?" she asked. "He might have friends getting revenge for him."

Cal nodded. She was a smart woman. "Maybe the dowager countess did it."

Her mouth turned down. "I thought you two were growing to accept each other. And can you really imagine the dowager countess getting on the ground beneath your vehicle to cut a brake line?" Suddenly she giggled. But then she quickly sobered. "What of the man who attacked me?" she asked. "Could it be him—whoever he is?"

"It could be. I'm going to find out who was responsible—and make them pay."

He saw her shiver. "I overheard the maids talking about the curse on the Worthington Wife." She lifted her chin. "A brake line isn't a curse. It's a deliberate act of malice."

"That's true." He took the glass out of her hand, put them both on the bedside table. "Don't think about this anymore. You don't have to worry about anything with me around.

"Tomorrow, I want you to pack, Julia. I want to take you to Italy, to Nice, to wherever you want to go. We'll get away from here." He fell back on his bed, pulling her with him. "Now let me make you forget about all this with a sweet roll in the hay."

And he was pretty sure he did.

22

The Dowager Countess

When Julia went to sleep, Cal got out of bed quietly, got dressed and went out. He drove the Worthington Daimler to the Boar and Castle, parked outside.

Maybe O'Brien had cut the brake line to give Cal a warning.

The publican was still up, serving the last round. Cal found O'Brien with a glass of whiskey. "I wondered when you would show up after I met your wife. Do I tell the newspapers about your past or do I get my dough?"

"I gave you money to get the hell out of England. You're not getting another penny from me."

"Do you really want your pretty wife to read about you in the headlines?"

Cal was aware of the other few men in the bar staring at them, at O'Brien's pale pink suit. In a low voice, he asked, "Did you cut the brake lines of my car?"

Kerry shrugged. "What if I did?"

Cal got up. He grabbed the bastard's arm, twisted it behind him. "I'll break your damned arm if you don't promise to leave Julia and me alone. I'm willing to take care of you like we used to do it back in the Five Points Gang. Understand?"

"You wouldn't. You'd be arrested—"

"I don't give a damn. You almost killed my wife."

He hauled O'Brien to his feet. Dragged him outside and sure enough, people looked at them, but no one said a word. Outside of the pub, he growled, "If you keep pushing me, you ain't gonna live long enough to enjoy Jolly Old England."

Once it wouldn't have been an empty threat. But it was now. He prayed O'Brien didn't figure that out.

O'Brien pulled out a knife, but Cal took care of that with a twist of the man's wrist. "You sell the story to the newspapers, I'll come for you. You do anything to hurt my wife, my family, or me, and I'll get you. You know what I am capable of, O'Brien."

His foe lost his bravado. "All right, damn it."

Cal dragged Kerry O'Brien back into the public house and ordered him another drink. He paid for it. He was walking toward the door when O'Brien said, "I didn't do it. Those brakes—that wasn't me."

He turned. "What?"

"I took credit for someone else's work. I wouldn't want to see you dead. Someone else wants that." Sniggering, he tossed back his whiskey.

Cal went out the door, almost staggering. He'd thought that O'Brien had done it, which would mean it had nothing to do with the missing women or the attack on Julia. Damn. He drove back from the village to Worthington. The shortest route took him past Lilac Farm. It was faster, even though it was a rougher, windier road.

Something jumped in front of him. He slammed on the brake. The car screeched to a stop and his headlights illuminated a small hunched-over person. A woman, and she put her hands up to shield her eyes and let out a shriek.

Cal jumped out of the car. In the streams of light, Mrs. Brand huddled in a ball. He crouched beside her, trying to soothe her. He knew he hadn't hit her, but she was terrified.

"Are you all right, Mrs. Brand?" Nothing looked broken, but as he tried to lift her to her feet, she struggled to scramble away, getting covered in mud. More forcefully than he wanted, he lifted her and drew her toward the car.

She took one look at his vehicle and screamed again. "The motorcar . . . You!" Frantic she shouted, "Sarah! I remember. The motor. It were here. What did you do with Sarah? I saw you!"

"I'm not the man who took Sarah," he said, in a gentle voice. But she still screamed. He caught her and wrapped one arm around her shoulders. "I'm Cal Carstairs. The earl. I want to *find* your daughter, Sarah."

"I can't find Sarah. It's too late. I told her to go away if she couldn't behave. What have I done?"

"It's not your fault." Gently he got Mrs. Brand

to the door. "This isn't the car that Sarah got into," he said. "That was a dark red car. This one is dark blue." Then, he gambled. "It was John Carstairs who took Sarah. Or was it Anthony?"

"That night . . ." She stared helplessly ahead. "The lights were so bright. I followed Sarah to the road. Sarah got into the car and I shouted at her not to go. That she was being wicked. That she would have a terrible reputation. They drove away. But I knew the shortcuts through the woods. I found the car. It was going slow up the lane. It had its lights off. I saw it turn. I followed, trudging and out of breath. But I found the car. I saw Sarah—she were asleep. I heard— It was a spade I heard. And I saw—"

She started to scream again.

Cal pulled out the small flask he kept in his pocket. "Irish whiskey. Like medicine." He forced her to take two swallows. She couldn't cry out while swallowing and he took care to make certain she didn't choke. "Who took Sarah?"

"He were all in black. Like a demon. Then the car went away. I ran down to the farm, but when I got there . . . when I got into the kitchen I felt all dizzy. I don't remember . . ."

"It's okay. I'm going to take you back to the farm. I'm going to find Sarah."

He got Mrs. Brand to sit in the car. Pulling a rug out of the back rumble seat, he wrapped it around her. That gave her lucidity long enough for her to look at him in shock. "My lord? Whatever am I doing here?"

"You don't remember?"

The question made her panic.

"You were out walking," he said. "I'll drive you back to the farm."

"Thank ye, milord," she whispered.

When he reached Lilac Farm he found Brand holding a lantern, calling out in panic for his wife. The man almost fainted with relief as Cal drove up and helped her out. He helped Brand get her to her bed. "Brand, I believe she saw the man who took Sarah. I found her on the road—"

"She always chases after cars, thinking Sarah's in one of them."

"I think she saw something, up one of the lanes. She saw the car there that night."

"She never told me. I didn't know she'd gone out that night. I found her in the kitchen."

Mrs. Brand must have collapsed because her mind had been unable to cope with the truth. Perhaps seeing his vehicle had made her remember. Which meant they might have been near where Sarah had been taken by a man who'd used a shovel.

Julia was still sleeping when Cal got back to Worthington. He left her alone, crawling into his own bed. At about three, he dozed off. When he woke, the sky had lightened to the color of steel. It was daylight, but the day was cloudy. Cal got up, got dressed. He got his car—the brake line was now fixed—and was driving past the house when a figure rushed toward him. He hit the brake.

This time it was Julia. She wore a skirt and blouse and held a shawl that flapped in the wind. "I saw your light go on. Where are you going so early?"

"I think I know where to find Sarah Brand. I'm going now so I can be there when it's light."

"I am coming, too."

"No, you're not, Julia."

"Yes, I am." She pulled open the passenger door.

"All right. But you will have to stay in the car."

As they drove he told her what Mrs. Brand had said. "I think she saw Sarah's killer."

"But why didn't she ever say anything?" she asked.

"Maybe it was too much for her and the shock of it made her mind snap. I think seeing my automobile made her remember. You'd have to get a headshrinker like Sigmund Freud to figure it out." He drove to the lane that led to Lilac Farm.

"It's so awful to think she saw it," Julia murmured.

"You don't have to do this."

"I do—I have to."

He admired her courage. He drove slowly, looking for—looking for anywhere that might make a good place for a grave. Or graves. It had to be secluded enough that the killer had felt he could carry a body and dig a grave and not be seen. It had to be close enough to the farm that Mrs. Brand had been able to catch up to him. Obviously the killer didn't know Mrs. Brand had seen him.

On his left was a lane that crawled up a hill. Tall grass filled in the track and tree branches hung over it. The grass had been knocked down recently. Some of the branches had been snapped. Someone had driven up this relatively unused path in the past few days.

I saw it turn. I followed, trudging and out of breath.

If Mrs. Brand had followed the car up the hill, she would have been out of breath. Cal crept up the track. He saw the fear on Julia's face.

The track ran out on the top of a hill. There was an outcropping of rocks.

Julia pointed at them. "There were legends that those were used for sacrifices. It is supposed to be haunted. All nonsense, of course."

"But it could explain lights being seen here. Headlights," Cal murmured.

He stopped the car as close to the large rocks as he could get. He got out, opened up the trunk and got out his shovel. He started walking around. Smaller stones were piled up—obviously by human hands. Behind those piles he scraped fallen leaves aside and discovered the ground was lumpier. The area had been dug up before.

He started to dig. Julia was getting out of the

car. He called, "Don't come over here, Julia. I don't want you to see this. If I find what I'm looking for—it's going to haunt you forever."

The summer morning was cool, with gray clouds overhead—but he was digging hard and started to sweat. In the War, he'd dug graves for bodies—especially the bodies of pilots, if there was any-thing left to bury. He stopped digging, wiped his face. He was actually wiping his eyes, because he damn well felt like he could cry.

"Are you all right?" Julia called. "Oh, I'm sorry—what a foolish thing to ask."

"I appreciate you asking. I thought I'd learned to be tough when I was growing up. But when I think about what it is that I'm doing right now, I want to be sick. Stay by the car."

The earth was compacted, which made it hard to shovel with care. He pushed the shovel in and went deeper than he'd expected. And hit something.

He uncovered more and his gut clenched. He was looking down at the head that had almost decomposed to a skeleton, still with some black hair. He dropped down on one knee. Around the skeletal neck was a tiny silver locket. "Sarah" was engraved on the front. With initials upon the back. "J.C."

John Carstairs? Cal carefully prized open the locket. A lock of black hair was inside.

He found another two piles of pebbles and figured that they probably marked the graves of the other girls who had vanished—Eileen Kilkenny and Gladys Burrows.

Julia walked toward him but he stopped her. "I'm taking you back home."

"I saw your face, Cal. I saw the horror and torment in your eyes. You found one of them."

He let the shovel fall. He went to Julia, wrapped his arms around her, burying his face in her hair. The wave of grief was staggering. "I found Sarah."

"Oh—oh no. Poor, poor girl." She let out a sob, then took a deep breath. "Is there any clue to who did it? Don't spare me if you believe you know."

"I don't know yet, angel. But there's a locket around Sarah's neck with some black hair in it, and the initials J.C. It must be John Carstairs. God, there's been so much tragedy here. Maybe they're right and this place was cursed."

"What do we do now?"

"Go to the police."

"But we— I would like to go to the dowager countess first. I would like her to know, before the police come."

"Why?" he asked, confused.

She touched his arm with that gentle, elegant way she had. "Plans must be made, because once the police constables know, there will be gossip. It can't be stemmed." She stroked down his arm, clasped his dirt-covered hand. "This has been awful for you. We will see the dowager and we will get you a cup of tea. That is the best thing for a bad shock."

He couldn't understand how Julia could be so cool and collected. His heart hammered and his eyes burned with tears of grief—even though he'd never met these girls—and his blood burned with outrage. John Carstairs would have thought of him as nothing—Cal knew that—and all along, he'd been a sick, vicious killer.

Then he looked at Julia and saw the tears streaking down her cheeks.

She wiped them away. "Falling apart does nothing. But I—" Tears came and he held her until they stopped. Then he took her back to the car. He drove to the dower house, a two-story brick building that looked huge for one woman. The countess was the only one who had gone to live there—he'd found it odd, but the countess told him the girls were to stay in the mansion until they married. They weren't to go with their mother. Cal found this world strange.

He walked up to the front door and knocked on it, Julia following him. Upstairs, a curtain moved. He saw the countess's frightened white face through the panes of glass. She let the curtain drop hurriedly.

He knocked on the door. Kept knocking. Finally it was pulled open. An elderly butler blinked at him. Cal didn't know the man—he'd let the countess hire whatever servants she'd wanted. "My lord?"

"I have to talk to the dowager countess."

"My lord, her ladyship attended a late party last night. I do not believe the dowager is awake."

"She is. I saw her at her window."

"I do not believe she is receiving. If you will kindly wait one moment, my lord . . ." The butler drifted away up the stairs, like a disembodied spirit. When the man returned, Cal could tell what he was going to say. "The countess is not well. She is not—"

"She had better see me. If she doesn't, I'm driving right to the police station. I think she'll know why."

"Cal, what are you talking about?" Julia breathed.

When the butler hesitated, Cal pushed past him. He stalked up the stairs. Felt that graceful touch—Julia's hand on his arm. "Cal, stop."

"She saw me coming and she looked terrified. Why else would she be scared of me?" The burned picture. The car under wraps, the shovel, the scarf hidden there. She knew he was looking for the killer of Sarah Brand. "I think she knew, Julia. That's why she's been afraid of me." He didn't have proof of that, but instinct had kept him alive in New York and in the skies over France.

"She couldn't—"

"I think she knew and she kept the truth hidden."

"But—" Julia gasped. "Once I overheard her say that John had taken his own life. She believed—or knew—it wasn't an accident. Oh, heavens, perhaps it meant . . . a guilty conscience."

He doubted it. A man like Carstairs likely believed he could do anything he wanted. What it meant was that the former Countess of Worthington had left Cal's parents to die and David and him to starve, while she knew one of her sons was a rapist and a killer.

He ran up the stairs.

Heavy footsteps followed him. Cal jerked around at the top of the stairs. Julia was behind him and the dowager's butler was behind her, already wheezing.

"I'm not going to hurt her," Cal said coldly. "Don't give yourself a heart attack trying to stop me. I just want the truth. Finally, after all these years. I want her to admit that it's her family that's rotten to the core. And that she denied justice to innocent families."

Julia touched him in her gentle way. "Cal, we don't know this for certain yet."

"We will soon." It didn't take long to figure out which room was the dowager's. A door slammed down the hallway. He heard the click.

Reaching the paneled door, he ran his hand over the doorknob. Locked. He took a step back, lifted his foot and kicked the door open. With a splintering shriek, it flew open.

The dowager screamed. "Don't kill me! You've come to destroy me!"

When he'd come here weeks ago, this was what he'd wanted. The dowager cowering from him. But now, all his rage just kind of ran out. He felt like a sputtering engine, trying to keep going, but failing.

She just looked like a terrified old woman. Not the devil he used to imagine in his head as a young starving boy. "Sit down," he said gruffly. "I came here to talk about John. And Sarah Brand."

She seemed to get older in front of his eyes. "I see. What is it that you think you know about John?" She lifted her chin and her blue eyes glittered with defiance.

For all the countess was no spring chicken, she dressed to the nines, even for bed. Her hair was bobbed, all silver waves. Her nightdress was embroidered silk, festooned with feathers and pearls. It screamed wealth. And she'd known her son had killed innocent women. He was sure of it now—sure she had known.

"My lady, should I summon help?" It was the butler, staring from the shattered door at his mistress.

"If you want to call the coppers, go ahead," Cal said.

"We do not have coppers. We have the police, but we do not need to bring them here. Please leave us."

"My lady, the American—I mean the earl—"

"Leave us now, Montrose. I do not see how I have not made myself clear."

Montrose, the butler, left. The dowager gazed haughtily. "I should prefer we speak in my dressing room. The door there is intact. I do not want this spread as gossip."

"All right." He would give her that. She swept on ahead of him.

Julia clasped his arm. "Cal, you must calm down. You broke the door. You are rather terrifying."

He'd scared Julia. But what did she want of him? He couldn't behave like an emotionless English earl. If the dowager had known the truth, she'd let three women's deaths go unavenged. She'd subverted justice. Three families had lived a hell for years, with no idea whether their daughters were alive or dead. All to save the lily-white arse of her precious, evil son.

Even now, what the dowager countess really cared about was the gossip. The scandal. The damn family.

And that made him mad.

She seated herself gracefully in a white chair in her dressing room. He took the one opposite.

"What do you wish to tell me about John? I presume you have unearthed a pack of lies?"

"I've found the truth. From your reaction, I'd say you know what he did. And you said nothing."

"What do you believe my son is responsible for?"

"The rapes and murders of three young women."

She flinched. She paled even more. In her eyes was the terror of self-preservation. But she said,

497

"What evidence do you have to support such a vile accusation?"

"We both know it's true," he said softly. "In 1916, Sarah Brand disappeared. I found evidence she'd been in one of the older cars in the Worthington garage. I learned that a woman named Eileen Kilkenny also disappeared. And a maid named Gladys Burrows. Today I found Sarah's body."

She gasped.

"According to your former chauffeur, there weren't many automobiles around here in 1916—but there was a red one at Worthington. Sarah had a crush on John's older brother, and I figure John pursued her, taking his brother's car. Maybe she was willing to go driving with John but I don't think she was willing to sleep with him. So he drove her to a reasonably remote place, attacked her, killed her and buried the body."

The countess shuddered. "Stop . . . stop."

"Having an automobile made it easy for him, except he was careless. He left evidence in the car. Left the shovel in the trunk that he used to bury them. Left a woman's scarf."

"How can you know it is John?"

"I found evidence on Sarah's body."

"Where is this evidence?"

Her blunt, calculating question surprised him. "I've kept it somewhere safe."

"So you have not gone to the police yet?" she asked.

"Not yet." He leaned close, aware of Julia standing by the fireplace. "How did you know the truth? And how in hell could you keep such a secret? You let those families continue to suffer. Mrs. Brand wanders at night in her confused state, still searching for her daughter. She walked right in front of my car and I almost hit her."

Tears dripped to the countess's cheeks. "What was I to do? He came to me and he confessed," she whispered. "It was just before his accident."

"You could have spared those innocent families. You could have told the truth."

"And my son would have been hanged! He didn't mean to do it. He was always . . . not quite right. And the girls—they should have known better than to go out alone in a motorcar with a man. One of them gave him photographs of herself wearing nothing but her undergarments. They were no better than—"

"Don't," Julia said fiercely. "Do not blame the girls."

"Your son was to blame, not them," Cal snapped "I don't care if Sarah paraded in front of him naked—he had no right to force himself on her. No right to kill her. Your son had every advantage—money, education, your precious bloodlines—and look what he was. He should have paid for what he did."

He spoke low, fighting to keep his voice controlled, but she had drawn back into the chair.

"Now that he is dead," the dowager whispered, "he's answered for everything he did. He paid with his life."

"The families need to know—"

The dowager jerked in the chair. "No! People cannot know!"

"I don't give a damn about protecting you from scandal. Not now."

"It's not me," she cried. "Think of my daughters. They are innocents in this, but they will be punished. What gentleman would marry them after such a scandal?"

"Of course they're innocent, so why shouldn't someone marry them?"

She sneered. "You have no idea how Society works."

"No. I can't say I do. And I'm glad of it. It's made me a hell of a better man."

"She is right, Cal," Julia said. "Cassia, Diana, Thalia will all be hurt by this. It will ruin their lives. They will be ostracized."

"No man would want to tie himself to a family that is notorious," the dowager countess cried. "The girls would be ruined by association. Spare them, at least. John is beyond punishment on this earth. He pays now in eternal damnation. I believe he took his own life. He deliberately drove off the ridge into the quarry."

"Cal, there is nothing to be served by destroying the family. It will even hurt us—and it will touch

500

David, also. Everyone will be ruined," Julia whispered.

"There needs to be justice," he growled. Then he realized . . . the countess had known he was looking for the truth. "Did you cut the brake lines of my car?"

"What are those? What are you talking about?"

He explained about the crash and she gasped. "I would never do such a thing."

He now had the ultimate power to hurt the dowager. To do the worst thing that she could imagine: making her the object of scandal. When his mother had died, he had promised to hurt them all. But now he kept thinking of the dowager's daughters, who were innocent. How could he let them be hurt by his actions?

"You won't tell anyone about this," the countess said quickly. "Or I'll tell the world the truth about your mother."

"What?" he growled.

"Do you know why I objected to your arrival so strongly?" she demanded.

"Why don't you tell me?" He spoke smoothly. But inside his gut churned.

"We knew what your mother was. We had reports sent to us. She entertained men in her rooms—"

"That's a damned lie." Cal rose from his seat.

"You know it is quite true. Your mother was a prostitute. And she behaved scandalously before

501

the marriage, having relations with your father and becoming preg—"

"Goddamn you," he barked. "Goddamn you to hell. You paid for an investigator and had him spy on us, but you wouldn't send any money when she was sick. Money that would have paid for a doctor and medicine. Money that would have saved her life. She sold herself for money to feed David and I. You forced her to do it. I've got the power now. I could destroy you. I could let you watch while Worthington Park is sold around you—"

He stopped, chest heaving. Julia had gone very, very white.

"Then what—you'll tell the world about John?" the countess said. "And I'll make sure no one believes you. I know all about your past, Worthington. I have been told about all of it. I am sure Julia knows nothing about—"

"You can tell her whatever you want. I'm going to lose her anyway when I destroy this place. And I'm damn well going to the police. I couldn't live with myself if I didn't get justice. Maybe nothing can be proved now, after nine years, but I want them to damn well try."

Slowly, he met Julia's eyes. He expected anger. Shock. She now knew one of the things he had been most ashamed of—that he hadn't been able to prevent his mother from selling her body, doing something that tormented her to her soul.

But Julia whirled on the dowager countess.

502

"How could you threaten such a thing?" she demanded of the dowager. "It is true that if the truth about John gets out, the girls will suffer in the stead of their brother. I understand your fear and I don't want my friends—my family now—to suffer. But you cannot be so heartless. You were never like this. You were always kind."

"I must protect the family I have left," the dowager croaked. "Julia, this will touch you. If you have children, a scandal would hurt them. Is that what you want?"

Cal felt Julia look to him. He said, "We could leave this place, get rid of this cursed estate, travel the world. Live anywhere we want, keeping our children away from here, so they'd never be hurt by it. We could go to South America. Santorini. Venice—"

"I don't want to run away, Cal, and leave everyone else to suffer. I won't."

With Cal she went to the police station. To Julia's surprise, he did not tell them of John Carstairs's confession to his mother. He told them he suspected John because of the car in the garage, the spade, the locket. After, as he drove them to Worthington, with rain pattering the windshield, she asked, "Why did you keep his confession a secret?"

"He didn't confess to me. I don't know what exactly he said to his mother. If there's evidence, they'll find it. Maybe, if they can't prove anything,

I'll tell them. But even then, it's not cold, hard, irrefutable proof. I know this is going to hurt my cousins. But you understand, Julia, that I couldn't keep the deaths secret?"

"I understand," she whispered. "I do want to go with you when you show the police sergeant the— the place." Scotland Yard was to be called in, too.

"No. I don't want you to see any more of that. I'm taking you home, then showing the police the graves."

"Cal, are you really going to destroy Worthington now—because of what the dowager threatened? It was wrong. Unconscionable. But—"

"I don't know. I— Hell, I want you to come away with me and I want to forget about Worthington Park."

His heart was raw and she understood. But she had to fight for Worthington. Not for the estate— for Cal. He needed to finally escape the pain of his past.

At Worthington, Cal left her there, then returned to the police station. She went to the morning room. She didn't tell the servants any of what had happened. She began a letter beseeching the dowager countess not to reveal a word about Cal's mother.

"My lady?" A maid bobbed a curtsy, holding out a folded page. "This note was delivered for you. A young lad brought it to the kitchen door. Said it was dreadful important."

Julia hurried to the maid, took the note.

The writing was shaky, terribly so. Julia struggled to read it. But when she did, an icy, sick feeling washed over her. It was from Lower Dale Farm. Their father was ill.

"I must go and fetch Dr. Campbell. Is the boy still here?"

"He ran off, milady."

And Cal was gone—with the police. She must deal with this herself. She needed her vehicle. She would drive directly to the hospital to fetch Dr. Campbell. She would test the brakes. The garage was always locked now, and the chauffeur took great care, checking the vehicles each day. Surely she would be safe enough if she traveled directly to the hospital to get Dougal.

At the front door, she put on her coat. But as she stepped outside to go to the garage, the Duke of Bradstock drove up. He leaned out the open window. "Julia, I was coming to see you. I want to apologize for upsetting you." His car purred as he shifted it into Neutral.

Then she had the perfect idea. "Would you be willing to do me a favor, James?"

"Anything, dear Julia. Ask me anything."

Should she involve him? She must. "I need you to take me to the hospital and collect Dr. Campbell, then take us to Lower Dale Farm. We must make haste."

Belowstairs, Tansy ran into the kitchen and burst into tears. Hannah almost knocked her bowl to the floor in her surprise. "Tansy, you must stop being so dramatic."

"You were right all along," the girl cried. "Oh, I've been so stupid."

"Tansy, what on earth—" Then Hannah knew and she touched Tansy's shoulder. "He had his way with you, didn't he? I know you saw him last night. You gave in and he broke it off with you."

Tansy shook her head. "I didn't see him last night. I snuck out to meet him but he never came. I wouldn't let him have his way—and I was afraid that's why he didn't come. And now I just saw him! With her! She's so hoity-toity, and there's her husband so much in love with her, but I saw her get into his motorcar just now. I saw the look in his eyes as he drove off. He's in love with her. He looked right at me, because I was standing there, and it was as if he didn't even see me."

Hannah was all mixed-up. "Who do you mean? Who is 'she'?"

"He came, and Lady Worthington got into his car. And the way he looked at her—well, he never looked at me that way. Never."

"He's probably a friend of Lady Worthington."

Tansy moaned. "She's his lover, more like. And I found out he didn't give me his real name. She called him James."

23

Disappearance in a Motorcar

James's motorcar rumbled along the road toward the village. Julia shivered in the seat beside him. Cold air had swept in and fog was settling on the countryside. They drove through it in valleys and it swirled alongside the road like ghostly apparitions.

This wasn't the main road, but it was a lane Julia knew well. A shortcut to Brideswell village. It would come out very close to the hospital.

There were few motorcars in the village—no one passed them. James was driving quite quickly, as she'd asked, turning the wheel with skill to avoid holes in the road.

He slowed a bit, then pushed down on the pedal and the car went perilously fast. With a rapid movement, he turned the steering wheel. The car seemed to skid onto two wheels and she shut her eyes out of instinct.

When she opened them, they were on a different lane—a rougher one that was just two tracks cutting through a field. "Shouldn't we be going the other way to the village?"

He kept his focus on staying on the tracks. "Shortcut."

Men. And they complained about women behind

the steering wheel. Julia's heart thudded. She didn't want to waste precious time. "The *other* road is a shortcut. I think it would be fast enough. This looks like the kind of track you can get stuck on." It couldn't be much used. She, who knew the estate well, did not know where it led.

"Be quiet. Leave the driving to me."

"Women are no longer seen and not heard, James. This track seems to be going away from the village. I don't think this is a good idea."

"It's a perfect idea." Then he added, "I learned your husband is taking you on a long trip. A tour through the Mediterranean, then on to Egypt, where you will explore the archeological digs and travel up the Nile. It appears I wouldn't be seeing you for a very long time."

"What? We didn't decide on a trip." She had said she did not want to run away from Worthington Park. "How did you know about it?"

"Your husband told your butler and a footman overheard."

She peered ahead. Fog swirled and it looked milky white in front of them, the headlights picking out trees that seemed to fly at them out of nowhere. What he'd said didn't quite make sense. "But how did *you* know?"

"I paid the footman to give me information."

"You paid a footman to spy? Why?"

"I wanted to know what your husband was doing to you."

She was stunned. How could James have thought such a thing was right? He was truly far too arrogant. "We should have been at the hospital by now." He must have gone the wrong way after all.

"Don't fret, Julia."

"James, Mr. Toft is ill. It could be very serious."

She gasped as the stream of light from the lamps on the car picked out looming trees in the mist. James slowed the car, picking his way along the track. He must know where it was; Julia could see nothing that looked like a road.

They passed through a wooded area. James stopped the car. Here, it was utterly gray, but for the two pinpoints of the headlights, which illuminated nothing but bracken and tall grass. She stared at him, shocked and confused. "What are you doing?"

"We've run out of road."

His wretched shortcut had turned out to be useless. She'd told him not to do this. And they'd wasted so much precious time. Panic rose and she struggled to fight it. "You have to turn around. We must go back—"

"Calm yourself, Julia. The bugger at Lower Dale Farm is not in any danger."

She flinched at his harsh description. "You don't know that—"

"But I do. I know it because I wrote the note and paid some village boy to deliver it."

"Why would you do that? Was this intended as a joke?"

509

"I needed to get you into my car, Julia. You should have seen your face when I drove up. You looked as if your knight errant had arrived."

"I don't understand."

"I've waited a long time for this. I didn't want to have to hurt you. I thought you might come to me willingly, become my mistress, once you found out the truth about that American thug you married. But then I learned I was running out of time."

"What are you talking about?"

"He is going to take you away. He would not bring you back here. I'd waited too long already. I paid a man to cut the brakes of his damn car, but that failed to kill him. I am not going to let him take you from me forever."

Shock had made her wits freeze, made it hard to think. James wanted her. Learning Cal wanted to take her away had made him determined to act.

Three women with dark hair and blue eyes. But that had been John Carstairs. What was Bradstock going to do—try to seduce her? "What do you want from me?"

"I want to be intimate with you. I've wanted it for so long. When I was going to propose marriage to your father—"

"Propose marriage to Father?"

"I had a proposition for him," he said impatiently. "It was common knowledge he'd frittered through his fortune. His debts couldn't be covered, and the income was dissolving because of his poor management. I was going to cover his debts, if he gave me you."

"This is not the eighteenth century. I wouldn't have allowed myself to be sold, no matter what Father said," she declared.

"Then your engagement with bloody Anthony Carstairs was announced," he said, ignoring her. "I'd waited too long. I was going to get your father to demand you break the engagement. He would have done anything to get his hands on money to cover his debts. I could have ruined him."

She sucked in a cold, sharp breath. Bradstock was mad.

"Before I could do that, Anthony volunteered for battle. All I had to do was wait. Reports were coming back—thousands of men were being blown to bits. Anthony was so stupidly brave I was sure he'd get killed."

"He was *truly* brave. How dare you mock him?" But even as she threw those words at him, she looked around. She could get out of the car and run. She was going to have to do that. She hadn't paid a lot of attention to where they had turned exactly, because she'd been so fearful for the Tofts of Lower Dale Farm. The fog made it confusing, but she thought she recognized where she was. On the other side of the hill from where Cal had found the bodies.

He had wanted her—and three dark-haired women had died. "Did you— Were you the man in the motorcar with Sarah Brand? What of John Carstairs? Did he—he kill Sarah or did you?"

The moment she asked the question, she knew she could not turn back.

He smiled. "I did. I met him and we both had our way with her. She looked so much like you. John loved you so much, Julia. I found out about how much John loved you, Julia, when I came to visit Anthony and Nigel. I came to see you, even knowing I couldn't have you. Once I learned about John's lust for you, I knew he was going to be the perfect scapegoat. I tempted him with photographs I got of Gladys, the maid."

Julia felt frozen. Of course. J.C. Not John Carstairs. But James. And he was heir to the dukedom then, known by his courtesy title, the Earl of Cavendish. "The photograph was signed to 'A.' I told the daft girl my name was Anthony." His smile widened. "John enjoyed our game, having women who looked like you, the woman who loved his precious brother. I knew I could lay the blame at his door if things went wrong. Then the War came. I managed to avoid conscription— my father ensured that. I returned from university, and wanted to play the game again, with Anthony gone. But John had an attack of conscience and killed himself, the bloody fool. That's why I had to stop for so long. But seeing you made it so painful that I needed another girl . . ."

While he was talking happily, she grasped the

door handle to the car. With a swift motion, she shoved open the door and she jumped out of the car as fast as she could. She skidded on the ground—the misty rain made it slippery.

Something grabbed the sleeve of her coat and she screamed. Using all her might, she pulled free and she began running down the track back the way they had come. Behind her, she heard Bradstock curse. "Bollocks. Don't be a damn fool. There's nowhere to run."

But she kept going. She plunged off the track, into tall damp grass. She could see nothing, and that must mean he couldn't see her. But he could hear her crunching through the grass, couldn't he? Julia dropped to her knees. She was going to move quietly, and low, below the height of the grass.

A car door slammed, echoing eerily in the vast silence.

He was coming after her.

"Stupid cow," he said, his words partly muffled by the mist. But now that she wasn't running, she could hear him much better. "We can be together now," he growled. "I won't let that American scum have you. I won't let him take you from me. I found out all about him. Told Lady Worthington what he was—everything I'd found out."

Julia bit her lip so she wouldn't shout at this evil, awful man. She was too scared to move, in case she made a sound.

"I'm going to keep you," he said, his voice filled with triumph. "Only I will know where you are. It will be my secret forever."

The police constable worked at uncovering Sarah's body, with the sergeant watching the procedure. The young constable had gone behind bushes to throw up once. Cal had helped him for a while. Then something had caught his eye. He bent down. Crisp footprints had dried into formerly wet mud. They had to be fresh—these couldn't have lasted years. He hadn't walked over here. Neither had Julia.

Someone had been here recently. Obviously not John Carstairs.

Julia had been attacked and not by Ellen's pimp, Lowry. Julia, with blue-black hair and stunning blue eyes . . .

He had to see her. Had to know she was safe. He would get her trunks packed today—they could be gone tomorrow, leaving Worthington Park behind. David could stay if he wanted, as long as he wanted. They could take Diana with them, head to Paris, send her on her way safely to Switzerland with the chaperone.

He told the policemen he needed to check on his new bride, needed to see her. He drove fast to get back to Julia. The wind whipped back his hair. Grit flew against his driving goggles. Despite the conditions of the road, he drove like a bat out of hell. His car springs screeched with each bang and jolt. His headlamps tried—and failed—to cut through a veil of swirling mist. He crunched a headlamp against a stone wall that appeared out of nowhere.

Still, he didn't ease up. Who could have been there? A farmer? One of the gypsies? But Cal doubted it—it was off a narrow track, behind a grove of trees.

He hit the brakes as he roared into the drive, skidding to a stop right in front of Worthington. Within minutes, he learned Julia was gone. She had received a note that Toft was ill. But the chauffeur told him Julia hadn't taken a car.

"His lordship's going mad upstairs. He thinks Lady Worthington has gone missing." Eustace had come into the kitchen to impart the latest and most exciting gossip.

Hannah lifted her head from her rolling pin just as Tansy gave a little cry and dropped her bowl. It shattered with such a loud sound that Tansy shrieked. Batter flew everywhere.

Hannah sighed. "Tansy, clean up that mess." To Eustace she said, "Lady Worthington went out for a drive with a friend."

"Don't tell him," Tansy urged. "Don't."

"Why not? She was driven away by a gentleman that she knew. She called him James. Go tell him that. I guess she didn't leave a note or anything."

Eustace went up to relay the message.

Moments later, Hannah and Tansy were shocked to hear heavy, fast footsteps pound down the stairs and the Earl of Worthington burst into the kitchen.

"Eustace told me you saw my wife get into a car," he said abruptly.

"I didn't—" Hannah saw Tansy make eyes at her and shake her head. Then she realized Tansy feared the earl would find out she had been slipping out to meet this man. "One of the maids did and she told me."

The earl frowned. "Why didn't this maid come forward upstairs when I asked if anyone had seen my wife?"

Hannah had to think quickly—because of course, it hadn't been an upstairs maid. "She was outside when she shouldn't have been. She was scared she would get into trouble."

"Who was driving the car?"

"I don't know. She didn't know, either. But Lady Worthington called him James."

"What did he look like?"

Hannah had no idea. She looked desperately at Tansy.

"This is very serious."

"My lord, will you promise you won't get the maid into trouble? You won't dismiss her?"

"If someone knows something, I need to hear it now," he said angrily.

Hannah shuddered. She was going to lose her place for Tansy. But the earl wasn't only angry, he was frightened. She could tell. "Don't get her in trouble. It was my job to discipline her, and I failed. She wanted me to keep her confidence. I'm going to break it, so I should pay."

He looked at her in surprise. Then said, "I won't fire the girl. Who was it?"

"Tansy, my lord." Hannah pointed at the cowering, white-faced kitchen maid.

The earl went over to her. "You're not in trouble, Tansy. Just tell me what the man looked like. Where were they going?"

Tansy looked down more demurely than Hannah had ever seen. "He said he'd take her to the farm. She wanted to fetch Dr. Campbell first. He has black hair and he's a gentleman. I never knew his real name. But he drives a beautiful car. Dark red and all covered in shiny chrome. And she called him James."

Hannah swallowed hard. "This man—he's been showing attentions to a girl when he shouldn't have done."

Tansy made a strangled sound, but Hannah knew she had to go on. His lordship had looked concerned about this man, and Hannah knew he was a bad sort. "He lied to the girl about who he was. Made her false promises. I thought maybe her ladyship should know about this gentleman."

The earl stared at Tansy—at her lovely blue-

517

black hair. "Tansy, were you the girl? You aren't in trouble—you won't lose your job. I need your help. Desperately."

"Yes. I didn't do anything really naughty, I swear. He used to take me driving."

"Where did he used to take you?"

Tansy tried to explain it, but she didn't know the surrounding land. Hannah did and she could guess where it was from Tansy's confused description. When she told the earl, he lifted her hand and kissed it!

"Thank you. Both of you." With that, the earl ran to the stairs. He grabbed the banister and took the steps three at a time.

Tansy tried to stir again, but began to cry. Hannah told her to sit down. As she brewed tea, Eustace came by her. "That was bally good of you, Han—Mrs. Talbot. Protecting Tansy when she was doing something so daft."

Hannah looked up in surprise to see Eustace regarding her with a soft, caring look in his eyes. The way he used to look at Tansy. But she was a cook now, happy with her career, and she knew Eustace had been wounded by Tansy's interest in another man. His attentions to her might be coming from his hurt pride. Anyway, she was quite happy with her future as a cook. She wasn't ready for a romance. But she prayed everything was all right with the new ladyship. Why was the earl so afraid?

Cal almost crashed into David, who was wheeling his chair down the hall, hands pushing on the rubber wheels.

"Cal, what's wrong?" David asked.

"Julia's gone. She's been taken." It had to be the Duke of Bradstock. Julia had called him James. And Bradstock had wanted Julia. Was that why he took black-haired women? Fear beat like a pulse in Cal's head.

David stopped rolling. "Julia got a note—"

"I know. I saw it. She went with the Duke of Bradstock in his car." Had Bradstock and Lord John Carstairs been abducting and murdering young women together? "I think he has killed women who looked . . ." God, his legs went weak with fear. "Like Julia."

David's face whitened. "We've got to find her—" He looked down at his artificial legs. "What can I do?"

"Stay here. I think I know where he's taken her." He was praying he was right. If he wasn't, what else was he going to do? Combing the countryside would take forever. There weren't many roads, but they covered a hell of a lot of land.

"I'll send everyone else out looking that I can, Cal. I'll call the village police station. That I can do," David said.

"Thank you," Cal said. He gripped his brother's forearm. There were a lot of things he'd always wanted to say to David. For some reason, he needed to say them. Fast. "I'm sorry I couldn't get enough money to save our mother. I'm sorry I was too late to save Father. I'm sorry I didn't keep you out of danger in battle—"

"None of that is your fault so shut the hell up, Cal. Go and get your wife."

Cal ran out to his car. Maybe he wanted to say those things because it was likely he wouldn't see David again. If he couldn't save Julia, he was going to kill Bradstock. Or die trying.

Christ, he had to save her. But his gut was like lead, his heart like ice. He had been too late to save his father. Too late to protect his mother.

He couldn't be too late now.

The fields stretched around her. Julia was on her hands and knees, hidden by the wet grass, terrified to make a sound. She heard Bradstock stomp through the grass. Moving away from her.

What was she going to do? She could double back to the car.

Cal had told her she was brave. She thought of Ellen Lambert being completely vulnerable, driving an ambulance through shelling. She owed it to all modern women not to be a coward.

Staying low, Julia ran back to the car. Wincing at the sound, she opened the door and climbed in. He would know where she was as soon as she started the car. As soon as the engine caught, she shoved the pedal to the floor. The engine screamed and the car lurched forward. Almost giddy with hope, she went a few feet, clinging to the wheel with hands that were frozen with fear.

A sound, sharp and explosive as a gunshot, made her scream. It came from the front of the car. The wheel moved funny. The steering wheel jerked in her hand. She'd hit a hole and buggered up the front of the car. She was moving downhill. The tire was flat, but still turning.

The lights picked up Bradstock as he reached the edge of the track. Showed the vicious fury on his face as he ran out into the track in front of her.

To escape she was going to have to run him down.

If she didn't, he'd kill her.

She had to do it. She couldn't leave him alive to kill anyone else.

She accelerated—

No, she couldn't do it. She took her foot off the accelerator, slammed on the brake. The engine stalled. The car stopped.

Oh God. She was a fool. She thought of Zelda Fitzgerald's words. She *was* an utter fool—a soft-hearted one. Strangely, she still heard the rumble of an engine. It sounded far away, lost in the rising fog. It couldn't be her engine.

Then the sound disappeared. Her imagination?

Bradstock slammed his hand on the hood of the car. He didn't seem aware of the low, soft sound of a motorcar—so she must have dreamed it. Rage emanated from him. Slapping his hand along the hood of his car, he prowled toward her.

She had no weapon. She was more scared than when Ellen's attacker had come after her. Her hand was still clutched around the key.

The key—

Julia pushed the car door open. It was a barricade between her and him as she scrambled out of the car. She ran several feet, then he grabbed her arm and jerked her back. He pulled her with him back to the car. Flung her against the hood. She cried out as she slammed into the metal.

He was on top of her, trying to force her arms back. She drove her knee at his vulnerable place. He howled. He didn't let her go, but his grip slackened. She broke her hand free and scratched his face with the key.

He roared. "Bitch!" His palm cracked against her face.

"You were the one. The one who tried to take me outside Ellen's cottage."

"You were spending so much time with Worthington. I was so angry with you," Bradstock snapped. He wrestled to get the key out of her hand. She hung on like a hunting dog. His hand wrapped around her wrist, forced it back. The key fell out of her hand. She looked desperately down the lane—

There was something there.

The beams of light illuminated a silver motorcar coming up the track toward them. She yelled, "Help me! He wants to kill me!"

Bradstock swung around, just at the moment the other car stopped and a large male shape jumped out. The lights picked up golden hair. Then Cal's face, contorted with a viciousness she'd never seen on it. He lunged for Bradstock. His fist sliced across Bradstock's face. He punched again, right into the duke's face. Bone crunched.

Bradstock hit back. She saw, in the light, silver in the villain's hand. The blade of a knife. "Cal, look out."

Bradstock stabbed wildly at Cal, but Cal blocked his every attempt. Cal fought like a man possessed. Better than a prizefighter.

She looked for a weapon. Something to use on Bradstock to protect Cal . . . Heavens, Bradstock would have a shovel in the boot. She could threaten him with that.

But as she slid along the side of the motor toward the boot, Bradstock let out a roar as Cal snapped his wrist back. The breaking sound echoed across the empty field. The knife glinted as it fell to the ground.

One more punch to Bradstock's face sent the fiend reeling back. His huge, broad-shouldered body slumped bonelessly over the hood of his motorcar.

"Julia."

Cal's arms went around her, engulfing her in warmth, in safety.

"How did you get here?" she whispered. "I thought— I was certain I—"

"Hannah convinced Tansy to tell me she saw you get into Bradstock's car and where he used to take her. Bradstock used to take her out in his car. I guess because she looks like you."

Hannah. Tansy. The women in the kitchen had helped save her life.

"I was scared I was too late," he said gruffly. "When I saw the car headlights coming toward me, my heart just about stopped. But when I saw him outlined in them, I knew you'd gotten behind the wheel. You almost saved yourself, you smart, smart girl. But you couldn't run him down, could you?"

"No. I simply couldn't bring myself to do it. It wouldn't have been right. It wouldn't have been cricket."

Cal laughed huskily, with a catch in his voice. His arms tightened. He laid his cheek against her head. "You even tried to escape a killer in a lady-like manner. What am I going to do with you?"

"I wasn't all that ladylike. I scratched his face with his key."

He kissed her. His mouth took hers in such a fast, overwhelming passion, she was literally lifted off her feet. When he set her down he said, "You should have gone for his eyes."

524

She shuddered. "Cal, I'm sorry. I'm just not that ruthless."

"You don't have to be. You're perfect, Julia. Perfect in every way. God, I love you. I love you with all my soul. And thank God, you're safe." He hugged her to him. "David telephoned for the police. They should arrive soon. Then I'll take you home."

She could hear the sounds of cars roaring up the path. "Home to Worthington? It is our home, Cal. Truly, it is."

24

America

For the next month, Julia was treated like a Hollywood movie star. Cal pampered her in every way. He brought her champagne, and asked for the most delectable dishes and desserts for dinner. He took her out riding in the mornings and she loved showing him how the mist rose from the fields and sunlight glistened on dew. They had tea on the lawns under the spreading branches of an oak, while the lawn mowers clacked. In the evenings, they walked through the woods with the estate's dogs following them. They would return and sit with the terrace doors open to the breeze, drink cocktails, then go up to bed . . . where the most decadent and naughty things happened. Day by day, Cal healed her from the shock of Bradstock's attack.

After all the fear and pain that had come before, it filled her with joy to be building this life with Cal at Worthington.

Diana wanted to stay longer at Worthington and she fussed over Julia, and seemed happy with her more sedate life and spending time with David. Julia knew they must take Diana away soon. They did not tell Diana, Cassia and Thalia about John.

The Duke of Bradstock never went to trial—he hanged himself, taking his own life, and Cal had not told the police about John's involvement. In the end, he decided justice had been served by John's death and he didn't want to hurt his cousins' futures.

But the dowager and Cal did not speak to each other. Julia believed the dowager would not hurt Cal by exposing what his mother had done, since Cal had protected John.

A week after the attack, on a morning Cal went out, knowing she was now safe, Julia visited the ladies she was helping. She saw Mrs. Billings, who lived in a cottage alone, now that Mr. Billings had passed on. They had lost all their sons in the Great War and Julia had suggested that one of her widows, a young woman with three children, share Mrs. Billings's cottage. Mrs. Billings was delighted to have children around her. Julia had also introduced Mr. Toft to a widow of another farm. They were working their farms together. She hoped that in time a romance might take root.

She drove to Lilac Farm, knowing that soon the Brands would be leaving it. They now knew what had happened to Sarah. It had broken their hearts, but Brand had insisted there was peace in knowing the truth. They were to move into a cottage on the estate.

But as she reached the farm, Julia heard a great deal of banging. She followed the sound, and stopped her car on a rise. Below her, men scurried everywhere around all kinds of newfangled equipment. Wood from the sawmill lay in huge stacks. Houses were being built on land that had once been the fields of Lilac Farm.

She quickly drove home. Heart in her throat, she found Cal in his study. "You are building houses? But what about Lilac Farm? The land is needed for the farm."

He shoved back his golden hair. "It's sold, Julia. It was the best land to begin building and I received a damn good offer for it. For the Brands, the farm is wrapped up in sad memories. I'm going to take care of them."

"But . . . but you never talked to me about this." She felt numb with shock. "Have you sold more?"

"Yes."

Then he told her what he had sold. Three farms belonging to families no longer able to farm. Nausea rose in her belly. "How could you?"

He paced on the Aubusson rug in front of the fireplace. "With the money I've made on the land, the families are living rent-free in new homes. The children of those families will be sent to school. I've seen the squalor of slums. It's the same here. People live on top of each other while I have acres of underused land."

She could see the benefit, but still felt fear over such abrupt change. "But you did not talk to me about it."

"You would have said no. The truth is, Julia,

I can't stay here. The dowager can destroy my mother's name if she wants and I've realized I can live with that. What matters is that I can still hear the condescending sneer in the dowager's voice. It cost my mother her soul to do what she did. It cost her life. Do you look at me now and see only a man with a mother who whored herself because her boy was too late to protect his father, too late to protect her?"

His words went through her like a blade of ice. The pain in them broke her heart. "I see a man who loved his parents and who would have risked his own life to help them."

He looked away from her. She saw that—but he didn't. How could she make him see?

"This place will never be a home to me, Julia," he said harshly. "What matters is us and not Worthington Park. We can be together anywhere. It doesn't have to be here."

Leave and never come back? Then she saw the truth. "Cal, you have to stop running away. You cannot run from your past. You have to heal from it."

"We could be happy if we were away from here. I want to build a future for us. Don't you want that?" His golden brows drew down.

"Yes, but I feel we do belong here. You're angry and you are doing rash things—"

"These changes aren't rash. My desire to leave here isn't rash."

"But when you proposed, you told me you wouldn't destroy Worthington."

"So it was the damn estate all along. Julia, do you even love me?"

"Of course I love you."

"But if I'd been honest, if I told you that Worthington wasn't part of the deal, you never would have said yes."

"Honest? Do you mean you lied to me?" Shock hit her.

"Yeah, I lied to you. I made a vow to my mother as she was dying that I would make the Carstairs family pay. How in hell could I ever be lord of this when she had to condemn her soul?" He raked back his hair. "Julia, which do you choose—Worthington or me?"

"This is ridiculous. It should not have to be a choice." They were echoing the night he had proposed in Paris and she had only the same answer to give.

"It is. For me."

"Cal, I can't accept this." She wanted Cal to find happiness in the same life that she did. And it hurt that he'd lied. Her father had lied to her mother. Mother had found out about all his affairs. His lies had made her desperately unhappy.

"Julia, damn it, tell me which you choose." He stalked toward the window, his shoulders stiff and tense. "It's Worthington, isn't it? You'll always love it more than me."

How could she trust anything he told her now? She would always worry about what was unsaid. "Why couldn't you have been honest?"

He turned. "That night in Paris, would you have said yes if I told you I still wanted to sell Worthington?"

"I—" She wouldn't have done.

"You would have said no. I can see it in your eyes."

"I am not to blame for this!" she cried. "Cal, Worthington is my place in the world. It is where I belong. I once thought love was all that mattered in marriage. But you've shown me I was wrong. Love is meaningless without one thing— honesty."

"Hell—" He broke off. "Julia, I've never been honest with you. What Bradstock told you about me was true. He may have been a vicious killer, but he was right about that. That's what Kerry O'Brien was going to give you. All the rotten details of my past. You're right—you deserved honesty. And you deserve better than a man like me."

Then he was gone. He walked right out of the room, walking past her.

She shook with pain. He'd lied to her from the very beginning. She didn't know how to fix this. She didn't know how to stop feeling sick with betrayal. Or how to stop what he was doing to Worthington.

For all her training to be a lady and to handle any situation, she felt powerless. Brokenhearted. Afraid.

Cal did not come down for dinner. Nor did he come to her room that night. The next morning, she marched upstairs and pushed open the door to his room. A modern woman would sort this out.

But the bed was smooth and a sheaf of white paper sat in the middle of it. Her heart stuttered when she saw her name at the top. It was a letter written from Cal.

I don't even know how to write this. I'm no good at putting things into words.

I made a vow, a promise, when my mother died. Mam told me to forgive the old earl. I told her she was worthy of justice. When the dowager looked down on Mam, it made me almost choke in my guilt, so I think I was lying to myself when I thought I sold the land for good reasons. I did it in anger.

I saw your face when I admitted that most of the things Bradstock told you were true. I did run with the Five Points Gang. It was work with them or be targeted by them. My mother told me to stand up for what I believed in, but in the end, I wanted the money. That was a lot easier to live with when I was a young, arrogant thug than it is now. I never expected that.

I'm sorry I lied to you about Worthington. I'm sorry I didn't tell you about my past. I knew I would lose you if you knew the truth about me.

So I'm gone. As my aunt said, I'm not fit for decent society.

I said I don't believe in curses, but my mam did. If there's a curse on you, Julia, it's me.

I'm going to London first to meet with the solicitors. Worthington Park will be yours. The title is entailed, so is the estate, but I could sell it for debts. So I'm taking out a big loan in your name, then I'll have the lawyers draw up the papers for you to foreclose.

The estate is yours. You are the sole owner.

I guess you changed me because I want Worthington to survive. You can make that happen. There's no one else I would trust with the estate. You called it "your place in the world." I would never take that away from you, Sheba.

I love you with all my heart, Julia. I'll come back in a few months and if you want me gone, I'll give you a divorce. I'm sorry if I caused you pain.

That's what I'm good at. The only thing I've done well, except for painting, is hurting people. And I can't paint now. It's all garbage, what I'm putting on the canvas. Now that I don't have your love, I can't seem to paint right.

You were my muse. I was right about that. It's killing me to leave, but it's the right thing.
Yours regretfully,
Cal

For a long while, she held the note, staring blankly at it.

Then, out of the small cupboard in the bedside table, she took out Cal's bottle of fiery whiskey. She poured some into a tumbler and walked back into her bedroom as Zoe walked in.

"What is that?" Zoe asked.

Julia took the tiniest sip. "Gah!"

Zoe's brows rose. "Julia, what on earth are you drinking?"

"Irish whiskey." She had literally just touched her tongue to the stuff and shuddered. Yet the burning sensation after was rather pleasant. "Cal says this drink relaxes him. I was hoping to discover that was true for me, as well. Would you like some?"

"No, thank you, I shouldn't. Besides, I much prefer cocktails. That's the only way hard liquor is palatable. But why are you drinking?"

Julia lifted the glass to take another sip, but her eyes watered. Perhaps the promise of feeling less upset wasn't worth the price of drinking this. "My husband has left me."

"What?"

She gave Zoe the letter. She adored her sister-in-law, and Zoe's business acumen had made her wise in other ways, as well.

Suddenly, the urge to cry overwhelmed her. Julia set down the glass and sobbed. Zoe embraced her. She cried and cried. Then sucked in a deep breath in an unladylike way. "I'm sorry. Falling into disarray is not something I do lightly."

"Disarray? Julia, your silly husband has gone away. You have the right to be upset." Zoe sighed. "Marriage can be so annoying. That was why I wanted to be independent. Fortunately I discovered the blessings of marriage outweigh the times when you'd like to bean your husband over the head."

Julia laughed—Zoe had taught her to not restrict herself to ladylike smiles—but almost as quickly she felt like crying again. "It's so complicated. He lied to me and he didn't tell me about his past. He was a mobster, apparently. I don't know what he did, but it sounds as if it was terrible. I wish he would have talked to me instead of leaving."

"I went through the same problems with your brother, Julia. He wouldn't tell me what caused his shell shock."

"But you convinced him to tell you. And you

both worked together to heal him. Cal has just . . . left. I should be angry with him for doing that. But I know he did it because he believes he is doing it for me. He gave Worthington to me."

She had made him see how important Worthington was. But this was not the outcome she'd hoped for. "He asked me if I chose Worthington or him. I couldn't answer then—I was too shocked and angry that he was asking me to choose. But I choose him. And now it's too late."

And just like that, the tears began again.

She'd cried buckets for Anthony when she'd learned he'd been killed. She had not cried when Ellen had been hurt—she'd been too outraged. She had cried when Mrs. Toft had died in child-birth. "I'm sorry. I don't know why I am crying so much. I feel rather sick—"

Zoe plucked the glass of whiskey out of Julia's hand. "I know why it is. You are pregnant, dear."

Could it be true? Could she be . . . enceinte? She'd been married just over a month.

"You're a married woman, and nausea and tears are two signs that you might be having a baby, Julia. We must go to London to see a specialist. But first, you must go for breakfast. Now is not the time to not eat. I'm sure Cal will come back."

"In months, he has said." She wanted him there, to share her news with him. But she went down for breakfast with Zoe as their guest—where David, Diana, Cassia and Thalia were in the dining

536

room. They did not need to know Cal had gone. But Cassia asked if it was true that he had left for America.

"Wiggins told our lady's maid that Cal ordered his trunk be brought down from the attic," Diana said. "And he saw the tickets for the *Olympic*, lying out on Cal's bedside table. He is sailing for New York. But there was only one ticket."

"He has gone to New York City. For a visit," she lied. "He left me in charge of the estate."

Diana's eyebrows lifted. "Is more of the estate going to be sold?"

"No. Worthington Park is safe now. I promise." And in a soft voice, she said to Diana, "I will take you to Paris as soon as I can."

But Diana shook her head. "I— No— Julia, it's so complicated." Diana got up and left and Julia understood the rush of painful emotions she must be feeling.

After breakfast, Zoe left and Julia walked through the corridors. She was supposed to run Worthington but all she could think of was Cal. She saw David in the library, gazing at a shelf out of his reach. She hurried in, fetched the book he wanted, handing it to him.

"Thank you," he said shyly. Then, "Julia, there's something I need to ask you. Maybe you'll think I'm crazy, too. Cal would. But I want to do it."

"What is it?"

"I know Diana is expecting. I know her beau let her down—Cal told me. I want to ask Diana to marry me. Cal settled a lot of money on me when he made his fortune. I can't give her a title, but I can give her a nice house. I know I'm not a catch without my legs—"

"David, you are a true gentleman, a hero and a good man." Julia's heart wobbled. She was so touched. But then, practicality set in. "But Diana . . . may still be in love with this man, even though he is utterly useless. I don't know what she will say."

"I can hear 'no.' But I want to try."

"Then I do hope, with all my heart, that she says yes."

After she left him, she found Diana. A lady would never leave such a thing to chance. "Could I speak to you for a moment? In the morning room, perhaps?"

Diana's loose dress floated around her as they went into the morning room and Julia carefully closed the door. A lady got to the point when it was necessary. "Diana, David has fallen in love with you and he intends to ask for your hand in marriage."

"David—marriage?"

"Yes. He adores you. He has accepted that you will be reluctant to marry him because he has lost his legs in the War. It happened in the most heroic way possible—he was saving the lives of other men. Be gentle when you refuse him. Be as kind as you can. He is a very good man."

"Julia, I'm not going to gently refuse David Carstairs."

"Diana, please—"

"I'm going to accept him. Could you tell him that, so he will get the courage to ask me?"

"Diana, please don't do it just because you need a marriage. He deserves much more—"

"Julia, sometimes you are terrible. You are completely insulting me. You really think I'm not capable of loving him, don't you? Why—because he was wounded in battle? I do love him. He knows about my child and offered to help me with money. I said I couldn't ask that of him. He is a good man. He knows the worst about me—all my horrible sins—and he doesn't condemn me for them. David says that when he sees me in the morning, it is as if he has awoken to a perfect day. He made me see there is more to life than a title, than being mistress of a large house that is really an empty home."

Julia jerked. That was what she was—mistress of a vast house that now felt empty, when what she had wanted more than anything was happiness.

"I will tell him. I will tell him right away." Julia clasped Diana's hands. "I would love to know you two are going to be married, before I go away."

"Where are you going?"

"America."

New, sleek, renowned for its speed, the *Athena* was like no ship Julia had ever seen. Everything was clean glass, polished silver metal, smooth lines. Her stateroom was done in white and black, crisp and striking. There were no frilled velvets, no Italianate smoking rooms and staterooms designed to look like fussy Victorian rooms in an English manor. Here the lines were streamlined, promising a voyage to a new, thrilling world.

Julia had been startled that even Nigel approved of her pursuing Cal. Cassia had taken command of her work with the widows while she traveled with Zoe and Nigel, along with Nicholas and his nurse They intended to visit Zoe's mother in New York, as Mrs. Gifford was thrilled to see her grandson and to know Zoe was expecting again.

Over dinner in the dining room with a modern silver-and-white ceiling, she said, "Cal gave me Worthington to keep it safe. I've realized *this* is my place in the world—to fight for important things that I believe in. And I believe in Cal. More than he believes in himself. But can I convince him to come back with me? He said he is not worthy of me. I don't know how to make him see that isn't true."

"Go to him. And you will find a way," Zoe said, with all her modern confidence.

"You're right, Julia. This is where you belong," Nigel said. "Taking charge suits you."

Julia was nervous until the day they docked. She stood at the railing, breathless. The city rose out of the water like something magical, with buildings that scraped the sky.

Once they disembarked, they hired a car. Zoe drove, as she knew the city well. David had given Julia the address of the house they used in New York. It was outside the city, in a place called "Great Neck" on Long Island Sound. Where wealthy people went to summer.

It felt like they had plunged into the country. Green trees shimmered lushly against the blue sky. Fields stretched around her and in the middle sat quaint clapboard farmhouses with large porches.

The roads became narrower and they got lost. Stumbling upon a house, Julia got directions from the butler who answered the door, who was quite stunned when she introduced herself as the Countess of Worthington. She learned that the roads and railways were kept deliberately in disrepair to discourage the city people from flocking to the area in the spring and summer.

Following the directions, their Chrysler motorcar pulled into a long drive. Julia put her hands over her mouth as the mansion came into view.

"This belongs to Cal?" Nigel stared.

The large mansion followed the curving drive,

giving views of the grounds from all directions. It was white as snow, striking with black shutters and a large black front door. Two large wings branched off the main portion of the house. From the drive, as they neared the house, they could see the gray crashing waves of the ocean beyond. The house stood at the end of a spit of land that bravely pushed out into the sea.

"I had no idea Cal had the money to buy this," Julia whispered. Coming to Worthington Park had not been so much of a shock to him. He hadn't told her the whole truth about his wealth.

Nigel stopped the car and Julia didn't wait for any servants to appear. She got out and rapped on the front door. The door opened, and she got to shock another butler with the announcement of her title.

"Is my husband in?" she asked. Her heart hammered—she didn't know for certain he'd come here. He could have traveled anywhere. Even left America by now.

She could have laughed with joy and relief when the butler bowed. "The master is in his study, madam."

"My lady," Zoe corrected cheekily.

Then Zoe squeezed Julia's hands. "Go and see Cal." To the butler, she said, "My husband and I would like to wait in another room."

"Allow me to show you the drawing room that overlooks the Sound, madam."

"That is the Duchess of Langford," Julia pointed out. "I'm afraid you address her as 'Your Grace.' It is rather complicated, but I know you'll get the hang of it."

His jaw dropped so fast he almost had to catch it in his hands. Julia had him point her toward Cal's study. At first, she walked there like a lady. Then she couldn't wait and she ran.

Her shoes clicked on the gleaming marble tile and skimmed across beautiful carpet. She knocked on the white paneled door to the study.

"Come in."

She felt a sharp jolt of delight at the sound of his voice. She gently pushed open the door. He stood by his window, looking out at the lawns and the white-capped gray waves of the sea.

"What is it?" he asked brusquely.

"Hi, Cal," she said, as casually and jauntily as she could.

He spun around and he staggered backward as he saw her. A tumbler with a small amount of dark gold liquid fell out of his hand. "Julia?"

"You've dropped your—"

She broke off as he gripped her around the waist and lifted her in his arms. His mouth covered hers, in a hot kiss that could have made the cold ocean water boil.

Julia had feared he might not want to see her or he might be determined to keep distance between them even when they were in the same room. But he pulled her so close there wasn't any space between her breasts and belly and his hard body.

"Julia, why are you here? Here in America?"

"I've come after you, Cal. I'm chasing you in a bold, brash, modern way. And you've dropped your drink."

His blue eyes went large with disbelief. "You came across an ocean for me? You shouldn't have done. If you wanted to see me, Sheba, all you had to do was telephone and I would have swum the ocean for you. You shouldn't have gone to so much trouble. The truth is, I'm not worth it."

"Cal, I know you are. And I enjoyed taking charge and traveling across the ocean for my very first time."

He set her down, cupped her cheek. "Before you say I'm worth it, you need to know the truth about me, my muse. You need to know where I've come from and what I've done."

With the fabric top up on his 1924 Rolls, Cal drove into the city, making his way to the area where he'd grown up. He drove through streets that still cried of squalor, where the stink of industry and the smell of sewage rolled up the streets from the river.

He didn't look at Julia. Didn't need to see her to know what she must be thinking.

"This is where you grew up?"

"Yes," he said abruptly. "The neighborhood is known as Hell's Kitchen."

"Hell's Kitchen. That's a curious name. Was it because of the heat in the summer?"

He gave a hard laugh. "No one agrees on where the name came from. A reporter from the *New York Times* called one of the tenements 'Hell's Kitchen,' back in the 1880s. It's at 39th Street and Tenth Avenue. The reporter went there to write a story on a multiple murder and called it the lowest and filthiest place in the city. Or some say the name came from a veteran police officer who was watching a riot with a rookie copper. The rookie calls the place 'hell itself,' and the veteran says, 'Hell's a mild climate. This is Hell's Kitchen.'"

Cal stole a glance, expecting to see her look disgusted. "I should have known," he muttered.

"What?"

"You're too much of a lady to show your shock on your face." It came out angrier than he'd intended. "I want to see it—don't hide it. Hiding it means you pity me."

He stopped the car on the road outside the sagging, worn, mean-looking walk-up tenement in which he'd lived as a boy.

Julia, her lips perfectly slicked in dark red lipstick, her skin glowing like the sheen of silk, looked up beneath the brim of her hat. "I do not pity you. You survived poverty I cannot even imagine and you got out. I admire you and respect you—how could I not respect a self-made man? s someone who inherited her position, her place in her home, I have nothing but intense respect, Cal."

"Julia, you earned your place in the world, as you call it. I'm a self-made man, but it's how I made it that you should hate me for. You know, it killed me to leave you—"

She had her hand on the door handle, ready to push the door open. He stopped her. "You aren't getting out here."

"I want to look inside. To see your old home."

"It's not a home," he said bitterly. "It was a small, dirty apartment, filled with stink, disease and violence." He put the car in gear—he hadn't turned it off in case they had to leave in a hurry. Before he started moving, a boy ran out of the shadows and stroked the smooth, curved fender.

"She's a beaut, mister," the boy said.

Cal's throat tightened. In the boy's low whistle, he heard himself twenty years ago. In the boy's look of longing and desire as he cooed over the car, Cal saw his own hunger, when he'd been a boy, to get money and go places.

"What's your name?" he asked.

"I'm Tom."

On a whim, Cal motioned Tom to come over to his window. He talked to the lad, found out the boy's father had been a mechanic, but was out of work after the War. "Pa lost his leg, and can't get any work," Tom said.

"How terrible," Julia breathed. "Even here, there isn't the kindness and care given to the war heroes that should be given."

"No," Cal said. "Which is why boys ended up in gangs, fighting for money, fighting to move up in the world." To Tom, he said, "Tell me where you live. I need a man to fix my engines. I keep a few cars out of the city, and my chauffeur's leaving me to get married and move out to California. I need a new man. Give me your address, and I'll come back and talk to your pa. If I think he's right for the job, there's a cottage out at my place on Long Island Sound."

Tom grinned, gave him the address, then took off. He ran up the steps into the open front door of the building.

Cal shook his head. "What are the odds?" he said thoughtfully. "He lives in the apartment I lived in."

"Will you give his father a job?"

"A missing leg won't make it impossible for him to tend an engine. That takes a man's hands and his head. The boy can help him and learn a few things when he's not in school."

"This is very good of you."

"I learned it from you, Julia. The pure, sweet pleasure that comes from helping someone. From changing even one life."

"Cal . . . that's so sweet. Thank you."

He saw her smile, a smile more radiant than any sunrise, or autumn-leaved forest, or stunning wilderness scene he'd tried to capture on a canvas.

As much as he wanted to turn around and drive away and have Julia, keep her, make sure he never lost her, he knew he had to be honest with her.

Cal drove away from the sidewalk. Julia reached out and touched his shoulder. More sad apartment buildings flashed by them. She smelled the river, heard a mournful horn.

They were driving toward the tall buildings of the center of Manhattan.

"When I was a kid," Cal said, "I wanted to make money for my family. I told you my father worked at the docks. He hated the brutality, the intimidating, the thieving. He stood up to the gangs and that got him beaten up. I ended up working for them. First I was running messages and acting as a lookout when they broke into warehouses."

"But you were just a boy—"

"I knew it was against the law. And I knew it would break my mam's heart if she knew I'd been helping the gangs. But I needed the money. After Father was killed, I swore I'd never be vulnerable like that. Mam worked as a seamstress in the daytime. Twelve hours a day, every day, she worked in a warehouse with bars over the windows and poor light, worked until she was losing her eyesight. And after she'd slaved all day making clothes, she spent the nights washing dishes at pubs. She worked so hard she got sick. That's when she got desperate. She feared David and I wouldn't be able to survive if she couldn't earn, so she swallowed her pride and wrote to the Carstairs family. She hated that they felt she was nothing. But she kept muttering that they were right and she was nothing because she wasn't strong enough to look after her boys. She was weak, thin as a tiny bird, because she let David and I have almost all the food. I wouldn't eat all of mine so she could have some.

"She got sicker, and she lost her jobs. Then she—she sold herself to men for money. I used to hear her cry at night. Some of the men were like the one that beat up Ellen Lambert. They didn't want sex unless they could use the woman as a punching bag."

Julia wanted to say something, but saw he needed to talk. So she let him.

"Having to prostitute herself finished her. It ate away at her inside. I wrote to Lady Worthington myself, begging her to help my mother. I hoped for some pity, some shred of kindness. But I didn't get any. I went back to the Five Points Gang. Then America entered the War and I signed up along with a man I knew, Wild Bill Lovett. When I got out, he was heading up the Jay Street Gang. Prohibition started and I got involved with them and with bootlegging. In war, I'd learned how to kill—"

"Did you—did you do that in the gang?"

"No. I was muscle. I threatened people, collected debts. I never took an innocent life." They were moving into the tall buildings. "I'm taking you to the Plaza for luncheon. There's something I've got to tell you there."

"Cal, you don't have to tell me anything more. I love you, you know."

They drove down Park Avenue to the Plaza Hotel. Cal stopped there. Cars zipped past them. A cacophony of horns rose around them. Girls strode past on clicking heels.

"I'll drive you back to Nigel and Zoe if you want, after I tell you this," Cal said. "I left the Jay Street Gang and started my own enterprise. Bootlegging and fake bonds." He hung his head. "A member of one of the gangs tried to kill me, to move into my position and get my turf. I had to fight for my life. He stabbed me and I beat him badly. Then he went and got drunk and got hit by a car."

"That wasn't your fault," she said.

"I'd almost beaten him to death, Julia. Rumors started that it was one of my men who ran him down. I don't think that's true and I didn't order it, if it was. Stories grew that I killed people. I didn't, but that night I had come close to becoming the kind of thug my father hated, the kind of thug who had killed him. I was afraid that next time I might cross the line. I had to fight to succeed without hurting anyone. I got out of crime and spent day and night studying companies so I could invest my money and make enough to look after David."

"Looking after David is what drove you. You never took anyone's life. And you got away from crime."

"That man's death is on my soul. I pounded him and he likely got drunk to ease the pain. I was sure Mam was turning in her grave over what I was doing. So I went to Paris and tried painting. My dad had taught me how to draw, and he'd brought some paints and pencils from England when he left for good. I found I loved painting, and I guess I could have let it completely heal my soul, but I didn't. I didn't want to give up on my desire to get revenge."

"Do you still want that? I understand if you do—"

"Julia, you crossed an ocean for me. I have to make myself worthy of you. I'm not going to hurt the family. Or destroy the estate. It's yours, angel, so I can't do that."

"You're helping that young boy. That's what we should do together. Help people."

Cal said softly to her, "I used to dream of having a rich man come up and offer me work. Give me a way to escape this place. So maybe I've made someone's dreams come true."

"You made most of mine come true," she

551

whispered. "My heart was in bits and pieces and you've given me the strength to make it whole. I understand that you can't see Worthington as a home. Cal, maybe I am too late, but I choose you over Worthington."

He shook his head. "You were right, Julia. I was always running away. But you can never outrun yourself. I don't want to run away from the life you want. I know now that I can't live without you. And, you know, I guess I actually miss Worthington Park."

She smiled. "Now, let's go inside, shall we? I have something to tell you."

"I think we should take a room in there."

"Really? Whatever for?"

"I want to spend the rest of the day making love to you, Sheba."

Her heart glowed with joy. "There is something I must tell you, Cal. I believe I am expecting our child. If all goes well, you are going to become a father. And I know you will be the most wonderful father."

"Julia!" He kissed her senseless. "Then we should go home. Back to Worthington."

He'd called Worthington home. Her heart soared.

"I don't want to go home just yet," she said. "I have a few months—and you promised to show me adventure. I want to travel with you and paint."

Cal looked stunned. But two months later, Julia drew the paddle of a canoe through crystal-clear water. Liquid dripped with each stroke, forming rings and ripples. The morning sun was rising over the mountains, sending warm light over the lake.

"You're a great paddler," Cal said, behind her.

Julia half turned, but carefully—she was still concerned she might tip the canoe. "I feel I'm doing it completely out of synchronization with you."

"It's perfect," he said.

"It is." She gazed over the water. Yellow and red leaves blazed around the lake. They had traveled by train into Canada, then up into the north of the province of Ontario. For weeks, they had traveled, as summer became fall, and had spent days here in a tent. At night they snuggled together in a sleeping sack.

"You know, you look damn sexy in trousers," Cal said.

Julia blushed. "I don't know how women ever did this in skirts."

"Are you really enjoying this, or is this too rough for you?"

They glided toward a rocky point. A huge fir tree towered there. Julia paused, resting her paddle. "I love this," she said. "I wasn't certain I'd love sleeping beneath the stars, but I do."

Cal steered them to the rocky shoreline and Julia got out, her leather boots balancing on the uneven rock. She loved the crispness of the morning air and the pure scent of it. It was wilder than the English countryside, but it spoke to her soul.

With Cal, she unpacked the canoe. He always wanted to do most of the work, but she helped him set up the tent and lay out the sacks and blankets they used for sleeping. Cal set up a fire. That night, they sat beside the fire and watched the stars. And she saw the glorious northern lights—stunning displays of dancing green, purple and yellow.

The next day, they worked together at the edge of the rock, sketching on small canvases. Cal painted the landscape and she tried to paint him. Much to her chagrin, he took the picture from her at the end of the day and looked at it. His eyes widened. "It's incredible. You have real talent, my beautiful muse. More talent than me."

She laughed. "I don't."

"You've made me more handsome than I really am."

"That is exactly how you look to me. Even here, in the wilds, I think you are the perfect Earl of Worthington."

He kissed her. "You know, Sheba, I think it's time to travel home. Since you're in a delicate condition."

She nodded. "If I get very large, I'll probably tip the canoe." And she laughed as Cal pulled her back into his arms.

● ● ●

In April, when snowdrops blossomed over the lawns of Worthington, Julia gave birth to two beautiful babies—twins! Cal was there, helping her through the birth. Dr. Campbell and a London specialist attended. She had just sent Cal home from the hospital for some sleep, Nigel and Zoe had come and left. Isobel had come, fascinated by the medical practicalities of birthing twins. Although many medical schools had closed their doors to women now that the War was behind them, there were still some places and Isobel was determined to leave that year to study.

Then Julia heard a nurse giggling outside her room, and she knew who had come. Seconds later, her charming brother Sebastian peeked around the door. "Only you would have one of each rather than having to choose. It's more perfect this way," he said, grinning.

She held both babies in her arms, which she felt rather nervous about doing. She asked her brother about John Ransome.

"Alas, I've realized I can't change John's mind. He won't turn his back on his family—and their expectations—for me," Sebastian said.

"As you said to me, he should be willing to fight for you. Perhaps if I bring you together—arrange dinner parties—"

"You will be too busy being a mother. I'm philosophical about this, Julia. Love will come for me eventually. I plan to return to Paris and paint. But I'm going to stay in England for the summer, to see my adorable nephews and niece."

"It will be wonderful to have you here," she said.

She sensed Cal just as he came in her room, carrying a bouquet of roses. He stopped in the doorway and just looked at her. She had never seen him look so happy. Diana had given birth to her daughter a few months before, after her marriage to David. David had even ridden a horse just before that, as Julia had vowed he would. It had been a delightful time. This was even more wonderful. "You are supposed to be resting," she said.

"I couldn't stay away. You look radiant, Julia. Perfect."

"You mean they are perfect."

"All of you are perfect," he said softly. "There is no curse now. There can't be. Your blend of modern compassion and old-world elegance and honor has broken the curse forever. You've brought happiness to Worthington. And brought the most wonderful miracles of all to me. Two beautiful babies, the perfect wife and love."

"Amen," Sebastian said.

Julia looked up. She saw the dowager countess in the corridor, afraid to come in. "Would you take our daughter?" Julia asked him.

He looked confused, then embarrassed, and she smiled. "Our daughter has the curls."

As he scooped their little girl into his arms, she

said, "You could introduce her to the dowager. I've had to think long and hard about it, but I think we should give her a second chance."

Cal nodded. "She wrote me a letter telling me that she would never breathe a word about my mother. I admit, I haven't answered it." He made a beckoning motion. As the dowager Lady Worthington came in, she whispered, "I'm sorry. So very sorry. For everything."

Julia looked to Cal. He said gently, "It's accepted. And thank you for your decision. Now, come here and meet the future Earl of Worthington and his perfect sister."

The dowager did, wiping a tear from her cheek.

Then her mother and grandmother came into the room. Julia saw the joy in her mother's eyes, and she had Cal help her mother hold each baby, one at a time. "They are beautiful," her mother cooed, her eyes bright with happy tears. "It is so miraculous. Two wonderful babies. And speaking of something miraculous, your grandmother has allowed Sir Raynard to court her more seriously."

"Court me? Rubbish," Grandmama declared. "But perhaps I have realized I have been blessed with everything—a home, a family, delightful grandchildren. So perhaps I could risk allowing a gentleman into my life once more."

"I highly approve," Julia said teasingly. And she knew she would be a Worthington Wife who had perfect happiness.

Acknowledgments

Many, many thanks to Allison Carroll, my editor for *The Worthington Wife*. Your enthusiasm for this story from the very beginning has inspired me and pushed me to make this book the very best it could be. From working back and forth with me on revisions when my life took a turn to brainstorming titles, you've been wonderful.

A huge thank-you to everyone at Harlequin and HQN. You have all put so much care and attention into this book. The lovely cover made me almost swoon with joy.

Also, thanks to my agent, Evan Marshall, for your support and for being there whenever needed.

I have to thank my family for putting up with a writer on deadline—and there are quite a few deadlines along the way to getting a book out in the world. Their faith and support have made me feel blessed.

And of course, thank you to all who read this story. It was always my dream to write about the Roaring Twenties, and I hope you enjoy the ride as much as I have.

Center Point Large Print
600 Brooks Road / PO Box 1
Thorndike, ME 04986-0001 USA

(207) 568-3717

US & Canada:
1 800 929-9108
www.centerpointlargeprint.com